I0773458

WATCHERS OF THE EVENFALL
First edition. October 31, 2022.
Copyright © 2022 Joe Field.
ISBN: 979-8-9862686-1-3
Written by Joe Field.
Cover designed by Joe Field.

WATCHERS OF THE EVENFALL

Joe Field

Sarcastic Griffin Books

To the first person who read my novel unedited and still called it "a masterpiece."

CONTENTS

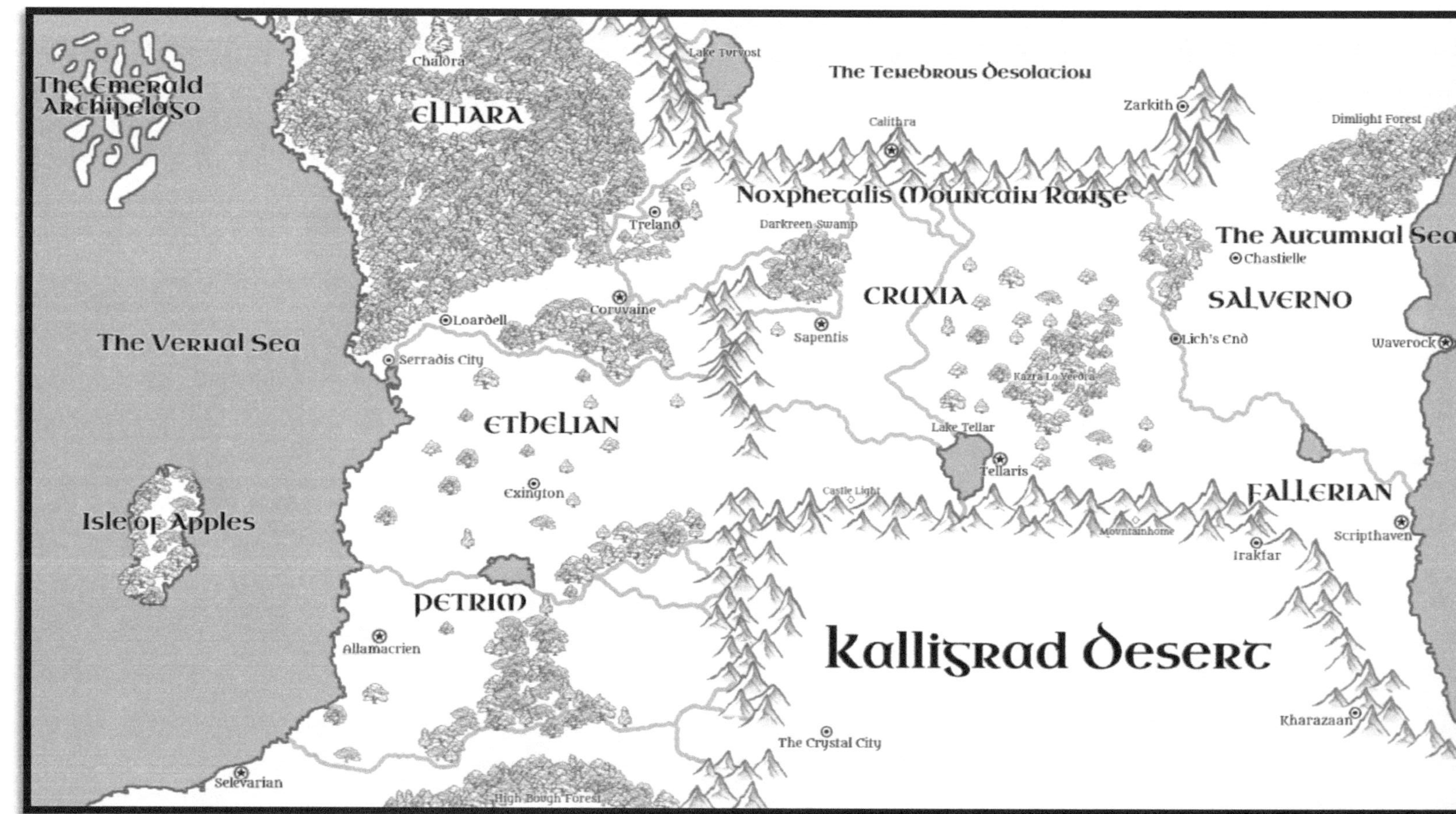

The Emerald Archipelago
ELLIARA
Chalora
Lake Turvost
The Tenebrous Desolation
Zarkith
Dimlight Forest
Calithra
Noxphetalis Mountain Range
Treland
Darkreen Swamp
The Autumnal Sea
Chastielle
CRUXIA
SALVERNO
Loardell
Coruvaine
Sapentis
Kazra Lo Verola
Lich's End
Waverock
The Vernal Sea
Serradis City
ETHELIAN
Lake Tellar
Exington
Tellaris
Castle Light
FALLERIAN
Isle of Apples
Mountainhome
Irakfar
Scripthaven
PETRIM
Allamacrien
Kalligrad Desert
Kharazaan
The Crystal City
Selevarian
High Bough Forest

Prologue
Rising Shadows

Garo dashed through a monochromatic landscape of smoke and fleeting images that stretched endlessly in all directions. The Shadow World—a murky reflection of Algendis—was a half-formed realm of warped temporal distortions and metaphor. These black images existed without asking to be viewed or altered, running a blind dance through the white landscape. No sound but distant echoes reached Garo's ears, like the creaking of a ship's hull, or the phantom songs of singing whales. Humans knew this place existed, but their knowledge extended no further than blind speculation. Garo had never encountered a human here and doubted he ever would.

He rushed through the nothingness, no grass or ground beneath his paws, nor sky above his head. The white surrounded him, only broken by ephemeral shapes in unidimensional grayscale, both near and far. He glanced to the side and beheld a black canine face grinning at him as it ran parallel before breaking off and disappearing. It was one of his brethren. A grim. Other creatures lurked in this realm, but Garo spent no time determining their identities or motivations. It was unwise to pause in the shifting darkness. Grims could traverse great distances swiftly by stepping through shadows, and were the most benevolent of the black dogs to use this realm.

Garo was unique among his kind. He was a shadowseer. The shapes of this domain extended through distance and time. Untouchable and cryptic though they were, they could be studied. The dark blots enclosing the surreal landscape were multilayered, telling a condensed story for anyone willing to look into them long enough. The tales they told were indefinite in the sense of names, locations, and dates, but provided clues to the past and to the future. Much as a tall shadow might hint at the qualities of a tree, the shadows of time gave the vaguest inkling of what would come when viewed from a specific angle.

He neared his destination at last. Glancing back, he saw his rear half had dissolved into a smoke trail. All things within this place were but shadows of their true selves. Once, noticing such alterations would have unnerved him, but it held no apprehension for him now. He was more ghost than dog—the Shadow World merely reflected that truth.

Garo's face fell as he approached a white mass extending out like an explosion. Something unprecedented had happened. His stomach churned as he neared the vision. The Shadow World was vague, but never wrong. He was certain he made no error. His predictions took time, but he endeavored to ensure the correctness of his work. What he gazed upon now told a fearsome tale—one he couldn't share entirely with anyone. A lengthy chain of events driven by an unseen force of unfathomable power to an impending cataclysm. This horror threatened to systematically rip existence apart. Every world would descend into primordial chaos. The white—reaching out with crooked and searching fingers grown fat—represented utter annihilation. The Shadow World was previously entirely black, but the once small cracks of white had overwhelmed the backdrop of the realm, no matter how far he ran. When the white overtook the black completely, nothing would remain. What was a shadow world without shadows? Still, he had hope; four dark figures repelled the nothingness. Besides these, there were others, but they were smaller and distant in comparison. The main players in this cataclysm stood before him with such distinctness that he had determined their identities beyond doubt. The werewolf brawler. The vampire prince. The dark elf warlock. The girl.

He peered deeper into the dark space of the girl, puzzled. *How? How can the shadows claim she's still*—he froze, his eyes locked on the image. Did the girl... move? He leaned as close as possible and that was when the shadow saw him. The girl stared at Garo with glowing green eyes. The grim stumbled back, every vaporous hair on his body standing on end. The green eyes tracked him but did nothing else.

He shook his head, trying to rid himself of the impossible thing he witnessed before bolting off and away from the vision. Even as he left, he felt the girl watching him. Green eyes in a monochromatic world. Was such a thing possible? No, nothing less than a god could accomplish such an inexplicable feat. And yet this girl... how?

He sprinted into the black image of a wide city with a vulpine crest. Something unfathomable had occurred. The time for questions had ended; he needed to act.

The Last Wall would rise, and Garo would be its architect.

Chapter One
To Sleep No More

Cradled in endless darkness, the girl gradually awoke from everlasting slumber. She knew nothing of herself, for she thought of nothing. A ripple in the void passed through her with infinite power and equal gentleness. Then, a deep and tender warmth pulled her up. She noticed a faint sensation, muffled and faraway. The warmth pulsed through her rhythmically, and a tingling moved over her as she realized the presence of her body. Colors and sounds encroached on her senses. A voice whispered coaxing entreaties, calling to her so distantly intimate. But... something was missing. Something was wrong.

Awaken.

Whose voice was that?

Live.

As if waiting for that command, her awareness exploded, and she emerged from the abyss like a swimmer reaching the surface of a bottomless lake with sudden buoyancy. This change startled her, and she spasmed.

"Ah ha! I've done it!" an older man cried victoriously. "I knew I'd done... well, *something,* but evidently that last bit was necessary to catalyze your perceptual faculties." He took a calming breath. "Can you speak?"

She attempted to open her mouth, but her lips barely separated and she only pushed a breath through.

"Oh, yes, apologies," the man said. "I had forgotten it's been a while since you've used that. Well, you can keep trying. The spell should allow you full control over your physical movements within the next few days, but within the hour, I predict you'll function enough to speak, respond, and so on. In the meantime, let's try something easier. How about opening your eyes, hmm? Oh, and these—" she felt light pressure at two spots in her head "—are your eyes, just in case you'd forgotten. It'd be nice to talk to somebody who can actually *see* me rather than just hear me. It's more personal."

She fluttered her eyelids—which were extremely heavy—until she finally held them open. Her vision was blurry and she could only perceive vague gray shapes. Those shapes gradually defined themselves, and she realized she gazed at a wood roof with stretched cobwebs between the rafters. She also saw the face of a man above her.

The man who'd spoken before stood beaming over her. His hair ranged from gray to white, and his overall appearance was disheveled. His clothing—while not hinting at dire poverty—looked like it could benefit from a thorough washing. Despite this, his clear and lively brown eyes were kind.

"Ah, good!" He rubbed his hands together. "You can finally see me, though I'm afraid you're getting the worse deal out of it." The man stopped and unthinkingly scanned her before rushing to retrieve a sheet from somewhere beyond her sight. He wrapped it around her and tucked it to the best of his abilities. "You must, ah, forgive me"— he blushed—"but any decent physician would tell you the procedures I put you through required minimalist attire on your part."

"Wh-who..." she whispered, as his eyes widened and he drew closer, "who a-are... you?"

The old man crowed triumphantly and bowed comically. "My dear," he said, "I am Hickory Allkirk—mage, scholar, and scientist." His eyes shot up. "Oh, and you're Hazel Enda, a girl who died. Just in case you forgot."

"What?" Her tongue felt heavy as she spoke. It also didn't help that Hickory talked rapidly and darted between thoughts haphazardly. She died?

He smiled as he consulted some notes on a table adjacent the wooden slab she was on. "Allow me to explain." He flipped through some papers and frowned, muttering to himself. "No... that can't be right. But it is. But—wait, no—yes. I... hmm." He scratched his head. "I'm sorry, my dear," he said to her. "I'll give you the abbreviated version of my research while I run a few diagnostic tests to ensure everything works properly. Necromancy is more art than science, I'm afraid, and I'm a terrible artist." He beamed at her. "The tests won't hurt, I assure you. I just don't want you exploding suddenly."

Her eyebrows raised.

"I mean, that's just an example. I assure you it's... unlikely." His eyes looked everywhere except at her.

Somehow, she wasn't convinced.

He touched her wrist, and she felt an electric zap followed by warmth. "I wanted to create a new variety of undead creature. You are the result of that experiment."

The zap to her wrist energized her. "There's... more than one kind?"

He nodded absently and moved his hand to her neck, placing his thumb and forefinger just under the back of her jaw. She felt a small sting. "Hmm? Oh, there are many kinds of undead, but most fall into one of four primary categories. Zombies are the most common variety. Do you know what a zombie is?"

She sensed the fog dissipating. The sting in her neck acted like a mental breeze. "Zombies..." she mused. She remembered a woman... her mother... calling her a zombie when she stayed awake too late. "...

they're mindless, right?"

He smiled and nodded. "That's what most people think, and it's not entirely incorrect." He moved his hand away from her neck and rubbed his fingers together, which glowed with a pale blue light. "Zombies are dead bodies with a control spirit put into them. The spirit animates them and has only one desire: to enact the will of its master."

Hazel met his eyes. "So... I'm not a zombie."

He put his fingers to her forehead, and the light shifted in color from blue to yellow. He nodded with satisfaction. "Oh, certainly not. You are yourself—body and soul—which makes you closer to a revenant or lich than it does a draugr or zombie."

She blinked several times. "Than... what?" She got the impression that even if her head hadn't felt thick, she would've struggled to understand Hickory.

He stepped in front of her and made several hand motions before putting the edge of his palm against her sternum. "Draugr are essentially strong and intelligent zombies with magical powers. Both of them decay over time, following the same general timeline as a corpse." He closed his eyes and breathed. He cocked his head and opened his eyes again. "Interesting." He wrote a few notes on the adjacent table.

"What?" Hazel asked, "Interesting... how?"

"I'll answer your question momentarily," he said. He slowed his breathing, and the creases in his face smoothed as he visibly relaxed. Hickory raised a hand, flickering intermittently with a radiant golden light. The mage opened his eyes and frowned at the sputtering magic. "Work, damn it!" he exclaimed. The light instantly extinguished. He sighed and repeated the process, producing the same unstable golden flashes. Hickory opened his eyes and touched her shoulder with his glowing hand. A peaceful warmth radiated into her shoulder in time with the pulses of light. He continued breathing calmly. "How does that feel?"

"Good."

"Huh." He withdrew his hand and scribbled more notes. He glanced at her between words. "You may well be a new type of undead. If you were of the decaying variety, you probably would've been destroyed by that bit of thaumaturgy."

"And you did it, anyway?"

"I—uh"—he avoided eye contact sheepishly—"I mean, I was reasonably sure it wouldn't happen."

Hazel frowned. Something told her she was *reasonably sure* there was nothing reasonable about this mage.

"In any case, that probably makes you a revenant." He shrugged. "Probably."

She sighed.

"What? It's not like I know *everything*..." He rubbed his hands together and thin tendrils of pinkish smoke rose from his fingers. "There should be one more simple and perfectly safe diagnostic—" He extended his hands toward Hazel and a blast of pink energy exploded through the room, blasting Hickory out of view. She heard a bottle shatter from the impact. He scrambled to his feet. His eyes darted around the room and his face paled.

"'Safe'?" Hazel questioned.

"It should've been..." He regarded her cautiously. There was something in his gaze she couldn't quite understand. It was almost distrusting. He seemed... afraid.

He shook himself and ran back to collect some paper from the ground and scribbled. He glanced back at her with nervous excitement. "You are really quite extraordinary, Miss Enda," he said. "You're similar to a revenant but show no vital deterioration, which is common to such creations. Semeleme is a jealous goddess and doesn't give back the dead without a cost. Revenants don't possess innate arcane ability, however, unlike you."

"But I'm not magical."

"You mean you *weren't* magical," Hickory corrected. "That spell simply measured the amount of innate magic within you. All creatures have *some* magic, but typically not much. The result I got from you implies much greater arcane potential than most spellcasters. In fact"—he hesitated—"you could say your power is almost lich-like in magnitude."

Hazel pondered what he said. Liches... she'd heard stories about them. They were monsters bards sung of in epic poems. To fight a lich was comparable to fighting a great dragon—an insurmountable task none but a legendary hero could accomplish and survive.

Hickory tapped the tip of his quill against his cheek absently, inadvertently putting ink freckles over his face. "A revenant with a lich's power. It's a terrifying prospect, but you *can't* be a lich. Those take *years* to make. Decades. You've only been dead a couple of months." He smiled nervously. "I guess you really were a stroke of divine inspiration. I created a new type of undead. It's hard to believe, frankly."

He gazed down at her absently for several long moments. Abruptly, he blinked and shook himself. "Oh, please forgive my negligence, dear child. Let me raise the bed."

A series of gears clanked, expanding her view of the room. The area was in a state of extreme academic disarray. Multiple tables with open books stacked upon each other with hastily written notes sat scattered around her. Various potions lying at odd angles were placed in no specific order over desks, chairs, and on loose pieces of parchment and paper. Mismatched candelabra rested precariously on uneven surfaces, and without regard for the paper now strewn throughout the room— possibly due to the earlier explosion. Half-eaten meals lay slowly decaying in random locations, and a kettle was whistling somewhere behind her. A wooden staircase leading up to a door, coupled with the absence of natural light, gave Hazel the impression she was underground.

When he finished bringing her into an upright position and further secured her wrappings, he smiled. He opened his mouth to speak when the room shook. Footsteps and voices clamored above them and from the top of the staircase. Hickory retreated furtively until he stood beside Hazel.

"It's okay. They won't find us down here so long as we're quiet," Hickory whispered. "I have the doorway carefully hidden. They'll never be able to guess where it—"

"Hey!" shouted a voice from upstairs. "I found a doorway behind the bookshelf!"

"Damn," Hickory muttered. "At least the door is locked."

"Hickory Allkirk," proclaimed a man from behind the door, "you are suspected of practicing necromancy. This is Chief Inquisitor Thomas Eller of the Department of Inquisition of the Council of Archmages. Open immediately. You have violated the laws established by the Council of Archmages, the Gray Empire, and the Sovereign Nation of Ethelian."

"No, no, no, no, no!" Hickory muttered as he reached under papers and clutched a gnarled wand. "I've come too far to have these naysayers interfere now... not now... why did it have to be now?"

The door burst open, revealing a man in his thirties, dressed in an elegant blue robe emblazoned with a single white rose. The robe fell just above his ankles and looked more functional than Hazel expected for such a garment. Behind him appeared several soldiers. His eyes flicked over the room, betraying no emotion.

"Based on your noncompliance and the presence of some mutated body, I assume our knowledge was correct. Hickory Allkirk, by the dual authority of the Inquisition of the Council of Archmages and the Kingdom of Ethelian, you are under arrest for practicing the unholy atrocities of necromancy. Surrender immediately or we will take you in by force."

"Don't think you can take me down so easily, young one!" Hickory snarled. "I've been practicing magic since before you were born!" Hickory drew an image in the air with his wand and thrust it toward the top of the stairs. A bright streak of blue light erupted from the wand, screaming as it flew toward the inquisitor. The blue-robed mage raised his hand as the blue light hit his palm, coalescing and writhing around it before dissipating. The inquisitor gestured with his wand,

and a blast of air, only visible from the dust it disturbed, rushed down at Hickory. Hickory—not expecting such a broad attack—was knocked from his feet. As he scrambled to rise, Thomas Eller descended halfway down the stairs. The inquisitor's countenance darkened as he walked, and his voice contorted into deep, reverberating tones.

"Come, Hickory, give up. Give in. It is easier to relax. Let your mind wander. Release. Calm down. Drop the wand. Sleep."

Hickory beat his head with his fists. "Do you really think your cheap sorcery will have any effect on me?"

Thomas shrugged. "I guess not." And like a coiled snake, he struck. A tiny, silvery wisp shot toward Hickory and struck him in the chest. The small mote of energy exploded with such force that his shirt disintegrated. The room shook with the concussive blast, and several glass containers shattered. Hickory hurtled backward, slamming into the wall with a loud *thud* and a splitting *crack.*

The inquisitor sighed. "I really hoped he'd come peacefully. Such a waste of time and energy." He reached the bottom of the steps with six amazed guards behind him. He took quick stock of the room before turning to the guards. "Two of you carry him to the cart and I'll make certain he tries nothing more foolish than he has thus far. I suppose he'll need to be healed by the thaumaturgist upstairs since I either broke his neck or his head. You two gather his research and *carefully* compile it for further inspection, and you two unhook that *creature* from its stand and load it into the cart. Beware of any traps Mr. Allkirk may have set."

One guard glanced uneasily at another. "Shouldn't we check for traps first?"

"Simple caution should suffice. I doubt he had the time or foresight to set any timed surprises over anything. Any additional spells are likely inscribed. Don't read his notes; compile them and I will sort them."

The soldiers moved accordingly. Two strode out of sight, collecting scraps of paper and items of interest, while others carried Hickory from the room, with the mage following with a drawn wand. The remaining soldiers stood before Hazel. Both wore the light blue brigandine armor common to the guards of Coruvaine, with arming swords at their sides. One was an older teen, the other was in his forties. The older man examined her bindings until the mage left the room with Hickory's unconscious body. Hazel remained silent as she processed everything that transpired in under a minute. She imagined she should feel shocked, but she felt... nothing.

"So," said the older man to the younger, jabbing him in the side with his elbow, "is this your first time seeing a zombie?"

"Yeah," the younger replied, glancing between Hazel and the soldier, "are they dangerous?"

"Not really. Once the necromancer controlling it is neutralized, they're usually pretty docile, unless he gives an order beforehand. I've been on at least eleven different raids. It's not common, but with an attending wizard or magician, we usually finish these things without a snag. Say what you want about the Inquisition, but they're real serious when it comes to the undead."

"It's hard to believe she's really dead. She seems so... alive."

"She must be fresh. It's strange for a necromancer to choose a new corpse. Also"—the soldier peered at her—"zombies aren't usually green. Huh."

Hazel blinked. "I'm *green*?"

Both soldiers jumped and retreated without turning from her, their hands drifting to their swords.

"Go get the mage—*now!*" the older man snapped at his junior. Hazel watched as the young man scrambled up the stairs. She raised her hand and saw it was a vernal shade of green.

What was going on?

Even as her thoughts sharpened and her other physical sensations returned, she noticed something else was different. Where previously she remembered joy and sorrow, fear and anger, there was... nothing. She rose from the dead with her thoughts and memories, but something was missing. All those feelings once bursting vivaciously within her had disappeared.

Despite rising from the grave as a living person, she'd lost the feeling of being alive.

Chapter Two
To Return and Still Be Missing

"Please sign at the bottom of the page, Chief Inquisitor."

Thomas Eller scanned the document and sighed impatiently. This was a mistake, a *grievous* mistake.

Nonetheless, he signed Hazel Enda's release.

The administrator nodded curtly. "The Sovereign of Ethelian thanks you and your magicians for continuing to support the kingdom."

"We're not magicians," Thomas corrected, struggling to contain his annoyance. "At least not all of us. Some are mages, others spellcasters but few are *just* magicians."

"Oh?" The woman blinked vacantly. "What's the difference?"

He read her thoughts using sorcery to see if she was as empty-headed as she appeared. She was.

"A spellcaster is any human who uses one of the seven schools of magic, a mage is a spellcaster who has proficiency in two or more schools of magic, and a magician is someone who has proficiency in the seventh school of magic which is called lesser magic."

She smiled. "Well, isn't that something? I'm not one for jargon, but I will try to remember that. Thank you for the information."

"Indeed," Thomas said, rising to his feet. The administrator stood opposite his desk within the Inquisition's safe house in Coruvaine. He maintained a neutral expression to mask his exasperation. What he mentioned hardly qualified as *jargon*, so much as common knowledge from the past five centuries. "I would like to speak with her before she departs."

"Certainly," the administrator replied, swiping a gray curl behind her ear. "His Majesty extends all courtesy and respect to the Inquisition."

Thomas resisted rolling his eyes. If the king respected the Inquisition as this sycophant said, then he wouldn't have forced the girl's release against Thomas's recommendation. She rose from the dead, which placed her squarely under the jurisdiction of the Inquisition. Remanding her to the Sapphire Guard would have been bad enough, but remanding the girl to her parents—who were little more than peasants—bordered on criminal.

"Please tell the inquisitor at the front desk to send her in when you leave."

"Of course. I'll wait outside with her parents until you've finished."

He nodded, and she exited, closing the door behind her. Naturally, she wouldn't leave until Hazel returned to her parents. The administrator needed to ensure the Inquisition did nothing untoward, not that they would. Still, having a delegate from the beloved ruler of Ethelian might put her parents at ease. At least, until they saw their daughter.

Or whatever was left of her.

A light knock on the door came moments after it was shut.

"Enter."

Hazel entered wearing a dark gray dress with long sleeves and a matching cloak. From what the chief inquisitor could determine, the material was expensive and a gift from the king brought by the woman who now waited outside. Hazel stood at the desk. Her eyes drifted idly around the office, but the rest of her face remained unchanged and emotionless.

Thomas forced a smile, which she didn't reciprocate. "Well, Hazel, it appears your parents have arrived to bring you home."

She didn't respond.

"Are you excited?"

"No."

He squinted at her. "No nervousness or interest in seeing your parents again?"

"Not really," she said. "Should I be?"

"That isn't for me to say. Would you prefer to stay here?"

"Not particularly."

"Then what is it you want?" He studied her face. Despite the three weeks he examined her, there were many mysteries to unravel and even more questions that needed answering. He had kept her with the Inquisition, but during her stay, the king commanded the Sapphire Guard to oversee every test and ensure her humane treatment. Even if the reason for their presence was noble, it slowed the normal operations of the Inquisition significantly and so they made frustratingly little progress.

"I don't want anything."

He didn't need to use sorcery to know she spoke the truth. She stood nearly motionless. Her behavior had remained constant since they happened upon her in Hickory Allkirk's laboratory. When they ran tests, she occasionally asked questions, but she was generally apathetic to her surroundings.

"Perhaps seeing your parents will reignite your emotions."

"If the Inquisition and the Sapphire Guard couldn't fix me, I don't know what good my parents will do."

"Do you need to be fixed?"

"Yes," she said, her eyes meeting his, but remaining impassive. "I'm not like I was. I'm incomplete. Broken."

"Do you wish to be as you were?"

"It's like I said"—her eyes fell—"I don't want anything."

He strummed his fingers on his desk. "I do not think your parents possess any magic comparable to what we've used on you thus far, but it's possible you may remember the bond you shared with them many months ago. That could rekindle your feelings."

"It doesn't matter to me."

"Well, if it doesn't matter, then going home with them should be acceptable."

"It is."

"Then I suppose you can go see them immediately. For the foreseeable future, I would like to meet with you once a week to ensure you are healthy and no sinister magic awakens that would cause you or your family distress." He rose and circled his desk, gesturing to the door. "Come, it's time to leave."

Hazel did as he requested. He previously noted her compliance in his research was consistent with the behavior exhibited by many zombies, but she was far from mindless. Furthermore, zombies would only listen to the one who summoned them or conjurers by proxy. Her obedience stemmed from no compulsion except a lack of motivation to resist. Even during examinations—which would have caused any other young woman her age to blush—she demonstrated no embarrassment.

He ushered her into the main hallway and to the exit. As he passed a window, he noticed a man and woman standing anxiously beside the administrator outside. He stopped before the front door and smiled at her.

"It's time for us to part. If anything changes, you can inform me during one of our weekly appointments. I'll let you meet your family privately."

She nodded and left the building.

Thomas strode to the window and watched. The windows to the building were obscured by magic, keeping others from looking in. He cared little about the actual privacy of their reunion, but desired to observe and learn what he could. As an inquisitor, he served as more than law enforcement; he was a researcher too. How Hazel reacted to her parents—and how they received her—might cast some light on this mysterious case. Were the parents secretly responsible for her death? Were they working with the king and answering to him? Did the king hire Hickory Allkirk to raise her from the dead? While the probable answer to those questions was *no,* he still needed to investigate. After all, he was an inquisitor.

Hazel's mother—a woman in her forties—raised both hands over her mouth. Tears formed in the corner of her widened eyes but did not fall. She took a tentative step forward. Hazel's father—of similar age to her mother but muscular and scarred from numerous burns common to a smith—stood ashen faced as he stared at his daughter.

Although Thomas could not hear the exchange, he saw her mother mouth her name. Hazel responded affirmatively. Lynn Enda—the mother—closed the gap between them and held Hazel's shoulders at arm's length. Thomas leaned closer, studying the parents. Kyle Enda approached his daughter and put one hand over his wife's, which rested on the girl's shoulder. The man looked away, quivering. His wife wept openly. Soon, the woman held Hazel in her arms, though Hazel remained indifferent. Kyle hugged both of them together, but still she moved not an inch.

The administrator interjected after several minutes and ushered them into a nearby carriage, which immediately departed.

Thomas left the window and returned to his desk. He leaned back in his chair, crossing his arms. Many emotions were at play between them that he doubted they expected to feel. He considered how he might have reacted if a loved one returned from the dead. Certainly, it would not have resembled the display he witnessed. The return of their daughter must have been an answer to their most fervent prayers and profoundest wishes. Was her return all they desired? From what Thomas gathered, she had been vivacious once, but that liveliness had disappeared. Would her parents thank the gods for returning their daughter, or would they come to regret their pleas? Was Hazel still their child, altered as she was? The initial answer—and one naturally assumed by the ignorant and optimistic—would be *yes*. In time, that could change. He recognized their hesitancy. They knew this girl with her green skin and lack of emotions was not the same Hazel they raised. She returned, but not unchanged. If she remained this unfeeling automaton, then the doubt would build.

Thomas tapped a feather quill against a page, debating what to tell the Grand Inquisitor. Hazel may not be an immediate danger to herself, but lesser trials had broken stronger people than the Enda family. In time, they might beg the Inquisition to take her a thousand miles away to Selevarian. When that happened, the Inquisition would be ready.

Chapter Three
Awake While Others Dream

"Who are you?" Hazel asked.

A gentle breeze swayed the trees, while the stream whispered endless nothings, but the night was otherwise silent. She stood far from home, more than a mile from the southern edge of Coruvaine's third wall. She watched a large, dark animal sitting twenty feet from her, regarding her with intelligent green eyes.

She folded her arms. "It's usually polite to introduce yourself to strangers."

The creature stood and smiled with bright white teeth. As it moved closer, she noticed the animal was a black dog, though bigger than any she'd seen. "You're correct, Miss Enda. My apologies."

"You're forgiven," she said, examining the creature. "What are you?"

"I'm a grim, and my name is Garo."

"A grim..." She thought for a moment. She remembered stories she read of black dogs given power by fae magic to protect certain areas from harm. Most were sad stories. "Have you come to return me to my grave?"

"No," Garo said, sitting down. "I do not belong to the cemetery where you were once interred. My business is different. May I ask why you're here?"

She considered the creature. Talking to fae in the forest at night was an excellent way to be kidnapped or ensorcelled by their strange magic. Still—despite the stories—she sensed no malicious intentions. "I'm here because my entire existence is tied to this spot. It's the only reason I am the way I am today." She gazed at the ash tree beside her. "I was here with friends when I fell from a high branch and drowned in the creek, unconscious. This is the one place I can go where I don't worry others."

"You don't fear the dark?"

"No. Here there are no... expectations."

The black dog nodded slowly. "I can understand that to an extent. What's changed since you returned to life?"

"Me." Hazel examined her green hand. The alteration should have been alarming—or even devastating—but it wasn't.

"I imagine your parents are pleased you've come back." The grim's tone gave Hazel the impression he was searching for something.

"No, they're not." She looked at Garo. "Hazel Enda died several months ago. The only child of Kyle and Lynn Enda, taken just before she reached adulthood. When I was discovered in that mage's house, they assumed it was me as I was—as they remembered me. But I'm not." She put a hand on the tree and ran her fingers over the bark. "They have now lost two things: they've lost their beloved daughter, and they've lost the perceived right to grieve for her passing. It's a toothless kind of mourning to be sorry for the living. It would have been better for them if I stayed dead."

"I doubt they see it that way."

"You cannot see if your eyes are closed," Hazel replied. "They would never admit it—even to themselves—because it defies all parental instincts. Parents should love their children regardless of what they've done, and to do otherwise is ungodly. My parents are good people and clung to the hope I would improve, but it's been three weeks and nothing has changed. Every day I'm with them they sink deeper into hopelessness and I'm the cause."

A breeze rustled through the branches. It was colder than usual, but Hazel felt no chill or desire to warm herself. The gentle sounds of the forest filled the silence between her and the grim.

"You are more open with your feelings than I would have expected, Hazel Enda, and more insightful than others your age. Few would share such intimate thoughts with a stranger."

"I'm not open with my feelings because I don't have any. As for my honesty, only those who feel pain worry the truth will hurt them. It's easy to be open and clearheaded without emotions." She approached the grim. "Why are you here?"

"I'm here to find you."

"Well, you've found me. What now?"

"Now"—he stood and stretched—"I give you the same offer I gave the others."

She nodded. This sounded familiar. "You've done this same thing three times so far, haven't you?"

Garo's head tilted, and he blinked. "I—well, yes, actually. How did you know?"

She sighed, looking up as a small cloud briefly obscured one of the moons. "I just know things sometimes. I have dreams where something happens and then later it does. Often it's vague, but other times it's direct. I saw you before as well. It was just a week after I'd woken up." She watched the black dog. It was hard to discern the emotions of the creature, but she could sense his growing anxiety as she talked. "You ran through a world of endless white, only disrupted by the passing forms of animated shadows. It was only half of you. Your back half was missing."

Garo retreated a few steps and sounded like he was clearing his throat. She smiled. "You were afraid of me there, too."

He barked a short laugh. "You're absolutely right, Miss Enda, though you had glowing green eyes in the Shadow World and now your eyes are…" he squinted.

She sighed again. "Hazel. My eyes are hazel."

His posture relaxed. "Were you named for the color of your eyes?"

"No. My mother craved hazelnuts when she was pregnant with me and my parents took it as a sign from the gods it was supposed to be my name. Honestly, I think they just couldn't come up with anything else."

He chuckled. "You can move from terrifying to humorous without effort. You have a gift for simultaneously disarming and alarming those around you. I suppose rather than speak to you as I have the others I've made this offer to, I might as well ask: what is it you know?"

"You told the others of some sort of occupation. It's something dangerous, but I don't know what. I think it involves white flowers…"

The grim tilted his head. "Flowers?"

"… or the flowers could've been part of an unrelated dream. I don't know."

His tail wagged slowly. "Well, the first part is correct, at least. Would you be willing to hear the specifics of the offer in exactly one week's time?"

"I would"—she looked back toward the city—"but my parents will never allow it. They barely let me walk near windows. I doubt they're eager to let me start a career."

Garo peered into the canopy, weighing his words. "Your previous insights seem to indicate otherwise."

"I think," she said, staring into the darkness and toward the city, "that they wouldn't want me to leave. They may be miserable with me, but they wouldn't welcome the thought of me disappearing, either."

"Allow me to be blunt," he said. "If you cause your parents' suffering, then it would be most to their benefit—whether or not they recognize it—if you left. I do not mean you should never see them, but if you believe that each time they gaze upon you, they die a little within, then the answer is to live away from them until your emotions return."

"Even the sorcerers of the Sapphire Guard couldn't get my emotions back. Do you think your fairy magic can?"

"No, but sometimes we find what we need when we stop searching for it. If your goal is behind a wall, it may be wiser to seek an aperture than to fruitlessly attempt to scale the stone. What I offer you is a gate to achieving what you desire. It may be a circuitous route, but it has more potential than waiting for a miracle."

She stared into the branches of the trees. "Even if I wanted to, my parents would never consent."

"Their consent is irrelevant. By the laws of these lands, you are an adult and free to do as you see fit. Besides, they recognize they're incapable of protecting you as well as they'd like. Your world has become more dangerous than you realize. Rumors already swirl around your neighborhood and it will only worsen. One day, others will seek to destroy or possess you. When that day comes, it will be crucial to have allies who can aid you. As it stands, your parents are alone in defending you, and they know it isn't enough."

She nodded. She thought back to her time with the Inquisition and Inquisitor Thomas Eller. He hadn't wanted her released, but the king demanded it. She understood little about the Council of Archmages, but she knew the Inquisition worked for them and *not* for the kingdom. How long did she have until they claimed her?

"I'll go."

He nodded. "I'm glad to hear it. You're more important than you realize."

"Do you know what I am?"

He shrugged. "No, not precisely."

"Then how do you know I'm important?"

He gazed at her. The breeze gently lifted strands of her hair. As she pushed them back, she saw her green fingers. She wasn't human. Not like she was before.

"I believe," he said, "importance is only partly related to *what* one is. Have you ever heard of Gazrilan?"

"No," she said after a moment.

"Gazrilan is a five-hundred-year-old dragon. How is it you've never heard of a creature as great and old as Gazrilan?"

"I"—she shook her head—"I don't know. I don't know the names of *every* dragon."

He looked at her slyly. "But you've heard of Gharazan'nar'rakesh, or Alza'varathede, correct?"

"Of course. They're in many stories."

"Then I suppose it doesn't matter *what* one is rather than *who* one is. Gazrilan is many good things, but his full title is Gazrilan the Indolent. He has sought nothing more than to spend his days idly hibernating in the winter and napping in the sun during the summer. He hunts when necessary, but rarely further than a mile from his cave. Occasionally he waylays travelers to hear a few stories, but nothing more. His life is spent doing neither harm nor good." He smiled at her. "Your importance isn't tied to *what* you are, but to *who* you are. I know you're important for who you are, even if I don't know what you are."

"That's nice of you to say, but I'm not sure that's true. I assume you're recruiting me for something you believe I can do, but I don't know what that is. How am I supposed to help if I don't know what I'm doing?"

He leaned forward a little. "I haven't any idea."

"You're uncertain how I can be useful but you want me to join you?"

"Exactly."

"I know I've only been alive a second time for a couple of months, but that doesn't make sense."

"One of the great joys of life is it is not constrained by our abilities to comprehend it," he said. "I know in time you will grow into something beyond my ability to fathom. I await that day, and the day after when you tell me I was right."

She scrutinized the black dog. He was only partly joking. Beneath the humor was a deep sincerity that made her want to believe him, even though he gave no evidence to support it.

She sighed. "I suppose it would be interesting to see what happens, but I have no relevant qualifications. Before I died, I'm pretty sure the only thing I was good at was climbing trees, but my present situation throws that into question."

He laughed. "I'm sure you have other useful skills. But we've tarried here long enough. I told your parents I would get you home safely, so that's what I'll do." He padded back toward the city.

She let him lead the way. They chatted the rest of the way about other matters, but her mind drifted elsewhere. The faintest flicker of emotion sparked in her chest as she walked. Would this really give her a sense of purpose? She doubted it, but she needed to be certain.

Chapter Four
Stranger and Strangers

It was late afternoon when Hazel arrived at the library. The day was clear and bright, which made the old building appear less forbidding than it might have otherwise, given the lack of attention it had received in the past twenty years.

The Calixford University Library had been abandoned for several reasons. Expansions made to the university grounds rendered the location suboptimal for students. Rather than update the structure, the heads of the college constructed an entirely new building that combined research laboratories with the library and brought it to the center of the campus. This older library was over a mile from the main campus, but since the college had gained in prestige, funding, and students, the shift away from this location had to be made.

The building was exceptionally large, and had housed thousands of books, manuscripts, and scrolls while providing ample areas for study, discussion, and reading. It was four stories tall and only slightly rose above the nearby buildings. It haunted the outskirts of the city, and few cared about the abandoned library. For a few years between its desertion and the adoption of the newer facility, this place stored additional copies of certain books, volumes which were outdated, or damaged but still readable works. A single elderly librarian lived among the shelves and fulfilled requests sent by the college. During those interim years, the university attempted to sell many of the books to the public with slight success—Hazel had been an eager patron some years back. When the librarian finally died, the old library shut its doors permanently without further attempts to empty its store of books and items. The university had everything it needed, and nobody else wanted them, and so the old library served no purpose. When its keeper was buried, all memories of the library were buried with him. It had been eight years since she last entered the library that now stood before her.

A slight breeze rustled her short-sleeved white dress and compelled her to hold down her wide sunhat. Before she died, she wouldn't normally have worn such a hat, but she found fewer people noticed the green tone to her skin when she was in shadows. She also wasn't fond of the green shawl draped over her shoulders, but it was a common enough accessory for the beginning of autumn in Coruvaine, and— given the warm weather—was preferable to wearing heavier and more concealing clothing.

The street was quiet, with only an occasional pedestrian leaving home to travel deeper into the city. Since the area surrounding the building was residential, carriages and horses were practically nonexistent. She approached the library and examined the structure before ascending the eight long steps leading to the main entrance. Two large, arched doors of mahogany with etched images of Athelea and Selevara—the goddesses of knowledge and magic, respectively—stood before her. Her brow furrowed when she noticed the chains connecting the handles, preventing entry. She only gazed upon them momentarily when the chains loosened and slithered to the ground. The doors opened to reveal Garo waiting inside.

"Hello, Miss Enda," the grim said. "You'll forgive me for keeping the doors locked. I didn't want just anybody to come in. Please, enter."

Hazel entered the dimly lit antechamber of the library. "Were you waiting for me?"

"No," Garo said, "I was on my way to retrieve another guest and decided to wait for you. Now that you're here, however, I fear I must leave immediately. I apologize for my abrupt departure, but it cannot be helped. I know you enjoy reading, Miss Enda, so use the library as you please. Others are here as well, if you should like to talk with them. Two of them—the last I checked—were resting from a rather long journey. If you want to seek them out, they're upstairs. If not, then I can introduce you when I return. I leave the choice to you." With a bow, the grim padded past her and outside as the doors shut, the chains snaking back into place.

As Hazel wandered into the library proper, she noticed several things as her eyes adjusted to the gloom. A thick layer of dust blanketed the room and gray motes waltzed lazily through the air. The floors were of marble, and columns of the same supported the wooden roof above. Tall windows lined the sides of the building and would have provided ample natural light if wooden shutters didn't prevent even the smallest ray of light from shining through. A vast number of high bookshelves lined the building, with occasional areas where armchairs and tables could be found. Upon the sides of each bookshelf rested dimly glowing spherical magelamps, which dotted the walls and sat upon each table. Rolling ladders leaned against each shelf, though many were broken or of dubious integrity. Thick rugs in the sitting areas provided quiet to the library, as did many aged tapestries which lined the space between the windows. Piles of books and scrolls littered the tables, chairs, and sides of the bookcases. In its peak years, this place might have been majestic or been a haven for the erudite, but now it served only as an echo of its former self. A hollow memory of its former self.

Hazel—not having any powerful desires to meet people without introduction—perused the derelict shelves. There was something sad but comforting about this building. In life, Hazel had privately imagined that her books had personalities and were akin to children. Taking in old and used books was much like adopting a child, Hazel thought.

This library would have seemed like a massive orphanage peopled by abandoned children now thin from malnutrition. These books waited, or perhaps they slept. As she strolled through the library, she squinted at a book written in a language she didn't recognize. Many of the books were similarly alien to her, while others were written as intermediary volumes bridging between missing tomes.

She let out a stifled sneeze as she browsed one shelf, scrutinizing titles in the dim light. She paused and listened. Was someone talking? She followed the whispers to the back of the library, winding her way through the maze of shelves, book stacks, and chairs to its origin.

"... no good. No good at all. Is this the best he could do? No, you shouldn't be here. What? *Why...* ugh. I don't care how much they respected you as a librarian. This is unacceptable..." Hazel found the source of the muttering. It was a tall young man with short dark hair, surrounded by stacks of books. He removed additional books from the shelf as he spoke.

"Karling's *Guide to the Iron Mountains* next to Ellion's *Sorcery and Its Practitioners*? What *is* this? Who thought this was a good idea? Why not follow the imperial archival standard? If the best scholars in Scripthaven devised it, then it *probably* works. Instead, you just—" the man looked up and noticed Hazel observing him calmly. "Oh! Oh," he said, rising to his feet and dusting himself off. "I'm sorry. I didn't realize you were standing there. I'm a little embarrassed. You caught me thinking out loud."

"That's alright, we all do it," Hazel said, eyeing the books. "What's the problem?"

"The problem is the former librarian either had no organizational scheme, had boggarts putting books in random places, or else had a method of categorization requiring some secret computation to figure out how to sort things. Just now I found a beginner's guide to magic next to a book on geography. Neither author was alphabetically close to the other, nor were the titles or dates of publication related. The most depressing thing of all is that nothing has escaped the chaos. They aren't even arranged by genre!"

"That is annoying," Hazel agreed. "I hate when my books are disorganized."

"*Exactly,*" he said, his eyes widening emphatically. "You understand, but I don't know why the librarian didn't." Then, realizing the abruptness of their encounter, he bowed. "I'm afraid I forgot to introduce myself properly. My apologies, miss. My name is Alistair."

"Alistair, it's nice to meet you," she replied. "I'm Hazel. I assume Garo met with you as well?"

"Yes, he did." Alistair nodded absently, straightening a book on the shelf. "Ambassador Garo is quite an interesting person."

"That's putting it lightly."

"Perhaps a little." Alistair flashed her a smile. "Did he tell you anything about why we're here?"

"No, he was very vague. What about you?"

"Equally cryptic to me as well. It seems we're both in the dark."

"Yes, and it's not just the aging magelamps," Hazel said. "How can you even see the titles? Wouldn't it be easier to open the windows?"

He scrunched his nose. "I'm a little sensitive to sunlight. Besides, it gets easier once your eyes adjust."

Hazel paused and studied him briefly. It was hard to tell in the dark, but he was pale. "I guess the sun wouldn't be desirable, given your complexion."

Alistair placed a couple more books on the shelf. "You are quite right, though judging by your own clothing, it seems you require similar protection."

She shrugged. "I burn easily."

"Then I suppose we are agreed: the less sunlight, the better. Besides, excessive sunlight can damage books."

"It can?"

"Maybe." He shrugged playfully. "I can't say I know for certain, but it sounds plausible, doesn't it?"

She crossed her arms. "For a moment, I thought I'd learned something new."

"Sorry to disappoint. I can only pray you'll one day recover from my momentary deception."

"It will take time, but I think I can eventually heal from this injury and trust again."

He put a hand over his heart. "Thank the gods."

Hazel smiled. "I like you. Let's be friends."

He returned the smile. "Nothing would please me more."

"I hope the others Garo met with are equally friendly."

Alistair wrinkled his nose.

"What?" Hazel asked. "Do you know anyone else?"

Alistair grimaced. "I only met one other, and I found that *person* to be... challenging. Rather than remain, I repaired here and got sidetracked by the lack of order. I can be a little obsessive regarding organization and precision."

"How long have you been down here?"

"What time is it?" He kneeled down, dusting off another book.

"About four in the afternoon, I believe."

"Huh," Alistair said, taken aback. "I've been rearranging books for the last five hours. Time passes swiftly when you're in good company."

"And what better company is there than a book?"

"None, save perhaps a fellow bibliophile."

Hazel smiled and leaned against a shelf. "Are you always so charming?"

"Only when there is someone capable of being charmed."

"You should save it, then. I'm sure there's a thousand others in Coruvaine who would swoon if you batted an eye in their direction."

He frowned with mock distress. "But not you?"

"Not me. I get the impression you're a little old for me. I'm guessing you're somewhere around twenty-five, or twenty-six?"

He wavered his hand in the air. "More or less. Nonetheless, I was merely teasing. Becoming romantically involved with someone closer to your own age would be prudent." Alistair chuckled. "You're an interesting one, Hazel. I will confess, after meeting the person upstairs, I had my doubts about whether I should stay, but I think your presence has persuaded me to remain for at least a little while. That, and I need to sort through this mess."

"I can help with that," Hazel offered. "I enjoy organizing books."

"It's a relief to find a kindred soul," Alistair replied. "But I think we need a plan of attack. Can you handle the shelf behind me? I think that row is supposed to be on various animals, so you can sort them accordingly."

"Will do."

They reorganized the shelves for a little longer, all the while speaking casually with each other. She learned more about Alistair's various interests, and shared information about herself when asked. It was nice to feel at ease with someone. Alistair was often formal with his mannerisms, but she never got the impression he was condescending to her or treating her like a delicate flower. His kindness appeared genuine, as did his reactions to everything she said. This continued another hour before they heard the whisper of Garo's voice say, "It's time. Come upstairs to the common area," before fading away as hauntingly as it arrived.

Hazel relinquished the book she held to a random shelf. She had little luck sorting the books in the low light and resolved to bring a candle next time.

"I suppose the rest will have to wait until a later date." Alistair sighed, gazing longingly at the shelves. "I was hoping to at least make a *slight* improvement before he returned. Oh well. We'll organize these books eventually, Hazel, and *maybe* we can do so according to the imperial archival standard. *That* would be quite exciting."

Alistair dusted off his hands and brought Hazel deeper into the building and up a wide marble stairway that branched off into two symmetrical spirals ascending to the second level. From the second level landing, he led her to a doorway across from the stairs and up another sharply curving flight of wooden steps. Upon reaching the top of the flight, Alistair guided her through a closed door while the stairs continued still higher. They entered a large hallway that opened up into a room with ample furniture on one side and a doorway leading to a kitchen on the other. The furniture looked either new or restored and was free of dust or blemish. Thick rugs covered the hardwood floors, and a large fireplace added to the homey characteristics of the common area. Ensconced magelamps cast a warm and gentle light upon the room, in contrast to those upon the ground level of the building. Only one thing seemed strange, and it was a pair of legs crossed over the arm of a couch whose back faced Alistair and Hazel. The legs bobbed and the feet—which were bare—moved in tune with a rhythm their owner was whistling.

"Is that you, pretty boy?" a woman asked from the couch.

Alistair's face twitched. "Did no one ever tell you it's impolite to sit on a couch that way?"

"Depends," the woman said, shifting into a sitting position. "Did no one ever tell you the wooden stake is meant to be shoved into your heart, not shoved up your"—the speaker rose to face Alistair but, seeing Hazel, aborted her retort—"hey, I didn't know someone else was here. Who's the green girl?"

The young woman who leaped from the couch appeared to be Alistair's age, or perhaps a few years younger. She had a light coppery tan, and medium length dark brown hair that fell in wild tangles around her head. Her clothing was worn and minimalistic. Despite this apparent disregard for appearance, she was exceptionally beautiful, and her amber eyes showed a wily humor. She approached Hazel inquisitively.

"I'm Hazel Enda," Hazel replied, unfazed by the abruptness and straightforward question. She turned to Alistair. "Is she the person you mentioned?"

"How did you guess?" Alistair asked dryly.

"Hazel, huh?" The young woman said, ignoring the exchange.

"So, what's with the green skin, anyway?" She held up one of Hazel's arms, examining it. "Let me guess: zombie. No, no, wait... banshee. Oh, hold on! Uh... tree spirit! Okay, now tell me."

"I don't really know, but I guess I'm kind of like a zombie?"

"Perfect. I totally guessed it right the first time. I have an intuition about these things." She grinned. "I'm Lara, I'm a werewolf. It's great to meet you, Hazel."

She gave Hazel a quick hug before turning to Alistair. She left one arm draped over Hazel's shoulders.

"So nice that the prince of sulking around and obsessing over details could join us today. I thought I scared you off. I know I'm probably pretty terrifying to your sensibilities, O Grand Eminent Lord of High Princeliness."

"I can think of many terrifying things about you, Lara," Alistair said, crossing his arms, "but most concern your hygiene and lack of decorum. It'd take more than that to deter me from being here."

"Oh-ho! So pretty boy actually *can* handle being around people who aren't dressed in silk and satin," Lara replied with a smirk. "I guess I misjudged you. Then again, I don't know much about vampires. Tell me something: do you crap upside down like a bat?"

Hazel blinked. "You're a vampire?"

"Yes," Alistair said, "a nosferatu, to be exact. As for your question, Lara, I will not dignify it with a response."

"But wasn't *that* a response?"

Alistair drew in a deep breath to reply when an exhausted, articulate voice sighed from the staircase they just exited.

"Is this really why I left Elliara—to hear senseless bickering?" A gray-skinned half-elf stepped from the stairway, rubbing his temples and clenching his jaw. He was several inches shorter than Alistair and only slightly taller than Lara, though he was slenderer than either of them. His red irises studied the room beneath two elegantly arching eyebrows until they settled on Hazel.

"You..." he said, striding to her, his thin black hair flowing gracefully behind him as he inspected her. "You... are most intriguing..."

"Hey, weirdo, how about giving her some space, huh?" Lara said, forgetting or actively ignoring her previous lack of boundaries. "I mean, it's not like you can just walk up to someone and—" He snapped his fingers in Lara's direction without taking his attention from Hazel. A light blue wisp of smoke momentarily wafted from his fingers and a transparent sphere of the same color appeared around Lara's head. Her mouth moved, but no sound pierced the bubble.

"That's arguably the best thing that's happened all day," Alistair said, approaching the half dark elf. "Thank y—" he snapped again in Alistair's direction and the vampire, too, was silenced by a blue bubble. All the while, his attention never shifted from Hazel.

"You are extraordinary." He gazed at her with subdued awe. From this close Hazel noticed he was close to her age, though his large eyes may have made him look younger than he was. "What are you called?"

"I'm Hazel," she said, observing the other two, who appeared thoroughly distressed. "Can they breathe in those bubbles?"

"The spheres of Elchoran block sound, nothing else," the half-elf replied whilst moving his hands around her. "Though I doubt a vampire even needs to breathe. The spheres only last a few minutes. Unfortunately."

She watched small sparks dart from his hands as he drew symbols in the air at different points. Some gestures reminded her of similar motions spellcasters used to determine what magic had brought her back to life. "Spheres of Elchoran?" she asked. "Are you Elchoran?"

"No, no, Elchoran was an archmage three-thousand years ago who studied sound. He taught the spell to his students to help them when studying during the construction of the first citadel of the Council of Archmages."

"Ah, I see," Hazel said. "Then what *is* your name?"

"I'm Lyvaelan. What are you called?"

"I'm Hazel—"

"No—no, I mean, what *species* are you?"

"Oh, I'm human."

"Human? Really?" Lyvaelan locked eyes with her. "I wouldn't have guessed that. Strange. You're not really human, are you?"

"Yes, I am," Hazel protested. "At least I was born human."

Lyvaelan arched an eyebrow. "What is *that* supposed to mean?"

"I was born human, died human, then came back to life like this."

"Ah..." His eyes widened, and he examined her with renewed interest, though his voice remained calm and even. Hazel noticed the other two appeared similarly surprised. "And yet, you're not a zombie, and likely not a revenant. Intriguing."

"What? How did you know I'm not either?"

"Your aura. Whatever happened to you changed you into something linked to nature magic, though I can't say for certain."

Alistair and Lara both stared daggers into Lyvaelan, though he was unbothered by the vehemence they showed toward him.

"Lyvaelan, really." Garo's smooth and dark voice slid through the air as he slipped from the shadows. "I don't even have a chance to introduce you and you're already making trouble. If you'd please, release them from their spheres immediately." Although his words were firm, Hazel could detect the slightest hint of amusement in them.

"If I must, Ambassador," Lyvaelan replied, "though I like them better with the spheres." He again snapped his fingers, and both bubbles disappeared with a small *pop*.

"The elf is as bad as you, pretty boy," Lara muttered.

"Enough," Garo said, moving to the middle of the sitting area. "I'm happy to see you're all getting along so well. I see your love for each other was inevitable. However, I didn't summon you here for playful banter. I would ask that you focus on what I have to say, as I dislike repeating myself. First, I will introduce our benefactor. We have him to thank for the use of this library and the opportunity you will all be offered. This is my good friend, Aldric."

Chapter Five
The Heroic Goal of Monsters

Aldric smiled from the hallway. He wore a turquoise tunic with geometric embroidery running in waves and loops through the cloth. A black velvet cape that reached his ankles billowed behind him as he walked. He was a few years older than Hazel's father, with salt and pepper hair and a beard. She hadn't met him before, and yet he nodded toward her with familiarity. Hazel glanced at Alistair as a range of emotions played over his face.

"Thank you all for coming," Aldric said. "I eagerly anticipate learning more about each of you later. Please, let's sit and hear what Garo has to say."

They sat around the grim who waited in the middle of the common area. Hazel sat on the couch Lara had vacated for a large blue armchair. Aldric joined Hazel. He greeted her with a warm smile. Alistair sighed and rolled his eyes, turning his attention to Garo.

"You all know me, and so I shall inform you of my occupation instead. I have worked several centuries as an ambassador for the Seelie Court, which encompasses the elves and the rest of the well-intentioned fae. My involvement over the years in human kingdoms has grown from that of an emissary to consultation beyond what the court-appointed philosophers provide. Most recently, I collaborated with the King of Ethelian, and together we've developed a plan that's equal parts promising and unusual. We hope the four of you can help test this new program."

The shadows cast by the fireplace danced across the room into discernable shapes. Images flitted across the walls as the grim spoke. Lara and Alistair sat upright, watching the magic display. Lyvaelan stared at Garo intently as the black dog continued, "I possess the ability to travel into a realm called the Shadow World. Within the darkness, I behold inklings of the future. I want the four of you to spearhead this endeavor because the shadows identified you as the ideal candidates.

"I now relinquish the floor to Aldric, who will present additional information along with details of the occupation I mentioned to each of you."

The shadows relaxed into a lazy flicker as Garo moved to the side. Aldric stood and strode to the center of the room, facing them. His pleasant expression was replaced by one of earnest seriousness.

"I would first like to thank you for answering Garo's summons. I know some of you traversed great distances while others were close. Irrespective of the length of your journeys, you all came. For that, you have my gratitude."

He took a deep breath. "I want you to form a unique branch of the military, specifically in law enforcement. In recent years, the city guard has been beleaguered with an increasing number of deadly nocturnal crimes. The guards can handle gang activity and burglary with few problems, but recent incidents have been... extreme, of late."

"How do you mean?" Lara asked. She had resumed a relaxed slouch in her seat with one leg over the arm of her chair.

"I mean, it isn't simple human crime anymore. Spellcasters, therianthropes, vampires, fae, daimon, and others create problems that the average soldier is ill-equipped to handle." He held up a hand to stave off protestations. "I'm *not* saying any entire group is wholly at fault for the crimes of the few. Only the guilty are guilty. What I *am* saying is when one criminal with considerable power appears, soldiers cannot handle it adequately, which usually results in death or severe injury. The problems have steadily worsened, and so a more proactive measure must be implemented. That proactive measure is you four."

"Forgive the interruption," Alistair said, "but isn't there already a division of the military dedicated to such tasks?"

"You're right. It would be that division of the military—specifically a subset of the city guards—you would join, at least until you establish yourselves as an independent group. For those of you unaware, by accepting this offer, you would become Watchers of the Evenfall Vigil. The Evenfall Vigil handles criminal activity surrounding superhuman phenomena, which may be criminals using magic, or powerful races committing crimes. As it currently exists, they are predominantly human, and I have wanted to diversify their ranks for some time. They're the best in the city, but being human comes with drawbacks, not the least of which is predictability. The easier criminals can guess the moves of my soldiers, the more likely my soldiers will end up dead." He sighed heavily. "Too many have fallen in recent history." He locked eyes with each of them. "All of you would provide some randomness to the movements of the Evenfall Vigil, which will shake nocturnal criminal activity to its core. Your designation would give you autonomy to do what you believe is best and to investigate independently."

"How does it benefit us?" Lara asked, twirling her hair absently.

His lip twitched, as if concealing a smile. "You will receive two silver merchants per month, which is a little more than double the payment any guard would receive." Hazel's eyebrows lifted. Her parents' modest home cost sixteen silver merchants. It was strange to think that in eight months she could afford to buy her own home.

"In addition," Aldric continued, pacing before them, "your room and board will be paid for, so the entirety of your salary would mostly be for any extraneous costs. Beyond that, you could submit requests for equipment, training, or anything you might require and—if the request is deemed necessary—then it shall be granted in full without impacting your remuneration. As time passes and I see the results of what you have done, your pay will increase, as will your authority within the standard ranks of the Evenfall Vigil. Depending on your success, I may grant you actual commanding power over the guards or the spellcasters in my employ, though that would be a matter to discuss in the future."

"What makes us qualified?" Lyvaelan asked. "Besides being oddities in the human world, I doubt any of us possess training in law enforcement. The vampire could be helpful, and the werewolf girl presumably has some strength—though she seems as likely to commit crimes as she does to prevent them. But what of us? This undead girl has no abilities relevant to combat. I've spent my life away from excitement, so I don't cause an arcane cataclysm that could threaten innocent lives. Placing me in the middle of circumstances where I need to act swiftly could be too much excitement. Why would the king want us working in his city?"

"What do you mean by *that*?" Lara asked, sitting up. "What arcane cataclysm?"

Lyvaelan averted his eyes and wrung his hands. Garo spoke softly. "Lyvaelan is half dark elf, half warlock."

Lara and Alistair recoiled at this information while Aldric winced.

"I hoped to avoid bringing it up, Ambassador," Lyvaelan whispered. "My lineage is not a source of pride."

"Be that as it may," Garo replied loudly, "I trust you. I know your limitations and would not have you here if I believed it would be ruinous. Besides, the others need to know so that they have faith in you as I do. The basis of all healthy relationships is mutual trust. That is what we must build."

Hazel remembered stories of warlocks, but each had a hint of whimsy that inclined her to believe the information contained in them was either inaccurate or metaphorical. Tales of these creatures focused on their destructive nature and typically ended with them destroying themselves. A "warlock" often seemed like an epithet for an evil spell-caster of great power, although she noticed no malice in him.

"I have to agree with him regarding qualifications," Hazel remarked quietly. "I don't have any special powers, or background, or knowledge in anything. I returned from the dead, and as amazing as that is, it isn't something I chose. No power of mine resurrected me. I'd just get in the way."

"Actually," Garo smiled, "you have a special role. You all do."

He rose and paced the room as Aldric returned to his seat. The grim stopped before each person, looking them in the eye.

"Whether you four recognize it, your abilities in combination make you a deadly force. Alistair has persuasive abilities, excellent hearing, and is a student of the sword. Lara has experience fighting in the arena against numerous enemies and possesses naturally heightened tracking skills and incredible strength. Lyvaelan knows much about magic and can use it faster than most. Hazel"—his green eyes glittered—"can see many hidden things."

"What's that supposed to mean?" Lara asked.

"She could see me traveling through the Shadow World. Only creatures of darkness can enter that realm in order to move from one location to another. Somehow, she saw me there. If she did not see me *literally,* then the metaphorical act of gazing through the shadows indicates possible precognition." He grinned. "The potential usefulness of knowing a crime may happen before it actually does is not lost on us."

The grim paused. "That aside, none of you are perfect, and it will take time before you function in anything more than passable fashion. No one expects immediate perfection. I urge you all to be patient with yourselves and with each other. Strive to work together as a team. You may all be individually strong, but if you use your powers in concert, you may well be unstoppable.

"I'm also part of this group, to an extent, but my involvement is necessarily minimal. I have many responsibilities as an ambassador and cannot legally be employed by a human kingdom. Nonetheless, I remain one of the chief overseers of this project. It's also worthwhile to note that although this initiative only currently affects this kingdom, it was also approved by the Seelie Court and the King of the Nosferatu. In other words, your jurisdiction extends into both territories, though your responsibilities will—for now—be contained to Coruvaine alone."

Lara sighed loudly. "Okay, I know I already asked this, but what's in it for me? I mean, the pay isn't exactly what I'm looking for. I could make just as much or more in the ring."

"For you, Lara," Garo said, "a chance to do something meaningful with your life. A chance to be part of a greater community. A chance to meet and overcome challenges worth your time."

"Hmm. Yeah... I'm going to pass on that. Thanks for the *chances*, though. I'd prefer to make the same amount fighting in the ring where I'm less likely to die horribly." Lara directed this statement toward Lyvaelan as she stood and walked toward the stairs.

"Wait!" Aldric exclaimed. "You're just going to walk out?"

"That's the plan."

Aldric bit his lip and looked to the side, considering. A slow smile spread across his face. "You make bets in Treland, don't you?"

Her hand rested on the rail, but she paused. "Yeah, so?"

"I have a wager for you."

Garo cocked his head at Aldric.

"How much money do you make in half a year?" Aldric asked.

"Well," she said, gazing at the ceiling, "each match I usually make four silver commons, which I would then bet on myself to make eight. Two fights a week, means sixteen silver commons each week, then four weeks in a month, and six months in half a year, which would bring the total to..." She scrunched her nose doing the mental math.

"Three hundred and eighty-four silver commons," Alistair said almost immediately.

Hazel's eyes widened. Her parents' house cost less than half that amount.

Aldric nodded. "Very well. Besides your weekly salary, I will make a bet with you. If, by the end of the six months you work here, you choose to leave because the work isn't for you, then I will compensate you with approximately double your earnings for that time period, a full seven silver nobles. If by that time you choose to stay, then I will still pay the amount you would have made in the arena: three silver nobles, eight silver merchants, and four silver commons."

She raised an eyebrow. "If you're trying to get me to stay permanently, you know that bet actually incentivizes me quitting in six months, right?"

He shrugged. "You can either leave now or leave later. If you truly have no interest in the group by then, you'll leave wealthy. If you choose to stay, it will be due to your appreciation for this work. Plus, you'll still get that pleasant bonus of your winnings to lessen the disappointment of losing out on double that amount. Even if you lose the bet, you essentially win."

Lara hesitated. She crossed her arms and leaned against the wall, fighting some internal battle. "Even if that was true, who are you to throw money like a witch throws hexes?"

Alistair rubbed the bridge of his nose. "He's the King of Ethelian." Lara's jaw dropped and Hazel's eyebrows raised. The king was sitting beside her just a moment ago and she didn't realize it. This situation got even stranger.

Aldric scowled. "Did you have to end the fun so quickly, Alistair?"

The vampire crossed his arms. "I think you've had enough fun for one evening, *Your Majesty*."

Aldric shrugged. "What about the rest of you? Will you join this endeavor? Part of the reason for my now-ruined anonymity was to provide you the chance to unite without feeling you are making the decision under duress. This is your choice, though I sincerely hope you accept."

The room was quiet as they contemplated the offer.

"My parents..." Hazel finally said. "Do they know how dangerous this is?"

"At a certain point, Miss Enda, we must decide whether we will do what we wish or what others wish of us," Garo said softly. "Will you make your decisions or let others make them for you?"

Hazel gazed at her fern green hands. She didn't need to ask for the ages of those around her; she knew she was the youngest. What role could she have to play in the fate of Coruvaine? Not half a year ago she ran barefoot with her friends through the nearby woods without a care, but now she'd somehow become important? She hadn't wished to die, but she hadn't asked to be brought back either. This didn't upset her, but she was aware how passive her role was since she'd returned from the dead. She was caught in a stream of others making choices for her that she couldn't escape.

"It's not our circumstances which define us," the grim continued, almost like he was reading her mind, "but what we choose to do when we are placed in them."

This statement resonated through the room as the group pondered what decision to make.

"I'll do it," Hazel said in her typically soft voice. "Ever since I was resurrected, I haven't felt right. I haven't felt much of anything, really. But this might change that. Until now, my choices have been made for me. This time, I choose to join the Evenfall Vigil."

The rest appeared visibly surprised, not only that she spoke, but that such a quiet girl should join so quickly. It was only Aldric and Garo who looked pleased, rather than astonished.

Alistair glanced to the side, clenching both fists. A moment later, he relaxed his hands and smiled at Hazel. "I can't very well let a fellow bibliophile undertake such a dangerous occupation alone. I guess I'm in as well."

"Despite that," Lara said, "I'll join too. You can only win so many fights before the competition gets monotonous. Maybe this'll shake things up a bit. Plus"—she grinned wolfishly at Aldric—"I have a bet to win."

Garo turned to Lyvaelan, who was deep in thought, leaning with both elbows on his knees, his nose and chin resting on his hands joined with interlocking fingers, staring at a fixed point somewhere in front of him.

"This will kill one or all of us," he stated softly. He was silent for several moments. "I think this may ruin me. Is the cause really so important, Garo?"

The room was quiet, and the building energy disappeared. Garo gazed kindly at Lyvaelan. "It is."

Lyvaelan closed his eyes and heaved a heavy sigh. "Then I, too, will join. Even though it seems like a terrible idea that will end in utter disaster."

"I can tell he's gonna be fun to work with," Lara muttered.

"I'm elated you have all agreed to help," Aldric said, not waiting to see if Lyvaelan would respond to Lara. "Your exceptional talents will benefit this city greatly."

"Perhaps you could go over the specifics of the contract we have," Alistair said. "What precisely will we be doing?"

"In the first place," Aldric said, rising from his seat, "I should give you these." He drew from his pocket several small, brightly polished steel badges. Each badge had emblazoned on it the seal of the Kingdom of Ethelian: a fox sejant with a spindle of yarn above it, surrounded by grape leaves. Outside this seal on one side was a star and on the other side the moon Progon in crescent, cradling the smaller full moon, Kythis. Above the images it read: "Evenfall Vigil," and below it was the motto of the guards: "vigilant in darkness."

"These are your official marks of service," Aldric continued. "Watchers possess a higher rank than the normal guard, and so you will be capable of issuing basic orders in case of an emergency. In the next couple of weeks, we will inform the guards of these changes. I would advise against using these until you meet your superior officer, however, as they still need to be magically infused and linked to each of you.

"My expectations are simple. There are many cases available which could benefit from your expertise. Frankly, any improvement is improvement enough. I suspect—despite your individual talents—you will need time before you can properly work as a team. With that in mind, I have a matter that has been increasingly problematic in recent months. Somewhere in this city, there is an alchemist—or alchemists—who have been creating illegal potions that turn average criminals into rampaging monsters. We've worked to discover the root of these deals, but every time the guards get close, they reach a dead end. Those who use the compounds lack coherence for some time after and their memories are significantly impaired. We suspect this alchemist is using these individuals as test subjects before trying something bigger."

"Okay..." Lara said, "but I'm pretty sure none of us are detectives or anything. What makes you think we'll succeed where the guards failed?"

"I have a couple of reasons," Aldric said. "First, your enhanced physical attributes should allow you to apprehend any suspects before they do significant harm. Second, you each have special gifts normal humans do not, which might provide an edge to discovering the whereabouts of the Alchemist. Because of your enhanced senses and skills, you may find the users of this potion before they take it and thus prevent them from destroying their own memories, which could provide the clues to their supplier. While I do have several investigators on this case, they are ill-equipped to deal with many magic-related crimes, and the time it takes to have a spellcaster appear to help often allows the trail to disappear before sufficient headway can be made. Having a pure team of spellcasters has also been unsuccessful."

Alastair nodded. "That's understandable. Spellcasters require time and focus to use magic, whereas guards can act immediately but ineffectively. An enhanced human could quickly subdue the guards and rush the spellcaster, which could cause spells to go awry, unless the spellcaster is trained in combative magic."

Aldric stroked his beard. "Precisely. Since the War of the Night ended, most spellcasters are inadequately trained for combat."

A clattering of pans in a room nearby startled the group. This was followed by a high-pitched gurgling voice which didn't sound like it was speaking in common imperial.

"What was *that?*" Lara bolted upright, looking at Garo.

"Ah yes," Garo said as if just remembering something, "I haven't introduced you to your chef yet."

All four responded in unison, "Chef?"

Garo sat up. "Yes, your resident chef and steward. If this is to be your home, you must have a housekeeper. He's a little unusual, but he makes excellent desserts and is fastidious in his more domestic chores." The grim turned in the voice's direction. "Charlie! Come here for a minute. The members of the team have finally arrived, and I want to introduce you."

A light knocking noise was heard, but no one was seen until the source arrived in front of the group, becoming visible. The creature before them was short, no taller than three feet, and had dark orange skin. Its body was lanky, which made its wide face stand out more on its beanpole-thin torso. A wide mouth spread in a nervous smile, with scores of small, sharp teeth, and a miniscule nose. Large, yellow eyes resembling a cat's darted between them, while its small and pointed ears twitched. It walked slightly hunched over, which highlighted the fact that its arms were almost the same length as its legs. Each hand possessed four muscular, but thin, fingers upon each of which was a long, sharp black talon. Finally, completing the creature's appearance, was a brown tunic, iron boots, and a simple red cap on its head. Lyvaelan, Lara, and Alistair all jumped at the appearance of this creature.

"A redcap!" Lyvaelan exclaimed, holding his hands before him as purple motes of light buzzed like agitated wasps between his fingers. "Are you insane? What is a redcap doing here?"

"This," Garo said, striding over to the creature, "is Charlie. Be nice to him, he's sensitive. His race is typically too dangerous to approach, but since he was discovered by brownies at an early age, he was raised to be an immaculate housekeeper. He's actually quite gifted, though his appearance and the reputation of his race throw most people into a bit of a panic. But believe me, he's trustworthy, and an excellent chef."

"A redcap as a housekeeper," Lara muttered, crossing her arms, "now I've seen everything."

"Pleeeeeassssse," Charlie hissed, removing his cap deferentially, revealing his hairless head, "pleeeease to... m-m-met you. I... will do b-b-bessss-besssst job to help youuuu."

"Aww," Hazel cooed. The earnest expression on the face of the little demented creature before her, and his stuttering attempt to communicate, made him oddly adorable. "Thank you. I hope we can be friends."

The redcap grinned literally from ear to ear before pointing one claw at his chest, "I, Charlie," then pointing at Hazel, "you?"

"I'm Hazel."

"Hazel. Yessss. Be friennndsss. What... what you like eaaaat?"

"I like chocolate."

"Choc-late." His yellow eyes twinkled. "I make." Charlie instantly disappeared, and the sounds of bustling in the kitchen resumed.

"It appears he's taken a liking to you, Hazel," Aldric remarked with a chuckle.

"He's so cute," Hazel replied with a smile.

"I wouldn't advise getting close to him," Lyvaelan said, frowning. "Redcaps dye their hats with human blood."

"While that's normally true," Garo said, "it turns out the need to dye their caps red consistently is rooted in a severe compulsion. Since he was raised from infancy by an extremely peaceful race, he only recently started dying his cap red. The red is a combination of cherries, cranberries, and pomegranate, if I'm not mistaken. His compulsion is not as severe as most, and relatively harmless. Charlie sometimes loses his temper, but only under extreme duress. He gets depressed faster than he gets angered. Please appreciate his work and don't judge him too harshly because of his species."

The redcap reappeared with a silver platter laden with a variety of chocolate desserts, ranging from truffles and cake to muffins and brownies. He proffered the tray to Hazel, who took a small muffin from the stack.

"Thank you, Charlie."

"Wel-welcome," he replied, "have-have rest?"

"Oh," Hazel said, "I couldn't possibly eat all this, but perhaps everyone else might want some?"

Charlie looked around the room and held the tray aloft tentatively. "W-want ssssome?"

"Why not?" Lara shrugged, but reached over cautiously to snatch a handful of truffles and brownie. "I'm sitting with a warlock, so I guess dessert is the least of my worries."

"I suppose it would be rude not to try some," Alistair said, taking a cookie. "Thank you, Charlie."

"W-welcome," Charlie turned to Lyvaelan. "You want?"

Lyvaelan rolled his eyes and grabbed a chocolate truffle. "I hope this doesn't kill me."

The King of Ethelian helped himself to a large slice of cake.

The grim refused with a smile. "I'm afraid chocolate doesn't agree with dogs, even of the ghostly fae variety."

Each person nibbled their food before looking up in astonishment.

Lyvaelan gasped. "It's *good*. You actually *made* this?"

"Yesss. All make, on own."

Lyvaelan's eyes widened as he stared at the redcap. "Incredible. Here, come back with that tray. I don't think I've tasted a dessert this good in Elliara before. You've outdone any light elf I've encountered."

Charlie grinned wider and puffed out his chest with pride. The others had similar praise. The entire experience had—in some ways—helped relieve the tension between the new members of the Evenfall

Vigil. The uncertainty before the arrival of the redcap had dissipated.

"Charlie," Alistair said, enjoying his second cookie. "How did you make these so quickly? Hazel requested chocolate, and you prepared these desserts in moments."

"I'mmmm jusssssst the bes-besssst chef." The creature's grin took on a mischievous curl.

"Charlie is not above teasing," Garo said. "I told him chocolate is a beloved dessert most here would enjoy. He *did* make everything, he just did so in advance and excess."

Charlie made a farting noise with his lips. "Pffff. Fun sssssspoiler."

"Hazel," Lyvaelan said, ignoring the conversation, "Garo mentioned you've been having precognitive dreams. Is that true?"

"You mean dreams of the future?" Hazel asked.

"Yes. Is that accurate?"

"Well... sort of. They've been little dreams. Dreams of things like a carriage breaking down a few streets from my home, or dreaming that my mother gave me a dozen daisies and then the next day receiving them as a gift. It isn't every night, and usually the dreams are vague. I can't control them."

Lyvaelan nodded intently. "That's because you haven't learned how."

Her eyebrows rose. "You can learn that?"

"Of course." Lyvaelan shifted in his seat, still looking at her. "Dreams are the first step in seeing visions of the future. I have trained in the art of farsight, and the principles are essentially identical. For you to harness your natural foresight abilities may take you only a year or so."

"Can you teach me?" The prospect of learning to control her dreams and understanding the future excited the smallest spark within her.

"Me?" Lyvaelan exclaimed with arched eyebrows, his eyes searching the room. "I'm sure you could find a better teacher."

"Do you mean you won't teach me?"

"Well..." he hesitated, shifting uncomfortably, "no, not exactly... I just think you could find someone better. *Anyone* better."

"I disagree," Hazel replied. "You know how to use farsight, which you say is similar. I also don't know anyone else who could teach me."

"I'm not much removed from being a total stranger."

"Yes, but we'll work together," she said, staring into his deep red eyes, "so this might help build that bond. Of course, if you don't want to, I understand. I don't want to burden you."

Lyvaelan searched the room with his eyes before shaking his head. "No, it's not that at all. I can instruct you. It would also give me a chance to examine you further. I've never heard of a revenant or zombie capable of foreseeing the future, though liches and draugr sometimes can. Perhaps working closely with you will help me better understand what you are."

"If you find out, please tell me," Hazel replied. "I'd like to know what sort of thing I am."

"The most important thing," Aldric interjected, "is who you are, not what you are. You're Hazel. So long as there's that, you have everything you need. Though I will let you know if my sorcerers extract any additional information from Hickory Allkirk that could prove useful."

"I was wondering about that," Hazel said with a thoughtful frown. "When can I see Hickory? My parents were told contact between us wouldn't happen soon, but I want to talk to him at *some* point. There are things I want to say that I haven't been able to."

Aldric hesitated. "Well... at present, it's difficult to say when you'll be able to meet with him, since we understand so little about how he revived you. I understand your desire for closure surrounding this entire ordeal, though. We'll eventually find some way for you to say your piece without the potential for a trap spell."

"I see," Hazel replied. It was mildly disappointing, but expected.

Lyvaelan studied her for a moment. "It's possible that by improving your abilities, you may discover what you are. That may lead to an understanding of the magic the spellcaster used to revive you."

"Do you really think so?"

He shrugged. "It's a possibility. I don't think it's likely, but there are few disadvantages to trying."

"There it is"—Lara jumped in—"that famous dark elf optimism I've heard so much about."

Lyvaelan shot her a steely glance through narrowed eyes. "You know, you're much more charming with a sphere of Elchoran over your head."

Lara winked. "Trust me, I don't need to talk to be aggravating."

"I believe it."

"I just realized something," Alistair said. "How are we supposed to start? Do we simply find and arrest people, or do we need special training?"

The Garo smiled. "I think it may be best for you to learn how to swim by jumping in the water. You will work under the jurisdiction of the Evenfall Vigil, and they'll fill you in on the basic laws. They know not to waste your time with commonplace crimes. As cases arise, a messenger will be sent here to gather you and escort you to the location. I expect your first few cases will be a little challenging, but I have confidence you'll learn." He paused. "Eventually."

"Your faith in us is overwhelming," Lara said, rolling her eyes.

"When do we begin, Ambassador?" Alistair asked.

"Half a week from today on the first of Elimia. This will be a demanding occupation that requires quick response times. Consequently, you will all live here. Your rooms are furnished and equipped with everything you might need. If there is anything lacking, you may tell me or King Aldric, and we will see if we can reasonably accommodate your request. Questions?"

Hazel raised her hand.

The grim chuckled. "Hazel, this isn't a school assembly. What's your question?"

"What about the books?"

"What *about* the books?"

"Can we use the books in the library?"

"Yes, you may. In fact, I should mention this library essentially belongs to all of you. It was originally going to be torn down before I convinced His Majesty to procure it from the university. We've outfitted it to be as useful as possible, but if you dislike something, it's yours to alter as you wish. Keep in mind we don't have unlimited funds. Any damage you cause, you will need to pay for or live with."

Lara whistled. "Think of the crazy parties we could throw."

"Can't you take anything seriously?" Alistair asked.

"Not if I can help it."

"I think it might be time to separate," Aldric said, rising to his feet. "Hazel, don't you live on the other side of the city? I'll take you in my carriage."

"Thank you, Your Majesty, but I wouldn't want to impose…"

Aldric smiled. "No imposition at all. In fact, I would welcome your company."

"Before you adjourn to your respective abodes," Garo said, "I would like to leave you with a parting thought. In a land predominantly composed of ordinary humans, you are a shield in the darkness. I do not know if the city will receive you kindly at first, for the unfamiliar and powerful are always frightening. As you learn and grow, so will this city. If the people view you now as monsters, realize the heights you will one day reach when they laud you as heroes. You may scoff if you wish, but I already see each of you destined for greatness."

Lara rolled her eyes. "Did your shadow realm thing tell you that? You might want to check again."

Garo shook his head. "No, it was nothing I witnessed in the Shadow World. It's simply what I see in all of you."

With that, Aldric and Hazel bade the rest farewell. They exited into the early evening to Aldric's coach. The carriage lacked the flair of royalty one might expect, but upon close inspection was made of higher quality materials than average. Aldric helped Hazel into the coach box before getting in himself and sitting across from her.

"I've never ridden in a coach before," Hazel said, looking around.

"This is a smaller one. I use this when I don't want to draw too much attention. The fortunate thing about riding in a coach is it allows for some privacy. It should be around twenty minutes before we arrive at your house. I wanted to talk with you privately, and this seemed like an excellent opportunity." He knocked twice on the side of the coach and they were soon moving.

She studied the king. He was earnest, but something troubled him. "What did you want to discuss?"

"Are your parents... religious, by chance?"

Hazel thought for a moment. "Yes, but not fervently. We mostly follow the cults of Hemericanth and Melantros, though my father makes offerings to Tavek before big jobs. Why?"

He looked out the window. "What do you know about the Cult of Semeleme?"

"I've heard they handle funerals in the city, but I don't know much else."

"That's understandable. Normally, one doesn't hear much about them unless someone close has died. The Cult of Semeleme is surprisingly popular, considering she's a chaos god and goddess of death. Her priests are known for embalming the dead and handling all the ceremonies surrounding funerals. It's not simply a law of ours that makes them responsible. They are extremely competent in their work and are more respectful because of the sacred nature with which they regard their occupation." He glanced at her. "In fact, they worked with your body when you died."

"Really? I didn't know that." She searched his eyes. "Why are you telling me this?"

Aldric frowned and his gaze became distant. "The cult's duties as undertakers only encompass one aspect of the group's work. A much larger part of their role involves routing out and destroying necromancers and their creations. They view the undead as unholy monstrosities that break the holy laws of Semeleme. Even revenants, when summoned under legal circumstances, are sought after and eliminated where possible." He hesitated. "They see it as their extrajudicial duty beyond any government's power to grant or forbid."

Hazel read his worried expression. She felt nothing. "They want to kill me."

"Well... not exactly. Not yet. I've been doing my best to keep what happened to you a secret. Unfortunately, even a king has his limitations. I could've kept you a secret far longer if I detained you indefinitely, but your parents deserved to know and you deserved to have a normal life. Instead, I've sworn both my personal mages and the guards who found you to silence. I've explained the situation to your parents, but there's only so much they can do. News gets out. At present, word has spread slowly, but rumors are gaining traction. I will need to meet with the High Priestess of Semeleme soon."

He leaned toward her. "Hazel, my powers are limited. You don't yet understand what your return from death has done, or how it will change the world. Ethelian is a strong nation, but authority greater than mine will eventually come for you. The Inquisition supersedes my power in undead matters. I can placate them and slow them down, but the further we go, the harder it will be to protect you from the Cult of Semeleme and the Inquisition of the Council of Archmages."

"I'm not afraid."

He blinked. "What?"

"If they come for me and I need to go, then I will. You've protected me more than I deserve. You've helped me and my family to a considerable degree, and for no personal gain. Thank you. I know you'll continue to do your best. Ever since I returned, I noticed my emotions are far from what they were. Fear, joy, pain... they're all so distant. I'm not afraid of the future, but I'm grateful for your concern."

"You... are a brave girl, Hazel. Don't be afraid to ask for help. I will continue to do my best to quell rumors, but I don't want you to be shocked if people accost you when they learn of your revival."

"Do you really think my return will change the world that much?"

"You are the first of your kind. It takes a hundred years to create a sentient lich, and you've long outlasted the lifespan of a revenant. Some may see you as some unique draugr, but others may view you as the answer to immortality. Others may find ways of using your power for personal gain. From what I know about magic, you're a complete mystery. Even if it's impossible to replicate what happened to you, no one will rest until they're certain."

"Will my parents be okay?"

"I think so. They weren't responsible for what happened and are otherwise ordinary people. The only harm which could befall them would be the secondary pain of seeing you hurt."

"That's good. I was... worried about them."

Aldric smiled kindly. "I'll do my best to keep them safe. No one will do anything without my permission first." He grew serious again. "I mention this not to scare you, but to help you make an informed decision. I could order you to stay at the castle for your protection, but you would lose your freedom. By letting you walk free, you may eventually lose your liberty to others who do not have your best interests in mind. I wish to protect you, but that may hurt you in the end. That's why I leave the decision to you. If you feel you're in danger, you can ask for my immediate intervention. If you need to escape—even out of Coruvaine—I will arrange for you and your family to disappear to a place where you'll be safe."

She smiled. He was a kind man. He offered himself as a servant despite being a king. "Your Majesty, thank you. I'll take your words to heart. I hardly know what I'm doing, but becoming a Watcher of the Evenfall Vigil seems like the right choice. If my opinion changes, I'll let you know."

Their journey continued for a short while, the conversation shifting to lighter topics. The king provided an entertaining discussion, though the gravity of previous matters was not lost on Hazel. Even as they parted ways, she mused on what he said. As she entered into her room, she considered her surroundings.

Her bedroom was filled with the ghost of who she was. A stuffed bunny—faded from age and the love of a young Hazel—slumped on her pillow. A small painting she made two years ago when she aspired to be an artist hung above her bed—she'd been so proud of how she shaded each leaf and apple on the tree. She gazed at the "Giant-Killing Stone," as she and her friends called it. Her friend Tommy had tripped over the rock, then—in frustration—kicked it, which caused him pain and moved it not an inch. When he hoisted it up, a large centipede had crawled from under it and over his hand, causing him to drop the stone which landed on his other foot. Hazel and Claire had laughed until they cried. From then on, the two girls jokingly worshipped the stone as a "giant-killer," and each time Hazel left her room, she would laugh and rub its surface for luck. Most recently, her mother had given her daisies, which drooped despite the water they were in. A small collection of petals surrounded the earthenware vase where it stood withering by the window. She remembered smiling and reading books, tending flowers she'd gotten for her birthday, and having sleepovers with her best friend. All these alien memories and feelings she once held dear echoed in her mind.

She had died. She had died in such a stupid, meaningless way. She wasn't angered by it, but she knew she'd put her parents through profound pain by being careless. She couldn't die like that again. Her parents wouldn't relive the pain of losing her without some higher purpose. She wouldn't die by slipping out of a tree, nor would she wilt away like the flowers on her windowsill.

If I'm going to survive, I need to get stronger, she thought. *I need to know who I am and what I can do. I need Lyvaelan to help me.*

Chapter Six
To Live in Separated Unity

Alistair helped carry Hazel's luggage into the library with some effort, the last few minutes of reflected sunlight casting weakening rays upon the vampire prince. Despite the sun, he insisted on fetching her from her home. After an awkward exchange between her parents and Alistair, they took the carriage to the library and enjoyed a pleasant conversation. He apologized for concealing his race when they first met. Many humans initially feared vampires, and that terror was exacerbated by proximity and seclusion. Alistair feared she would react poorly, and so decided against mentioning it until the others were gathered together. Hazel cared little and forgave him the temporary deception on the condition that he answer some of her questions about vampires, which he naturally agreed to. She learned there were varieties of vampire beyond nosferatu—which Alistair was—and discovered that sunlight no longer killed vampires but rather crippled them. Vampires were not undead in the strictest sense but reacted to thaumaturgy in similar ways to undead creatures, which caused much confusion among humans in how to classify them. Alistair also confided that he was learning to fly without the use of wings, though she noted embarrassment when he told her. He had lived with King Aldric for the last two decades as a political hostage, which was apparently less terrible than it sounded. They discussed his family briefly, and how he was the youngest child of five born to Venarius zar Erythis, the King of the Nosferatu.

As they strode through the library, Hazel noticed that disorganized piles of books had disappeared, and the entire entryway had been cleaned and swept. Cobwebs—which added to the disconcerting décor of the place—had been removed. The library that once exuded a borderline haunted appearance now merely resembled a dimly lit building.

Hazel marveled at the changes. "Did the king send in a cleaning crew?"

Alistair smiled thinly. "Not directly, no. I'm afraid I'm to blame for its current state of relative order."

"Really? You did all this yourself?"

"Yes, I did. I had free time, so I cleaned what I could. I can't abide walking through messes, so I organized and shelved the books. Then I beat the dust out of the furniture and swept it up. Despite my best efforts, the dust returns every time I leave this place. Behold!" He swept his index finger over a table, creating a light trail. "I cleaned this table *yesterday* and yet it came back! I swear, it's like these old places *want* to be dusty."

Hazel continued noticing the differences from a week ago as they walked. "Did you organize the books?"

"No, that endeavor was a little much, even for me. I've done my best to arrange them into something resembling order, but it's only marginally better than it was before I reorganized. Besides"—he winked—"I didn't want to organize them and spoil our future date."

She looked at him sideways. "How thoughtful of you. My heart's aflutter." She squinted in the dark after the door shut behind them. "Do we know when the magelamps are going to be fixed?"

"I think an order was placed with the king's magicians, but it may be a while before they arrive."

"Why bother waiting?" Lyvaelan said, causing Alistair to jump. Hazel turned toward the voice. She could barely make him out sitting in an armchair twenty feet from them. A large, thin volume that appeared to contain artwork sat on his lap.

"Can you *please* make some sort of noise to let people know you're there?" Alistair exclaimed, poorly masking his surprise.

Lyvaelan raised an eyebrow. "I just did."

"Yes, but I meant something so that I—we—would know you were present immediately." Alistair paused. "Actually, why didn't I hear you? Even those who try to be quiet are easy for me to sense."

Lyvaelan sighed and closed his book. "Vampires are exceptional in their five senses, but dark elves are extraordinarily stealthy. They are the Children of Shadow and disturb the world around them like shadows. I overheard your conversation and you, Hazel, mentioned the magelamps. Are they too dim?"

"Yeah, I can barely even see you," Hazel said.

"Hmm." Lyvaelan looked around the library. "I suppose it might be hard to see for a human."

Lyvaelan stood and walked to the nearest magelamp, touching its dim surface. "Ideally, magelamps need to be adjusted once every thirty years. The last time these were charged was..." he closed his eyes for a moment "... almost forty years ago. That would explain why they've lost their luster. Fortunately, the problem is magical, not material."

"Why is that fortunate?" Hazel asked.

"Because I can channel magic, but the materials would need to be obtained, which would take more time. Let me give you a small lesson in magic..."

"Much as we would enjoy that," Alistair said, "we must convey Hazel's personal effects upstairs."

Lyvaelan narrowed his eyes at the vampire, then at Hazel, then her bags. With an eye roll and an exasperated sigh, he pointed both hands toward the luggage and with a series of gestures, the bags levitated and left Alistair and Hazel's grasp.

"Lift!" Lyvaelan commanded, and Hazel's baggage flew to the end of the room and up the stairs. "There," Lyvaelan said, turning to the astonished prince, "now you have some time to listen." He closed his eyes and touched the magical device, running his fingers over its smooth, round surface. "When crafting magelamps, a temporary recharging enchantment is preferable to a permanent enchantment. Creating a magelamp that requires occasional recharging is so simple any magician could do it. Maintaining such an enchantment is easy, providing the original construct is undamaged. A broken magelamp may need to be completely replaced if one of its components is damaged and a new enchantment would need to be placed instead of a simple recharge. Since the components are fragile, it doesn't make much sense to make the enchantment permanent." He paused, muttering a few words under his breath. He turned to Hazel. "Do you know why libraries prefer magelamps to conventional candles or eternal torches?"

Hazel shook her head.

"Magelamps are easier to enchant since they only give off light, unlike eternal torches which give off light and heat. They also can't cause fires, which is useful when dealing with such flammable things as books."

Light glowed in the magelamp he touched, but only fractionally more than before. As Hazel studied her surroundings, however, she noticed the entire area had brightened, like she stood outside on a sunny day.

"Come, Hazel," Lyvaelan beckoned. "Since me and the vampire see better in the dark than you, the intensity of the light shouldn't matter. I doubt the werewolf girl cares for literature, so it's only necessary for me to show you how to adjust the lights. Place all the fingers of one hand on it—it shouldn't matter which." She approached the lamp and followed his instructions. "Turn your hand clockwise. Good, notice how the light is brighter in this area? To dim it, turn your hand counterclockwise. Yes, exactly. Now, to change the area of illumination, move your fingers up along its surface to increase the range, and to decrease it simply bring your fingers down along its surface. Very good." Lyvaelan dusted his hands off. "Shall we go upstairs?"

"How do I turn them off?" Hazel asked.

"No need. They could remain at this intensity for several years without requiring charging. If you truly want it darkened, turn it counterclockwise. To dim them completely would require an addendum to the spell, which would take substantially more time. I can adjust the present enchantments in an hour or two."

"Oh, no need," she said, not wanting to trouble Lyvaelan further. "We can go upstairs."

"Good. I'll finish the rest later, but for now, the range should suffice to prevent you from tripping and falling over anything."

"Thank you."

Lyvaelan nodded and walked toward the stairs, with the other two following. When they reached the top, they found Hazel's bags placed neatly to the side, and once again Hazel saw Lara's bare feet dangling off the side of the couch. The werewolf poked her head over the top of the sofa and grinned.

"Hey kid, it's good to see you again."

"You too, Lara."

"Well, how about that? She remembered me!" Lara said, rising from her seat. "Honestly, I'm terrible with names, but I never forget a face, which is why I remember you but can't recall your name."

"Her face is green," Lyvaelan said placidly. "It'd be difficult to forget it."

Lara wrinkled her nose at him. "Rude." She turned back to Hazel. "Let me see... was it Ashley? Oakley? No... Lily? Rose? Violet?"

"Hazel," Lyvaelan said, brushing past her to sit in a large armchair.

"Hazel," Lara repeated, glaring at Lyvaelan. "I was *just* about to say that."

"Well, you *were* about to run out of plant-related names," Alistair remarked dryly.

"I still had a few I could've guessed. Anyway, no offense, Hazel."

"None taken."

"Have you been to your room yet?"

"No, I'm on my way there now."

"Oh!" Lara said, leaping up with a smile. "I'll show it to you! Let me take some of your things."

"We're fine," Alistair said, reaching for Hazel's bags. "I was just about to help her—"

Lara grabbed the luggage from Alistair with surprising speed. "We don't need your help, Prince." Lara glanced down the hallway. "Where is her room again?"

Alistair pinched the bridge of his nose. "I thought you said you didn't need help?"

Lara raised her eyebrows and stared at him expectantly. Alistair finally sighed. "Fine. It's upstairs at the end of the hallway. It's opposite your bedroom, Lara."

"Great, that's all I needed to know. C'mon, Hazel!" Lara turned and ascended the stairs.

Alistair nodded at Hazel. "Shout if you need any help."

"I heard that!" Lara called over her shoulder.

"So funny she assumed I was talking about her," he mumbled as Hazel climbed the stairs.

Hazel studied the building as she walked. The library had undergone few renovations in the past decade, and yet much was in excellent condition despite its age. Elegant wood paneling adorned the walls of the winding staircase, and although the spiral of the stairs was constructed simply, it was clearly designed by someone with an eye for the artistic and a mind for the pragmatic. Every ten steps terminated in a semicircle with a tall window, which would have welcomed abundant natural light if the shutters were opened. She realized then that the library stood with its entrance to the south and its back to the north.

They summited the fourth floor, which immediately let out into a large common area, similar to the one immediately beneath it, but with a shift from the functional and fashionable to the comfortable and fa-miliar. A couple of large couches and a few worn armchairs with ottomans made a broad semi-circle around a welcoming fireplace. Several large pillows were strewn about the floor and a couple of large blankets completed the sense of sleepiness which the room exuded. They continued left through the common area, passing a small kitchen and entering a hallway with a row of closed rooms. The two last doors appeared different from the others. On the door to the right was a carved wooden placard of a howling wolf. The left bore a similar plac-ard, except instead of a wolf, it depicted a tree with a single large nut placed in the center.

Hazel touched the surface of the image with a smile. "A hazelnut."

"Yeah, I think these signs are kinda silly, but I guess it's a nice touch. And, hey, at least it helps remind us which room is which. I'd hate to accidentally walk in on the vampire while he's primping." She inclined her head. "You mind opening the door?"

Hazel complied and found herself in a spacious bedroom with large windows adorning two sides. It was more lavish than Hazel was accustomed to, but not excessive, and actually strayed a little on the drab side. She noticed a closet and a bathroom through adjacent doors on one side of the room. On the other side stood multiple empty bookshelves of dark wood. A table with a couple of chairs sat near the window.

"It's not much," Lara said, putting the bags down near the bed. "A little boring, if you ask me. Lucky for us, we can change the rooms however we want. New paint, art, furniture"—she followed Hazel's eyes to the shelves—"books... you name it. Anyway, I'll let you unpack and get settled in."

"Thanks for carrying my bags."

Lara grinned. "No problem. I mostly did it to piss off the vam-pire." And with that, she exited, closing the door behind her.

Hazel perused the shelves and discovered a note and a small vol-ume. The book was a gift from King Aldric.

Hazel smiled lightly and leafed through the pages of the empty journal she was given. She held it close to her for a moment before replacing it on the shelf. Absent curiosity led her eyes around the room. Ensconced magelamps in pairs were arranged around the perimeter of the bedroom by each doorway and on either side of her bed, though only the first two by the entryway glowed. She approached the magelamp closest to her and increased the light the way Lyvaelan had shown her, then wandered to the window on the eastern side of her room. As she shifted the curtains back, she realized it was more of a glass door than a window. She opened it and stepped onto a small metal balcony with a railing which reached just higher than her waist. The sky had darkened and stars were visible.

From her high balcony, she could see almost a mile into the city where streetlamps in the distance flickered on with the same constant glow as the light in her room, while less densely populated areas possessed conventional lamps. In the nearby vicinity, the area remained dark and quiet. When Calixford University thrived in this specific district, the surrounding area teemed with life and activity, but not anymore. The library was literally a stone's throw from the third wall of the city. Beyond that wall was a dense forest which would have required almost an hour on foot to access by the nearest gate. This was not, Hazel thought, an ugly place; it was simply abandoned and inconvenient.

She stood for a few moments, breathing in the air as a light breeze from the forest blew toward her. With a light sigh, she opened her eyes and quit her room to join the others. Tonight, they would receive their first assignment.

Chapter Seven
The Burden of Command

"Why didn't the grim come with us?" Lara asked as she trudged behind Alistair. "Wasn't this whole scheme *his* idea?"

"It was," Alistair said as he led them through the city, "but Ambassador Garo clarified we would do this with only minimal involvement on his part. He thought we might be better off talking to the commander without having an official present to alter the nature of our exchange."

"Wouldn't it have been wise to have someone introduce us?" Lyvaelan asked.

"I..." Alistair paused, collecting his thoughts. "I think he knows what he's doing. Perhaps the commander is an agreeable individual who requires no introduction?" He didn't sound convinced.

Lara snorted. "Yeah, so agreeable Garo didn't want to be here."

It had only taken fifteen minutes on foot to reach the headquarters from the moment they left. It was situated halfway between the library and the northern gate of the city along the thin curved route that encompassed the northwestern edge along the interior of the third wall of the city.

The headquarters was an austere shade of gray. In part, this was because of its stone construction. It stood nestled directly beside the inner part of the third wall of the city and had the same unbreakable appearance of the wall it was situated against. The building had two levels, with most of the windows on the second floor. As Hazel gazed at the building, she noticed the windows were much thinner than any she'd seen. Each window was about four feet tall, but less than half a foot in width. It resembled an oblong box in its dimensions, with a large door on the eastern and western sides of the building. The emblazoned crest of the organization loomed over the entrance and underneath—written in plain but bold lettering—was the name of the division: The Evenfall Vigil.

Alistair smiled at the group, his hand on the door. "Well? Are you all ready?"

Lara rolled her eyes. "Just open the door, Your Highness."

Alistair complied with a frown. Magelamps illuminated the room. People bustled between overladen desks. Soldiers wore the same style uniform as the regular city guards but dyed a shade of blue so dark as to almost appear black.

"Huh," Lara said, looking around. "I was expecting there to be more weapons."

"Well, we *can't* just have weapons lying around the front door for someone to walk up and use," said a man's voice beside them. "Can I help you?"

They turned to their right to see a young man with two slightly curled back goat's horns and light brown curls with a beard to match. He sat, watching them with eyes half closed. The soldier seemed young by human standards, but it was difficult to know for certain. He wore the same uniform as the other guards, with a crest resembling that of the badges they carried.

"Hello Officer," Alistair addressed him. "We're here to see the commander of the guard."

"Oh?" he said, an eyebrow shooting up. "What business do you have with Commander Comrear?"

"We were sent by Ambassador Garo under orders from your king," Lyvaelan said.

A slow grin spread across the satyr's face as he stood and looked them over. "O-ho-ho! Is that right?" he asked, stepping out from behind his desk, revealing his goat lower half wearing matching dark blue shorts. "I see, I see! Well, let's not keep the commander waiting, then! Right this way." He turned and sauntered further into the building, his cloven hooves lightly clacking on the stone floor. "I apologize for the frosty welcome; the commander has been expecting you."

"What's your name?" Hazel asked the satyr. She noticed his pupils had the same rectangular shape she'd seen in goats and sheep.

"I'm Sergeant Concornus. But we can talk later. I have to introduce you."

The satyr led them to a wooden door with the name "Commander Marcus Comrear" emblazoned on the surface.

"I don't like this," Lara whispered. "*No one* shifts moods that quickly who is up to anything good."

The satyr knocked on the door before poking his head in.

"What is it, Mel?" a voice yelled from inside.

"It's the new recruits the king recommended to you, Commander." Sergeant Concornus replied.

"Veratheragan have mercy." The voice sighed. "Send them in."

"He's ready to see you," the satyr said.

"Thanks," Lara said, her voice dripping with sarcasm.

"Anytime," he replied brightly. There was a skip in his step as he returned to his desk.

The group entered to the watchful eye of a man just past middle age. Thick stubble grew on his face, and a tonsure of graying hair encircled his otherwise bald head. Bags under his watchful eyes implied he slept little. He wore the uniform of the guards, but with a dark red sash over his left shoulder.

"So," he said after a moment, "I suppose you're my new Watchers."

"Sir," Alistair said, stepping forward, "allow me to introduce us, I'm—"

"I know who you are," the commander interrupted. "You're fifth in the line for the throne of Noxphetalis. You've lived here almost twenty years and still can't hold a sword against Jorvan at the castle. You're Prince Alistair." His eyes shifted to the dark elf. "And you're Lyvaelan of the Dark Union. Whether your presence in this city is a blessing or a curse remains to be seen. If the king himself hadn't commanded otherwise, I would've either neutralized you or ejected you from Coruvaine immediately. Gods save us if you can't control yourself." Lyvaelan paled at the comment. "And you, Hazel, I know little enough about, but I don't know what sense there is in putting a child on my team." He focused on Lara. "And finally, we come to the last member of this little troupe. Lara, the werewolf." He stared at her, and she met his eyes, unflinching. "Lara, I have to say I'm... actually a fan of yours. I visited your fight in Treland against that minotaur a couple years back. I lost good money on that bet, but it was worth losing. The way you finished it by throwing him by his horns... well, that was a fight I'll never forget."

Lara blinked. "Ah, uh... thank you?"

"But don't misunderstand me, your typical ability to knock things around does not make you any more qualified than the rest of these misfits the king sent me." He stood, crossing his arms. "I suppose my opinion should be clear to all of you: I don't like that you're here. Normally, I'd require each of you to have several weeks of training and obtain basic weapon proficiency. After that, each trainee would work with a seasoned soldier for the next year before being responsible enough to partner with another. His Majesty, however, has told me to put you all into the field *immediately* and informed me I may separate none of you. Now, I *could* just send you into the heart of danger, but—like it or not—you're all my responsibility and I do my best to protect my soldiers. Besides, I'm not sure letting you show yourselves in the heart of the city is a good idea. That's why I'm going to send you on a special mission, one requested by a very important citizen. A friend of the king's, actually. He's been dealing with some troubles regarding the construction of the outermost wall. He's the foreman, you see." Commander Comrear sat back down, his posture relaxing slightly as he pushed a piece of parchment across the table to them. "You're to speak with him tomorrow morning at ten. Don't be late."

"Ah," Alistair said, "there seems to be a misunderstanding, we—"

"There has been no misunderstanding, Prince," Comrear said. "The Evenfall Vigil handles any problems related to nocturnal and superhuman activities. This is both. You must be there to formally interview him. Of course, *you* don't have to be there at all, Prince Alistair. Not *everyone* needs to be present. Would the rest of you be fine with this?"

Lara leaned on the desk. "I think what the prince means is there's a mistake. We're supposed to be doing important stuff, not just taking the lowest priority grunt work. What about all this business of alchemists making illegal stuff in the city? Why aren't we handling that?"

Comrear strummed his fingers on his desk. "How would you start?"

"Well—"

"Do you know enough about the law to recognize what compounds would be illegal and which are perfectly fine?"

"I mean, we—"

"Do you know how to make an arrest or question a witness?"

"We could—"

"I didn't think so." He sighed and held up a hand. "Look, I get that you're eager to get started on a big case. I also know Aldric probably filled your heads with promises of glory and action, but I can't have four powerful people running around the city with no concept of our laws and leading people to slander our name any more than it has been." His jaw tightened. "Half the time we're called ineffective because crimes still occur. The other half of the time, we're labeled an unnecessary relic of the past that should be cut out of the city budget.

The king has kept our department because he sees the merit in our work, but the last thing I need is an extra dozen complaints that a bunch of reckless hellions are running around in our name. In time—with official training—I'll let you take on greater tasks, but until that time, you work small jobs. Understood?"

The others nodded hesitantly, but Lara glared.

"Then there you go. I understand this isn't the ideal situation for any of us, but we can only seek to do our best with what we have. With that said, your time to shine will have to come later." He leaned forward slightly. "Do you have your badges?"

Everyone nodded affirmatively.

"Good, take them out. Honrick! Honrick, get in here!"

The door opened and a blonde woman stepped in, her hair tied neatly behind her in a loose bun. She wore the same dark colors as the rest of the guards, but the tunic flowed down to her ankles and she wore a dark cloak over it, giving a slightly more elegant look. She appeared as tired as the commander who called her.

"Yes, Commander?" she said, ignoring the others in the room.

"Honrick, these are the new recruits, and I need you to charge their badges. All of you come forward one at a time. Ellen Honrick is our staff mage, proficient in lesser magic, sorcery, and enchantment, isn't that right?"

"Yes, sir." Her expression hadn't changed from a surly frown.

"She works for the Evenfall Vigil on important cases, so you'll talk to *me* before you talk to *her*. She has better things to do than listen to your questions and requests. Now hold out your badges, one at a time."

Hazel stepped forward; her badge held in the palm of her right hand. The mage placed her hands slightly above and below Hazel's hand, and Comrear placed his index finger on the shield.

"Hazel Enda, do you swear to protect and serve the people of Coruvaine? Do you promise to save those lives you can save, help those you can help, prevent crimes when you can prevent them, and aid the

Evenfall Vigil in the defense of this city and the rest of Ethelian? Do you swear fealty to the King of Ethelian, His Royal Majesty Aldric Valmore, and to the country of Ethelian? Do you swear to assist, by every means possible, the occupants of this city in the case of foreign invasion? If you agree to these terms, say 'I do.'"

"I do."

Honrick, who had been whispering under her breath and moving her hands ever so slightly, stopped and held them rigid as miniscule forks of lightning flowed from her hands and over Hazel's. Hazel noticed the slightest tickling sensation as blue tendrils of electricity snaked over her skin and coalesced around the badge until it glowed bright blue.

Comrear removed his finger. "There, you're done. Next."

He repeated this process for each member. When they were finished, he looked at the group. "The badges will glow faintly blue when you and *only you* hold it. No trading them between you. Those who see it will know not only that it is an official badge, but that you're working under the purview of the Evenfall Vigil. They will not always shine, however. If you use it in any capacity other than obeying my orders or observing one of the promises you made, then it won't glow. The citizens know the difference between each badge, so they'll know if you're working beyond your capacity. Furthermore, those badges are *not* interchangeable. If you lose them, you'll have to repeat this process over again and get a lecture from me. Maybe I'll also have Honrick turn you into toads for a while. Who knows?"

Honrick groaned and shook her head at this last comment.

Lara leaned forward on the desk. She had been tapping her foot impatiently, and Hazel could hear some faint growls come from her. "Look, *Commander*, I didn't join in this to take notes from random citizens. I've busted heads and dealt with pressure before. I don't know about the rest of these weirdos, but I'm prepared to pick up their slack in the field if I can't go solo on missions. This Alchemist guy doesn't sound so tough. Let us take the mission."

Comrear only half listened to her as several voices came from outside his door. Honrick stepped out and spoke in hushed tones to others and then returned to Comrear. She whispered in his ear and he immediately stood, nodding to her. She exited, and Comrear buckled his sword belt on.

"You want to see what the Alchemist can do? Fine. It's your lucky day. One of the Alchemist's creations is wreaking havoc on Selebar Street. You can all witness how the Evenfall Vigil handles criminals. You'll be observing only, but trust me, that'll be enough."

Chapter Eight
Carnage of the Street

Four minutes after boarding the wagon, Hazel and the others reached the crime scene. The horses moved faster than she had ever seen within the city, and the low number of people in the streets made travel easier. They rode in silence, with Commander Comrear sitting with the driver in order to assess the situation. Alistair's expression changed as they moved, shifting, as if listening to a distant conversation. Then the wagon stopped.

"Shit," she heard Commander Comrear say.

They jumped from the wagon and saw two other wagons arrived ahead of them. Over twenty soldiers rushed to assume position before the Alchemist's monster. They all wore the dark blue brigandine armor of the Evenfall Vigil and carried crow's beaks, which differed from the armaments she saw other guards equipped with. Hazel wasn't certain what she expected to see. A dragon, or griffin, perhaps. A manticore also seemed like a possibility, though few lived this far north. Regardless, the monster was none of these.

The monster was human.

A man, just over seven feet tall, stood covered in blood some fifty feet before them, a wild grin on his face. She was too far away to see his eyes, but in the relative dark of the street, she noticed his veins appeared bluer than normal and massive muscles rippled across his body. He watched them without responding, repeatedly smashing his bloody fist into a wall. As Hazel squinted, she realized he was holding something in his gore-covered hand.

A human head.

Hazel tore her eyes from him to search the rest of the road. Seven massive bloodstains littered the street. Cracked fragments of bone and what she assumed were brains lay trodden over. The stench of refuse and iron permeated the air. She looked at her companions. Alistair glanced from Comrear to the monster and kept his hand hovering over his sword, an expression of desperation on his face. Lara had paled and all pretense of bravado had disappeared as her jaw set with humorless determination. Lyvaelan closed his eyes and appeared calm, although Hazel wasn't sure.

"Into position!" Comrear roared. "Four crow's beaks in front of Honrick. Hold nets at the ready. Mellius and Oleisia, perform the thyrsus maneuver! You three, bring out the barrels from wagon five for the naiad."

Soldiers fulfilled his orders, running where he ordered. Sergeant Concornus chuckled and swaggered toward the deranged man. A woman with light blue skin and dark blue hair skirted the monster to where the barrels were placed.

"Hey-o! Big and ugly!" Concornus called out. "Are you going to keep staring like an idiot, or are you going to show me a good time?"

The monster moved his head in the satyr's direction but continued his repetitive action. A faint wheezing laugh issued from him.

"It's just my luck to fight someone who's as stupid as he looks," the sergeant continued. "I suppose I'll need to be the one to start the dance."

Hazel blinked, and the monster had fallen back as the satyr rammed into his stomach with his horns. At the moment of impact, Mellius curled his legs under him and pushed off of him to land on his feet after performing a backward flip. The man rose to his feet slowly, still shaking with silent laughter. Instantly, the man crossed the twenty-foot divide between them, matching the satyr's speed. Mellius leaped to the wall next to him and off it as the man's fist crushed the cobblestones. Just as quickly, he smashed the brick wall with his other hand but narrowly missed his limber opponent.

"Oh my, you're more eager than I thought. I guess I'll have to use this after all." Concornus clapped his hands together and as he drew them apart, a wooden staff topped with a large pinecone appeared. He twirled the staff in his hand and then transferred it to the other. It was an impressive display, but Hazel couldn't help thinking he was showing off.

The monster turned his head and bolted at the satyr. Mellius dodged nimbly between the hands of his enemy, sticking out his tongue and making crude gestures at the creature.

"Enough, Mellius!" Commander Comrear shouted. "Bring down the bastard already!"

The satyr nodded and bounced over his opponent's head, rolling into an aerial somersault as he tapped the back of the man with the pinecone tip of his staff. Although the blow appeared light, the man went sprawling, and the impact caused a rush of air that blew Hazel's hair back. The man rose to his feet with a wobble. Foam appeared along the edges of his grinning mouth.

"Oh?" Concornus said, his smile fading. "You handled a blow from my thyrsus surprisingly well. I suppose I'll just have to hit you a few more times until you're *really* enjoying yourself."

As the satyr dashed at his opponent, the other soldiers moved into a practiced formation. Four soldiers stood shoulder to shoulder in front of Ellen Honrick with the spear-points of their crow's beaks leveled at the monster, waiting. The magician muttered words under her breath and closed her eyes. When she opened them, she looked at Comrear and shook her head.

"Damn," he muttered. "That would've made matters simpler."

Oleisia—the naiad with blue hair and skin—gestured at the barrels and water burst out, following her every motion. The stream coiled around her as she held her position. Concornus struck twice more with his thyrsus and after each, the creature staggered more and struggled to move in a straight line. The monster retained his speed, but his inability to maintain balance made his alacrity a greater detriment than an asset.

Honrick stared at the monster and gestured in the air and intoned. "Bane and pain are all you'll see so long as you shall gaze on me!" Twin beads of red shot from her hand and into the eyes of the monster. The creature shook its head and glowered at Honrick with radiant crimson eyes. The moment she uttered the spell, the naiad sprayed water along the street, which immediately hardened into ice. The crazed man rushed at the mage, but his lack of coordination and the frozen ground caused the monster to fall forward and slide across the ice—which curved as the naiad directed—to the armed soldiers. The ice instantly melted and reformed around the creature, freezing him in a solid block. Four soldiers lunged forward as Honrick and the other four backed away. They threw a large net woven with several small black stones over the monster, covering each part of his body to the best of their abilities. Honrick touched the net and whispered as light spread across the surface and the ice burst. The monster had broken out. Honrick retreated a few steps but showed no pain from the shower of ice shards.

The monster gyrated on the ground, but the net kept him down. Again, he spasmed, but the net moved hardly an inch. Commander Comrear approached and examined the net. When he was satisfied, he nodded to the four who were defending Honrick. "Get to work, but avoid the net." The men nodded and repeatedly stabbed the criminal with the spear tips of their crow's beaks.

Alistair gaped. "Isn't that a little excessive?"

Comrear scoffed. "You have a lot to learn, Prince. Look at the wounds they're inflicting. Does that son of a bitch seem to care?"

Hazel peered closer and noticed no blood emerged from the man's body. Each wound closed as soon as the weapon withdrew.

"We're not just stabbing him in the middle of the street for fun, vampire. We're doing it so we can transport him back to headquarters for questioning. That potion could last until dawn if we did nothing. The concoctions the Alchemist uses increase healing or return the body to a previously healthy state. According to Paxton Averly, they prevent incoming damage from achieving any permanent wound unless parts are removed from the individual. Given that these monsters are strong as an ogre and fast as a sylph, using precise attacks rarely work. Honrick tried to use sorcery but—like I expected—this guy's mind was so jumbled she couldn't do anything."

"What about the net?" Lyvaelan asked.

"The net uses an enchanted lodestone weave," Honrick answered, joining the commander. "Each of those stones currently weighs a hundred pounds. It's one of the few ways we can immobilize them."

Lara's eyebrows shot up. "A hundred each? There's a stone at every knot! How isn't he crushed to death?"

"We've tried to use fifty-weights," Honrick replied, shaking her head, "but the last time we tried it, the criminal nearly broke free. It took some creative thinking to survive that night."

A soldier ran up and saluted Comrear. "Sir! How would you like us to handle the fallen?"

"Gather as much as you can into piles. Keep any badges you find with the bodies for identification. I'll see if I can get some wizards to reconstruct their bodies so they can have a decent burial." Comrear sighed and ran a hand over his head. He turned to Lara with tired eyes. "Well? Did you have fun?"

No one answered.

"Tonight, I get to tell several families their beloved sons, husbands, and fathers are never coming home. The bloody pulp you see used to be good soldiers. Now they're gone." He shook his head, his voice still quiet. "Go home. Meet with the foreman in the morning.

Enjoy life while you have it. You're dismissed." Comrear turned from them and barked orders as Hazel and the others departed in silence.

They were as quiet as the streets they traveled for the next ten minutes. Hazel understood the bleak and emotional scene and yet could not connect to it. She remained respectfully silent for her allies.

"It occurs to me," Lyvaelan said softly, "that I don't know where the construction site of the fourth wall is. Do any of you?"

Lara winced and looked at Alistair.

The vampire sighed. "Perhaps. I took a tour of the wall one night out of curiosity. I'm not certain, but I may know where the current construction site is. When I spoke with His Majesty, he mentioned the workers required a significant amount of oversight, even if they were highly efficient. Still, it isn't especially helpful for me to know, since I won't be going with you tomorrow."

"Good point," Lara said. "Hazel, have you been out there?"

"No, I'm afraid not. My house is in the southern part of the city and the construction site is a few miles to the north. I only know about it from my parents and school."

Lara bit her lip and turned back to Alistair. "Could you show me on a map?"

"Yes, I can do that. I might suggest leaving earlier than necessary if you're uncertain where to go."

"Heh, I'm not too worried," Lara said, looking much relieved. "I've got great instincts about these things."

"Should we determine who will go tomorrow?" Lyvaelan asked before Alistair could reply. "I know little about vampire physiology, but you stated attending was impossible. Are you weakened by the sun as well, werewolf?"

"Not really. I'm not as strong as I am at nighttime and I can't turn into a wolf during the day, but otherwise I'm good to go! I'm pretty formidable at any time."

"And you, Hazel?"

"Me?"

"Yes," Lyvaelan said mildly, "I assumed our group was selected in part because of our peak performance at night. Are you weakened during the day?"

"No. No more than usual. I'm not even sure if I would know how to tell. I guess the only issue is I try not to be seen during the day, but besides that I have no problems with sunlight. What about you, Lyvaelan?"

"I'm stronger at nighttime, but I have no other problems with daylight, except for being noticed by others. There is a reasonable distrust of dark elves anywhere humans dwell, and this city is hardly an exception. I can join you two at the wall. I'm curious to see what sort of magic may have been happening there."

"Okay, so it's everybody except for you, Your Highness," Lara said with a smirk. "We'll try not to have too much fun without you."

"I'm sure you will," Alistair replied dryly. "But more seriously, I'm disappointed with our assignment, even after everything we saw. I think we could do more."

"I hate to agree with you, but I do," Lara said. "Honestly, if I would've known we'd be doing boring stuff like checking construction sites, I would've stuck around my old place and kept fighting."

"They are right to distrust us," Lyvaelan said.

Lara scoffed. "Oh, really? And why shouldn't they trust us? We haven't done anything wrong."

"That may be true, but we've done nothing right either," Lyvaelan replied with a shrug. "Each of us are members purely on recommendation. Not a century ago, vampires and therianthropes destroyed many towns and killed thousands of people. Both groups have made reparations and neither were entirely responsible for their actions, but there are still many humans who distrust the predatory nature of your races. As for warlocks and dark elves, both live to the far north of Elliara in the territory of the Unseelie Court and savor the destruction and manipulation of humanity. And you, Hazel," Lyvaelan continued, turning to her, "are little more than a child in the eyes of the guards. A child who has never been trained in combat and whose origins are—I'm guessing—unknown."

Hazel frowned. "But I *am* an adult. I'm sixteen."

He shrugged again. "I doubt the commander cares in the slightest."

"Now hold on," Alistair said. "His Majesty himself recommended each of us. How can you say he would be less than reliable? Does his word mean nothing to his own soldiers?"

Lyvaelan glanced at Alistair, then ahead. "I know of the interactions between Aldric and the Seelie Court. The King of Ethelian is unique among rulers for following his intuition. It's because of those impulses the peace treaties with Elliara have been successful. Judging from the office we left and the battle we witnessed, I suspect the Evenfall Vigil functions on a limited budget, despite the increase in superhuman crime. This city sits on a well of arcane energy, and so anything that wished to attain greater magic would be drawn here. Those things are now causing destruction and chaos at night and the commander's soldiers are dying or getting injured beyond his ability to do anything more than reallocate insufficient funds to protecting them."

He continued forward, almost talking to himself. "Finally, when the king does something, he sends a group of beings who represent many of the threats they combat. None are trained, they receive their own special treatment, they cannot be terminated from the organization, and the commander is still responsible for their actions. The most reasonable course of action is to put us aside and hope we aren't as terrible as he believes."

They walked in silence until they reached the library, contemplating Lyvaelan's words. While the dark elf spoke with soothing impassivity, his words unsettled them. The temporary escape from thoughts of the bloodbath they witnessed was replaced by musings on their inability to do anything meaningful for the Evenfall Vigil. Hazel sat up late into the night, considering what had happened while contemplating the future.

Chapter Nine
The Problem of the Bluecap Worker

The next morning found Hazel, Lyvaelan, and Lara in good spirits, despite the previous night. A light breeze rustled through the trees, and the warm sun tempered the chilly autumn air. The city proper was just waking up and foot traffic was relatively low. The true beauty of the morning was not fully realized until after they had exited the third wall and entered a much more wooded area. Along the road were occasional cottages interspersed with trees, flowers, and grass. The city had slowly expanded, and each successive wall signified more than protection: it meant citizenship.

The first wall surrounding the king's palace, the first garrison, the royal gardens, and the Hall of Relics, was built in the early days of Coruvaine, when the capital had moved from Exington in the south and into the northern region of the kingdom. The palace had been constructed there to provide additional support to its constituents in the whole of Ethelian, but also to escape the undue influence of its neighboring nation, which had pushed for a united country under the flag of the Knights of Petrim. Coruvaine had been little more than farmlands and a scattered collection of huts when the king built his palace upon the tallest hill in the region. The countryside was primarily forests and fields with minor variation in altitude. The wall encompassed the entire hill of Coruvaine and was made much larger than was initially thought necessary. As the fledgling capital required more trade and promised increased protection, more citizens sought safety beneath the shadow of its wall.

The second wall rose two generations after the completion of the first. Wandering merchants found few reasons to travel through the region because of the lack of a protected marketplace. Recognizing the need for growth, the king constructed another wall which brought in permanent businesses and became a location for markets and trade. Farmers sold their crops within the safety of the wall, and travelers found rest for the night.

The third wall was built when bandits raided homes in the night and escaped with little problem. An increasing number of people were drawn to Coruvaine included members of the Council of Archmages who wished to erect a school near Exington but—at the request of the king—was instead established in Coruvaine with the promise that those who attended the school would assist its residents. And so, the third wall whose overall area encompassed sixteen times the area of both previous walls combined was designed with the purpose of not simply increasing the city size itself but of eclipsing the glory of the previous capital. The population grew after the creation of the third wall for several centuries, with no one seeing the necessity of a fourth until the War of the Night came to Coruvaine just over two hundred years ago. The lush farmlands had been soaked with the blood of farmers and massacred livestock in acts of wanton destruction. The king had lost his son three miles from the third wall. In his grief, the king vowed to protect his people by building a wall where his son had been found and surround the city. Such a project was ambitious to a degree that required multiple generations to fulfill.

The meaning of each wall changed over the years, Hazel's teachers in school taught her. The first wall was viewed as part of the palace itself. The second wall had become more affluent in time with increased security and low quantity of land. The third wall represented the people and the university. It was the hub of trade and the primary area through which the main road ran. It was varied in its makeup, with some loud and bustling areas, while others were nearly empty and quiet. It had greater connection to nature than the inner two walls while still being safe from predatory animals and bandits. So, what did the fourth wall mean? With the conclusion of the War of the Night almost a hundred years previously, many questioned the decision to continue construction on such a time-consuming venture. The citizens had many ideas, and while a few supported—or opposed—the wall's construction, their opinions hadn't changed the outcome.

As Hazel walked in this lush countryside, she wondered if the creation of this wall would change the peaceful scenery. She had learned a decent amount of the city's history from her school, and she knew the third wall had once been just as connected to nature. Some areas were more heavily wooded, and a small river flowed through the eastern side of the city which helped maintain a natural appearance. She'd seen more buildings rise within the third wall when none thought it could ever become so populated. In her mind, this fourth wall was ambiguous in its implications. The walls could be seen as embracing the landscape or surrounding it. It could seek to trap and stake its claim on the land, or it could make the city itself more natural without compromising its safety.

Like most subjects these days, she didn't know how she felt about the matter. The same apathy which existed in her prevailed even now. She thought her old self would've felt strongly about the wall and been angry, or perhaps fearful that the wall would destroy something she enjoyed spending so much time in, but at the moment she doubted even a massive fire would've excited much care in her.

The further they traveled along the road, the fewer the houses became. As they walked, Lara occasionally commented on the landscape and how it compared to Treland, or regaled them with a lively story of a previous fight. Lyvaelan remained unaffected by either the werewolf's stories or by the beauty of the day. He'd spoken hardly a word since leaving the library, although it didn't seem to be linked to any foul mood. Lyvaelan left wearing a hood and a scarf to cover his appearance while he was within the third wall. While the rising temperature made wearing such garments uncomfortable—late autumn was often still warm in Coruvaine—it was only once they were well beyond the third wall that he removed his scarf. His garments, Hazel noticed, were primarily in subdued tones of gray, though the cloak he wore appeared to be an exception, as it was dyed a deep shade of green.

"Lyvaelan, I have a question," Hazel said.

"Yes?"

"I know you're gifted in magic, so why not use magic to disguise your appearance?"

Lyvaelan looked at her for a moment. "The sorcery I would use which alters appearance is imperfect. The spells involved aren't difficult, but they unravel easily and draw more attention as a result. If you cast a spell to look like someone else, it depends on your ability to recall that person's appearance. Unfortunately, most find it difficult to reconstruct a precise face and so certain details look... off. It's hard to explain without showing you, but simply put, it's easy to put on a mask but challenging to make it convincing. The same problem arises when altering details of how one looks, say, elongating a nose or changing eye color. Memory thinks about such things differently than they actually are. Details are lost for the overall picture, and so a person who is paying attention can often see through the illusion. But assuming one can construct a decent disguise, the problem with Coruvaine is the third wall has a low-powered anti-magic field which specifically detects and removes illusions. I learned this the hard way upon entering the first time. It took a solid hour to explain things adequately to the guards, even after showing them my signed papers."

"Oh, I see. Is there some other way of making a disguise that's more convincing that wouldn't be dispelled in the same way?"

He thought for a moment. "Yes, though it comes with its own problems. Illusions—which are under the practice of sorcery—draw inspiration from one of two things: oneself or others. Illusions inspired by oneself are drawn from the mind of its creator. Thus, others will see my idea of a person when I make myself look like one. When focusing on another, it uses that person's image of a person instead."

"Well, why not use that? Wouldn't that be more effective, anyway?"

"It would be... for a single person. When casting an illusion on someone, it requires the knowledge that a person is there. After all, if the focus of the spell is someone else, then it makes sense that knowledge of that person would need to precede the spell. Others might be added to the spell after it's cast, but if the caster isn't aware of a specific person's presence, then that individual will not be under the influence of the spell. Each individual will probably have differing perspectives toward that person, which can lead to confusion, especially if the spell isn't specific. If I used such magic to appear like a light elf to one guard, but then another I hadn't noticed saw me, I would appear as I actually am. The strength of an illusion depends on belief in it, so my control over the ensorcelled person would grow tenuous until the spell failed altogether. Illusions can be potent, but they are difficult to use effectively. There are other ways to maintain anonymity, but changing appearance is harder to make convincing than you'd think. I may actually use that specific technique to set the foreman at ease with me."

"Interesting," she said as a blue dragonfly flew across the path. She wasn't sure she understood everything he said, but she had the feeling that asking more questions would only deepen her confusion.

"Yeah, interesting," Lara said, both hands clasped behind her head as she walked. "I never knew much about magic. Werewolves can't really use magic like humans. Don't misunderstand, some of us can use a little, but nothing powerful like illusions."

Lyvaelan raised an eyebrow. "Most illusions are not especially powerful."

She shrugged. "Yeah, well, even the best among us struggle to use alchemy, so even lowbrow illusions are unheard of. Other therianthropes may have greater access to magic than werewolves, though." Lara glanced at him. "Speaking of great access to magic, how is it you use it without killing yourself? I heard warlocks practically explode when they just think about casting a spell."

His expression hardened. "Many years of rigorous training and meditation. Not everything you've heard is true about warlocks, even if some of it is." He tilted his head. "It sounds like we're approaching our destination."

Hazel listened but heard nothing beyond the sounds of nature. It was another minute of walking in silence before she heard the scrape of pickaxes in the distance.

After leaving the main road, they headed west of the northern gate. They journeyed through the grass and trees for a few more minutes behind Lara, who noticed evidence of people creating a natural path in the direction Lyvaelan heard noises. A large clearing opened, revealing piles of gray stone, gravel, dirt, and a large square yellow tent around fifty feet from the tree line. The site sounded busy with the clang and scrape of industry, and yet there was no evidence of carts, horses, or tools Hazel could see at this distance. As they approached, she noticed dozens of wheelbarrows, chisels, and hammers littered the area, but each tool was too small to be used by a young child. Hazel turned to her companions to ask their thoughts when she saw the puzzled look on both of their faces. Apparently, they were as lost as she was.

A wavering blue blur rushed between them, chattering like an agitated squirrel before darting into the tent. It resembled a tiny blue flame.

"What was *that?*" Lara said, looking around wildly.

"What?" said a rumbling and slightly accented voice from within the tent. "What do you mean there are monster-people outside?"

The same wild chattering responded incoherently.

"No, no, yes, I understood the words you were sayin', I just don't know what you *mean* by them. Huge? Do you mean dragon-huge, or regular sized human-huge? Ugh. Look, just because they're new doesn't make 'em a threat, and no, you're not bein' replaced, I—oh for the love of Tavek, I'll just see 'em myself."

The tent flap moved aside to reveal a dwarf with a dark brown beard braided short. While he was shorter than Hazel by several inches, his broad shoulders and thick, muscled arms gave him a physically imposing presence. His frame was nearly square and reminded Hazel of a barrel. He wore a brown apron over workman's clothes and had a long piece of charcoal behind one ear. A hammer hung from his tool belt, along with a chisel and various other implements. He swiftly appraised them and smiled amiably.

"Welcome, strangers," he said warmly. "What can I do for you today?"

"Ah..." Lara looked at Hazel and Lyvaelan, as if requesting permission to speak. "We are with the Evenfall Vigil. We were sent to talk with—"

"With me!" He rushed forward to shake their hands. "Yes, please come inside. It's a pleasure to meet y'all. I'm Riglin Carstaff, chief foreman of the fourth wall."

The group entered the square tent to find a few wooden stumps which served as makeshift chairs with blankets on each. The tent was ten feet on a side and a few feet shorter. At the back of the tent was a desk with notes strewn across it and a map of Ethelian, along with a more specific map of Coruvaine. A few barrels were off to the side, along with some stacked books.

"I hope you'll forgive the mess," Riglin said, indicating the seats they could take, "but I work better in clutter. I'd offer you all a drink, but I don't have any additional cups and the workers, well... their portions would be more annoyin' than anything."

"Who are your workers?" Hazel asked, taking a seat.

"Oh? You didn't see 'em?"

"No," Lara said. "Or rather, we might have seen a blur of one."

"Ah, right. Well, I'll have you meet the one who saw ya. It's rude he didn't introduce himself. Zigglepet!"

The same blue blur darted past them from a hiding place within the tent to rest on the desk of the dwarf. The creature wavered in place like a blue flame hovering just eight inches above the desk. The same fierce chattering issued from the little flame and was directed at Riglin.

"Yes, I know," Riglin said as if trying to pacify the creature, "they're big. *Very* big. Bigger than me, even. I could see why you'd be worried. But—no, hold on—stop, Zigglepet, just—stop, damn it!" The creature stopped chattering for a moment. "That's better. These people are working with the guards of the city to help. They're checking to make sure everything is fine and ensure we get finished on time. They're not a threat; they're nice folks. Now please, take off your hat and greet our guests."

The blue flame ceased flickering and took a more solid shape. The flame now appeared like a small hat. Just as the flame became a hat, the rest of the body appeared that was attached to it. He resembled a tiny human miner in virtually every way, except his facial proportions were comically exaggerated. An enormous mouth with a wispy white beard and a tiny nose sat under two small but expressive eyes that were set beneath large eyebrows. The creature frowned at them and stared before spouting some chattering nonsense and promptly disappearing from the room.

"Ah, you'll have to forgive him. The workers are a bit jumpy. They're the best at what they do, but that leaves 'em imbalanced socially."

"Are all of your workers bluecaps?" Lyvaelan asked. Hazel only now noticed Lyvaelan's skin and hair had turned pale and fair, and now more closely resembled a light elf.

"Yeah, all of 'em. Not all construction workers are, but it's more expensive gettin' the human workers to travel three miles each way to get to work than it is to get these little guys who live in the forest. Plus—for as much as they complain—they love the job, so it works well. They're not suited to workin' further in the city since they distrust new people—as you've noticed—and that would set things back. Besides that, they also have a hard time with precision work, and most construction within the city is too detail-oriented to work well with them. So, here they are."

Hazel had heard of bluecaps but had never seen one. According to her father, bluecaps were wild little men who enjoyed working in mines and were fae. She recalled the slightly pointed ears of the creature she'd just seen, and it confirmed at least one aspect of what her father told her.

"Do you speak their language?" Hazel asked.

"Ha! I don't think there's a soul alive who does. I'm not even sure they speak the same language to each other. I can understand what they're tryin' to say, probably some kind of fae magic or something, but I can't speak their gibberish. They have no problem understandin' others, however."

"Well, as interesting as it is hearing about your workers," Lara said, leaning on the desk, "I imagine you probably want to talk more about the problems you've been having rather than the people who work for you."

"Well, you're not entirely wrong," the dwarf said, stroking his short beard and looking at the ceiling of the tent. "But I suppose it'd be more accurate to say my workers *are* the problem."

"I thought you said they were good workers?" Lara said, raising an eyebrow.

"They are," he said, "but I think they've been goin' missin'."

"Okay," Lara said. "Can you tell us more? Maybe start at the beginning?"

"Sure. I guess I should start by explainin' how the law works with fae creatures differently than it does with humans and dwarves. The king decreed that whatever compensation for labor is agreed upon by both parties is acceptable. Fae aren't allowed membership in any guild, nor do they gain residence as members of the city, but they are still bound by its laws and protections. This may seem unreasonable, but certain groups of humans tried to capitalize on having fae join groups only to bring disaster on themselves. Since none register as human workers, the accountability in terms of official documents is relatively low. In short, if they work then they get paid, but we don't need names nor do we need specific accounting. Of course, an unscrupulous foreman could hire fewer workers and claim there were more, which is why the king only allows a select few to work specifically with fae while workin' directly for him.

"About a month ago, I was goin' over some of my personal notes and I noticed a trend that was mildly confusin'. We had a surplus of funds for the workers that had been gradually increasin'. It looked like over the past month, workers had declined in number. As you can see, these guys are mostly invisible and they take random days off without sayin' much. Early on, their disappearances were unnoticeable. But now... I don't know. It's strange. There used to be triple the number of workers than there currently are. I've tried questionin' them, but they aren't exactly the most reliable witnesses. Besides that, they may work extremely well together, but they're not community-oriented, if that makes sense."

"What trends have you noticed regarding their disappearance?" Lyvaelan asked.

"Well, for starters, they were those who worked mostly on the night crew. We do construction here at night and during the day and switch off shifts. I would plan the basics of what the night crew would do, and then the more specific stuff could be done under my supervision durin' the day. That was another reason I hadn't noticed until recently."

"Did anyone see what happened?" Lara asked.

"Well, not exactly. I came a few nights, but everything seemed normal and it was throwin' work off track. Instead, I asked one of my workers—a bluecap by the name of Garvey—to watch over the scene and report what he saw. He was one of the few I really got along with that seemed consistent and trustworthy. After that night, I hadn't seen him again." The dwarf rubbed the bridge of his nose. "I contacted the king about this and he stated progress was still important and he'd send some members of the Evenfall Vigil to look into it for me. I take it he meant you three?"

"Four," Hazel corrected. "Our fourth member has a hard time in sunlight."

Riglin squinted at her. "You're a pretty strange bunch. What exactly makes each of you so special, if you don't mind my askin'?"

Lara pointed at each person as she answered, "Werewolf, green girl, half-elf, and the other is a vampire."

Riglin whistled and sat back in his seat. "Well, when the king sends for help, I guess he doesn't waste time. I'm glad y'all are here. I'm not much of a detective myself, but I can show you the area and give you some of my conjectures, if that helps."

They all agreed, and the foreman led them outside and showed them the worksite. Because of the swift constructive capabilities of the bluecaps, the site was recently established. Trees had been cleared away twenty feet on both sides of the wall, and the lumber was stacked close to the inner tree line. Little flickering bluecaps rushed back and forth with small wheelbarrows, or occasionally lifting massive stone blocks which were far bigger than any of the small creatures. What the creatures lacked in communication skills, they more than made up for in efficiency. The entire process ran like clockwork, with each worker never hesitating to do its job or waiting. It looked even stranger to Hazel, given that each worker looked exactly like a small blue flame. The foreman would occasionally stop to inspect the work and offer a suggestion or request a change that would be implemented quickly and with little protest. Riglin appeared simultaneously laid back and enthusiastic about his work. It was clear to Hazel that the success in the wall's construction was due in no small part to the foreman in charge.

"Unfortunately for you investigative types, I haven't found much. I've seen some animal tracks, usually deer, cats, or maybe a wolf, but few things are out of the ordinary."

Lara sniffed. "Have you come across any sulfur deposits when you were searching for bedrock?"

Riglin frowned. "No, no sulfur... why do you ask?"

"I smell a faint trace of sulfur in the air." She explored, following her nose. "It's mostly around this section of the wall, actually."

"Really?" the dwarf said, sniffing the air. "I don't smell anything..."

"True, but you're also not a werewolf," Lyvaelan pointed out. "I don't smell anything either, but I'm willing to trust Lara on this. Riglin, have you ever come across sulfur when working on the wall?"

"Never."

"Well," Lara said, "maybe we'll find the sulfur source while we're here, too. What time does the shift usually change?"

"The day workers are usually done around seven. If ya'll could be here around that time or slightly after, I'd be most appreciative."

Lyvaelan had been muttering to himself and a small swirl of smoke appeared between his palms, shifting colors before settling into a dark green with occasional faint red ribbons. "Tell me," he said, "have you had any spellcasters use magic in the area?"

"No, not that I can recall. Mostly it's just the bluecaps."

"Hmm. Yes, I can sense their magic but there's something a little different that's difficult to pinpoint..." He scrutinized the swirl of smoke and fixated on a small part of sparkling burgundy, "that red bit represents something different from the bluecaps. It's something a little more... sinister. Possibly fae, but the trace is weak which means either not much magic was used, the creature covered its tracks, or the use of magic happened a while ago." He stared at the smoke for a few moments longer before clapping his hands together and dispersing it. "We will be here tonight to patrol. Until then." He gave a curt nod and left the foreman.

Lara glanced back and forth between him and the dwarf. "Uh, I, ah... I guess we'll see you later!" And she followed Lyvaelan.

Hazel hesitated. "I have a question for you, Riglin."

"Certainly," he said, walking back into the tent.

"How have things changed with your workers in the past few weeks? Were they always so jumpy about visitors? How have they been feeling?"

Riglin sat back, stroking his beard. "Ya know, they have been a little sullen lately. I figured it was just weather changes, honestly. They get a tinge melancholic in the autumn. As for visitors, they're usually cautious, but they have been quicker to report disturbances to me than normal."

"Is there anything..." Hazel searched for the right words. "Is there anything that could catch them? Or any predator that might want to eat them?"

Riglin's brow creased as he considered. "That's a curious question. Truth be told, I don't know of anything as fast as they are, and their invisibility would be difficult to circumvent. But now I have a question for you, miss: why do you ask?"

Hazel averted her eyes in thought. "I guess... it was just a feeling."

"Alright then," Riglin said with a reassuring smile, "thank you for coming, miss...?"

"Hazel." She smiled back.

"Miss Hazel. I look forward to seein' you and your associates again soon."

Hazel hurried to rejoin them. Lara rushed after Lyvaelan and berated him for leaving so abruptly. A couple hundred feet from the site, Lyvaelan stopped and gazed at Hazel with that same impassive expression she was growing used to.

"What is it?" Hazel asked.

"You didn't tell him the truth," Lyvaelan said. "You saw something, didn't you?"

"What do you mean?" Lara interjected. "We were both there.

There's no way she would've picked up on something that neither an elf nor a werewolf could sense."

"That's true," Lyvaelan said with a nod, though his attention was still on Hazel, "except Hazel knew something about what was happening to the bluecaps before she even came here."

"Wait, what? Really?" Lara exclaimed, glancing between them.

"You're right," Hazel said, meeting his gaze with her own calm expression. "I didn't want to tell him about the dream I had last night. My dreams don't always make sense, but I felt like somehow it was connected to this. It might not be real. Besides, the dream didn't make much sense. I didn't think he'd understand, especially since even I don't understand it and it was *my* dream."

"I see," Lyvaelan said. "You withheld information which could be detrimental to someone without the ability to comprehend its true meaning. You made a responsible decision. I wonder why you didn't tell us, however."

"I still don't know which dreams are worth mentioning and how much of each might come true. Some dreams I have are pretty weird. Besides, I didn't remember my dream until I saw the bluecaps working because they reminded me of these little blue fires I saw."

"Well," Lara said before Lyvaelan could reply, "I think if your dream has significance, you should tell us all about it with Alistair here. I may not be his best friend, but we should all be on equal footing. You can tell us about your dream after we brief him on what we've discovered."

"I must reluctantly agree," Lyvaelan said. "Much as I wish to hear more, it'd be best to discuss this back in the library. Perhaps I should start educating you on your dreams, Hazel. After we've spoken with Alistair, your first lesson will begin."

"Really?" Hazel said with faint surprise. "You want to start today?"

"Of course," he said, turning from her with a wan smile. "There's no time like the present to learn about the future."

Chapter Ten
Sight Beyond Seeing

"**I**s that everything you discovered?" Alistair asked after they recounted the day's events. "That's not much information to act on. Though it is strange that bluecaps are disappearing."

"Indeed," said Lyvaelan, leaning back against the couch in the upper common room. "But minimally, we have two sources pointing toward something strange occurring, if not more. In the first place, Lara detected the smell of sulfur in the area, even though no sulfur deposits had been found in the nearby area. Second, my trace spell found some magic different from what the bluecaps were using. Third..." he looked toward Hazel, who sat drinking her tea. "Hazel had a dream."

"I did, but I don't know how useful it'll be," Hazel said, staring into her teacup. "Dreams make more sense when I'm in them. When I wake up, it's just a lot of vague impressions and not every dream comes true, so this might mean nothing."

"And yet you thought it relevant enough to ask the foreman about it," Lyvaelan said.

"Maybe you're right. I'll tell you about my dream," Hazel said, watching the tea leaves swirl in her cup. "I was in a forest at night when I noticed a small blue flame. Then another. And another. And dozens more. They were together in the darkness between the trees. I lost sight of the trees and only the many blue flames in the night remained. The blue flames shrank as they faded into the distance and as the darkness shut on them, I realized I the blue flames burned in the gaping jaws of some monster. I couldn't make out its details, but there were bright white eyes, and it was made of shadows. That's all I can remember."

The group sat in silence for a moment, digesting what Hazel revealed. After a while, Lara raised her eyebrows. "So... does that sound familiar to anyone? I get the bluecaps are like the fire in her dream. But what about the shadow thing that held them? It sounds a little like our grim friend, honestly."

Alistair gasped. "Garo would never—"

"I'm not saying he *would*," Lara interrupted, holding up a hand. "I'm saying that as far as creatures made of shadows with jaws go, there are similarities."

"She isn't wrong," Lyvaelan said. "Grims are among the few fae who use shadow magic and yet are not destructive by nature. Plenty of fae of the Unseelie Court possess similar powers. It's strange, though. None of the ones I know of care for capturing or eating bluecaps. Actually, most tend to not care what other kinds of fae do and prefer to focus more on the affairs of humans."

"Are you certain it's a fae?" Alistair said. "Given the vague nature of what we've discussed and learned, it sounds like it could be a daimon, a vampire, or perhaps even a human using magic. We also aren't sure how literally we should interpret her dreams. For all we know, a giant shadow monster eating bluecaps could be metaphorical."

Lyvaelan's eyes narrowed. "I can't say for certain that it *is* fae, but I strongly suspect it is. The magic I detected seemed more chaotic than most humans or daimon, but there was so little it'd be difficult to say definitively. The sulfurous smell also indicates malevolent intent in magic, though that's a trait shared by fae, daimon, and spirits. As for it being certain kinds of vampire, I find that improbable. Based on what I've gathered from being around you, Alistair, the magic trails you leave behind are next to none. Aside from that, your aura is relatively calm, which is not the case for the magic I sensed at the site."

"Hmm." Alistair mused, holding his chin between his thumb and forefinger. "There are other species of vampire that are magically gifted, but it's not a point worth debating. I suppose we should report this information back to the commander."

"Why bother?" Lara yawned. "We haven't learned anything of value yet. The best we have are hunches and what the foreman said. Anyone could've gotten that much."

"I'm inclined to agree," said the deep, ethereal voice of Garo as he stepped from the shadows.

"Shit!" Lara exclaimed, bolting upright. "Do you *have* to do that?"

The grim grinned. "No, it's just more fun to." He looked at the others. "You can make your report after you have new information."

"I thought you were going to Elliara," Lyvaelan said, unsurprised by his arrival.

"I did and now I'm back. I wanted to hear the details of your mission. I would like to act as a counselor of sorts for the group. The least I could do is help you through your first assignments."

"Do you know about the shadow things in my dream?"

Garo looked at Hazel. "There are many creatures capable of bending shadows. Lyvaelan has already said as much as I would know on the subject, unfortunately. Did you find any tracks?"

"No, there were none," Lara said. "Even if they had covered their tracks, I would've found *something,* but there was nothing nearby. Not even local wildlife, despite what the foreman said. The only signs of wildlife were a distance from the wall, but specifically avoided the sulfurous smells."

"That narrows it down." Garo sat. "It means these creatures are almost pure shadow. They likely avoid daylight."

"How could they steal or hurt something if they were pure shadow?" Lara asked.

"Shadow creatures are intangible in their default state," Garo said. "They can, using their innate magic, make themselves partially tangible or entirely tangible. This can include going from virtually weightless to possessing great mass. There are limits to these abilities and they vary with the creature, but one thing these creatures have in common is they rarely leave much of a trace except for some vague aroma."

"Like the sulfur."

"Precisely." He thought for a moment. "It may also be useful for you to know that my powers are similarly weakened by light. Creatures of shadow have similar flaws, though they vary in how effective and deadly light is against them."

Lara twirled her hair between her fingers idly. "So... how do we know this thing wasn't actually just flying around? I mean, succubae and other creatures leave behind a smell and also fly, which would negate the footsteps."

"A good point," Lyvaelan said, "but those creatures are not shadow-based. I think Hazel's dream ought to be taken literally. Still, when we patrol tonight, I think we can determine whether the creature is of shadow. Ambassador Garo, is there anything you require of us?"

"Not at all. I'm simply here at your disposal. I may retire to the library if any would like support or advice. For at least a little while, I shall be here to help you navigate the Evenfall Vigil, but I will not command you."

"I think I'll join you downstairs." Alistair rose to his feet. "There may be some books on this subject and there's always more organizing to do."

Garo gradually disappeared into the shadows until no trace of him remained as Alistair descended the stairs. Lyvaelan glided quietly to his room without a word, while Lara reclined on the couch and was soon snoring. Hazel hesitated, unsure of where to go. Eventually, she walked to Lyvaelan's room.

His bedroom was closest to the stairway leading down to the formal common area. She'd paid little attention to the doors, but she noticed a similar placard to the one on her door, which bore a hazelnut and a tree. This was less identifiable. The center of it was a conjurer's circle with myriad shapes and geometric designs within. The circle was broken sharply in three different areas through its center in jagged cuts, like the circle had been smashed. Beneath the circle was an arrowhead pointing down, whose backward facing barbs flowed around the outside of the circle like wisps of smoke. The complete image was intricate, disturbing, and sad to Hazel, but she didn't know why. She reached to touch the symbol when the door opened. Lyvaelan sat cross-legged in the center of the room, about fifteen feet from the door. His eyes remained shut, but Hazel got the impression he opened the door magically.

"Come in, Hazel."

She stepped in and scanned her surroundings. The room resembled hers, but austere. A small window in the far corner admitted little light compared to the floating magelamps positioned around the perimeter. No decorations or extraneous art adorned the walls but a statuette of Selevara stood by his bedside.

Lyvaelan frowned, his eyes still closed. "You wondered about something in the hallway. Something about me."

She studied the dark elf warlock. "Yes, how did you know?"

"There are many forms of sight a spellcaster can use," he said, his breathing and voice maintaining a constant level. "I used *insight*. Insight—when one is relaxed enough—can reveal realities beyond the physically knowable by opening oneself to the constant flow of magic. It's less intrusive than direct telepathy, though I could've used that on you if I wished. What was it you wanted to know?"

"What does the symbol on your door mean?"

Lyvaelan sighed and opened his eyes. He looked away from her. A strange sadness mixed with shame and apprehension played over his face as he wrung his hands.

"Those are the symbols of my people combined. The arrowhead disappearing into shadows represents the dark elves. Creatures of subterfuge and night. The broken circle represents the warlocks. The oathbreakers. Together they make the Dark Union."

"I remember Commander Comrear said something about you being an oathbreaker. What does that mean?"

He folded his hands in his lap. Hazel could see tension as his hands squeezed each other. "How much do you know about warlocks, Hazel?"

"Not much. I know they use magic and they're dangerous. They also look human."

"All accurate, though the last part is incomplete. Warlocks *are* human." Lyvaelan separated his hands as swirls of gray smoke weaved between his fingers. "A few thousand years ago, a contingency of mages separated from the Council of Archmages. They believed humans were flawed in their use of magic. Most other races such as elves, faeries, and daimon use magic innately, essentially making their will manifest directly through magic. Humans had to learn. As a result, the lifespan of humans only increases in proportion to magical ability. Some reasoned this was unfair and sought to make magic more accessible. They didn't want to use magic; they wanted to become magic. It may seem like mages cast spells quickly, but their access to the flow is limited and takes considerable effort and time to master.

"This group was anathema for speaking such blasphemy. Humans were given magic by Selevara, who, the legends say, only required their willingness to study and dedicate themselves. The warlocks realized there was more to the story than simple myth and reasoned that if the oath which bound humanity to Selevara's gift was ruptured, they would have direct access to magic others lacked—power to an unprecedented degree and the ability to change reality on a whim without all the laborious study typically required. They called upon the gods of chaos, specifically Gnostrevaine and Terekmalamae, and created a powerful circle near the Noxphetalis mountain range, at the edges of Elliara. A great well of arcane magic. With the combined might of each mage, they broke the circle. It was only upon the third break they became true warlocks. They were cursed with black eyes, like a bottomless void reflecting their insatiable lust for power. The darkness spread through their veins and bodies, giving them a frightening appearance. They were successful. They had broken their ties to the Lady of Magic. They did not anticipate the flood of power each received. Every warlock could channel a nearly endless amount of magic through himself, which could cause considerable wonders at will. Their ability to contain the magic was, however, flawed."

"What do you mean?" Hazel asked. "How was it flawed?"

"When a warlock uses too much power, it becomes... intoxicating." She saw a flicker of hunger in his eyes. "Overwhelmingly so. Immense arcane forces flow through too rapidly to control, and the warlock's body dissolves into the flow of magic. When the warlock dies, he creates an arcane cataclysm which warps the area around him for many miles, unless it is contained. It destroys everything and twists the world into a chaotic distortion wherein the most improbable things become the most probable and safety, reason, and strength are rendered meaningless." He sighed and appeared calm. "A warlock is immensely powerful and lethal. If he ever releases his power... if *I* should ever release my power... many people could die."

"But I've seen you use magic. You didn't seem to have any problems."

"Small uses do nothing to me, especially when I'm calm. It's my emotional state that triggers it. Strong emotions such as anger, hate, or fear can all lead to overexerting my powers."

Hazel pondered this. "What about other powerful emotions, like joy?"

Lyvaelan raised an eyebrow. "Joy? I'm not sure I'm capable of experiencing such a thing. While I've lived my life surrounded by joy, it has never touched me. I lived with light elves, and yet I shrank from their kindness and frivolity. Even my mentor brought me little in the way of happiness. He showed me contentment, and that's really all I've ever needed."

"Contentment does not compare to real joy."

"If you say so."

Hazel stood in silence while Lyvaelan stared unfocused at the floor, his expression difficult to read. This person before her, so placid, had never known happiness. It was hard to fathom. Although at present she couldn't feel such things herself, she had memories of laughing with friends, celebrating birthdays with her family, and the many little delights of childhood. The present emotional fog she was in was ever present for Lyvaelan, she thought, except he must choose it for the good of others. His seriousness and subdued affect now made sense to her.

"There was a time I felt something close to joy," he said after a while, "but it nearly killed me and many residents of Elliara. I let my power flow, and I've never experienced anything so intoxicating and freeing. It was euphoric. The only thing I desired was more power. It was only because of Kiran that I didn't destroy everyone."

"Who is Kiran?"

Lyvaelan averted his eyes. "He was my mentor, my friend, and the closest thing I had to a father, as far as I understand the concept of one."

Hazel watched him. "Your parents didn't raise you?"

"No. You could say I was... adopted. During one of the many conflicts between the dark and light elves, Kiran found me. He was human, which is why I'm still alive today. The light elves have an un-disguised dislike for dark elves, and the sentiment is mutual. Kiran was helping the light elves retake territory in Elliara when they found me abandoned by my parents. Many urged him to kill me, anticipating the damage I could inflict, but he saw an opportunity. He thought I deserved to live and prove no one is born evil. From then on, he mostly stayed in Elliara, although he would take intermittent trips out to meet with other spellcasters."

His voice quieted as his gaze fell to the floor. "He taught me almost everything I know, but most importantly, he taught me how to cast spells without going too far. He showed me how to wield magic like a human spellcaster instead of a dark elf or warlock. I learned how to meditate and feel the magic around me and breathe with its contours and understand the sensation of it without seeking to control it. He taught me many things, one of which I will show you now." He shook himself. "Please, sit."

Hazel nodded and sat cross-legged across from him on the floor, assuming a similar position. He looked at her with his dark red eyes as he spoke evenly and softly. "Your power is one few possess. People gifted with foresight—or precognition, as some call it—often experience dreams first. When we sleep, the flow of magic pervades us without our conscious minds to block it. Your mind naturally draws magic into it in such a way that it predicts the outcome of reality itself, since magic is the quintessence of all things—even things which have not yet come to exist. Because your mind draws magic to it on its own, all that's necessary is for you to learn how to allow magic to flow through you while you're awake. It begins passively, but as you open yourself to its use, the visions will grow clearer and you will control it."

He closed his eyes and took a slow, deep breath before looking at her with sharpened focus. "My foresight is limited and only functions with considerable effort, and there are others much more gifted with seeing what lies ahead. I am better with farsight—or clairvoyance, as it is also known. I can share a sense of what it's like and it may help you understand your own abilities better." He reached out and lightly tapped her forehead.

With a rush of air, Hazel felt herself flying at a great altitude, soaring over a vast plain of green grass and gnarled trees. As she soared over hills and streams, she drew nearer to a dense canopy which stretched out as far as she could see, an almost unreal shade of vibrant green. The trees linked, admitting little light between them as she dove between the branches without disturbing so much as a leaf. Squirrels scurried across branches, chasing each other. Deer grazed, their ears occasionally flicking to ward off a fly. Blue jays flitted through the trees, announcing their presence with a squawk, while a hawk preened its feathers in the high branch of an oak. Several amphisbaenae rolled across the ground, propelled by their small legs, and resembled small serpentine wheels. The deeper she explored the forest, the darker it grew, and she had the strangest impression there was more beyond her sight. Rings of toadstools appeared regularly, forming perfect circles. Lights periodically blinked and disappeared, shifting with some hidden purpose. The animals were larger and older than those before. Great elk strode glowing through the dark with an air of solemn nobility, while crows watched her as she passed. She heard innumerable faint whispers through the branches. As she sought the voices, seeking to understand what was said, the whole of her vision filled with two large, almond-shaped eyes radiating a pure white light.

Begone.

Hazel felt like she had been slapped as her vision hurtled backward at an extreme speed. She fell in reverse until she landed back in her body with a jolt and searched Lyvaelan's room wildly as the dark elf warlock watched her.

"What happened?" she asked when she understood where she was.

"That was farsight," he replied, folding his hands together.

"That was incredible. I've never experienced anything like that before."

"Really? Never?" he asked doubtfully.

She looked at him quizzically. Was this sort of thing common in Elliara? "No, never."

Lyvaelan cocked his head at her. "Interesting. You were directing my sight. Normally I would've been in complete control, but you were more insistent than I expected, so I decided to see where you'd go. It's unusual for someone who hasn't used farsight to know how to use it."

She was still trying to orient herself to the room. "Where was I?"

"It's easier for me to see places I've been to before, so I took you along the path I traveled to get here from Elliara. I was not expecting you to delve so deep into the forest."

"What happened? I could hear whispers and then it was like someone told me to leave." She felt like the giant white eyes were still staring at her.

"Your inquisitiveness intruded upon the privacy of the land. You met one of the constant guardians of the forest. A wood elf." He noticed her glancing around the room. "You needn't worry. The wood elves have no interest in you. Any residual feelings are likely a consequence of their little reprimand."

"How did it know I was there? Wasn't I invisible?"

"Elves are magical and can sense how magic flows around them. Imagine a still pool you might rest in. Now imagine someone drops a small rock in. Barring the noise, would you notice the ripple?"

She considered this. "I think it would depend on the rock."

"Precisely. The bigger the rock, the closer it is, the easier it is to sense. Of course, it may also depend on how vigilant you are as well. One person might be more inclined to notice slight changes around them, whereas another might miss the obvious. Wood elves are the most vigilant of the elven races. They monitor what occurs in their forests and maintain balance while protecting against intruders. The whispers you heard were the elves communicating telepathically, which is the primary way elves speak. While they likely noticed your presence from the moment you entered the forest, when you spied on them, they cast you out. A simple feat, assuming one is attuned to such things. It seems you only slightly bothered them, which is why they chose not to do something more unpleasant."

"What could they have done?"

Lyvaelan shrugged. "Many things. They could've trapped you so you couldn't disentangle yourself from the vision. They could've caused considerable psychic pain or placed an enchantment on you to make life more difficult. Occasionally—if they are truly annoyed— they may choose to mark you. There are many things."

She frowned. It would have been nice to have known the potential dangers *before* experiencing farsight. She decided not to bring it up.

"How would they have marked me?"

Lyvaelan narrowed his eyes, searching for the right words. "Wood elves commune with—and control—the creatures of the forests. Beasts, birds, insects, and even some reptiles and fish aid the wood elves. If they had marked you as an enemy, such creatures—if you encountered them—would make life miserable for you. They wouldn't risk their lives, but there are myriad ways animals could make life less livable. Fortunately, the mark usually only lasts a few weeks. Wood elves need to maintain the magic, and few have the patience to keep a grudge longer than a few weeks.

"In any case, I showed you how to see at a distance for a reason, and it was not for the sake of learning about my distant kin. I wanted to demonstrate how the sight can work and feel once you have developed it as a skill. Initially, when I would use it, it was how you experience your gift now: I beheld unknown places in a dream. As I developed the skill, I found I could use it whenever I wished. I simply had to improve at dreaming it first. Once I knew the experience, I could call upon it at will. While foresight is markedly different from farsight, there's enough overlap in use and understanding that this advice holds some weight."

"Okay," she said slowly, "so, how do I get better at it? Is there anything I can do to practice?"

Lyvaelan nodded. "One of the easiest ways to increase your understanding and retention of dreams is to record them. Many people do this hoping to find esoteric meaning or prophecy. While most dreams people have will in no way be predictive, it's fortunately helpful to you, regardless. Do you have something you can record your dreams in?"

Hazel thought back to the blank book Aldric had given her and nodded.

"Good. Use it. Record as many details as you can, however insignificant they may seem. The more details you write, the clearer your dreams will become, and the clearer your dreams are, the less guesswork you'll have to do. The more you trust them when you wake, the more they'll come to you during the day as well.

"Besides that, I would like you to practice with me daily. What we do each day will vary, but I think it'd be most beneficial to show you how to notice magic and use it."

She cocked her head. "But I don't have any magic."

He mirrored her confusion. "You rose from the dead and you can see the future. Is that not magical? I know when children are young, they're tested for arcane proficiency, but whatever you were told when you were young has changed. You can predict the future, so you're using magic whether or not you're aware of it. By understanding how magic works and how it feels, you'll eventually be able to use your foresight at will. Even as we train, you may find more of your dreams predict aspects of the future you hadn't expected. You may notice more details or see further into the future. It could be anything, really."

Hazel frowned in thought. Could it really be as simple as he made it sound? She didn't *feel* magical, despite all evidence to the contrary. Still, his words made sense, even if she had reservations. Lyvaelan watched her, his neutral expression unchanging as his eyes read her.

"With time, you'll recognize magic for what it is," he said, his words had a soothing and patient tone to them. "Magic is like the air: it would be impossible to live without it and yet we rarely notice its presence. Most don't even think of the air they breathe unless it becomes poisonous or takes on odors. If you consistently train yourself to observe aspects about the air, such as temperature, humidity, and so on, then you could likely predict events such as an impending storm, or how warm it will be later, or whether it's spring or winter. To others, it would seem impossible to get such an understanding, but to you, it would seem as natural as anything. Magic is no different in that regard, except it's far more fundamental to the universe than air.

"Eventually, you will understand the basic workings of magic and notice when others use it. Any trained spellcaster knows how to use magic subtly, so even other casters cannot recognize it, but it's important for a beginner to get a feel for it first. Besides, there are many creatures—especially fae—that poorly conceal their magic."

Lyvaelan uncrossed his legs and stood. "Each time we meet, I'll show you some magic in an obvious fashion, each day being less and less conspicuous until you're attuned to the presence of magic. By seeing through my farsight today, you've begun to get a feel for it. You may not realize it, since the magic was so obvious, but eventually you'll understand the common thread in every spell. That common thread is the stream of magic.

"For today, this lesson is concluded. You should rest a little before we leave. It has been almost two hours since you first entered my room."

Hazel's eyes widened. "Two hours? We only talked for maybe half an hour."

"True, but using farsight took more time than you realized. Over an hour, actually."

"But... it only seemed like a couple minutes."

He shrugged. "Magic. Perhaps you can take this away from the lesson as well: magic affects time in unexpected ways. It must also be equalized. To see so far away requires a counterbalance. I used less magic than I needed to, simply to show you a small piece of the wonders of magic."

She shook her head. "Amazing."

"Indeed. You should get ready for tonight. I will prepare myself. If you remember any other additional details of your dream, let me know."

"I will. Thank you, Lyvaelan." Hazel got up and made her way to the door before turning to him. "Also, I hope one day you'll feel joy without exploding."

He looked away and shut his eyes. He crossed his legs into a sitting position, except instead of sitting on the ground, he levitated at his height, as if he were still standing. Hazel returned to her room with much to consider.

Chapter Eleven
The Quandary of the King

Gods, I hope this goes well.

King Aldric sat in the nearly empty throne room. Two guards stood by the entry and another two attended twenty feet from the throne on either side of him.

It was strangely quiet. Typically, the room served as a great hall and general reception area for visiting diplomats. The dark marble pillars lined the hall on polished floors of stone. Ornate rugs depicting flying dragons and hounds chasing foxes ran the length of the room on both sides. Tapestries hung between tall windows showed the grand achievements of past kings of Ethelian. To either side of each row of pillars stood tables and chairs where visitors would frequently wait, or where philosophers and aristocrats congregated to discuss politics. Aldric preferred this chatter to the silence now present, but he needed the room empty. This was too important.

Aldric leaned against the palm of his hand, covering his mouth and tapping his cheek absently. He hated sitting on this high throne. It reminded him of his father's imposing figure and rule. While his father had strengthened Ethelian, Aldric knew many of his laws were severe and may have hurt his people more than intended. The economy of the kingdom—and Coruvaine specifically—had been stunted during his father's rule. Safety in the kingdom was also significantly better in his father's time. What changed?

Commerce and immigration.

Aldric was the first King of Ethelian—and the first ruler in the Gray Empire—to sign trade agreements with the nosferatu of Noxphetalis. He was named Elf-Friend of the light elves in Elliara, which conferred the same benefits as a conventional trade agreement. In his twenty-two-year reign, he allied himself with two of the non-human nations bordering Ethelian. He'd given his people the opportunity to travel and do business in both regions, which helped his kingdom grow. The elves provided valuable orichalcum that was used in trade with spellcasters and increased the use of magic throughout the city for more mundane matters such as the public streetlamps. The vampires quarried stone from the mountains, which made the completion of the outer wall possible and enabled him to build further garrisons throughout the country.

Other potentates respected Aldric for his strategic mind. Diplomats praised his incisive wit. His people loved him for his compassion and earnestness. In this moment, he hoped their views were justified.

The great double doors opened as a guard entered, followed by a young man in elegant blue robes emblazoned with a white rose. This was a spellcaster of the Inquisition. The young man walked with a confident, even stride, a pace behind the guard. His blond hair was tied behind him in a tight ponytail which drew Aldric's attention to his piercing blue eyes. Despite his confidence, there was no presumption in his gaze as he approached the king.

"Your Majesty," the guard said, "I present Chief Inquisitor Thomas Eller of the Inquisition of the Council of Archmages."

Aldric looked down, idly stroking his short beard. "Thank you, Derek, you may go." The guard bowed and left the chamber. Aldric's eyes followed the guard until he exited. The king closed his eyes and took a deep breath. When he opened them again, he smiled at the mage. "Thomas, it's good to see you."

The mage smiled and genuflected. "Likewise, Your Majesty. To what do I owe the pleasure of your summons?"

Aldric regarded Thomas. This man was shrewd; Aldric didn't believe for a moment he hadn't known the reason for the summons the moment he was asked to appear. He wouldn't play this game. "I think you know why I asked you here."

The mage studied Aldric. "Hazel Enda."

"Precisely." He took a deep breath. "I would like you to delay sending news of her to your superiors."

Thomas sighed. "Your Majesty, as I told you before, my hands are tied. I must report Hazel Enda's existence to the Grand Inquisitor. I'm bound by duty."

"And what of the royal seal I placed upon the case?" he asked, sounding more hopeful than he meant to.

"Your Majesty knows that the Council of Archmages respects the individual sovereignty of each nation, and Ethelian is no exception. The seal you possess gives you eight weeks to settle any arcane matter before the Inquisition intervenes. It was also mandated by imperial decree that the Council of Archmages and their assets would have final say in matters pertaining to arcane abuse, particularly as it relates to necromancy. I don't serve the Kingdom of Ethelian so much as I work alongside it. I aid where I can and subdue dangerous individuals. Part of my mission is making regular reports. My superiors know Hickory Allkirk has practiced necromancy, and we raided his home. They know nothing else. How can I keep such important information from them?"

Aldric shook his head. "The Inquisition would steal a girl from her family?"

A muscle in his face twitched. "The Inquisition would remove a dangerous threat to the kingdom."

"Do you truly think Hazel is dangerous?" Aldric asked, leaning forward. "Does she seem filled with murderous intent?"

"Looks can be deceiving. She didn't appear dangerous, but necromancy is a volatile craft, which can have dire repercussions. Underestimating a being created from necromancy is courting disaster." Aldric knew that Thomas was right. A single undead creature could kill many people besides inciting panic. "Would you really be comfortable risking the lives of the many for the convenience of a few?"

Aldric's eyes became serious. "Hazel is being watched and carefully supervised. Based on what we've seen and the tests my Sapphire Guards have executed, we have no reason to believe she will hurt anyone. I've surrounded her with capable individuals who will observe her in multiple settings. Beyond that, how I handle my people is strictly my business as king. I have worked tirelessly to ensure the safety and happiness of all citizens, and that includes Hazel. Exiling her on the chance she might be dangerous contradicts my beliefs as sovereign of Ethelian."

"Of course, my lord," Thomas said, bowing his head. "I meant no offense. Regardless, I still need to make the report."

Aldric stood and walked down to Thomas. "How long have you worked in Coruvaine?"

"Almost six years."

"Six years. When have I ever interfered in your mission as an inquisitor?"

Thomas searched Aldric's expression. "Rarely. You've been generous in your dealings with us in general, and me specifically."

"I have." He walked back up to his throne slowly. "I did this not to curry favor with you or your organization. I've sought to befriend you while many in the city still distrust the Inquisition. I've given you permission to work alongside my soldiers to uncover any necromancy or arcane abuse. More than that, I consider you a friend. You know me. I wouldn't ask you to do this unless it was of the utmost importance. This exceeds what either of us expected. Hazel disrupts our notions of how the world functions. We find ourselves in a strange situation neither of us fully understands. What I know is this: Hazel is back among the living, whether by the act of a god or a man. She is alive and just realizing what that means. Don't take this girl away from her family."

Thomas held his hands out helplessly. "I don't have a choice. I need to report our findings."

"Thomas, please. As your friend, I'm asking you—*begging* you— don't send Hazel to Selevarian. Find another way."

A hush fell over the throne room for what seemed like hours before the mage sighed and rubbed his brow. "I'm going to get in a lot of trouble for this, Aldric. I hope you're right."

A grin broke out on Aldric's face. "You're a good man. Thank you."

The mage held up a hand. "I have some conditions. In the first place, I cannot violate my post. Instead of piecemeal reports, I will gather additional information until a solid picture emerges, at which point I will submit it to my superior. That also means you *must* inform me of everything that happens with Hazel, and spare no details. I can delay my initial reports because we lack relevant information and are uncovering more. If matters get out of hand, then I'll step in and contact the Grand Inquisitor herself to make certain nothing dangerous occurs. I promise I'll only send such a report if the circumstance is most dire. Otherwise, I want you to send all findings—complete and unexpurgated—to me. If I sense you're hiding something, I'll contact Archmage Alvaria Saccarra and she'll send for reinforcements to collect Hazel Enda."

Aldric nodded. "I understand and agree to your terms, though I hope it'll never come to that."

Thomas looked at Aldric intently. "I will also be the official correspondent for the Inquisition on every matter pertaining to the Evenfall Vigil division that Hazel Enda belongs to. Every case they are assigned shall be overseen by me."

Aldric worked to contain his shock. "How do you know she's

working for the Evenfall Vigil?"

Thomas gave him a meaningful look. "Your Majesty, the Inquisition makes it their business to track potential dangers. This is another reason I am reluctant to delay my report. Putting someone like her in harm's way could have devastating consequences."

Aldric rubbed his beard. "Very well. I'll alert the commander, though he won't be pleased."

Thomas's face tightened. "Like it or not, he'll comply. The Inquisition is not as terrible and frightening as commoners erroneously believe. Normal people have nothing to fear from us. Our practices are regulated extensively and we answer to the Council of Archmages." He glanced at the entrance of the throne room. "Unlike others who are more religious in their dislike of the undead. Speaking with the High Priestess of Semeleme will be a less pleasant conversation than ours."

Aldric glanced behind Thomas to the doors. "Oh? Did you see her recently?"

"Just outside, actually." Thomas smiled ruefully. "She gave me a lecture on why my work is both dangerous and meaningless. Charming woman, really."

"She does her best," he said with a nervous chuckle.

"I'm sure she does. Good luck, Aldric, and remember: *no more secrets.*"

"You have my word."

Thomas bowed and exited. Aldric slumped on his throne with a groan. He already felt exhausted after meeting with the mage, but he suspected his next guest would be the harder of the two. That much he agreed with Thomas on.

He gestured for a guard to bring him water. He contemplated asking for something stronger but thought better of it. Despite his apprehension at speaking with the High Priestess of Semeleme, he realized he needed to be as alert as possible. A servant came bearing a goblet of water. He drank a few sips and set it down. He signaled to the guard before the doors, who nodded and stepped out briefly.

The guard opened the double doors and announced loudly, "The High Priestess of the Cult of Semeleme, Caeli Relinon!"

The already quiet hall took on a reverent hush as three people entered. To either side stood two older bearded men, both muscular through their dark brown clothing and cloaks, the hoods of which fell over their eyes, obscuring their faces. They each held shovels they carried like staves that appeared ornamental with a silvery head at the top of each. Between these two strode the High Priestess. She glided as she walked, the stone floor absorbing the sound of her footfalls, as if it feared to evoke her ire.

Aldric gulped as she approached. She was only a few years older than his daughter but possessed an ageless maturity. Her solid black kirtle balanced form and function. A thin black veil covered her dark brown curls and her lightly freckled face. Her expression was neutral as her large blue eyes gazed at Aldric. The High Priestess was equal parts beautiful and terrifying; her bright eyes seemed capable of accelerating one's heartbeat and stopping it altogether. The aura surrounding her commanded respect and the slight shiver most felt at her passing was for good reason: she was the beloved of Semeleme. She was the chosen daughter of the goddess of death.

"Welcome, High Priestess," he said.

Caeli gave a small smile and inclined her head in deference. "Your Majesty, thank you for granting us this audience." Her voice had a cold quality that made Aldric shiver.

"Of course." He took another small sip from his goblet. "How may I be of service to the Cult of Semeleme?"

"Your Majesty," her tone was friendly, but Aldric felt it could change at any moment, "it has been a matter of several months since a malefactor desecrated one of our gravesites and stole a body we laid to rest. We wished to know if any progress had been made in finding the culprit."

"Ah, yes, well, the case is complicated and I don't have the specifics in front of me at the moment, but I've been looking into it. We found the grave robber, and he's currently in our custody. We are presently interrogating him." Aldric suddenly felt like he was tripping over his tongue.

Caeli placed a hand lightly over her heart and sighed. "Semeleme be praised. We appreciate your hard work and the information you've gathered. It's a great relief to know this defilement won't go unpunished. When will we be given the remains?"

"Well, we don't currently think his crimes warrant a death sentence, so I see no reason to give over his remains—"

"No, no, not the criminal," the High Priestess interrupted, shaking her head. "Perhaps I wasn't clear. I speak of the remains of the body that was stolen. We must return it to the earth so the cycle may be complete and this child's spirit may rest in the caring arms of our mother."

Aldric struggled to maintain composure. Despite her calm demeanor, she utterly unsettled him. She was all that separated him from the goddess of death herself. He cleared his throat. "Yes, of course. There are some extenuating circumstances that complicate matters. Things are not as they were—"

"I understand a corpse may be violated in numerous ways, but whatever remains must be brought back to its resting place."

"That may be true, but in this case, there aren't remains to speak of."

"Nothing?" Caeli frowned. "Even if the body were burned by magic or transmuted into another substance, there would still be grounds for interment."

"I'm afraid neither of those is exactly the case," he said, trying to think of something he could tell the priestess that would appease her and prevent further questioning.

"How would you know for certain he'd exhumed the body if you didn't obtain possession of it? Grave robbers don't simply take a corpse and then admit to it later. That's *not* their way." She stared hard into Aldric's face. Her frown deepened and her voice sharpened to a quiet, dangerous point, "Where is Hazel Enda?"

Aldric's jaw worked, but no sound came out. As his mind worked to develop an explanation, Caeli's eyes widened and her hands tightened into fists. "She walks among us."

Aldric jumped. "Hold on a moment, it's not—"

"She's been brought back," she whispered. She stared at the king with fire in her eyes. "She's undead."

Aldric wiped a bead of sweat from his brow. "We aren't sure what she is, but we don't believe her to be undead."

"Then she *has* returned to the world of the living," she said, focusing her eyes on the king. She took a step forward. "And you know where she is."

"Yes, she has. We don't yet know all the details, but the Inquisition is looking into it. We don't understand what's happened to her yet, but we're doing our best to—"

"It must be destroyed."

"What?"

"We must obliterate the abomination this desecrating mage invented. Such atrocities must be eliminated." The cold in her voice—so reminiscent of the grave—had transformed into the burning zeal of a pyre that sought only to consume. "Give it to me. We will destroy it."

As she spoke, black wisps of smoke gathered and slithered around her hands in ever-increasing size and speed, pulsing rhythmically with agitation.

"I am given power by the goddess herself to eliminate any creatures which rise unnaturally. My touch is the healing salve of death, which returns the undead to the Lady of the Void. My power is as unlimited as my desire to destroy them. Give. It. To. Me."

Aldric watched as dark spirals encircled the High Priestess. This magic was beyond any spellcaster. It came not from innate ability or individual mastery: this magic issued from the goddess herself— unlimited, powerful, and divine. Merely seeing it filled him with mortal dread and reminded him of the single knowable fact of his life: it would one day end.

He took a breath to steel himself. "High Priestess, with all due respect, the matter is being handled. Your involvement—while appreciated—is unnecessary."

"If undead exist, then my involvement is entirely necessary." The dark energy continued to swirl around her. The priests on both sides shared her vehemence as the smoke coiled around their legs.

"The Inquisition will take care of this," Aldric said placatingly.

"The Inquisition!" she shouted. The dark tendrils buzzed like a swarm of aggravated wasps. "The Inquisition works only to take care of itself! Mages cause the problem, not the solution!"

"The undead can come into being without the interference of human mages, High Priestess." It was a weak excuse, but the best he could think of.

"Yes, but who—besides a human mage—can become such a horror as a lich? Who possesses the vile ingenuity to raise undead armies to ransack homes, kill the innocent, and bring pestilence wherever they tread?"

"Hazel has not become a lich."

"Then what?" she demanded, the dark fingers stretched out along the floor, spreading from her. "A revenant? A zombie? Some mutated new strain of undead to terrorize the world?"

"We don't know."

"You don't know." She stared into Aldric. "And neither does the Inquisition. They are incompetent. Return the dead to me. I will lay it to rest. Forbear to deliver such dangers into the grasp of mages who do not comprehend the damage they might accomplish by their foolish schemes."

"The Inquisition is highly competent, and trustworthy," Aldric said, only briefly aware of the irony of his earlier conversation. "The current Grand Inquisitor has been the most ambitious of any Grand Inquisitor in the last three hundred years. She has brought to heel countless potential threats."

"And how many did she eliminate completely by seeking our aid?"

"You know the Council of Archmages has a strict noninterference policy with various cults. Including you in their work would create an imbalance of power within the other cults, and soon others would seek to ingratiate themselves to the Council. It would ultimately serve no one."

"Alvaria Saccarra does not destroy threats, she merely saves them for later. Does it not occur to you that maybe her ambition is for her own gain and not for the good of others?"

"The results speak for themselves. She's done much good, and the Inquisition has proven helpful to me on numerous occasions."

"And the Cult of Semeleme has not?"

Aldric sighed. "Of course. The Cult of Semeleme has been indispensable and beyond reproach. Your burial rituals have helped millions come to terms with the loss of loved ones, and your care for the dead is unmatched."

He felt his courage returning, even as the dark magic curled around the steps to his throne. "I won't give Hazel Enda to you. She has returned and retains all her memories from before her death. She makes her own decisions. I've been counseled that eliminating her would be an error. I've spoken with her myself and she's a wonderful girl—like any other. You cannot have her."

"A girl like any other," Caeli repeated. "How many girls recover from death after four months? If she keeps her faculties and has existed longer than two weeks without deterioration, then she's a lich and must be destroyed."

"It takes decades—*centuries*—to create a lich," Aldric said, shaking his head. "There's no way she could've become one in such a short time."

"'The living lich of half a day is greater trouble than the lich of two tomorrows.'"

"That old saying doesn't apply here." The saying referred to the necessity of dealing with present problems before they got worse. Liches grew in strength the longer they existed and so a lich of two tomorrows—or in two days—was substantially stronger, but less immediate a threat than the lich which rose most recently.

"Does it not? Hazel may not appear outwardly dangerous yet, but she could spell the end of the world." The black energy continued to writhe, but slower.

Aldric waved his hand, dismissing the thought. "You're being melodramatic. Hazel wouldn't make the difference between the world ending or being saved."

"You don't know that."

"Not every strange thing is necessarily calamitous, Priestess."

"And not every girl rises from the dead in full command of her faculties, Majesty." She stared defiantly at the king.

Aldric rubbed the bridge of his nose. Despite the gravity of the situation, he couldn't help remembering tonally similar conversations he had with his daughter. "Regardless, you cannot have her."

"Where is it?"

"*She.* Where is *she?*"

"I stand by what I said."

"I'm afraid I cannot divulge that information. She is kept under careful watch across multiple settings to assess for any abnormalities in functioning."

"You mean she's out and among the people?" Caeli exclaimed.

"She is one of my people."

"Not anymore. Now she belongs to Semeleme and I will see to it she returns." The black tendrils receded. The attitude of the priestess had shifted from fury to cold determination.

"No, you won't," Aldric said, rising to his feet. "That girl is under my protection. She was taken too soon from this world and now she has the opportunity to live. I will not let you harm her."

"'I am the salve that heals, the cord that binds, and the water that cleanses,'" Caeli recited with closed eyes as the darkness melted away.

"'I am the fire that purges, the air that speaks, and the earth that welcomes you home.'" She looked up at the king. "I will find Hazel Enda and return her home. You cannot protect her in this because I am her true protector. I shall heal her of this undead existence and return her to the ground where she belongs. The goddess herself works her wonders through me, and none may escape her embrace for long. I would've wished we could work together, but if I must ameliorate the situation without you, then I shall do so."

"You will break none of my laws."

"Of course," she said coolly. "But not all the people will agree. When they hear of an undead creature among them, they may be excited to action."

"If you start any riots—"

"I will start nothing of the sort, but I cannot promise riots will not happen, regardless. My duty is to inspire the living so they may expire in a spirit of joy and rest. Some followers may get overzealous—and I would never condone such things—but I can hardly control the actions of others, now, can I?" She turned from Aldric to depart the palace as the last black wisps dispersed. "Thank you for your help, Your Majesty. I apologize if I may have been... intense. I take undead threats seriously. The information you've given me has been invaluable. We will take our leave."

"Of course," Aldric said weakly, sinking into his throne.

As they left, Aldric felt he should wait a while before standing. While he believed he'd done a decent job disguising his fear before the High Priestess was present, his quaking legs and queasy stomach made it difficult for him to move. He took a shaking drink from his goblet. This terror wasn't just of High Priestess Caeli, but for the object of her zealotry as well. Hazel was in trouble, and there was little Aldric could do.

Chapter Twelve
To Watch for Unknown Dangers

"Do you think we should've brought more weapons?" Hazel asked as they traveled the path to the construction site. The sun had set when the group left the library. For Alistair's sake, they'd chosen streets that put buildings between them and the final embers of daylight until the sun was completely gone. They were now only a mile or so from the work site and the smaller of the twin moons, Kythis—the rose moon—had risen in the east. Progon—the larger moon of icy white—crept up from the west. Both moons waxed crescent, providing little light.

Lyvaelan shrugged. "I have magic. I need no other weapons."

"As for me," Alistair said, rubbing the spherical pommel of his longsword, "my sword is a blend of alchemical silver and steel, which covers a wide range of creatures. Most vampires don't use weapons at all, but I know how to use a sword. Additional weapons and armor would be excessive."

"Aren't you concerned that your cape might get in the way?" Hazel eyed the fine black garment the vampire wore.

Alistair smiled. "I'm fast enough to prevent it from getting entangled. Besides, in an emergency, it could be a bandage or used to blind someone. If it hinders me, I'll tear it off. Besides"—he winked—"I'm fairly dashing with it, wouldn't you agree?"

Hazel gave him a blank look, which made him grin.

"Okay, but what about you, Lara?" Hazel examined the werewolf, who was dressed in her normal attire of shorts and an old shirt. "You don't have any weapons on you."

"Don't need 'em." Lara smirked. "Not when I got these two babies right here." She held up both fists and kissed each.

Lyvaelan frowned. "That seems... unnecessarily dangerous."

"Nah, I'm not worried. They've never failed me before. Besides, I know how to take a hit."

"Let's hope so." Lyvaelan turned his attention to the road.

They walked in silence for the next several minutes until they arrived. Riglin wasn't present but left a note in his tent thanking the group profusely and gave them additional information about the sleeping habits of the bluecaps. A few bluecaps continued to work in the night with chittering noises and the occasional *ping* and *clang* of metal on rock.

They moved closer to the temporary homes of the bluecaps Riglin had designated in a crude, hand-drawn map. Various small burrows rose like tiny hills around the open space and into the forest that had not been present earlier in the day and served as lodging for the tiny fae.

They decided to watch over the burrows instead of surveying the rest of the woods. The creatures who hunted the bluecaps were too stealthy to detain in a general search, but the odds of catching them near their intended prey seemed much better. If a creature attacked the wall, they would hear it.

When they'd positioned themselves near the bluecaps, Lyvaelan whispered under his breath with his eyes closed as his fingers weaved intangible threads of shadow. The strings expanded around the entire group until they were within a dark circle. Lyvaelan then stretched his fingers apart as the loose dark strands went taut momentarily and expanded into a thin vapor that hung about them.

"There," Lyvaelan said with a sigh. "We may talk more freely. They cannot hear us, and it should block them from sensing or seeing us. We're mostly protected from whatever hunts the bluecaps."

"'Mostly'?" Lara questioned with a raised eyebrow. She crossed her arms and leaned against a tree.

"Yes. Until we notice them, they won't notice us. This is more of an awareness spell than a concealment spell. The moment one of us sights them, they'll be capable of seeing us as well. Also, don't move too far away from me or you'll no longer be covered by the magic."

"How far is 'too far away'?"

Lyvaelan narrowed his eyes with slight annoyance. "You ask a lot of questions, Lara. Don't go further than fifty feet from me. You need to be within a distance I can see or sense. In a forest this dense the range is limited. Fifty feet should be the maximum."

"Sounds good to me," Lara said with a stretch. She slid her back down the tree until she was sitting and yawned. "Wake me up when it's my turn to watch."

"What?" Alistair said. "You're going to sleep during our stake-out?"

"Yep." She was now lying supine, her head resting between the roots of the tree.

"But we're supposed to be watching!"

"Yeah, but it's nighttime and I'm tired." Her eyes were closed, but she was smiling. It seemed to Hazel she was intentionally antagonizing him.

"That's not an excuse!" He stood over her with his hands on his hips. "This is literally our job. It's in our *name*. We are the *Watchers of the Evenfall Vigil*. What about that don't you understand?"

"Look," she said, opening one eye, "we have a pretty special group here, alright? I'm guessing your hearing is so good you could probably hear every person's heartbeat if you were concentrating. Our magical friend can probably send out magical pulses or sense life magic stuff and figure out when people are around. Me? I work by instinct. If something bad comes up, I'll know, even if I'm asleep. Having all of us standing guard is a waste of resources. Some of us will get bored, and that's much more dangerous than being asleep." She closed her eye. "At least for me."

"She may have a point," Lyvaelan said. "While not all of us need to sleep, resting from an active watch will keep each of us fresh. Lara may do us a favor by resting first. I'm too apprehensive to relax, and you two might feel likewise. After a couple hours of nothing happening when we feel like taking a break, she'll be refreshed for her watch and ready to relieve us."

"Yep, that's me," Lara said with a yawn as she nestled deeper into her place. "Giving everything I have for the good of the group. You can give me your 'thank you' letters after I've woken up."

Alistair rolled his eyes and trudged to the outer edge of the circle, muttering to himself. He closed his eyes and drifted off the ground and into the air. The vampire ascended haltingly, occasionally moving his arms as if he feared he might lose balance. True to what Alistair had told her, it was an inelegant demonstration of the ability. She wondered if he would've flown if Lara kept her eyes open. As he passed through the treetops, Hazel lost sight of him. Despite the clumsiness of the action—or perhaps because of it—watching Alistair gently float up was a surreal experience.

"Where do you think he's going?" Hazel asked Lyvaelan.

He briefly glanced up. "I think he's going to get a better vantage point. On the ground, he'll have some distractions, but up there he might hear the overall forest better." He moved into a meditative position on the ground and exhaled.

"Do you think they'll come tonight?"

"I'm certain of it," Lyvaelan replied. "The only question is: when?"

Four uneventful hours passed. Lyvaelan roused Lara from her sleep just after midnight so Hazel could rest. The girl tried to relax, but she couldn't shake the impression that something was wrong. She didn't feel nervous, exactly, just lost. It was like she had misplaced something and was currently searching in all the wrong places. She tried to shake off the nagging sensation, but it grew the longer she ignored it.

A rustling came from bushes about sixty feet from them on the other side of the burrows. Lara crouched, nodded to Lyvaelan, who nodded back, and crept toward the sound. Lyvaelan's attention was rooted to the spot as he waited, ready to cast a spell.

Despite this rustling, the nagging didn't dissipate. Hazel stood and strode in the opposite direction. She tried to imagine the sense of peace she experienced when using Lyvaelan's farsight, and the freedom she felt. Instead, she desired to direct her eyes elsewhere, like a gnawing but aimless curiosity. Gradually, the sensation changed from one of frustration to dawning realization. Finally, at the outer edges of the shadowy barrier Lyvaelan had created, Hazel saw it.

The creature.

Chapter Thirteen
When Shadows Have Teeth

At first, she saw nothing. Hazel's eyes fixated on a point of darkness beneath the canopy. As she tried to determine what was there, the gloom shifted. It was like staring into a void. The creature was utterly black, save for two lidless glowing white eyes without pupil or iris which leered at something on the ground. It was difficult to determine the exact shape of the creature, but it resembled a massive wolf with mutating proportions. Beneath one of its great paws, now shaped like a black hand, a shivering bluecap watched in paralyzed terror. The monster opened its mouth, revealing pointed fangs. It leaned close to the bluecap and grinned.

"Lost. So lost." The creature rasped before swallowing the bluecap whole.

Hazel's eyes widened. The creature shifted its gaze to Hazel, its grin growing wider and simultaneously less lupine and more hideous. Slits in its stomach and ribcage moved apart to reveal several bluecaps trapped within the prison of the beast's belly, all looking out with the same expression of utter fear that prevented them from moving or uttering even the smallest sound. The creature stalked toward Hazel.

"Mommy? Where are you, mommy? The woods are so dark and

I'm afraid of the shadows. They might have teeth." Its distorted and grating voice issued from its entire body and not just its mouth. As the creature spoke, it grew and morphed from four legs onto two as its forelegs became long and muscular arms, ending in skeletal fingers with jagged claws.

Hazel stood transfixed by the creature. The strange words it spoke made no sense to her and its odd shape, its lack of surprise, and the slow and deliberate steps it took toward her were entirely otherworldly and bizarre. Despite the horrifying being, she couldn't tear herself away.

The creature raised its arm slowly back, spreading its claws out from each other. It leaned its face to hers, and she could smell the stench of sulfur as it exhaled. She noticed movement in her periphery as more of these shadowy creatures surrounded her with those same lidless white eyes and fanged grins. The one in front of her whispered, "*Help me, mommy. I'm scared.*"

In a whir of movement, Alistair threw his arms around Hazel and swept her back, narrowly avoiding the claws which raked through the space she previously occupied, digging three gashes into the ground. The creature snarled and hissed in frustration at the vampire's interference.

"Are you alright?" Alistair asked as he rose. Hazel nodded, not trusting herself to speak. No sooner had he spoken and confirmed than he rounded on the creature that failed to strike her. The other monsters fanned out and encircled them when Lara dashed forward and punched. Her fist flew through the creature's head as if it were made of nothing more than smoke. It drew the attention of that creature who stood with three arms on one side of its body and an alligator head.

"*Hey? Did you hear that? I thought I heard something in the bushes,*" the creature rasped as it brought a claw down. Lara dodged nimbly to the side and kicked at the creature's arm, but it did nothing more than her previous punch and passed through without resistance. The fingers of the creature brushed part of the werewolf's leg, leaving a bloody red gash.

She blew a strand of hair from her face. "Alright, let's see how a tree does." Placing one hand against a twisted oak, she struck the opposite side with her fist. With an explosive *crack,* the trunk split, shaking leaves and branches free to the ground. She grasped it and swung it in a wide arc, as Alistair and Hazel ducked beneath the massive cudgel. Lara threw it with surprising force and speed as it crashed into the monsters and twisted upon colliding with the other trees. The forest had not settled into silence when a number of cackles filled the air.

"It was just a breeze," croaked a voice. Inky black smoke lifted from the tree and reformed into the monsters with their white eyes returning last. Each jeered at Lara and appeared unperturbed by the attack. The werewolf glanced between the creatures and brought her hands up into a defensive stance. Although Lara hid it well, Hazel noticed her hesitancy.

Alistair brandished his silver and steel sword and lunged toward the creature that had previously attacked Hazel. He slashed toward its head, cleaving it in half between its eyes. The creature reeled back with a chilling screech and roar that rippled across its torso, distorting its shape. With both hands, the creature pushed the two halves back together and retreated cautiously, recovering from its wound while it glared.

Alistair glanced at Lara, who now bobbed and weaved between the shadows, unable to connect regardless of where she struck. His head whipped around to see two more of the monsters approaching Hazel. "Lara!" he shouted. "Get to Hazel! If you can't hit them, make sure they can't hit her!"

Lara sprinted to her, lifted her with one arm and leaped twelve feet high, grabbing the bough of an elm with her free hand.

One of the shadow creatures glowered at Hazel and Lara with six glowing white eyes and reverted into a quadrupedal form. *"Waste... of... time. Return to the Alchemist... now."* The creature spoke to the one who initially attacked Hazel in the same chilling and raspy voice but with greater effort and intelligence.

The monster it addressed regarded the vampire with open contempt before responding. "*Come on, mom. Five more minutes? It's not that dark outside.*"

"*Fool.*" The other growled. It screeched as it and at least three others fled through the darkness.

The bipedal creature grew larger and more ursine, grunting toward two allies as they circled Alistair. The vampire glanced from one to the other, his expression calm and his stance ready, holding the sword with his right hand in front of him at a medium distance. The nails on his left hand had extended and looked dangerously sharp.

"Damn it." Lara growled, pushing Hazel into a higher branch to avoid the two creatures now attempting to climb the tree. "Where is Lyvaelan?"

The three shadows stalked the vampire, their grins returning as each stared at Alistair with a variable number of glowing white eyes.

"*Mommy? Mommy, where are you?*"

"*There it goes again; I swear I heard something!*"

"*The dark can't hurt you, not at all,/It's only in your head/That scary things are hiding there,/Or underneath your bed.*" The third one sang in a wheedling, sickly voice.

"Alistair, please get out of the way."

Alistair turned to see Lyvaelan forty feet back, concentrating on a spell with his eyes closed. He waved his left hand lazily through the air before his face with every finger, save his ring finger, extended as small motes of yellow light danced between them. His right was held out as if he expected someone to hand him something.

"Get out of the way?" Alistair said, his eyes fixed on the monsters. "But they'll rush you if I don't hold their attention."

"No, you've done that long enough," Lyvaelan said calmly. "I know what they are, but I don't want to hurt you. Move. *Now.*"

The motes of light flew into the center of Lyvaelan's open right hand, which he immediately clenched as bright golden light spilled through.

"I think you all might want to close your eyes."

The creatures noticed Lyvaelan and rushed him as Alistair dashed to the side. The two monsters attempting to climb the tree followed their companions. Lyvaelan stared at the creatures running hungrily toward him. He smiled humorlessly, stretched his fist toward the snarling mass of shadows, and opened his hand. A radiant blast of golden light burst from his palm, illuminating much of the forest. Hazel closed her eyes and felt a summery warmth flash over her skin. For a moment, the entire area was as bright as midday. The creatures had no time to react mid-leap as they dissolved into nothingness, spilling bluecaps onto the ground from their obliterated bodies.

Hazel searched the darkness as the explosion of light disappeared. Even with her eyes closed, the light hurt, and she was blinded. She heard someone retching close by. As her vision cleared, she saw a small floating orb of blue light illuminating Lyvaelan and the surrounding darkness. Lara noticed this and jumped from the tree while holding Hazel. Hazel blinked as her eyes adjusted.

"Where's Alistair?" she asked.

"Here," Alistair said from behind a tree. He crawled forward, quivering weakly.

Hazel rushed to him. "Are you alright? It looks like there's blood on your chin..."

"I'm fine... it's just my last meal, I'm embarrassed to say. That was... a lot to experience."

"Alistair isn't exaggerating," Lyvaelan said, approaching with the ball of light. "I used concentrated sunlight to ensure they died. I knew it wouldn't kill him, but it could still hurt."

"Yes," Alistair said weakly, "it did." He leaned against a tree and rested for several moments. Finally, he looked at Lyvaelan. "Was it really necessary?"

"It was," Lyvaelan said, averting his eyes. "Sunlight is the only way to be certain one has destroyed an aufhocker permanently. They avoid most forms of light, but even torchlight only repels them. It doesn't kill." He looked at Alistair with an expression of regret. "Sunlight was the only way. I'm sorry it hurt you."

"If it was necessary, then... thanks." He smiled at Lyvaelan. "I can feel the pain subsiding already." Based on his still shaking body, Hazel guessed it was a lie. "What did you call those things?"

"Aufhockers."

"What are they?" Lara asked.

Lyvaelan leaned against a tree and folded his arms in thought. "Aufhockers are fae of the Unseelie Court. They prey on travelers at night, although they'll attack others who are outside after sunset. Usually, they ambush humans and tear through the neck, but failing in that, they attempt psychological torture instead. They are thoroughly unwholesome beings."

"What about the things they said?" Hazel asked, remembering their nightmarish voices. "They didn't make any sense."

Lyvaelan nodded. "Aufhockers don't have their own language, nor can they learn the languages of others. Part of the reason they rip out the throats of their prey is because it allows them to use the same words and phrases they used in their last hour of life. Their bizarre utterances were some of the last words of their victims."

The group stood silent, as only crickets chirped.

"I will say," Lyvaelan noted quietly, finally breaking the silence, "it's strange seeing them in a group. From what I know of them, they're solitary creatures and prefer to hunt alone. There were at least eight here tonight—or more—which is not a coincidence. Their prey is almost exclusively humans. Attacking bluecaps at a construction site makes no sense."

Lara studied Lyvaelan with a curious expression. "You seem pretty calm, all things considered. Are you doing alright?"

His eyes narrowed. "It was rudimentary. Do I seem bothered?"

She shrugged. "Not at all, just making sure all is well."

Hazel ignored the bulk of the exchange and crept toward the

jumble of small bodies with blue hats. The bluecaps hadn't moved or spoken since the ordeal. She kneeled next to them and picked one up. It was no bigger than her hand. It continued to shiver, and she could've sworn she felt its heart beat through its entire body.

"It's okay," she said, petting its gray head with a finger. "You're safe."

The bluecap stopped shivering, and a sigh rippled through its body. It gazed at her with large purple eyes and smiled. The bluecap spotted its peers still lying on the ground. It jumped down and pulled one of her fingers toward the other bluecaps. Hazel moved her hand closer and comforted the others and each seemed released from the paralysis.

She hadn't noticed the other three members of her group watching her.

"You have a healing touch, Hazel Enda," Lyvaelan said.

"Yeah, it looks like you helped the little guys out! Of course, I've always found you relaxing to be around personally," Lara said, throwing an arm around Hazel's shoulder.

"This isn't anything." Hazel shrugged. "What all of you did was much more impressive than me comforting bluecaps."

"That's more a matter of opinion than fact." Alistair smiled. "Sometimes comforting a person after a tragedy can do more than destroying the cause of the tragedy itself."

The bluecaps all resumed their chattering and raced around Hazel, some of them climbing onto her shoulders, while others were swinging from her arms. She smiled as she watched them, but then her brow furrowed.

"Where is Zigglepet?"

The bluecaps' eyes opened wide as massive tears rolled down their cheeks. The first one Hazel held pointed in the direction the other aufhockers had gone in.

"They took him? The aufhockers took Zigglepet?"

They nodded.

"Well, I think we've done what we can for now," Lyvaelan said, looking at the others. "We've found the creatures that took them, and so the first mystery is solved. When we report back, I'll recommend that magelamps be installed around the perimeter with some daylight enchantments. The bluecaps may not like it, but they'll enjoy it much more than being swallowed by an aufhocker."

"That's true," Alistair said, resting his chin on his thumb and forefinger, "but what about the person responsible for their actions? This alchemist, they mentioned? Is it the same person who's caused all the problems in Coruvaine we've heard about?"

"Just another mystery to solve," Lara said, rising to her feet. "Let's go back to the city."

"Yes," Lyvaelan said, looking toward the city gates. "Wherever the missing bluecaps are, they're closer to us than we thought." He turned to them. "We should hurry. If I can track some of the magic trail they left behind, we might know whether they're in the city itself."

Chapter Fourteen
The Grand Inquisitor

Alvaria Saccarra gazed upon the city of Selevarian and sighed. From her office she could watch most of the city stretched out before her, extending all the way to the Vernal Sea. This city was the heart of the Council of Archmages. Everywhere she looked, she beheld evidence of the wonders of magic. Magnificent towers built in days, floating platforms carrying mansions, street vendors selling baubles of minor enchantments, and a massive population fed on crops that yielded produce throughout the year. These wonders paled compared to where she stood. Palace Valsidan, which represented the Council of Archmages, transcended the city, more a mountain than a castle. In all her years, she'd seen no construction to match its splendor. Not even the emperor's palace was as imposing or expansive. The Palace of the Archmages contained numerous gardens, training grounds, and zoos within its outermost wall, which was to say nothing of the innumerable libraries, studies, laboratories, and apartments within its interior.

Upon entry through the main gate, one was instantly struck by the immensity of the marble statue of Selevara, the goddess of magic. In one hand she grasped a staff topped by a large crescent moon cradling a smaller full moon, while the other hand, outstretched, held a tome with the sun emerging from its pages, made of gold and orichalcum. She regarded the world with austere determination.

It was Alvaria's mission to discover abuses of magic, before or soon after they occurred. The Inquisition had a frightening reputation built through years of paranoia and misinformation. She didn't mind the notoriety, so long as others complied. Entire towns were obliterated due to hidden transgressions which could've been avoided had the Inquisition intervened. If fear motivated others to obey them, then it was necessary to be fearsome.

The vaults of the Department of Inquisition were replete with confiscated artifacts and research too dangerous to be allowed into the world. They kept these items to better understand the minds of errant spellcasters.

From Alvaria's perspective, the greatest danger was not when mages failed; it was when they succeeded. Magic was unpredictable. While certain constants—such as the law of equilibrium—remained across multiple contexts, even those most fundamental rules could break or change sporadically. This was challenging for all researchers, but those who delved too deeply into this mystery often found themselves in the hands of the Inquisition. The Council of Archmages encouraged research within pre-defined limits.

Alvaria surveyed her office. The room mixed utility and beauty in ways only spellcasters would appreciate. Feather quills wrote notes on paper themselves while never dripping ink. The colors of the walls and decorations changed to suit the mood of its inhabitants. Decanters that could fill with any desired beverage of any temperature stood close at hand. Even the size of the room shifted according to her needs. Most of these features required only a light magic touch in order to function.

As she looked over her room, she frowned. The letter in her hand troubled her.

The capital city of Coruvaine in the northern part of Ethelian was having some... challenges.

Some challenges were to be expected. In the first place, a great arcane university was present in the city, which lent itself more to magic incidents. The city itself sat on a well of magic. This was—by far—a much bigger problem. Wells of magic existed in various locations and drew many magic users from the lowliest spellcasters to the most potent fae. A well of magic meant a spellcaster could use more external energy for various experiments, which would be more likely to cause catastrophic problems. It was like lighting a match in a room of dry tinder and oil.

The issue in Coruvaine should be dealt with, but how?

She fell gracefully into her chair, rubbing her temples.

She wasn't born into wealth, unlike many of the archmages. Her mother died in childbirth and her father was a common craftsman. He died before she was ten years old when an agitated horse kicked him in the face. She didn't have a chance to say goodbye.

Some good came of the tragedy, however. She pushed herself daily to become stronger in magic. Her sorrow propelled her, and eventually her skill and ambitions were realized. Becoming an archmage was challenging, but being one was even more so. Of course, it didn't help that the position of Grand Inquisitor was an important but undesirable role. In a profession that favored erudition and contemplation, she needed to act as an investigator and administrator. There were other archmages dedicated to similar tasks, but her role was viewed less favorably. The existence of the Inquisition meant there were limits to research, and real dangers if those limits were crossed.

It was a role that needed to be filled, and Alvaria was the woman to fill it.

A light knock at her door interrupted her musing.

"Enter."

A mage in a blue robe emblazoned with the white rose of the Inquisition stepped in with a low bow.

"My lady," he said, "Archmage Garson Varaldan seeks an audience with you."

A twitch of a smile lit the side of her lips. "The Archmage of

Dragons is here? Show him in."

The spellcaster bowed and left. Alvaria rose and turned to the window. Drawing herself up to her full height, she smiled. Her black hair flowed in long, elegant waves down her back and her bright green eyes danced with merriment. She was tall among the women and looked more like she belonged to royalty than research. She kept herself in impeccably good health and appearance, much to the occasional displeasure of some of the other archmages who took pride in their advanced age and shunned what they perceived as vanity. But there were still some who appreciated her eccentricities. Archmage Varaldan was one of them.

She heard the thump of heavy footfalls when the door opened, admitting an enormous figure.

"Alva! How good to see you," he said in his booming voice with a toothy grin. "I see the High Archmage hasn't fired you yet for slacking."

Alvaria looked at the archmage. While his shape was mostly human, he'd been irrevocably changed into a dragon-human hybrid. Golden scales covered his body, and horns resembling those of a gazelle adorned his head. A reptilian tail followed behind him from a slit in his green robes. His jaw extended out much like a lizard's but was softened by a more human face. Fingernails had become whitened claws and folded against his back were two great bat-like wings. He had no hair to speak of, merely spikes and scales. His eyes were perhaps the most human. Baby blue eyes amidst the gold of his scales gave the impression of a reversed cloudless sky and sun. The archmage wore robes with various depictions of dragons on it that shifted and flew as he moved. He held a coppery-gold orichalcum staff inlaid with rubies and sapphires topped with a huge pointed piece of clear quartz. The apparent opulence of his dress was almost completely at odds with his mannerisms, Alvaria noted with amusement.

"It's good to see you too, Gar." She smiled as she approached him. They hugged, and she noticed how much he dwarfed her. At nine feet tall, he was one of the biggest archmages. "But if I were you, I wouldn't worry about the High Archmage getting rid of *me* for slacking. I think you'd be first on the list."

Gar gasped. "Little Alva, it sounds like you made a joke! Have I been absent so long that you've grown a sense of humor?"

She pushed him lightly. "You've been gone long enough to grow an entire forest of humor—and with you gone, you might say it grew in ideal conditions."

He reared back. "O-ho! That is a sharp tongue you've got, and that's coming from someone with a forked tongue!"

Alvaria laughed for the first time that day. "Please, sit," she said, gesturing to an armchair.

The chair shifted in size and shape to accommodate Gar. Alvaria sat across from him.

Her eyes twinkled as she regarded him. "So, Archmage of Dragons, to what do I owe the pleasure of your company?"

Gar leaned back in his chair. "I just wanted to make sure you were settling in alright."

"'Settling in alright'?" Alvaria raised an eyebrow. "I've been an archmage for thirty years, and I've worked with the Inquisition even longer. I've had plenty of time to 'settle in.'"

"Perhaps, but our lifespans differ from most, and we take longer to get accustomed to our surroundings. Thirty years as a mage is not as long as being thirty years a baker, or thirty years a builder." He leaned closer. "Remind me, how old are you?"

Alvaria squinted at the ceiling. "I'm nearing my hundred and tenth year."

"Exactly. You're barely more than a child. Magic may extend our lives, but it can also stretch out transitional periods. There were some who didn't agree with your appointment and elevation to archmage status. Those kinds of prejudices take time to overcome, and your particular occupation doesn't help."

"That may be true." She relaxed back into her chair. "Although the other archmages don't see us as the bogeymen the average individual imagines."

"Yes, instead they think the Inquisition is a necessary evil to enable them to focus on research. With the active nature of the Inquisition, there's little time for its members to engage in arcane scholarship."

Alvaria shrugged. "I find the time when I can."

"I'm sure you do. You've had this position longer than most would. Do you not wish to head a different department?"

Alvaria rose and gazed out the window before responding. "I know others scorn the Inquisition. In the view of many members of the Council, we're little more than pest control or trash collectors. But for me, I prefer the active role it provides. I consider it a form of experiential research. I can see the latest blunders and successes of the unsanctioned spellcasters who thought they could use magic without consequence. In some ways, their research helps us recognize threats before they get too dangerous.

"As for the opinions of my peers, I don't mind what they say behind my back. If they whisper, it means they're afraid I might hear, and fear is at least a form of respect."

Gar chuckled. "A cold comfort, if you ask me." He relaxed into a friendly posture. "I thought you were likely fine. Nonetheless, I know it can be helpful having a friend to lean on and I doubt you'll get the same support from the Archmage of Nullification or the Archmage of Crystals."

She gave a half smile. "I would think the Warden of Arcanathema Prison would be sympathetic to my position. As for the Crystalline King, he shows little affection for anyone, so at least his dislike for me is hardly personal."

"Ha! Fair enough. If you want to know the truth, he was never cuddly, even before he transformed. The Warden might be in a similar position to you, except I think he has even less of a sense of humor. Tell me, who among the archmages has shown you genuine friendship?"

"Few," she admitted, "but I've always preferred quality over quantity. Besides you, there's the Archmage of Lights, the Archmage of Sorcery, the Archmage of Education, and the High Archmage himself. I also have allies within my department."

"That's not many."

She smiled wryly. "I'm an adult, Gar. Even before I became an archmage, I recognized the friends I would make as I aged would be few. Friendship is more important to children than adults. Besides, many archmages are gone for such extended periods you could say I hardly have time to befriend any. It's been, what, three years since you last visited?"

He crossed his arms defensively. "Yes, well, the dragons don't like me leaving without good reason..."

Her smile grew. "I'm not *blaming* you. I'm just using you as an example. Others have their own projects, and like you said, time slips away from us. For what it's worth, it feels like only yesterday you were here, bothering me like you are today."

His golden scaled face was unreadable. "You're not lonely?"

Alvaria strummed her fingers on the window ledge. "I've been contemplating my role as archmage for some time now. What sets us apart from other mages? It's easy to see how a wizard or sorcerer differs from the average farmer, but what differentiates archmages from other spellcasters?" She watched a dappled pegasus soar in the distance. "I know we must obtain at least high mastery in two arcane arts and simple mastery in all others, be voted in by the Council, and the High Archmage must explicitly bless the appointment; but if a simple vote was all that was necessary, what would stop a talentless charlatan from becoming an archmage?"

"No archmage would choose such a person. That's ridiculous."

"Exactly." She turned back to him. "It *is* ridiculous. Like asking a blind man to count stars. When we vote to admit a new archmage, it's because we see parts of ourselves and recognize not just breadth of experience—for such learning is universal to all archmages—but also depth. All of us want something more than what life has given us. We doggedly pursue our deepest passions to the exclusion of all other extraneous pleasures. As a result, we change and become more like the things we seek. Look at you. You study dragons and now you essentially *are* one."

He hummed, unconvinced. "My circumstances were unique, Alvaria. This was more a change made by draconic magic than by my labor."

She shrugged. "I disagree; but for now, let's consider other archmages. What about the Archmage of the Green or the Archmage of Crystals? Those are two who have become outwardly different based on their interests, but how many have become the living symbol of their disciplines? The Archmage of Lights is a genuine joy to be around, and whatever room she enters she makes more beautiful and dazzling. The Archmage of Nullification seems like an impassive void which is equal parts calming and terrifying. We're extreme. We become the thing we seek the most.

"Some archmages have students or research assistants, but many prefer working in solitude. But do they work alone, or do they have a different way of existing in the world? With the constant flow of magic that touches each of us so intimately and uniquely, are we ever alone? Perhaps human contact is unnecessary—or merely a stepping stone— to achieve this kind of transcendent tranquility. Maybe the love we have for magic surpasses the love most would have for others. By eschewing human relationships, we may have reached the pinnacle of communion."

"Alva," Gar said slowly, "understand that I'm not making light of what you've said, but... are you all right?"

She raised an eyebrow. "Of course."

"I ask, because what you're saying—while reasonable—lacks a human quality that shouldn't be missing in any archmage. We may be at the summit of human ability, but we're still human. It's easy to lose sight of that if we're not careful."

She smiled thinly at her draconic friend. "We're human until we're not; all we can do is seek improve without losing ourselves. I understand the dangers of devaluing human life. I've read the old cases left by my predecessors. The Living Conduit used similar justification for murdering an entire village in order to save—so he claimed—an entire region from a dire calamity. Immersed in magic as he was, there was no compunction, no understanding of the moral wrongness of killing innocent children, even if it meant saving others. It became a simple game of numbers to him. The ethical considerations aside, he acted without the weight of a conscience and yet claimed to be doing the *right* thing.

"I haven't lost my desire to help humanity. Death—*any* death—is tragic. Life is a treasure many don't realize they have. Humans, more than any other sentient species, have less time to accomplish great deeds. If I could help others live longer, happier lives without the shadow of death looming on the horizon, I would."

Her gaze softened. "Gar, you're sweet to worry about me. I really, truly appreciate it, but I'm fine. I love my work. I have many competent associates and I've helped other archmages by performing duties no one else wanted while enjoying it. To find one's most consistent activities fulfilling and beneficial to others is the best one can ask for in this life."

He smiled. "I'm glad to hear you're happier than your melancholic speech gave me reason to believe. I hope you'll tell me if something troubles you in the future, even if nothing's wrong now. Perhaps I was wrong to worry, though it did seem like you were bothered when I entered for reasons other than my visit."

She nodded and returned to her desk, picking up the report. "You are correct to say I am troubled by something. Perhaps you can help me figure out a conundrum I've found myself in?"

"If I can be of assistance, I'd be glad to."

"I can't discuss the finer details, but I am faced with a dilemma. A metaphor might be useful. Suppose a man has the opportunity to acquire a horse. He will be buying this horse from a man who is a close friend. The friend has no other family, and no other friends to speak of. This man realizes that when this friend eventually passes—in this example, he is quite old—he will likely inherit the friend's estate and possessions, meaning he would get the horse regardless of his patience. Waiting means he will—in fact—possess multiple horses, another home, and additional wealth. Buying the horse will allow the friend to live in retirement off the coin received from the other. There is no immediate need for the horse, though the man truly desires this horse above any other and waiting means he won't have the horse as soon as he'd like and would be unable to utilize it until this ally dies. Is it better to buy the horse now, or wait?"

Gar rubbed his forehead. "You know, this would be a lot easier if you just told me what your actual dilemma is instead of talking about hypothetical horses."

She pursed her lips and squinted, considering for a moment. "Very well. I recently received word from Coruvaine that there has been necromantic activity. An undead creature was created, but my inquisitors have been incapable of identifying it. To confound issues, the king has stepped in and ordered the creature's release since it possesses sentience and has no violent impulses we've observed. We could let this fall on the king's head and step in once it's clear he has no idea what he's doing, or I can travel to Coruvaine personally to oversee the transfer and countermand the king's orders by citing section thirty-seven of the Imperial Decree On the Inquisition of the Council of Archmages. The former risks the lives of innocent people, which is not something I take lightly. The latter, however, would damage my relationship with them, which would make work difficult in Ethelian, and the Inquisition needs no further impediments to its reputation."

Garson shifted in his seat. "It sounds to me like your metaphor didn't do your actual situation any justice. In your scenario, the man would win in either case, whereas here it seems like you would lose in either case. The horse-man must choose between a good thing now or many good things in the future. You have to decide between making a mess now or making a potentially bigger one down the road."

She sighed. "I suppose you're right. This has been weighing on my mind and I haven't gotten as much sleep lately as I'd like. What do you think I should do?"

He gazed absently at the ceiling. "I wouldn't want to upset the hierarchy by giving advice to the Grand Inquisitor."

Alvaria rolled her eyes. "Fine, you're absolved. I take full responsibility for my actions. What should I do?"

"If it were me, I would wait. If this ruler believes the undead poses no threat, this may be a good learning opportunity. Besides that, there is a university in Coruvaine and Lysander is the chancellor. If anything goes truly wrong, he can jump in to save the day. He's terribly good at that. This would give the king space—which he desires—while also providing insight to those who find the Inquisition redundant or evil. Your inquisitors can intervene if matters get out of hand. Going now seems risky, though I can understand your reticence at endangering lives by inaction. You should destroy this creation later."

"You're right." Alvaria smiled. "Thank you, Gar."

"You're certainly welcome. As a way to thank me, would you join me for dinner this evening? It's been some time since I dined in Selevarian and the palace food can be so bland. My treat, of course."

She smiled. "Nothing would give me greater joy than having dinner with an old friend and treasured mentor."

The Archmage of Dragons stood. "I'm glad to hear it. I'll be back an hour after sunset and we can walk from here. There's a new restaurant near the sea that looks promising."

Alvaria sighed. "I trust you as a confidant, but I am wary of your sense of taste. We can look at the new restaurant, but I'm not eating fried manticore spines again, or any other strange things."

"Hey," he said, pointing his staff at her accusingly, "you *liked* that fried manticore. You said it was better to have it on a plate than breathing in front of you."

"That's not the high praise you think it is, and that was before I had any." She shivered at the memory. "My views have changed since then."

"Well, *I* still think it was good," he said, crossing his arms in mock petulance. "But have it your way, Grand Inquisitor, I'll let you have final say in where we dine so long as they favor quantity over quality."

She gave him a flat look. "I'll do my best to ensure both."

He grinned and tightly hugged her. "I've missed our banter."

"So have I," came her muffled reply.

"I'll see you soon," he said, separating from her. "Make sure you're ready."

"I'm always ready." She crossed her arms and smiled. "You're the one who never arrives anywhere on time."

He chuckled softly. "True enough, Alva. Farewell."

The towering archmage left Alvaria in her study. The room seemed bigger and quieter when he left. Alvaria sat down, reminiscing on her past with Garson Varaldan. His physical transformation from human into semi-dragon had happened before she was born. He'd outlived most of his peers and maintained his youthful vigor. The dragons made him into a being of great magic and indeterminate longevity. Alvaria often wondered how it felt to see his peers grow old and die while he remained the same. While he'd never intimated such information to her, she imagined it couldn't be easy. Still, his temperament was more sunshine than storm, and she suspected that protected him from falling deeply into melancholic thoughts. Those who practiced magic lived far longer than those who didn't, but that fact did little to make the passing of a friend hurt less.

Alvaria stared at the report on her desk before putting it aside. The business in Ethelian was being taken care of by one of her trusted inquisitors. The city would survive another day.

Chapter Fifteen
Success Through Failure

"The city is doomed!" Lara yelled, slamming her hand onto the desk of Commander Comrear, scattering several papers to the ground.

The officer cocked an eyebrow. His demeanor showed no hint of concern. "Bit dramatic, don't you think?"

"Only slightly," Alistair interjected, before Lara could respond. "We know what's been causing bluecaps to go missing by the fourth wall. There are aufhockers capturing them."

Comrear's brow furrowed. "The Evenfall Vigil has dealt with aufhocker threats in the past. They're dangerous on the roads at night but pose no major peril beyond that. Besides, they're capturing bluecaps, not citizens. My job is to protect humans within the city walls. Bluecaps don't live in Coruvaine proper. It's unfortunate, but hardly worth all the fuss you're making."

"*They're in the city,*" Lara said, leaning in.

"What?" He sat up.

"It's true," Lyvaelan said, stepping forward. "We were attacked by a group of them. At least eight, but likely more. Several of them attacked us, but the others fled into Coruvaine. I tracked them to the city gate but lost the threads they left behind when they split up. They're among the citizens."

The commander reclined in his chair. Ellen Honrick, who stood beside the commander, spoke as he mulled over the information, "This doesn't make sense. Aufhockers naturally avoid small towns and villages. Why would they risk entering a city as big as this? This is far from their preferred hunting grounds. There are magelamps on the streets that would severely limit their abilities and bring them extreme discomfort, not to mention mages who could destroy or manipulate them."

"That isn't the only strange thing," Lyvaelan said. "Aufhockers have no interest in other fae, yet they targeted bluecaps. Humans are their prey of choice and yet—despite being much closer to human than the bluecaps are—only half of them fought us. One developed the ability to speak on its own and reminded the others that they needed to return to the Alchemist."

The mage pondered this. "Interesting. They were working for someone. Unfortunately, alchemy is one of the most widely practiced arcane arts. In this city alone, there are hundreds of practicing alchemists and a thousand more who could practice alchemy but don't claim it as their chosen occupation. However..." she turned to the commander.

Comrear returned the look. "We don't know if it's *the* Alchemist we've been looking for. This is the first we've heard of aufhocker *or* bluecap involvement. Still, it's worth investigating." He directed his attention to the others. "Did you destroy any of them?"

"Yes," Lyvaelan said, "we killed five. I used a sunlight spell to destroy them. We reduced their number by about half, if I had to guess."

He nodded. "Good. Fighting one of those things is an ordeal for even experienced soldiers. You've done surprisingly good work tonight."

Lara squinted at him. "Thank you? That sounded like a backhanded compliment."

Comrear ignored her. "You should all get some rest. I suspect the aufhockers won't invade the forest again soon. We'll install some proximity magelamps attuned to their presence. That should deter them from approaching the wall again. I expect, on your way out, that you collectively fill out a report form. We may need to review it again within the context of other crimes that may be connected.

"On a separate note, rather than come here, you have a new contact who will handle your future debriefings. He will then speak to me if necessary and bring your reports back to the office for filing. I expect you to be open, forthright, and respectful to him—at least on record. Personally, I hope you're a massive pain in his ass."

"Who is our new contact?" Hazel asked.

Comrear laced his fingers, resting his elbows on the desk. "Chief Inquisitor Thomas Eller of the Inquisition of Archmages."

The announcement was met with momentary stunned silence.

"You can't be serious!" Lara blurted out. "Why would we work with them?"

"It seems excessive, given the circumstances," Alistair said. "Why would they want to collaborate with us?"

"Why indeed?" Comrear replied, his gaze fixed on Hazel. "The order supersedes my authority. This command came directly from His Majesty, King Aldric." He viewed their surprised faces. "So, I really can't countermand a mandate like that. If you want to know why, maybe talk to the mage himself. I'm sure you'll be spending plenty of quality time together, after all. He'll be dropping in on you tonight after you've had some time to rest, so be prepared to greet him.

"If that's the last of your questions, you're dismissed. Remember to see Sergeant Concornus on your way out. He has all the relevant paperwork."

They left, weaving through the mass of desks and soldiers until they came to the bearded satyr who sat watching them with a smirk as they approached.

"It's really too bad, but it happens to the best of us. Most don't make it through their first night, and there's *nothing* to be ashamed of. You all tried your hardest. Here are the forms you need to sign acknowledging rightful termination, and I'll need all your badges and equipment."

Lara leaned on his desk. "We aren't fired, dumbass. We just need to write a report."

"What?" Concornus said, feigning surprise. "You can write?"

Lara leaned in. "Do you know what wolves do to goats in the wild?"

He leaned in as well. "Not exactly, but I've heard whatever it is wolves want, they always come back for more." He winked.

She blinked. "Well, uh, yeah, because wolves eat them. Eat goats. And that's what—I mean..."

"Sergeant Concornus, please give us the forms we need," Alistair said, rubbing the bridge of his nose.

"Sure. Here," he said, holding up a small stack of papers without shifting his rectangular pupils from Lara. "I had them prepared from the moment you walked in. Standard procedure, and all that."

Hazel observed the other soldiers. Many ignored the exchange, focusing on work, but some suppressed smiles and glances passed between others.

"Well, off you go. Shoo," he said, making a sweeping motion with his hands. "I'm sure the inquisitor will have lots of fun with all of you."

Lara growled as Alistair pushed her through the doorway. Lyvaelan sighed and followed with Hazel behind him. The night had been tiring for all of them in different ways, and the sun was just an hour away from rising.

Hazel found little rest that morning. While sleeping during the day was an unusual experience, the curtains to her room blocked out most outside light and dampened the sound of carriages and passersby. In fact, it was quieter, more spacious, and more comfortable than her bedroom back home. There was nothing wrong with her room.

She was tired—mentally especially—but it was that same exhaustion that kept her from sleeping. She replayed the events of the night in her head: the shadowy monsters, the terrified bluecaps, how the others had done so much work to protect her, and how she did nothing. Maybe she didn't belong with the group after all.

It was in the middle of these thoughts she heard a knock on her door. Before she could answer, it opened and Lara's head poked in with a smile. "Hazel, are you awake?"

"Yes..."

"Good." Lara sauntered in and reclined on the bed next to where Hazel was sitting. "I was hoping I wasn't the only one awake."

Hazel half smiled. "How would anyone stay asleep with a person knocking on the door?"

"Well, I guess I should say I'm glad there's at least one person who didn't *pretend* to be asleep."

"Why aren't you resting?"

Lara leaned back with a sigh. "Probably for the same reason as you, I'd imagine. That was some pretty crazy stuff in the forest last night."

"Yeah, it was."

Lara paused, staring at the ceiling. "Hey, Hazel?"

"Yeah?"

"You know, I'm actually pretty great," Lara said, taking a swig from a wine bottle that had escaped Hazel's notice.

Hazel studied the werewolf. "What?"

"I'm pretty great," she repeated matter-of-factly.

Uncertain of the point of the conversation, Hazel agreed. "Yeah, you're really amazing."

Lara looked at Hazel and scrunched her nose. "It just wasn't fair, you know? How was I supposed to know I couldn't hit them? I've been up for hours thinking about those stupid things in that stupid forest capturing those stupid little men, and I just feel stupid."

Hazel cocked her head curiously. "Why? You were amazing. You saved my life and got me out of harm's way."

Lara scoffed bitterly as she took another gulp from the bottle. "I jumped into a tree and then failed to do anything else."

"What about me?" When Lara raised an eyebrow, not understanding, Hazel continued, "I was absolutely helpless. I couldn't even run away. If you and Alistair hadn't stepped in, I would've been killed. If you failed to do anything except jump in a tree, then I failed to do anything at all."

Lara nodded, her face serious. "I know how you feel. It's a little different for me, though. How old are you, ten? Twelve?"

Hazel frowned. "Sixteen."

"Whatever." Lara waved a hand dismissively. "I'm fifty-eight."

"What? You don't look older than twenty!"

"Yeah, werewolves age differently than humans. By around twenty, we mature into adults and master our wolf and human sides, and then we stay at that peak for a few human lifetimes before getting our gray fur.

"Anyway, I've spent my life trying to be the most badass fighter I can be. No silver medals for *this* girl. I worked hard to be as strong as I am and with sheer brawn, I could mop the floor with anyone. I've beaten up vampires, werewolves, satyrs, centaurs, minotaurs, and even a few ogres. No one was really all that hard to beat, given the training I had when I was younger. I was a professional fighter, hoping to find my match. You know, a *real* challenge. I kept improving, but I fell into a rut. When you can beat anybody—no matter what—it's kinda boring.

"That's why tonight *really* pissed me off!" She sat up. "I could've beaten them if they'd fought fairly and let me hit them."

Hazel smiled. "Couldn't your opponents before have said the

same thing? 'If only Lara wasn't so strong, then I could have defeated her!'"

Lara's eyes narrowed, and she took a long drink from her bottle, maintaining eye contact with Hazel as she gulped. She looked ready to belch when a hiccup came out instead. Lara couldn't maintain her composure and laughed. "You're pretty smart for a twelve-year-old, but you should be careful about how you speak to a drinking brawler." She squinted at the ceiling. "It's just tough not knowing how to handle defeat. The other hard thing is I don't think there's anything I could do to improve.

"Not to mention," she pouted, "that vampire prince did more than me."

"That's true, but he also used his sword. You just had your fists. Have you thought about using any weapons?"

"Nah, they're not really my style." She raised her index finger and nodded as her eyes widened. "You might be on to something, though. His sword is made of steel and silver, right?"

Hazel remembered him mentioning something to that effect. "I think so."

"I know what I have to do!" she said, jumping off the bed. "Thanks Hazel, you've been a big help." She bounded to the door but stopped to glance at the green-skinned girl. "You know, you helped the bluecaps, too. I saw the way they responded to your touch. Comforting the injured is underrated. Gods know *I've* never been gifted that way." She paused, and her expression softened unexpectedly. "No one is born strong. It takes time and work. Don't kill yourself trying to become powerful all at once. It isn't worth it."

Before Hazel could respond, Lara vanished into the hallway. Her words were kind, but Hazel was still troubled. While the werewolf was always genuine, there was something in her look that seemed like pity, or perhaps regret. She could sense a similar sentiment in Alistair. They both wanted to keep her safe. She knew she was the youngest of the group, but she hadn't really realized how much younger she was. Lara was probably the closest in age to her, and she was old enough to be Hazel's mother.

She rose and left her room. There was one person who hadn't treated her specially, even if he was odd.

She approached his room and was about to knock when Lyvaelan opened the door.

"You wanted to talk?" His black hair flowed behind him, and he wore a simple gray tunic.

"How did you know?"

He shrugged. "I could hear your footsteps and it seemed like you were coming to my door specifically."

"How could you hear all that? I didn't think I was being noisy."

"You weren't. My hearing is better than most. Aside from that, I was meditating. My insight told me someone intended to speak with me. Come in." He slid back, admitting her.

She entered Lyvaelan's room, taking in the austere decorations and the statuette he kept. He stood by the door with arms crossed, watching her with his elegant eyebrows lifted expectantly. He wanted to know why she was here.

For her own part, she didn't know what to say. The nagging inside her needed to be expressed, but she struggled to find the words.

"Lyvaelan, am I... useless?"

He leaned against the door. "In some ways, yes. Why do you ask?"

She looked to the side. "Last night I couldn't do anything. I was just in the way."

"I can see why you'd think that, but allow me to offer a slight correction. Each of us helped defeat the aufhockers, yourself included. I destroyed them, but I needed the time you gave me to cast my daylight spell. The contributions of you three were about equal. You provided bait, Lara provided a fun target to chase and toy with, while Alistair provided a sense of challenge to the aufhockers who wanted to test their strength. None of your methods would've killed them, though the vampire might have been able to in other circumstances. But it would have been more challenging for me if none of you were around, since the spell is very localized. You were all distractions and provided an equal level of utility in their destruction."

She frowned at him. "Knowing I was the bait isn't reassuring."

"I wasn't trying to make you feel better." Lyvaelan sighed and sank into a chair. He seemed slightly exasperated. "Your father is a craftsman, right?"

"Yes, he's a blacksmith. He mostly works on the metal components for carts."

"Alright, what are some tools he uses?"

"Tongs, hammers, his anvil, those sorts of things."

"Does he use his tongs to hit the metal to shape it?"

She frowned. "No, he uses his hammer."

"Why not use the tongs?"

"They don't work as well as the hammer does."

He stared at her flatly. "Exactly. To accelerate this line of reasoning, the tongs aren't useless. If he didn't have them to handle hot metal, I imagine he'd probably hurt himself. They're ineffectual, however, if they're used in the wrong way when there's a better tool at hand. You're like those tongs. Last night, you were mostly incompetent. That doesn't mean you're always useless. You were quite useful when you predicted what sort of creature was stealing the bluecaps. That bit of intelligence helped me consider the best way to deal with them. I'm slow to react in emergency situations, so having the information beforehand helped me strategize how I was going to use such spells without hurting anyone else. If you hadn't told me, I might've used fire. Fire might have worked against them, though not as well, and it would've burned part of the forest and harmed you and the others. As things are, only the vampire was adversely affected, and it was a temporary injury."

"But I didn't know it was going to be useful."

"So? Does a hammer need to know it's good at hitting nails in order to be useful? No. Your argument is irrelevant. Besides, being useful is overrated. Do whatever you can and let others handle the rest. For what it's worth, the other two also feel like you do, even if you don't know it. I imagine you're mildly aggravated, but they're practically eating themselves up about it. Their surface thoughts are loud enough that I barely need to use sorcery to understand what they're thinking. You're young and learning. No one expected more of you than what you did."

"That's good advice, but I still don't feel much better. I appreciate the help, though. Thank you, Lyvaelan." Hazel moved to the door, but Lyvaelan stopped her.

"Hold on, Hazel. I didn't let you in just so you could vent. Kiran, my mentor, taught me that the only way to overcome our weaknesses is to increase our strengths until they eclipse our flaws. You have much training ahead of you. I suggest we start now."

Hazel smiled. The dark elf was odd and blunt, but somehow, she felt just a little better.

Chapter Sixteen
Reluctant Allies

Night came sooner than expected. Hazel's training with Lyvaelan had gone on for close to eight hours, though it seemed like far less than that. He pushed her to rely on her intuitions and act accordingly. She sensed truth in what he told her, but it was difficult to grasp. It was like she heard a tiny voice speaking to her but couldn't tell where the voice came from or what was being said. Still, she noticed. Lyvaelan was mildly pleased with her progress, which was the most enthusiastic he'd been about anything since he arrived. Not that she was exceptionally expressive herself, of course.

After training, Hazel returned to her room to sleep for a few hours. The additional work and the growing confidence she had in her abilities gave her the peace she needed to rest at ease. By the time she awoke, the sun had already set, and she smelled the aroma of cooking beef with spices and baking bread.

Charlie prepared dinner for them. Roast beef seasoned with rosemary, salt, and black pepper with diced onions exceeded Hazel's expectations for a main course. She was momentarily disappointed in the lack of garlic but remembered Alistair would eat too, and garlic wasn't agreeable to vampires. Biscuits, salad, stew, and a variety of sliced fruits were similarly prepared in excess. Alistair had a little of the meat and salad, but primarily drank a thick red wine, unlike anything Hazel had seen her parents drink. Lyvaelan ate some of everything but preferred the meat and salad over the rest of the array. Lara—in contrast to the other two—ate voraciously and didn't seem especially picky about what she devoured or in what order.

Hazel observed the vampire. "Alistair, have you eaten enough? It didn't seem like you had very much."

He smiled at her. "I'm fine, thank you. I only eat a little food to supplement my main meal." He swirled his wineglass.

"Blood?" Lara asked through a mouthful of biscuit.

"Sort of. This is blood wine."

"Blood wine?" Lyvaelan looked at the glass curiously. "I'm not familiar."

"I recognize this winery," Hazel said, noticing the label on the bottle. "It's made in Ethelian, south of Coruvaine, but I don't know much else."

"I'm not surprised," Alistair replied. "Blood wine is a beverage specifically for vampires. When the War of the Night ended, my people agreed to limit the intake of blood to non-sentient mammals, birds, and reptiles in partial reparation for the atrocities committed against humanity. This limited diet led to many vampires sinking deep in lethargy. It was possible to live, but far from pleasant. King Aldric put many arcane researchers and various vineyards to work, devising a way to make wine a greater export for the city. They created blood wine by using only one drop of human blood per bottle and then transforming much of the wine into a combination of the two with magic. The wine can stay shelved longer than blood. In fact, blood wine tastes better if one waits a little while. This allowed Ethelian to secure an alliance with my father, and it enabled them to establish trade agreements. Since Ethelian required considerable quantities of quarried stone from the mountains around Noxphetalis, the arrangement was mutually beneficial. That's part of the reason the outer wall can be completed at all."

Hazel leaned back in her seat. "I didn't know all of that. I just knew it was a big business."

"Indeed. Since its introduction twenty years ago or so, the different wineries have a never-ending demand for blood wine along with increased interest in different varieties. Introducing the method to multiple vineyards, and making the method obtainable to citizens of Ethelian upon request, increased the desire in each to compete to make the best blood wine. Since it was first introduced, it was immediately loved. Wineries have reached out to various vampires to get sommeliers who could determine the best course to take with both grapes and blood samples. It has become quite an industry. The average vampire needs little more than a glass of blood wine a day to survive, but most will drink two to three, simply to feel full and"—he weighed his words—"appreciate the effects of the alcohol. Blood wine affects us to the same degree normal wine would affect a human, unlike conventional alcohol. I would recommend against drinking any of this, though. I'm told most humans aren't fond of the taste of blood."

"That's a surprising level of ingenuity," Lyvaelan said, deep in thought. "Given the longevity of vampires, it seems likely the bond is one that will last several generations beyond Aldric. He's made allies with powerful individuals who will remain loyal long after he's dead."

Alistair smiled into his glass. "You're not wrong. Among my people, King Aldric is quite popular. From what my sister has written to me, they've erected several statues of the king holding wine bottles. To them it's reverential, but if such a statue were made here, I think others might question the king's drinking habits."

"I think some already do," Hazel said with a smile.

"Well, with his capriciousness, it isn't hard to jest about it."

"Whimsy isn't always detrimental," Lyvaelan said, brushing a strand of black hair behind an ear. "The only way he could open relations with the Seelie Court in Elliara was because of that flippant nature. I wasn't there, but I heard from Kiran he impressed the entire Council of Light with a simple mechanical toy that interested them.

He thought they might appreciate it, so he brought it along in case the other gifts failed to dazzle them. Apparently, the High Lord threw aside a powerfully enchanted orichalcum diadem in order to hold the trinket."

Lara leaned back. "Okay, but is that a true story or just a rumor?"

Lyvaelan shrugged. "I cannot say for certain. I do know, however, that they keep the toy on a pedestal in the main council room in Chaldra, the Great Tree. It's under constant surveillance, and not a council meeting begins without at least fifteen minutes of playing with it."

Lara shook her head. "Elves are weird."

Lyvaelan sipped his white wine. "They certainly are."

"I imagine all races have their eccentricities. Even among my people, we—" Alistair stopped and cocked his head to the side. "Someone just entered the library."

"You could hear that from here?" Lyvaelan said. "I have keen hearing myself, but even I heard nothing."

Alistair shrugged. "Vampires' hearing is among the best. We can echolocate with it, after all."

"It's probably the guy from the Inquisition," Lara said. "I'm not exactly excited to see him."

"Truthfully, I don't think any of us are thrilled," Alistair said, "but we should at least try to be polite. He may not be as bad as I've heard. Minimally, let's try not to make Ambassador Garo look bad in his absence."

Lyvaelan cocked his head like Alistair had. "Well, I think a good step might be to avoid talking behind his back. He's on the stairs."

The group fell into silence as Lara fidgeted in her seat. "Uh, what should we talk about? We can't just sit awkwardly quiet when he gets here or he'll know we were talking about him. It was a pretty crazy night last night, wasn't it? Lots of crazy things with the evil shadow dogs and stuff."

"Yes, crazy indeed," Alistair said in a stilted voice.

Lara chuckled nervously. "Yeah, Lyvaelan, I thought it was pretty great how you used light to defeat them. That was... yeah, that was awesome." It was interesting to see Lara, who usually seemed so confident, affected by the coming of the inquisitor. She sought to contain it, but Hazel noticed her tapping nervously with her hand.

A voice Hazel recognized came from the hallway. "I'm half tempted to let you carry on this conversation in the belief you're tricking me into thinking you weren't talking about the Inquisition derisively, but I'm not as sadistic as most claim."

A young man in blue robes with a white rose entered.

"Inquisitor Eller!"

He smiled. "I'm glad to see you're well, Miss Enda. It's been at least three weeks since we last spoke."

Lara glanced between them, her anxiety shifting to uncertainty. "Hazel, how do you know this guy?"

"He was one of the first people who saw me. He discovered I'd been brought back to life when he stopped Hickory."

"Hickory?"

"The mage who resurrected me."

"I'm still a little confused," Alistair said. "You were revived over two months ago, and yet you last saw him a few weeks back?"

"Yes," Thomas said, stepping into the room, his blue robes swishing with the movement, "I was the mage in charge of Hickory Allkirk, but Hazel's existence meant the case remained open until we determined who she was and what magics he used. I talked with her on multiple occasions and oversaw various examinations. Although she was released from our custody after only three weeks, she continued to meet with me biweekly until three weeks ago, just so I could monitor any changes in her behavior or symptoms."

"Did you learn anything from all that?" Lara said.

Thomas smiled humorlessly. "Frustratingly little, actually. Still, we did all we could within ethical boundaries and determined that—consistent with Mr. Allkirk's nearly incoherent ramblings—Hazel doesn't fit into any of the undead conventions. This brings me to why I'm here." He looked at each of them slowly. "I'm Thomas Eller, Chief Inquisitor of the Inquisition of the Council of Archmages. Like all members of the Inquisition, I uncover corruption wherever it hides. We handle the problems which are above the abilities of local governments. We don't handle conventional crimes such as theft, murder, or assault, unless there's a component which is arcane. A sorcerer using magic to get others to be his 'willing' slaves; an alchemist creating powerful drugs that affect the mind and body to a dangerous degree; a conjurer who's gained control of all the rats in a city and is causing a horrifying infestation; and, of course, the necromancer who brought the dead back to life for whatever dark purposes he wished. The Inquisition has dealt with these cases and saved many lives. To prevent these spellcasters from escaping into the public, the Council of Archmages created Arcanathema Prison which features the most powerful anti-magics at our disposal along with impregnable walls and a variable teleportation engine so none can plan to break others from the prison or choose when to escape themselves.

"The reason I bring all of this to your attention is to clarify my specific mission. My goal is not to hurt others, nor to steal individuals away in the night. Our austerity represents our acknowledgment of the atrocities perpetrated by fellow spellcasters against common people, and our zeal demonstrates our conviction to carry out our duty."

"Tell that to the werewolves and vampires you slaughtered," Lara muttered under her breath.

The mage appraised her calmly. "I grant our history can seem intimidating and our methods have occasionally been severe, but the werewolves and vampires we captured and experimented on during the War of the Night were necessary to break the curse that rendered both races little more than ravenous beasts devoid of morality. Your people were right to fear us once, but there are no further reasons for caution. Those captures and experiments ended months before the war itself concluded, and they saved many lives. Think what you wish of the Inquisition, but your opinion is only possible because the Inquisition liberated you from the curse. Otherwise, you'd be incapable of having an intelligent perspective, or the ability to voice it."

Lara crossed her arms.

"In any case," he continued, "I'm here for multiple reasons. In the first place, the institution of a group of guards with such unique backgrounds could be disastrous if not monitored carefully. I don't doubt the ability of Commander Comrear, but the Evenfall Vigil is terribly overworked and understaffed. His ability to oversee you sufficiently would require him to overlook most of his duties as commander, and that would be ultimately detrimental to the city. Second, you have a warlock dark elf in your midst. According to the theory of multiplicative arcane potential, Lyvaelan has the possibility of leveling this entire city on his own if he lost control and had no one nearby to assist. In that capacity, I can check to see if he's keeping calm and healthy. Third, I wish to monitor Hazel's condition. We still don't know what magic revived her or if it could be progressively more hazardous as time passes. She may not be a danger at the moment, but she could be in the future.

"Honestly, I'm flabbergasted the king didn't think to include the Inquisition in the formation of this group to begin with. It strikes me as borderline reckless, even with the advice of Ambassador Garo. In my mind, this is simply rectifying a major oversight.

"I would also like to add," Thomas said, leaning in, "you can hate the department I work for, you can hate me, you can hate all the mages you want, but in the end, I'm the best friend you have. I want this project to succeed. I want this partnership between my department and yours to flourish. I want you to feel fulfilled in your various crime-fighting roles. And I want, more than anything"—he looked at Hazel—"to keep all of you together. I haven't submitted my last report on Hazel Enda's case. Why? Because it would require her to return with me to Selevarian, where she would be put under the direct supervision of the Grand Inquisitor herself and likely never returned. The Inquisition is zealous. It's for good reason, but it's extreme. Based on my interviews with her," his voice softened somewhat, "I can tell she's a sweet girl. None of this is her fault. She's ultimately a victim of circumstances beyond her control. Do I want to take her away from her parents, her home, her friends, and her country? No. At the same time, I'm bound to my duties as an inquisitor. The only compromise I can strike is this: I'm simply gathering data on Hazel Enda to prove she's harmless. These reports will probably fall beneath the notice of the Grand Inquisitor, and so it'll be unnecessary to take Hazel back or for me to fear serious reprimand. I'm really doing my best to help all of you, so I hope you'll at least give me a chance and be honest about what's going on in your current cases. Understood?"

They nodded silently, each pondering the words the mage had spoken.

"Good. I'm sorry I brought the mood down, especially since you seem like such a lively group. You need to understand where I'm coming from and what I expect from you. I don't consider myself your superior, and I don't need you to address me by any title. I'll take care of the paperwork that is submitted to your department, so please give me the information you can and I'll take care of the rest. Spare no details.

"On that note"—he sat at the table with them—"I heard you had a busy night. Tell me about that."

Slowly, the group recounted the story, starting with their initial interview with Riglin, the foreman. They spoke of each event with some chiming in with additional details, while another took over the main narrative. As they talked, they gained confidence, and the previous openness of the group became more apparent. Thomas reacted to each additional detail with genuine interest. He asked only a few clarifying questions and was content to listen with rapt attention until the conclusion of the tale.

"Well," he said, leaning back, "it sounds like you've uncovered some very interesting clues. There may be stranger business going on in

Ethelian than I realized. We may also help each other in more ways than I'd previously expected."

"How?" Lara asked.

"My work revolves around finding those who are abusing magic. This alchemist—if it's a true alchemist—would fall under my specific jurisdiction. If arrested, then he or she would be detained by the Inquisition and taken back to Selevarian for additional questioning. Of course, it's unclear if this 'alchemist' is really a practitioner of any magic at all, or rather a codename or something else entirely. Aufhockers are incapable of speech beyond what they've heard so 'alchemist' could simply be a substitute term for something similar, such as another mage, or someone in a similar field such as a doctor or herbalist."

"That *is* a good point," Lyvaelan said with a thoughtful frown.

"What it is," Lara said, "is frustrating."

Thomas nodded. "I understand. Most cases I handle take months to years before they reach any satisfactory conclusions. Fortunately, you won't have to do *all* the legwork on your own. You work with a department of law enforcement that can gather and share information with you. None of you are expected to be detectives, from what I understand. You're more of a countermeasure against others with similar abilities that are beyond normal human capabilities. Of course, that means when your time comes to act, you must do so swiftly and efficiently. That's another reason I'm here. I spoke with Commander Comrear and he requested I ensure you all pass the basic requirements to become full members of the Evenfall Vigil, which includes various tests and hours of instruction."

"What?" Lara complained. "We have to do schoolwork for this?"

"I'm afraid so." He smiled. "But it's all the things you need, so when you work in public, you don't bring down any punishments on your own heads. The physical fitness tests are waived, although instead of doing those and preparing, it would be good for all of you to help Miss Enda with basic self-defense maneuvers and help her become physically fit if she's in combat scenarios. For the next three weeks, we'll work on rigorous mental and physical training. You'll learn the laws of Ethelian and of Coruvaine specifically. You'll learn of the various law enforcement branches and where the Evenfall Vigil fits in. Then you'll learn its history and the methods it employs."

"That sounds really boring." Lara groaned.

"It may well be, but it's necessary. Consider yourself lucky for the shortened curriculum. Most have to learn everything over the course of twelve weeks. You only need three weeks with some additional lessons as necessary.

"If anyone has any problems with this arrangement, I'm told there's an enthusiastic satyr in the Evenfall Vigil who volunteered to teach instead."

Lara shot up in her seat. "No, nobody has any problems with you. Let's stick with just us. No satyrs."

Thomas smiled wryly. "I thought that might be your response. That's all I had to discuss. I'll leave you to your evening and begin setting up my office on the library floor. It's one of the doors before the staircase. If any of you have questions, feel free to stop by."

The inquisitor stood and gave a small head bow before exiting the room. The group bade him farewell and retired to the living area, where Lara flopped onto the couch.

"He's not as bad as he could've been," she said with a shrug. "I mean, I've met some pretty big jerks from the Inquisition, but he seems nice. He also smelled like thyme."

"I agree," Alistair said, sinking into an armchair. "About his friendliness, not the thyme aroma. He was also very patient and forthright with us, which I wouldn't have expected. I was always under the impression the Inquisition would make arrests and take people away without justification. I heard King Aldric reference Inquisitor Eller before, but I never met him. The king holds him in high regard on a personal level, which makes sense now."

Lyvaelan studied Hazel, who sat on the opposite end of the couch from Lara. "I'm curious to know what you think, Hazel," he said at last as the other two followed his eyes. "You met him before. Did this change your impression of him?"

"Well, no, not exactly," she said with a slight frown. "It's hard to explain. When I was first brought back, he was frigid and dangerous. He was performing important business, and others needed to obey his commands immediately. Hickory—the one who resurrected me—tried to ward him off, but Thomas was much too strong and defeated him quickly. It also didn't seem like he held anything back when he knocked Hickory unconscious.

"As I got to know him through tests and interviews, he still seemed driven, but he was nicer, too. I think he has a lot of different faces he shows depending on what he has to do or where he has to be."

"I think that's expected from someone in his position," Alistair said. "After all, in his occupation, a moment of hesitation could be the difference between life and death. The stern immediacy he may have shown previously was to prevent any potential loss of life."

"That's true," Hazel said, "but it's hard to totally trust someone who could hurt someone so easily one moment and then joke around the next."

Lara bit her lip. "I mean, that's kind of what most of my life has revolved around,"

"Yes, but you fought for entertainment. You would go into matches fighting someone who knew they were going to get hit. You weren't running into a house to punch a defenseless old man."

"That's true."

"I see what you're saying, Hazel," Alistair said, "but from his perspective, Hickory may not have been a defenseless old man. Many of the strongest wizards appear ancient. Besides, necromancy is dangerous for a multitude of reasons, not just because it brings the dead to life. I've heard some necromancers can suck the life from an enemy, instantly killing them while multiplying the necromancer's own power. While I don't know if such rumors are true, I think erring on the side of caution was likely the right choice."

"Maybe." Hazel shrugged.

Alistair half smiled. "You don't sound very convinced."

"Honestly," she sighed, "I don't know what to think. What you're saying makes sense, but there's still something about it that bothers me. I can't explain it."

"You don't need to be convinced of anything," Lyvaelan said. "You should trust your intuition. The gift of foresight is a rare and difficult gift to master and shouldn't be ignored. It may be manifesting through your intuition. There's always reason behind the uneasiness one has for such things. I'm not saying Alistair is wrong, but if something troubles you, it makes sense to reflect on what it is. Perhaps as we work more closely with him, your feelings will change or become easier to define. Lean into that intuition and get to know him better. It may help you identify what's so difficult for you to accept about him." He looked at the others. "I don't trust him. He's too friendly for a viper, which inclines me to think he's dangerous."

"A viper?" Alistair said. "Don't you think that's a little harsh?"

"Kind words can hide cruel intentions," Lyvaelan said. "None of us had a high opinion of the Inquisition before. They are noteworthy less for their cruelty than for their dogged pursuit of their own goals. They're almost single-minded, from what I've heard. I suspect he's luring us into a false sense of security."

"I don't know," Lara said. "That sounds a little paranoid to me. I don't trust him completely either, but I don't think all of that was an act. He might actually be a friendly person in an unfriendly job."

"I concur," said Garo, emerging from the couch's shadow.

"Shit!" Lara exclaimed, bolting upright. "Stop doing that!"

Garo gave her a canine grin. "No." He turned to the rest of the group. "King Aldric informed me of the situation a few hours ago. I know you may not like it, but at present, the only choice we have is to work with the Inquisition. You'll need to cooperate to the best of your abilities. Hold whatever prejudices you want, but it will do little to change the matter at hand."

"Did the shadows of the future show anything about this inquisitor?" Lyvaelan asked.

"No. If he plays any role at all, it's relatively secondary. Whether good or bad, he isn't a powerful enough presence to make a noticeable difference in the shadows. That said, there's something coming. I know I mentioned it before, but it looks like it's becoming more inevitable with each passing day. There's a strange magic to it that makes me uneasy."

"It makes *you* feel uneasy?" Lara said. "Then it must be *really* unsettling."

"I wish I could respond to that jab humorously, but I can't. It's unlike anything I've ever experienced. I don't know how long it'll be, whether weeks, months, or a year, but it's imminent. Be on your guard. I'm gathering more information and allies, but I can't be everywhere at once."

"What do you want us to do?" Hazel said.

"I want you to keep doing what you're doing. Get stronger, learn to work together, and become a formidable force against whatever the upcoming danger is. Most importantly"—he hesitated a moment—"learn to trust each other. I've observed each of you, and not one of you is selfish or cruel. You all genuinely want to do good in the world. Trust that desire in each other." He turned toward the stairs. "I must speak with Inquisitor Eller to fully understand the arrangement. All of you should relax tonight. You had an exhausting experience with the aufhockers and you could all benefit from a long rest."

Chapter Seventeen
The Dream

Three weeks passed more quickly than expected. The Watchers of the Evenfall Vigil were placed on temporary leave, while the rest of their education was supplied by Thomas Eller. The days fell into a regular schedule with a large portion dedicated to the history and laws of Ethelian. Some of the information was familiar to Hazel, acquired from her country's education. This quickly moved into unknown territory when it delved into the origins of the organization.

The Evenfall Vigil was founded three-hundred years before the War of the Night ended to combat the then-persistent threat presented by vampires, therianthropes, unseelie fae, and other beings beyond the scope of most soldiers. This was accomplished by increased collaboration between spellcasters and the guard, combined with special armaments that would be too expensive for most. This heavy emphasis evolved into recruiting others with special talents and abilities. Certain daimon—such as satyrs, centaurs, and nymphs—lent their talents and added an unpredictable power to the organization. This later expanded to include seelie fae in a limited capacity. When the War of the Night ended, the Evenfall Vigil remained in existence to thwart other nocturnal threats, but their importance, numbers, and funding all diminished until King Aldric ascended the throne and signed trade agreements with the Seelie Court and the vampires of Noxphetalis. With relaxed borders, nocturnal crimes increased. It was only a few weeks before King Aldric left to meet with the king of the nosferatu to establish their alliance that the Evenfall Vigil received an increase in their funding to nearly double what it previously was with the specific order that the Evenfall Vigil division would act as the primary guards of Ethelian after sunset.

Hazel found the gaps in her education slowly filled. The others found much of this intriguing as well, with Lyvaelan the least interested in the specific history. It struck Hazel as ironic that the organization they'd joined destroyed and defended against their kind: unseelie fae, vampire, werewolf, and an undead creation. The initially frosty reception from the commander made more sense, given the original intent behind the Evenfall Vigil.

Beyond the history, much of the education dealt with procedures and specific laws of Ethelian with special attention to the local laws of Coruvaine. They suffered as a group through rote memorization and practice. Because most of the group had physical experience it was deemed unnecessary to go through the same training as the other members of the guards, although this omission—Thomas mentioned—presupposed that members of this group would train with each other and help increase their individual combat effectiveness. Hazel felt very much like that was directed at her.

During this time, the group settled into a schedule of sleeping an hour or two after midnight and waking in the early afternoon so Inquisitor Eller could instruct them. It was suboptimal for many of them—given their nocturnal preferences—but Inquisitor Eller had other obligations, and so they acquiesced to his schedule.

When not learning about the Evenfall Vigil, Hazel split her time between training with Lyvaelan, writing in her journal, and visiting her parents. She stayed with her parents on the weekends, usually spending the first five days of the week with the Evenfall Vigil and the three weekend days with her parents unless Thomas scheduled additional instruction. After living away from them, she wanted to see them more. Her mother asked after her health and ensured she was eating well, while her father regularly checked to see if any of the tools he gave her were being used. Hazel remained transparent but hesitated when it came to the confrontation with the aufhockers. She hid behind the veil of legal confidentiality to quell their suspicions. Her father teased her, but she refused to relent.

The training with Lyvaelan continued, and now she found she could connect to those around her when she let her mind wander. It felt similar to what she experienced through Lyvaelan's clairvoyance. He explained this as similar to insight, but more general and less refined. She could sense all kinds of life around her, but for some reason her attention was fixated on plants. The ability was strange but wonderful. It took her several minutes of meditation to get to that point, but once she did, she could stay that way for hours. Her dreams had also gained clarity. Lyvaelan explained that using other forms of arcane sight and recording in her journal would naturally increase the clarity and frequency of her dreams. Most still made little sense, but some presented snippets of the future. Occasionally she could complete the sentences of others because she heard them spoken in her dreams.

One early morning, a couple of days after they completed their training, Hazel jolted up in bed. Her heart raced and as she touched her forehead, she noticed sweat dripping from her brow, though she was cold as ice. The shadows in her room loomed longer and darker than she remembered, and she felt something she hadn't experienced in half a year.

Fear.

She rose from the bed, drawing a robe over her nightgown, and rushed barefoot down the hall. She had to talk to Lyvaelan. This couldn't wait.

She reached his door and knocked. It was only a few moments before he answered, opening the door. He stood blinking with a cocked eyebrow and bleary eyes. His expression and tiredness altered immediately upon seeing the intense concern written on her face.

"Lyvaelan, we need to talk."

He let her in and shut the door. "What's wrong?"

Hazel sat on the ground where she would practice meditating. She worked to slow her breathing. "I had a dream."

Lyvaelan sat close to her, his eyes searching her face. "What happened?"

She shivered. "It wasn't like the others. It was... something else. I saw many things, but these words are battering around inside my head and I have to say them first. *The living lich of half a day shall rise—*" instantly Hazel noticed she wasn't making any sound as a blue bubble formed around her head. Lyvaelan now stood, his eyes wide and his face the palest she'd seen. A blue film formed over his hand as he made a circular motion with it. He threw the blue magic to the floor, where it spread over every surface in the room. He made a quick gesture, and the blue bubble disappeared from Hazel's head.

He sat again, though alarm still sparked in his eyes. "Hazel, you can't say things like that when an inquisitor is close. Your relationship is tenuous with him. This could set things over."

Hazel silently nodded her understanding.

His gaze softened. "I've cast a spell so no one can hear through the walls, and anyone trying to use clairvoyance will have a difficult time. You can speak freely. What happened?"

Hazel met his eyes. "*The living lich of half a day shall rise with legions of undead that none can kill. Through betrayal of friends and oath, the living lich shall trample bodies and hearts. The world will quake as the impossible becomes the inevitable. The living lich of half a day may only be stopped by the slow progress of time.*"

Lyvaelan sat stunned.

Hazel sighed in relief. "I saw a vast plain with a large house or castle in the middle, and an army marched toward it. Then—from the house—a green light flickered and rose above everything. At first it was small, but then it grew bigger and brighter. The land opened and bodies climbed from the earth. They were all dead. Their eyes glowed, and they rushed at the army. The green light in their eyes was the same as the light above the house, and then I realized the light was a person. That person gestured and then it wasn't only dead bodies that rose, but the ground itself twisted as it desired. Then the green turned blood red as people screamed. I can't adequately express it, but there was such incredible power behind it that it felt unbeatable." She swallowed. "Lyvaelan, what should I do?"

He stared at her with an expression of such helplessness he seemed almost like a child. "I... I don't know. Liches are beyond powerful. I haven't studied them extensively, so I can't say more with certainty." He shook his head for a moment before looking at her with focused intensity. "Hazel, you must tell no one about this dream. Speak to me again if you need to talk, but telling anyone else could have terrible repercussions. Lara and Alistair might be alright to tell, but only do so if I'm present. Even then, I'm not sure you should say anything, since they don't know how to properly shield their minds from sorcery.

"Liches are the ultimate enemy of human mages and all living things. They possess power beyond even the strongest archmages and command hordes of undead that are all but impossible to destroy. If Thomas Eller uncovers this prophecy, he'll take you away."

"But what if it's dangerous *not* telling him? What if the Inquisition could help?"

Lyvaelan shook his head resolutely. "The Inquisition doesn't understand the nuance of prophecies such as this. They take all information and put it behind a closed door where no one can reach it. They confiscate and confine. The only reason you weren't taken immediately is because Aldric maintains considerable control over the Inquisition's activities here. If you reveal this, he can't protect you.

"Besides, there's always the chance this could be metaphorical. The future is only predictable in a roundabout way. There's so much variability it's borderline impossible for you to say any vision of the future means something specific. I swear to you, Hazel Enda, I'll help you through this and help you understand what this means. If I don't understand, then we'll find the answer together, but you must not rush into actions you can't take back."

Hazel nodded. Lyvaelan talked for another couple of minutes about the difficulties of using foresight, but Hazel couldn't focus. The images of the green figure rising above the others were too present in her mind to let her consider his words. She excused herself after promising to tell no one and returned to her room. She sat on her bed and looked at her green hands.

What was she, and what was she going to do?

Chapter Eighteen
The Hiemal Gala

Chateau Zarielle buzzed with activity. Floating lights dotted the road leading to the mansion, sleepily dancing to some unheard song. Carriages lined the way as pegasi, wyverns, griffins, and hippogriffs drew levitating carriages overhead as they soared to the chateau. The building itself radiated a white light from its walls, drawing the attention of any who were within several miles of its doors. The grounds extended dozens of acres in every direction, with carefully maintained gardens adorned with polished marble statues and flowing fountains. A short wall with climbing, perpetually flowering white roses surrounded the perimeter with a fragrance that gently enclosed the property without entirely blocking the view others would have of the interior from the height of a horse or carriage.

A high arch between the walls welcomed guests to the grounds of the estate. Overhead, at the summit of the elegantly carved stone, flowered an engraved white rose whose luminescent petals fell softly and perpetually, dissolving before touching the earth. Trees on either side of the road yielded to looming statues of robed figures on each side of the path. Each graven sentry was unique in appearance, but all shared the same stern expression and posture. The figures each held one glowing orb extended over the path to light the road. The avenue terminated in a large circle where dozens of attendants waited to direct the carriages appropriately. White stone steps led to the entrance of Chateau Zarielle, where two massive, carved wooden doors stood, overshadowed by the motif of the white rose.

The chateau boasted a massive ballroom, one which might have awed even royalty. Engraved silver and gold lines and circles created intricate patterns along the floor and walls. Strange symbols were etched into each pillar, and torch sconces were entirely absent. No chandelier hung from the vaulted ceiling, but swirling lights moving with gentle grace remained suspended instead, humming a gentle tune that put one at ease. No, this was not the castle of some baron or count, this was the home of a mage. An archmage.

This was the home of the Grand Inquisitor, Archmage Alvaria Saccarra.

She stood at the top of the staircase, overlooking the ballroom but beyond the sight of most on the ground level. Guests had filtered in over the last hour and would continue to do so for the next hour at least. She decided after talking with Archmage Garson Varaldan that reaching out to the other archmages might be beneficial. It wasn't altogether uncommon for an archmage to host such an event. It *was* unusual for that archmage to be the Grand Inquisitor. The invitation—which went out to every archmage and several high-ranking spellcasters within Selevarian—was in part a test. She wanted to see who would and wouldn't attend. She was mildly surprised to find such a large number arriving. Of course she'd prepared for more, but the number of guests—by her estimation—numbered several hundred at least.

She hadn't made her entrance yet and would wait until everyone arrived. While archmages weren't usually interested in upholding specific social rules, proper etiquette dictated that the host should wait until all guests arrived before welcoming everyone. Since the line of carriages could get rather long—and archmages were notoriously bad at getting anywhere on time—it made sense for her to delay her address. Those who arrived early—or rather, punctually—enjoyed refreshments and socialization while the others trickled in.

Alvaria stepped back from the staircase toward a man waiting a few paces behind her. "Arlith, remind me, who has declined the invitation?"

The chamberlain approached her with a smile, his bald head shining slightly in the light. He drew out a slender book strapped to his side. Arlith Kovak appeared middle-aged—but was much older—and wore white clothing with a half-length cape covering much of his torso. He was as excellent a mage as he was a chamberlain.

"Your Eminence, the list is short, considering the number of invitations you sent. Of the archmages, only a dozen declined. All but three of them are out in the field. Those in Selevarian are the Archmage of Magomechanics, the Archmage of Ceremonies, and the Archmage of Records. The latter declined on grounds that she's ill, while the Archmage of Ceremonies stated his duties made attending regrettably impossible."

The Archmage of Ceremonies was one of the oldest human mages in Selevarian and preferred to remain close to the High Archmage at all times. "And the Archmage of Magomechanics? What reason did he give?"

Arlith frowned, reading the book. "He said, and I quote: 'parties are a waste of time. I'd rather lose my other arm than parade around with a bunch of self-indulgent peacocks.'"

Alvaria chuckled. "Typical. Who else could not attend?"

"There are several spellcasters within Palace Valsidan who work as substitutes for the other archmages who declined, although their invitations were more for courtesy."

Alvaria nodded. There was a certain tact necessary when hosting an event. Given the increased lifespan of magic users, it was unwise to upset anyone who could hold a grudge longer than most humans could live.

The chamberlain continued, "Beyond these individuals, the High Archmage also sends his fondest regards but declined the invitation. That said, the number of archmages who confirmed is staggering. Some may forget and not show up, but even so, it's unusual for so many to agree to attend a gala."

Alvaria nodded, absently curling a lock of hair between her fingers. The High Archmage declined. She expected he would, but still reserved a bit of hope he'd surprise her. The High Archmage had never been to a purely social gathering during her tenure as an archmage, and she'd gathered from what others said that he never did. Having him here tonight would've been both a talking point and legitimized her presence as the youngest and newest archmage.

She smiled and dismissed the thought. It was unbecoming of an archmage to have such petty and prideful concerns. When he blessed her in the name of Selevara and anointed her an archmage, she became as much an archmage as any of her colleagues. Still, it was difficult to feel that legitimacy, even if she knew it had been conferred.

"I think I shall dress for the gala, Arlith. Are my chambers ready?"

"The spellweavers and your regular attendants have prepared everything to your specifications and await your arrival. Is there anything else?"

"Yes, please let the chef know of any changes to the number of guests. I think we may want to have some additional tomatoes gathered from the garden. Also, have some blackberries collected as well. I think a blackberry pie or two for later would be nice."

"Would you like the blackberry pie to be put into the dessert rotation, or is this a private request?" His tone was respectful, but she noticed a twinkle in his eye.

Alvaria smiled and blushed slightly. "I see no reason to pick *all* the blackberries and make the staff worry about adding a new item to the menu."

Arlith gave a small bow to conceal a smile. "Private, at my lady's wishes. Is there anything else?"

"Yes, check with the wine steward and have him bring out the midrange bottles immediately. Alert him that in an hour and a half he should uncork the best bottles we have in most plentiful supply. Ensure the archmages are served first when possible, but make no show of avoiding serving others as well. Send a messenger to me when the Archmage of Dragons and the Archmage of Education each get here. Beyond that, mingle with the guests and show them firsthand the immeasurable hospitality of Chateau Zarielle."

The chamberlain bowed low. "It shall be done, Grand Inquisitor."

Alvaria turned and strode up the hallway toward her quarters. Within, she found three spellweavers and a half dozen attendants, ready to assist her. Two attendants removed her clothing and jewelry, while the others arranged her hair. While she normally wore the subdued yet beautiful black and white velvet gown of the Grand Inquisitor, tonight she hired spellweavers to create a dress that would contrast with perceptions of her station.

The spellweavers brought a translucent gown as thin as a spiderweb before Alvaria. As they let go, the fabric shimmered but remained where they released it. The gown opened and enveloped Alvaria as the spellweavers traced their hands over the dress, pulling strings of pure light. She felt the magic in the garment as it touched her skin and attached to her. Once she was wearing the dress, the spellweavers released the strings of light which drifted softly into it. The fabric—once so close-fitting—took on a more substantial weight, like satin of the highest quality. The color of the gown rippled opaque as the attendants wove and pulled the strings of light with deft skill, like a master harpist. It shimmered gradually down from her shoulders to her feet as a wave of color washed over the dress, starting at the top with a dark midnight blue which descended into dark violet before turning light purple and shifting into a bright pink reminiscent of dawn once it reached the floor. Colors in the fabric rippled as she moved, giving them a life of their own. The arms of her gown altered colors as well, depending on where she held them. A short train behind it glided across the floor like tiny coral waves, always remaining just a hairsbreadth above the ground. An ethereal, silvery shawl was placed about her shoulders that glistened like tiny stars. A diamond necklace adorned her neck with a large circular diamond on a white background resembling Progon, and a smaller circular pink sapphire beneath it resembling Kythis. With the stars and moons arrayed about her neck, her appearance was complete.

She wore her long, curling black hair behind her with braids made from her frontmost curls containing the rest which cascaded down her back.

Her attendants finished the minor touches on her appearance while she thought of her guests below. A gentle knock on the door interrupted her thoughts.

"Yes?" she said without looking.

"Grand Inquisitor," came the page's voice from the door, "the chamberlain instructed me to tell you the Archmage of Dragons *and* the Archmage of Education are here."

She cocked an eyebrow at the voice. "Both of them? I instructed I was to be notified when each arrived."

"Your pardon, my lady," the page said with a quiver in his voice, "both archmages arrived in the same carriage."

She smiled. "Very good. Do you know if the guests are all present?"

"I think there are still a few entering the grounds. If I had to guess, I would say they should all be within the chateau in the next fifteen minutes."

"Tell the chamberlain to return to me in fifteen minutes with a more exact report on the guests in attendance. You're dismissed."

"Yes, my lady."

She closed her eyes and evened her breathing. Her mind swam into the stream of magic, the permeating force that flowed through, between, and from all living things. She felt the electricity of the magic as she pulled it into her. Her consciousness drifted into the stream as it snaked into the hallway and through the estate. She noticed her guests—the frivolity and excitement of some, the boredom of a couple, and the nervousness of others. She sensed the indistinct chatter, but more than that, she observed the immense power of those gathered. The most gifted spellcasters in existence were gathered together for no special purpose other than to socialize. She smiled. She remembered being a child and perceiving even the lowliest magician as godlike. Now she'd far surpassed the grandeur she'd first observed in the simplest spellcasters. It was daunting to think of, like living atop a high mountain and contemplating the distance to the ground. She'd come so far.

She opened her eyes. Her attendants had finished and waited in a line with their heads bowed. The spellweavers circled, examining their work with a critical eye and less deference. Finally, they nodded to each other and stepped back.

Alvaria smiled at them after admiring her reflection in a standing mirror. "Your work is remarkable. Truly. You have my thanks and promise of continued patronage."

The leader of the spellweavers, a slender young man, smiled and bowed deeply. "Your Eminence, all we ask is if you like the work we've done, you let others know your raiment came from the Shimmerveil Spellweavers."

"That, and your monetary compensation, of course," Alvaria said, her eyes sparkling with concealed merriment. "And you're amply deserving of both. My attendants will pay you. Of course, you're all welcome to stay for the event as honored guests."

"My lady is too kind."

A knock on the door interrupted the exchange.

"Lady Alvaria," the chamberlain said, "the guests have all arrived."

"Good. Enter."

He obeyed, bowing low and holding the door open.

"Would it please Your Eminence that I should accompany her?"

She glanced at him as she exited. "It would. Bring the alabaster staff as well."

He bowed and took a finely carved white rod from a tall cabinet that stored a variety of different staves. She found she enjoyed moving in the gown more than she expected. The undulating nature of the train disguised her steps, so she appeared to float as she walked. Arlith followed close behind her.

When they reached the top of the stairs, she scanned the mass of people before her. Each archmage brought several attending mages, and she now stood before and above all of them. It would have been terrifying if it had not been exhilarating. She took a deep breath and signaled to the chamberlain.

Arlith descended onto a broad landing that split into two symmetrical sets of steps leading to the ballroom. He moved to the center of the landing and to the stone railing. He stamped the butt of the staff three times before announcing in a booming voice, "I present the Archmage of the Inquisition, the Grand Inquisitor, Protector of the People, Alvaria Saccarra."

The crowd quieted as he turned to her and kneeled, offering her the staff. She descended the stairs, taking each step with regal importance. When she reached the landing, she took the staff in one hand and looked at the guests. She felt the cold of the alabaster rod and directed the flow of magic into it. Though they could not see or hear, she spoke poetry into it and a spell took form and grew. The staff glowed gradually brighter as a shimmering white stem extended from her hand and up the rod. As it reached the end, it blossomed into a great white rose that released constant glowing particulates into the air with serene grace. The transformation took mere moments. She returned her attention to the guests, emulating the rose's elegance in her mien and tranquility.

"I thank you for choosing to attend on this, the first of Melantria," her voice echoed out. This landing was designed with acoustics in mind and was also enchanted to amplify the voices of those who stood here. Although she spoke placidly, her words carried through the room. "I know it's strange for the Grand Inquisitor to host a party, and even stranger that it should have no connection to a holiday or major accomplishment beyond being the first day of winter. Today we're here to celebrate the simple act of living. Too often, we forget our human limitations. While others are rarely given eighty years to live, we may exist for hundreds before Semeleme claims us. Yet, despite that increased time, it cannot be always said that we *live* more than other humans than that we simply live *longer*. Today, I wish to celebrate life with all of you. Let tonight be a time to relax away from obligations and necessities.

"Eat your fill and drink to your content. Chateau Zarielle produces its own wine but has never had guests to drink it. It's almost as if people were afraid to visit the home of the Grand Inquisitor."

Several guests chuckled at that remark.

She smiled. "I hope by evening's end to have gotten better acquainted with each of you. You're all remarkable individuals who are deserving of a remarkable night. To life!"

"To life!" the guests echoed.

She slammed the butt of the staff to the ground and the larger floating lights exploded into a rainbow of colors that dimmed the hall while simultaneously providing a show of minor fireworks for the guests. When the lights settled, they were smaller beads that shifted slowly in coloration, providing a more relaxed ambiance.

Alvaria handed the staff back to Arlith, which returned to its previous state, and descended the steps. She took a deep breath, letting the excitement die down within her. She enjoyed the drama of addressing a large crowd, but that didn't make it any less stressful. As she walked down the steps, she saw the guests had returned to talking among themselves except for a couple of archmages who stood waiting at the bottom.

"You know, Alvaria, if you wanted a boring speech, you could've just asked me. I've had more practice," the Archmage of Education said with a grin. The man had blond hair tied behind in a short pony-tail. He wore elegant white robes with gold trim and epaulettes that hinted at his background in the Imperial Army. His eyes were an icy shade of blue and his features were gentle yet strong. He was broad shouldered for an archmage, and there was a strength to his physicality that was only slightly concealed by his robes. His fair face and ears ending in a slight point, coupled with the light golden glow around him revealed he was half light elf.

Alvaria scrunched her nose at him. "I know you could've. I just wanted others to think I could take the job of Archmage of Education if I desired."

The Archmage of Education laughed warmly before coming in to hug her. "It's good to see you, Alvaria."

"It's good to see you too, Lysander." She looked at the tall draconic archmage behind him. "I hear you and Gar took a carriage together."

"I was going to fly over here myself"—Garson Varaldan approached for a brief hug—"but he insisted."

"I insisted because you drank three *bottles* of wine before leaving to come here. Who knows how many birds you would've collided into, flying inebriated like that? You might've even ended up in a different country. The Knights of Petrim might've mistaken you as a call to adventure on some endless holy quest to slay the drunk dragon-man."

"I was *not* drunk!" Garson protested, a small gout of flames bursting from his nose. "I have a dragon's tolerance for alcohol and I didn't want to empty the stores in Alvaria's cellar."

She chuckled. "I think you underestimate the amount of wine we have."

Gar narrowed his eyes. "Are you challenging me, Little Alva?"

She shrugged. "Take it as you wish. I will say"—she lowered her voice conspiratorially—"we won't be breaking out the best wine until everyone else has gone. I also have special pies being made for later..."

Lysander leaned in with interest. "Blackberry?"

She nodded seriously.

The two visiting archmages looked at each other and nodded.

"Alright, Alva," Lysander said, "I think we can stay a little later than usual. But only because we're such good friends."

She smiled insincerely and put a hand on his cheek. "You two are *such* good friends. Who else could I bribe if I didn't have you?" She punctuated this last statement with a quick and small slap.

"Ow!"

She rolled her eyes. "Oh, don't be a baby. I didn't slap you *that* hard."

"You underestimate your strength," Gar grinned. "Besides, we both know Lysander doesn't know how to deal with physical pain."

This last statement was a shared joke. The Archmage of Education was one of the most accomplished battlemages living and possessed an officer rank in the Imperial Army from when he served during the War of the Night. If anyone at the party understood pain, it was him.

"I think I have a decent sense of how strong I am, Gar, and I can tell you Lysander is being dramatic."

A thin, half dark elf man in a marengo-gray embroidered robe approached the three. His skin was a dark gray—almost black—while the irises of his eyes were a milky white. Hair matching the color of his eyes was tied behind him. "I saw the Archmage of Education get slapped," he said in a neutral voice. "Is this the entertainment you promised, Alvaria?"

Lysander frowned at him. "Aren't you supposed to confine dangerous criminals, Archmage of Null?"

He shrugged. "In my capacity as Warden of Arcanathema, yes. But so far, I've witnessed nothing I would call criminal. Of course— even if I did—I only imprison those the Inquisition arrests. Are you going to arrest yourself, Grand Inquisitor?" His disinterested expression and tone made it difficult to determine when the Archmage of Nullification was joking.

Lysander folded his arms. "And they say there isn't corruption among the archmages."

"Ha! Don't take it so hard that Avrael is as sour as ever, Lysander. Has my successor been giving you trouble? Should I scold her?" asked another half dark elf man behind Lysander. He was built similar to Lysander in stature, but his short black beard, piercing violet eyes, and broad grin gave him an almost lupine appearance. His skin was a lighter gray than Avrael and had a slightly bluish tinge. He wore an embroidered white cassock with a wide white sash about his middle.

Alvaria looked down her nose at him. "I think you gave up the right to chide me, Malvex, when you stopped being Grand Inquisitor."

His grin widened. "I would never give up such rights. As Archmage of Sorcery, I may not be the Grand Inquisitor, but I'm still the one you come to when you need someone's mind read. In my book, that gives me every right to chide you on inappropriate behavior."

"I might agree"—Alvaria leaned in and lowered her voice—"if you hadn't worked my entire department into a mess before you left. It took me a decade to organize everything you never took care of."

He averted his gaze, scratching the back of his head. "Well, in those last years it was difficult to find motivation, and, uh…" he looked at the others, who waited expectantly. "Alvaria, why don't you slap Lysander again?"

"Something we agree on," Avrael said.

The others laughed until a server approached with wine glasses.

"All joking aside, Alvaria," Malvex said, taking a glass, "what you've done is impressive. In my tenure as Grand Inquisitor, I didn't accomplish as much as you did in your first ten years. And I know"—he held up his hand to stop others from jumping in—"some will jest it's because I had little interest in it. That isn't it, though. Your inquisitors are more efficient and act better than they did in my day. You've simultaneously made them more relatable and more efficient. It's hard to do either without creating a deficit in the other."

"I agree," Lysander said, taking a sip of white wine. "While most of my work keeps me at Calixford, I've had the pleasure of talking with the chief inquisitor you have up there. I think his name is Ellen? No, Eller! Thomas Eller. He's allied with King Aldric and much of the court, and the number of criminals he's subdued is impressive. I know he only got his start because of you, and that speaks volumes about how you judge character."

Gar nodded. "Didn't you fire many inquisitors shortly after your appointment?"

"No," Alvaria corrected, "I *released* several inquisitors because I heard their complaints and judged they weren't best suited to our line of work. It was nothing against them. They were all competent spellcasters, but competence as a spellcaster doesn't make an inquisitor. It requires more than that."

"You're right," Malvex said. "It takes a unique individual to be an inquisitor. It isn't for the faint of heart. It can be a hard, thankless job and becoming disillusioned and cold makes things worse."

"I suppose I have you to thank, Alvaria," Avrael said evenly. "After you let go of so many inquisitors, many came to work for me. Fortunately, disillusioned and cold is exactly how I prefer my prison guards. I think some may have even become more upbeat after joining the prison so they could see the fruits of their labors."

Gar gently shoved Alvaria. "How about that? It sounds like you've been helpful."

She rolled her eyes.

"By the way," Lysander said, "that's a lovely dress. Really, you are radiant tonight. It's clear to me you're as thorough with criminals as you are with your wardrobe."

"Well"—she took a sip from her red wine—"I've never been a woman of half-measures."

The night wore on and Alvaria greeted other guests. Many complimented her raiment and the party, and all voraciously enjoyed the food and drink. Most present were interested in talking about academic pursuits and philosophizing about different uses of magic. It was to be expected of a group who lived surrounded by magic. The ballroom was used less for dancing than for discussing. Groups broke away, some going onto the roof to see the aerie where some left their flying mounts.

Gradually, guests left. It was almost twenty miles to Selevarian, and the archmages had other matters to attend to. As individuals departed, others followed. Since so many arrived in groups, the party dissipated with surprising speed. Finally, it was just Alvaria, Garson, and Lysander.

Alvaria brought her friends to the roof and had the wine steward fetch several small casks of wine. The chamberlain retrieved the blackberry pie Alvaria requested, with the note there was another on the way, with a potential peach cobbler available if interest should be high enough.

Alvaria and her friends laughed, and talked, and drank on the roof until the pie came. Eschewing the dignity of separate plates, each dug into the pie with individual forks. It was well past midnight and Alvaria couldn't help but feel a joyful melancholy. A contented sense of nostalgia washed over her as she stargazed and listened to her friends joke about conversations they had earlier. She felt like a little girl again, staying up with friends, sneaking food from the kitchen, sitting outside with bare feet. The warmth of Selevarian in the winter reminded her of summers in years long past. How different things were now. Her friends, now talking animatedly, had more than half a millennium of years between them, and although she looked young, she was nearing a hundred and ten years herself. Her childhood friends died long ago.

She watched the archmages, teasing each other and playfully threatening to fight. If only her father could see her now, she thought. He wouldn't believe the world she lived in. Telerius Saccarra had been a simple man. He was a craftsman. He died when she was in adolescence. She never knew her mother. Alvaria put everything she had into magic and becoming the best magician she could. When she mastered that, she studied the other arcane arts and flew through them. Her teachers and associates threw around terms like "prodigy" and "savant" but only she knew how hard she worked every day to get to where she was. There was nothing in her lineage that gave her an advantage over others. She recognized her good fortune in becoming an archmage, however. Many gifted mages went unrecognized. It was only through others witnessing her talent and hard work and *acknowledging* it that she had gotten here, to the rooftop of Chateau Zarielle.

"Well, Alvaria? What do you think?" Lysander asked.

Alvaria shook herself from her reverie. "Hmm? What?"

"Who would you rather battle?" Gar said. "Me, or this scrawny half-elf? I'll admit he knows a few things, but he isn't friends with actual *dragons.*"

"There are scarier things to fight than dragons, my friend," Lysander said. "I've fought a dragon before and I'm still here."

"Anyway," Gar said, ignoring the last comment, "if you had to choose, who would you fight?"

Alvaria sighed and smiled. "I think I'd choose neither. If I fought either of you, I'd be on the wrong side of the battlefield."

"Spoken like a true diplomat," Lysander teased.

"Pff. That's a *boring* answer, Alva. Come on, give us something more to discuss. Who would you rather fight?"

She looked from one to the other. "I'd rather battle... you, Gar."

"What!" the Archmage of Dragons exclaimed. "Why would you want to fight me instead of him? I'm far scarier than he is!"

"I'm interested to hear your reasoning too, Alva." Lysander looked amused, but curious.

She gazed into the dark and smiled as a cool breeze whispered past. "You seem scary, Gar, but you're a big softie. You're strong and would rather die than let a friend get hurt, but when it comes to fighting, you don't really want to harm anyone so much as you want to protect."

He folded his arms petulantly and puffed two plumes of smoke from his nostrils. "Well, I could be mean if I wanted to."

She smiled. "I don't really think you could." She turned to Lysander. "As for you, I know you've had to make hard and decisive choices in the past. If you were really trying to fight me, you would end the confrontation as quickly as possible."

"I sound cold when you put it that way, Alva," he replied with a frown.

"No." She shook her head. "Not cold. You just know it's more painful to wait than it is to finish something immediately. It's because of your warmth you'd put an end to it swiftly, and against such an accomplished battlemage I would have little chance of winning." She stretched her arms. "But again, I'd rather not fight either of you. I'm strong, but you've both got the weight of years and experience. I'd rather have you with me than against me."

"Likewise." Gar rumbled.

Lysander merely smiled and nodded.

"Anyway," Alvaria said, "Lysander, I'm curious: how are things in Coruvaine? The reports I've been getting are brief, so I wanted to hear if anything interesting has happened."

"Oh, you know, it's much of the same. Like I said, Inquisitor Eller does a decent job. I also heard there was a necromancer recently who brought a girl back to life, but I don't know much else beyond that. I know it's got the Cult of Semeleme ruffled."

Alvaria sighed. "That cult is a problem wherever we go. Necromancy is such a sticky business with them involved."

"Have you returned the body? Surely that would simplify the situation."

"True, but according to what I've been told, the body isn't ready for interment, and giving it back could prove dangerous. The necromancer used strange magic that the inquisitors have been trying to untangle."

Lysander frowned. "Wouldn't it be better to bring the body here, then?"

"In theory, yes. Unfortunately, neither the cult nor the king are altogether thrilled with the idea of taking away the body of a young girl who'd been laid to rest. Requisitioning it without the consent of both parties would create more problems than I'd care to deal with at the moment."

He grimaced. "I see your point."

"Besides, Thomas has assured me the situation is carefully controlled and poses no threat to the population. If matters get worsen, then I'll have him bring it here immediately, or I'll go myself. In most necromancy cases, it's rare the zombie is a great danger. Even when the undead is a draugr, it's rarely an issue for my inquisitors once they've subdued the necromancer.

"All that aside, have there been any other problems?"

Lysander slowly shook his head. "Few I can think of. I've heard there are some people taking enhanced potions to commit crimes. Several guards died fighting the criminals, and all they learned was an alchemist did it. This alchemist has been causing problems but nothing too serious. Considering the amount of magic in the city and the university, there are fewer cases of arcane abuse than expected. I should say, though, that I've been gone for close to a month, so my news may be outdated."

"The news about an alchemist is troubling. When such criminal activity carries on, it reflects poorly on the Inquisition. I'll ask Thomas to devote more time to solving this problem. When are you returning to Coruvaine?"

"I'll be leaving in a few days, which should get me into the city in a little over a week if I use the gates."

Alvaria smiled sadly. "Leaving so soon?"

Lysander returned the smile. "I'm afraid so. My students need me. The school functions autonomously, but if I leave for longer than a month, the heads of each department get funny ideas about ousting me."

"They wouldn't dare."

He chuckled softly. "No, they wouldn't want the work. Regardless, I still have to hear their complaints and when I'm gone for more than a month, they all talk about how terribly my absence impacted the instruction of the students."

"Which is ridiculous."

"Welcome to academia."

They smiled and gazed at the sky that was just showing shades of slightly lighter blue with the coming dawn.

"We should get some sleep," she said, standing up. She looked at Gar, who was already snoring on the ground. "It looks like he got a head start on us. Come, I'll show you to your room."

"Alvaria, wait," Lysander said, grabbing her sleeve.

She turned to him. "Yes?"

"I have one more thing I'd like to do before turning in."

She cocked her head. "Oh? And what's that?"

He swirled his left hand in the air producing an inkpot and swirled his right hand, producing two paintbrushes. He raised his eyebrows suggestively.

She looked from him to the slumbering Archmage of Dragons and then back at him. She grinned and sighed, shaking her head at him. She snatched a paintbrush from his hand and kneeled next to Gar. "You're a terrible influence on me."

He grinned back. "Yeah, I know."

Chapter Nineteen
The High Priestess

Hazel breathed a sigh of relief. She was finally alone.

She returned home for the weekend and brought Lara along. Her family had asked her about others in the Evenfall Vigil, so when Lara expressed interest, it provided the perfect opportunity. Hazel found having Lara as a guest fun but tiring. She missed having time to herself, and her outgoing friend—combined with her parents' delight at meeting her—made the situation more exhausting than usual. Not that Lara was a terrible guest; despite her insouciance, she was polite and easygoing. Lynn and Kyle enjoyed speaking with her immensely. Still, prolonged exposure to Lara drained her, if only because of her high energy. It was fun, but best in small doses.

Today, her mother was going to the market, and she invited Lara and Hazel. Hazel went with them but brought a book along in case she had an opportunity to escape. After the first few minutes of strolling around carts, Hazel informed them she would be in a nearby park. Interpreting Hazel's reticence as caution, the other two agreed and promised to check in on her soon. With that, Hazel had left them.

While going out was always a potential danger, on sunny but cold days like this, it was easier to hide. She wore a wide-brimmed sunhat, a shawl around her neck and face, and a jacket over a gray kirtle. Through her parents' input, Hazel devised an ideal disguise that was believable but concealing. She retreated into a public park near the market. It was a small area of grass with surrounding trees and a pond. A large stone was carved into a long bench beneath a shaded willow.

Hazel took out her book and read. The park was quiet, and the sounds of the market, distant. Even the few children running nearby were muffled by the hush of the Luthain River, which ran through the southern and eastern parts of Coruvaine. The river, at the farthest edge of the park, sounded as if it were constantly urging silence, and the rest of the world obeyed.

The peace she experienced reading her book lasted only a few minutes when she heard soft footsteps in the grass nearby. A chill creeped into the air as they approached and retreated as they passed away. The footfalls paused at the other end of the bench.

"Do you mind if I join you?" asked a woman.

Hazel didn't look up. "Not at all."

The woman sat, and Hazel continued reading. She was vaguely aware of how rude she'd been by not doing more to acknowledge the stranger, but her book had gotten to an interesting point and it had taken an effort to respond, let alone tear herself away from the page. She also knew looking at the woman could reveal her green skin, though under the shadows of the willow and the sunlight filtering through the leaves, it could be construed as a trick of the light. The woman sighed.

Although Hazel was engrossed in her book, something nagged at her. She had a hard time pinpointing the cause. Guilt? Embarrassment? Curiosity? It was hard to say.

"It's a beautiful day, isn't it?"

Hazel glanced at the woman. She had a friendly face with freckles, outlined by dark brown curls. She looked only a few years older than Hazel, but her air of dignity made her seem older. She wore a black dress.

Hazel smiled at her, but quickly turned her head aside. "It is."

The woman looked at what Hazel was wearing. "You seem prepared for warm weather."

Hazel shrugged. "I burn easily."

"I'm sure you do."

They sat in silence as Hazel returned to her book, confused by this stranger engaging with her.

"I'm sorry, I haven't introduced myself. I'm Caeli."

Why was this woman striking up a conversation with a complete stranger? Hazel had no idea. "Caeli? It's nice to meet you. I'm Hazel."

"Hazel," Caeli said slowly. "What a pretty name."

"Thank you." *Why did she say my name like that?* Hazel wondered.

"You know, Hazel, you remind me of someone else I used to know. She was just about your age."

Hazel frowned. "There are many girls my age."

"Yes, that's true." Hazel glanced at her again and saw the woman's jaw tighten and relax. "She was a wonderful young woman. Loved by her family and her friends."

"She sounds nice."

"She was."

Hazel stopped. "'Was'?"

"Yes, was. She died recently."

Hazel felt her heart drop as a sense of impending danger filled her. "I'm... sorry to hear that."

"It was sad," Caeli continued speaking, but her tone shifted into biting conviction. "Unfortunately, her story didn't end there."

"It didn't?" Hazel looked at her.

Caeli's eyes drilled holes into Hazel. "No, it did not."

Hazel retreated further along the bench. She didn't know who this woman was or how she knew, but she did. "What do you want from me?"

Caeli's eyes locked on Hazel. "I want to honor the memory of the beloved friend and daughter, Hazel Enda, who was desecrated by a graverobbing mage and turned into a walking undead nightmare."

Haze's eyes widened. "Who are you?"

Caeli rose from her seat to her full height. Although she wasn't much taller than Hazel, her grim and stately demeanor made her tower over her. "I am the High Priestess of Semeleme, the chosen daughter of the Dark Queen. It is given to me to destroy the undead and all creatures abominable to the goddess of death. Whatever you are, you're not Hazel Enda, just a mockery of the girl who once was." As the priestess approached, shadows in the canopy dimmed and the world darkened as if a cloud had passed over the sun. Black tendrils swirled around the priestess's hands and arms as her expression grew zealous and determined. She reached out a hand and moved toward Hazel's head. Hazel heard a single, deep tone emanating from the high priestess like a hive of angry bees, drowning out all other sounds.

Hazel sat transfixed by the woman. The change in demeanor and the unexpected revelation shocked her. She wondered with morbid curiosity what would happen when the woman touched her. Would she die? Would it hurt?

The high priestess's hand stopped inches from Hazel's face when another hand grabbed Caeli's wrist.

"Don't you know it's impolite to touch others without asking first?" Lara said with a ferocious grin.

Caeli's gaze shifted to Lara. "You dare—"

"Yeah, I dare." Lara threw back her wrist and interposed herself between them. "You don't know the first thing about Hazel. She's a good friend and beloved daughter now, as much as she ever was. I may not know what she is, but I know who she is. She's my friend. If you want her, you can go through me. Between the two of us, I think I'm more likely to send you to meet your goddess than you are to send me."

The priestess blinked. "You know who I am and *dare* touch me?"

"I've flirted with death more than once," Lara said, folding her arms, "and you're just her priestess."

Caeli shook her head in disbelief. "This is idiotic. You don't know what she is, and yet you insist on protecting her? She could be any number of dangerous undead—even a *lich*—and yet *you* seek to protect her? She could turn on you at any moment."

"No, she wouldn't. I've got a good instinct about these things," Lara replied flippantly.

"What you have is a baseless hunch grounded in blind optimism." She looked Lara up and down. "Clearly, you're not undead, otherwise my touch would have annihilated you. I don't think I can fight you physically, but you won't always be there to defend this creature, and when you're not, I will return the body of Hazel Enda to the ground so her spirit may rest peacefully in the arms of the Dark Mother."

As she strode past them, Hazel shivered at the coldness of her countenance. Just before she reached the edge of the canopy, she glared at Hazel. Hazel shivered and felt no relief Lara had stopped her. Caeli's gaze showed Hazel she didn't view her as a person, but as an abomination.

After relaying this news to her parents, Kyle and Lynn both decided it would be best for her to stay at the library indefinitely until matters had cooled down. They hypothesized the priestess had observed the house and—upon seeing the three go out that morning—had followed. For that reason, Hazel wouldn't be safe at the house. The library was still unknown to the Cult of Semeleme, which afforded some safety. Her parents stressed this was only temporary and soon Hazel would be safe to come home again.

She wasn't convinced.

Hazel knew it was vain to hope the high priestess would relent or lose interest until she was laid to rest. She also decided—much to the relief of her friends—to avoid leaving during the day. One person she didn't savor the idea of telling was Inquisitor Eller. She decided to tell him on her own, though all three of them volunteered to join her. The others—she believed—would somehow make her situation worse. This was her problem, not theirs.

She knocked on his door, which sat on the ground floor of the library in what once may have been a large study room or book sorting area. He invited her in, and the door opened. The room was brightly lit, despite the lack of windows. Candles sat on his desk and a few orbs of light floated above sconces on the wall. The room was tidy and smelled faintly of thyme. Thomas sat at a wide desk, writing on some paper with a quill. When Hazel entered, he flashed a brief smile and continued his work. "Hello, Hazel. Please, have a seat."

She approached and noticed a variety of implements behind him that she vaguely remembered from when she first met him. Wands of various sizes and woods with different decorations were laid out in neat rows adjacent to alchemical equipment, such as a mortar, pestle, and alembics of varying sizes. A small censer burned and was the source of the thyme smell.

When she took a seat across from him, he said without looking up, "You'll pardon my rudeness, but I have several reports to make and"—he winked—"I procrastinate." When he finished writing, he folded the letter and closed it with a seal resembling a rose. He closed his eyes, muttered a few words, and the paper shrank until it was smaller than Hazel's little finger. When he opened his eyes, he picked up what looked like fine white sand from a drawer, which stuck to his fingers. He drew a circle and a series of glyphs and geometric shapes. When the circle was complete, he waved his hand over it and the sand glowed brightly as the light coalesced into the shape of a pixie. Large dark eyes, almost impossibly large for its head, glittered on a delicate purple body accented by two opalescent dragonfly wings. The creature's face resembled a small child's, but the proportions of its body were that of a young teen. Wild red hair and an impish grin with long, pointed ears completed the characteristic fae look.

"Take this letter and deliver it to the Grand Inquisitor Alvaria Saccarra in Selevarian. You can find her at Chateau Zarielle. If you cannot deliver this to her directly, see that the chamberlain, Arlith Kovak, receives it. Let them know it was from Chief Inquisitor Thomas Eller."

The creature bowed dramatically, its scant leafy-green clothing rustling as it turned toward Hazel. She studied it curiously. It winked at her.

"Ensure it is delivered," Thomas said, a little more forcefully.

The pixie turned its grin back to Thomas. "Of course, In-qui-qui-quisitor. The pretty lady will get it."

"The Grand Inquisitor," Thomas corrected with a frown.

"I said that, yes. The pretty lady will get it." It turned back toward Hazel. "But not *this* pretty lady." The creature's wings buzzed, releasing silvery dust all around the room. Hazel instinctively shut her eyes, and by the time she opened them, the creature was gone.

Thomas reclined with a sigh and smiled. "Pixies can be a chore to deal with. Have you ever seen one before?"

"Only from a distance." She searched to see if it had truly left. "How did you get it to come here?"

"Most inquisitors can summon a pixie. I'm a decent conjurer myself, so conjuring one was easy even if they're a little challenging interpersonally. To answer the intent of your question, using the summoning circle, I can call upon any creature I wish, provided I know its name. If I don't, then I can only summon creatures randomly and usually within a certain range. You've been working on extending your abilities, haven't you?"

"Yes, though I mostly just sense the plants in an area."

"Well, the more you practice, the larger that radius is. In my case, I can push my awareness just short of a mile beyond the fourth wall on the northern side. Fortunately, there was a pixie nearby who I could summon. Of course, if I needed to, I could've conjured more than one, but I only had one message, so only one pixie was necessary."

"Do you often use them as messengers?"

"The Inquisition likes to use them, so they've become standard." He cleaned the circle off the table and rearranged his desk.

"Why pixies? It seemed like you had some problems with it."

He flashed a rueful smile as he worked. "Pixies are persistent mischief-makers, but if you know how to handle them, they're extremely helpful. Since they're attuned to the natural world, beasts and birds rarely accost them. They're also full of energy and swift. I estimate the letter I sent will arrive in Selevarian within three days."

Hazel was impressed. Selevarian was over a thousand miles away. "Are pixies the fastest?"

"Not exactly. They're the easiest to summon and the hardest to intercept. We've tried using sylphs, which are arguably the fastest creatures in existence, but the results were... mixed. They were harder to control and required more magic. Besides that, the letters—while swiftly delivered—were more often than not in shreds. Letters could be delivered over vast distances in minutes, but it was often too risky to be used. Most reports are not extremely time-sensitive, so a week is acceptable. If it's an emergency, we have ways of contacting others immediately. We also tried using irids—which are undoubtedly faster than pixies—but they're notoriously bad at keeping confidential information private.

"Now then, Hazel"—he leaned back in his seat, giving her his full attention—"I imagine you didn't come to see me just to learn about the Inquisition's mail-delivery system. What can I help you with?"

"Well," she hesitated, "it's about something that happened earlier."

"Go on."

"I met the high priestess of the Cult of Semeleme."

His smile disappeared. "Hazel, *what happened?*"

She sighed. "I was out with my mom and Lara earlier today. We split up for a little while and I went to read in the park when this woman sat down with me and started saying strange things. She knew who I was before she sat down. Anyway, she was going to touch me with some dark magic, but Lara arrived and kept her from getting too close."

"She didn't come into contact with you?" His eyes darted around, visually diagnosing her.

"No. What would've happened if she had?"

He relaxed substantially. "Hard to say. The high priestess is granted powers from the goddess to obliterate the undead."

"So she would've killed me?"

"If you are undead, then her touch wouldn't have simply killed you. It would've annihilated you. Her power renders undead things not only dead but incapable of being used. Usually, that takes the form of reducing the creature to dust. That goes for revenants and the other forms of undead. It is the deadliest magic against reanimated beings, greater even than thaumaturgy. You seem to be some kind of extended-life revenant, so be careful."

"Is there any way to protect against it?"

"Practically, yes: don't get touched by her. Magically, there's nothing any spellcaster can use. Not even the High Archmage himself could counteract her magic. Her power comes directly from a god, and such powers are essentially infinite. Fortunately, that power is limited because humans are limited. She has to touch you in order to destroy you. That's her limitation. That said, she could wade into a sea of undead creatures and not one could so much as scratch her as each would instantly be destroyed. Such power would devastate if it weren't limited to such specific beings as the undead."

"What should I do?"

Thomas sat back, strumming his fingers on the desk, searching her eyes. "Are you afraid, Hazel?" he asked after a moment.

"No, not really. I guess I should be scared, but when she was about to touch me, I just felt... curious. I wanted to know what would happen."

"Did you want to die?"

"No, but I didn't really want to live, either. You know how I was before, when I was brought back. I felt nothing. My feelings are stronger now, but not as powerful as before. Should I be afraid?"

He shrugged. "Only you can answer that question. I suspect you don't want your parents and friends to be saddened by your dying a second time, but that differs from wanting something for its own sake."

"I suppose I shouldn't visit my parents anymore."

"If you say so."

She cocked her head. "You won't make me stay here?"

He smiled. "Nope."

When she looked at him quizzically, he continued, "Hazel, the Inquisition will always be here and the Cult of Semeleme will always be here. Most people only have one shot at living, but you've been given a second chance. I can't tell you how to live your life, but if you were to confine yourself to this library, then I might as well take you back to Selevarian tonight. I can't promise you'll always be free, nor can I promise you'll have a long life. All I can do is tell you to do what you think is best. You don't need to throw caution out the window in order to lead a fulfilling existence. Maybe go out at night. Have your friends accompany you. I'm sure Lyvaelan knows some spells that might help you in public without fear of the cult.

"Maybe it's irresponsible of me to suggest such things, but I'll let this be my one irresponsible action for the year. All inquisitors are entitled to one irresponsible thing a year, you know."

"Oh, really?"

He smiled warmly. "Absolutely. After all, we're only human."

"Well, I'm glad you're using your precious irresponsible decision on this. I had another question for you, based on my meeting with the high priestess."

"Ask it."

Hazel hesitated. She had already been given more freedom than she expected from this encounter, and she knew asking without fear of suspicion would be difficult, but she had to know. "What makes a lich so dangerous?"

He sat back, studying her. "What makes you ask?"

"One thing Caeli mentioned was I could be a lich for all anyone knew. I've heard other people talk about them before, but they were just stories. Whenever I've heard of them, they seemed like these big scary monsters that will steal people away and turn them into monsters. Since you're an inquisitor, I thought you'd have the most experience since you've probably fought or destroyed some before."

He continued studying her for a moment and she felt the slightest brush of a thought in her mind, as if someone had walked by. He sighed. "Well, Hazel, I suppose the first thing I should tell you is I've never encountered a lich and likely never will. To say I could fight or destroy one is almost hilarious. Forgive me for saying so, for I know your question is asked in earnest.

"Liches are the most dangerous undead creatures in existence. They were adept spellcasters before death, but something about dying and returning amplifies their previous powers a hundredfold. In particular, a lich's ability to summon undead is unparalleled. A gifted necromancer would struggle to control a couple dozen undead at a time. The weakest of liches can control thousands, seemingly without effort. We don't know exactly how this is possible, but there are reliable accounts of liches destroying entire civilizations because of this power. You know of the legend of Dranderis the Mad and the sacrifice of the Seven Companions? That story is told in many ways, but the historical records we have of that time show Dranderis had no less than four hundred-thousand undead soldiers. The real danger is not the soldiers themselves, but their limitless supply. Imagine sending an army to destroy them. No matter how powerful the fighting force is, a few soldiers will die in battle. The lich who can feel the presence, absence, and loss of life, notices the fallen soldiers and brings them into his army. Then, the soldiers of the other army have to fight their own undead kinsmen before they've even had time to grieve their demise.

Could you strike down a friend who fell under such a spell? What of a family member? Or perhaps an undead infant? Liches are possessed of no such qualms and lack any sense of morality."

Hazel exhaled. "That's terrifying. How can you defeat them?"

"There are a few methods. Liches can't be killed by anything that could kill them in life. Thus, most weapons and magic are little more than a nuisance to them. However, liches—and all undead—are weak against life magic. Life magic is most frequently used by thaumaturgists when healing those with injuries. It's magic which, when used on the living, does no harm but strengthens, inspires, and heals. This magic destroys the undead. By abandoning the precepts of life, liches are condemned by such healing magic. Death could not kill the dead, but life unmakes them.

"There are also some kinds of holy magic that are effective as well. The high priestess you met possesses a form of this. When disciples of a specific god show fanatical devotion, they are sometimes bestowed extraordinary blessings that are limitless within a specific range. These may be like the high priestess's abilities or may allow them to overcome certain challenges with slightly greater ease.

"This differs from those who work within the bounds of magic we know but may seem religious or holy. For example, the Paladin Order of Kalendril dedicates their mission to the triune worship of Veratheragan, Melantros, and Caleptis, while guided by the mission of their founder, Kalendril. Those who are initiated and withstand numerous trials and considerable education show their dedication in their ability to destroy undead and possess several magic abilities that are the same for each member but appear to be limited in usefulness. For example, their swords may glow in the presence of undead or perverse creatures, and their weapons—though unenchanted—may cause considerably more damage than normal. If they question their order, or cease to believe in the mission, their powers disappear. This appears— on the surface—to be divinely inspired magic but is truthfully nothing more than practiced thaumaturgy. Since thaumaturgy requires a certain confidence, humility, courage, and spiritual alignment, it makes sense that questioning those beliefs would lead to a loss of abilities.

"Aside from that, liches can sometimes be stopped using certain spells that contain magic and dispel it from an area. Liches are so much more magical than any other human that the removal of magic rapidly can cause them to collapse. This appears to only work on new liches, however. The longer a lich exists, the more powerful it becomes. We believe destroying an older lich is more difficult, partly because of their increased power but more because of their experience. This is conjecture, however."

"So... you said a spellcaster can become a lich. Is it possible someone who wasn't one could be?"

He scrutinized her with his piercing gaze. "Hmm. I assume you're talking about yourself? Truthfully, I don't know. It has never been done before. Most spellcasters who focus on becoming liches tend not to care about others. Theoretically, it could be possible, but it'd take a talented mage who was crazy enough to not seek the power himself."

"I see."

"If you're worried about yourself, I don't believe you are a lich. That said, I can't prove it and your case has been so oddly specific it's hard to rule out what you may or may not be. You shouldn't fear it, though. Liches are selfish, and I sense no selfishness in you."

"Maybe." She smiled a little sheepishly. "Though I'm glad you're taking a risk and letting me still go outside."

He smiled. "It isn't selfishness to want what everybody else has. Besides, if I didn't want to live a risky life, I wouldn't have joined the Inquisition."

Chapter Twenty
Present Troubles, Future Plans

That's a rather cavalier attitude to take," Alistair said when Hazel told them of her meeting with Thomas.

They sat in the uppermost common room near their bedrooms. It was around seven o'clock, and the group had only awakened an hour ago.

"Yeah, maybe he isn't so bad after all," Lara said, lying on a large pillow on the ground.

"Perhaps," Lyvaelan said, his gaze distant.

Lara raised an eyebrow. "Not convinced, Lyvaelan?"

The dark elf warlock folded his arms and shrugged. "No. I was expecting an extreme reaction in the opposite direction. This is borderline careless."

"While I might agree," Alistair said thoughtfully, "we should keep in mind he knows more about Hazel's condition than any of us. Maybe it only seems careless because we lack sufficient knowledge."

"I considered that," Lyvaelan replied, "but if that's true, then it's knowledge he's hidden from us, including Hazel."

"Well, I may not trust him"—Lara propped herself up on her elbow—"but we can still take advantage of his permissiveness. Why don't we go out?"

Everyone stared at her.

"What? We haven't gone out to any bars as a group. I know stuff is crazy, but I say we enjoy what we can when we can."

Lyvaelan gazed at the floor, nodding slightly. "I agree."

"You do?" Lara and Alistair said in unison.

"Yes. I can place glamours on me and Hazel that'll make us appear normal in the eyes of those who see us. It might be good to leave the library for a little while." He looked at Hazel meaningfully. "It could give us a chance to catch up with each other so we're all on the same page." He turned back to Lara. "Do you have any bars you would recommend?"

Lara shook herself from her surprise. "Uh, sure, I know a place. It isn't far from here. It's usually pretty balanced between crowded and empty."

"Perfect. Shall we leave in an hour?" The others looked dumbfounded at Lyvaelan's interest in having fun.

Lara looked at Alistair, who said, "An hour should be fine. I'll let the little guy know we won't be in for dinner. Is that alright with you, Hazel?"

"Sure," she shrugged.

The group walked to the tavern Lara recommended. The streets were empty save for the occasional pedestrian or member of the guards. Smithies, tanners, and other similar businesses lined the street. These establishments were built in the familiar city fashion, with shops on the ground level and living quarters on a second level. Construction was brick with wood to reinforce, although some of the newer buildings implemented quarried stone. On the corner of Plum Street and

Calivine Road, a large building stood whose rustic wooden carvings and weathered exterior showed it was one of the few places that hadn't been renovated in many years. In chipped white paint and simplified calligraphy, the sign above the doorway read: Skilliven Tavern.

Approaching the tavern, Hazel looked at Lyvaelan uncertainly. He didn't hide his face or appearance and told her such things were unnecessary. When he put the glamour over her, it looked like nothing so much as the pixie dust she saw earlier. He assured her that although she didn't look different, it wouldn't be a problem.

Lara led the group into the tavern. A long bar with a variety of bottles behind it reached across the entire building. A door behind the bar led to a kitchen from which smells of cooking meat wafted. Several sturdy tables ran parallel to the bar, with chairs in various states of disrepair. A larger dining area to the left offered open tables and more secluded booths in the corners. Lara hailed the bartender, a strong looking older man with a beard.

"Welcome, friends," he said in a deep, booming voice. "Sit anywhere ya'd like! I'll get your order in a minute!"

They sat at a table in the corner next to a staircase leading to individual rooms for weary travelers. A group of men sat nearby laughing, while a few men and women sat on stools at the bar, conversing. Several candles placed at tables or on the walls in lanterns lit the establishment. A large fireplace across from the bar and on the other side of the tables provided additional warmth and light, though the room was still comfortably dim. There were several people, but it wasn't busy for the time of night, Hazel thought.

Alistair scrutinized the chosen table and frowned. Drawing a kerchief, he wiped it over the table and chairs. He pulled a chair out for Hazel. When he moved to Lara, she chuckled. "I can fight a minotaur and win, Prince. I can pull out a chair on my own, thanks." He shrugged and took a seat.

The bartender approached, beaming. "Greetings, young people. How nice it is to have new patrons! You must be friends of Lara. I'm

Eustace, but please just call me 'Eu.' Now, what can I get for ya? I have some pork with a lentil soup that should be ready in a few minutes if ya fancy something to eat. If ya'd like a drink, might I recommend the Sleeping Giant Ale? It only came in yesterday, but it's popular."

Lara leaned closer to him. "Does it get you good and drunk?"

Eustace mirrored her. "I'll tell ya; it isn't called Sleeping Giant Ale for nothin'!"

"I'll have that, and I think we'll all have dinner too."

"Very good. And what would you like?" He smiled at Hazel.

She blinked several times. "Oh, I don't really drink all that much..."

"Ah, I expect not," he said apologetically. "I wasn't a fan of drink myself when I was your age. Let's see... Oh, I know. I can boil some water and get a nice tea going for ya. I have chamomile or lavender tea. I drink it myself after a busy night."

She wrinkled her nose. Apparently, death hadn't improved her thoughts on lavender as a flavor. "Chamomile for me, please."

"Certainly, miss, one chamomile tea. For the gentlemen?"

Alistair opened his mouth, but Lyvaelan interrupted. "He would like blood wine, preferably from last season, and I'll also have a cup of tea. Thank you."

Eustace bowed and went to the kitchen. Hazel sat mildly stunned at the exchange. He talked to her like she was normal.

"Lyvaelan," she said, "how do glamours work again?"

"Glamours don't alter the appearance of a thing so much as the attitude one has toward it. Fae use them often when interacting with humans to make their presence more readily acceptable. In our case, I placed a normalcy glamour on both of us. Those who see us will recognize you're green and I'm a dark elf, but instead of becoming curious or afraid, they'll instead see the appearance of two such individuals as commonplace. They might recognize we're unique, but it won't seem like a major issue. Glamours are easy to cast if one has elven or fae blood, but they are easy to break. If you attack someone, or perform some incredible feat that draws attention, then the individuals observing may question their perception of you and see through the glamour. The more people who shake off the effect, the more the spell wanes on you until it is broken. Sitting here, in a bar talking, however, is nondescript. If we don't call attention to ourselves, no one will care. The beauty of the normalcy glamour is it indirectly affects memory. Because we'll be viewed as nothing more than nondescript patrons, there will be nothing anyone will report or realize. Thus, we become socially invisible.

"I think, however, we should shift subjects." He paused while the bartender brought their drinks. "You should tell them about your dream."

Hazel looked around. "Is it safe?"

He nodded slowly. "Safer than the library, I think."

Hazel nodded back. She told Alistair and Lara about the dreams she had. Dreams of an undead horde with a powerful figure robed in green light rising above the masses beneath. She spoke of the urgency of the vision.

"There were words that burned in my mind I felt the need to say: *The living lich of half a day shall rise with legions of undead that none can kill. Through betrayal of friends and oath, the living lich shall trample bodies and hearts. The world will quake as the impossible becomes the inevitable. The living lich of half a day may only be stopped by the slow progress of time.*"

Lara exhaled loudly. "Well, one thing's for sure: I won't be using *that* idiom again soon."

"Indeed." Alistair mused. "What do you think this means, Hazel?"

She shook her head. "I don't know. I'm not sure, but... I think I might be the living lich of half a day."

"What?" Lara shouted, leaping up. Several patrons looked at her, but she smiled sheepishly and sat back down. When the others returned to their drinks, Lara lowered her voice, "Hazel, no! You couldn't be a lich. How would that even be possible?"

Hazel looked into her tea. "Well, we don't know *what* I am. I could be anything. I seem to be alive, but I was also brought back from the dead and I have my own will power."

"Yeah, but liches are supposed to be magical powerhouses, right?" Lara said, looking at the other two for confirmation. "I mean—no offense—but you haven't done anything except tell bits of the future. Liches can raise the dead and do crazy, powerful things."

"Lara's right," Lyvaelan said. "Liches are powerful, but Hazel shows some arcane aptitude she lacked before she died. Whatever was done to her may have altered her in some way we don't know."

"So what, are you saying she's a lich, Lyvie?"

"No, I'm not saying that at—" Lyvaelan raised an eyebrow. "'Lyvie'?"

Lara leaned back. "Yeah, it's your new nickname. I made it up just now. If you aren't saying she's a lich, then what are you saying?"

He shook himself. "I'm saying we should consider everything we know before ruling anything out. That color in her dreams? It's no coincidence her skin has changed into that color. Whatever is happening, she is pivotal."

"Couldn't that bit about the 'living lich of half a day' simply be metaphorical?" Alistair asked, leaning back in his chair. "It doesn't seem coincidental that her vision included an idiomatic phrase."

"What could it mean?" Hazel asked.

The vampire squinted at the ceiling in thought. "Usually, the phrase means it's wiser to deal with immediate problems than fixating on potentially worse problems in the future. Perhaps the living lich refers to a person who's imminently threatening?"

"So, what you're saying," Lara said slowly, "is the living lich of half a day could be a person who's already with us but isn't as lethal as someone in the future? What about the hordes of undead?"

"Couldn't those be the unthinking masses? The undead have a reputation for lacking intelligence and freedom of thought. Maybe it's a group of people who blindly follow someone."

"Hmm. That's... possible." Lyvaelan paused before letting out an exasperated groan. "Honestly, almost anything could be possible. This was only a brief page in the book of everything I've learned, not that my education has been altogether extensive. I may know more on the subject than anyone in this room, but that's saying very little. If we need to know more, we should speak with an expert."

"If that interpretation is right," Hazel said, "then I could still be the living lich of half a day."

"Damn it, Hazel!" Lara exclaimed. "Why do you insist you're the lich?"

Hazel stared at the table, not meeting their eyes. "When Hickory brought me back to life, he used some kind of spell that could test how much magic I have. It was supposed to be safe, but it caused a minor explosion. I could see something in his eyes back then. He was afraid. He knew he created something undead, or possibly alive, but he didn't know what."

Hazel raised her eyes. "When I saw the high priestess today, she looked at me like I was a monster. I know you don't see me that way, but what if she's right? What if I turn out to be something terrible? I don't know what was done to me, but I heard the words of the vision so clearly. It was like it was speaking directly to me. The prophecy says the living lich of half a day will betray her friends and her station. I have friends and I'm a member of the Evenfall Vigil. Becoming a lich would betray everything I work for and betraying my friends... I don't want to do that."

"You won't," Lara insisted.

Hazel averted her gaze and shook her head. "You don't know that. I may not want to, but maybe the magic in me will change and cause me to betray you against my will. Maybe I will end up betraying myself."

Lyvaelan stood and walked to Hazel. He put his hands on her shoulders and kneeled before her. His dark red eyes were more earnest than she'd seen. "Hazel," he whispered, barely audible to the others in the group, "I won't let that happen. Every day—every hour, if need be—I will work to heal whatever was done to you. You deserve so much more than to live a life of isolation on the chance you might hurt others. Please, *don't give up.*"

Hazel met his eyes and saw something there. It felt like the words he said were once spoken to him by another. There was desperation and sadness in those strange eyes. She looked at the others and they mirrored his concern. She turned back to him and put a hand on his wrist. "Thank you, Lyvaelan. I won't give up. Just promise you won't let me do anything stupid."

He smiled the most genuine smile she'd seen. "I promise."

"You have our promise, Hazel." Alistair said. "Just don't forget your promise to us either. After all, we still need to solve the mystery of the aufhockers and the Alchemist."

She nodded. For the first time in several months, she felt a comforting warmth in her chest. The kindness and love of her friends. While she enjoyed the sensation, she couldn't help but notice the tugging in the back of her mind of something ominous, like distant storm clouds on a sunny day. Something was coming. It was only a matter of time.

Chapter Twenty-One
Shelving Problems

I'm glad we finally got the chance to do this," Alistair said, dusting off the cover of an old tome. "I was afraid you might've changed your mind."

Hazel smiled at him. "And leave you to organize the books on your own? Never."

They stood in the library, close to where they first met. They'd used the main entrance to the library many times, and although Alistair said nothing, she noticed the distress in his eyes at seeing so many books in disarray. Upon returning from their excursion to Skilliven Tavern, Hazel proposed the two of them work on fixing up the library the following day. Much had improved from the beginning, due to Alistair's incremental cleaning and Lyvaelan renewing the magic in many enchantments. Still, much needed to be done. Every book seemed to contain more dust than knowledge, and the high roof showered additional detritus whenever a strong enough gust of wind rocked the structure. Some furniture was broken, while others were stained or placed in random locations. While the worst of the moth-eaten banners were removed, the few that remained were faded from age and cobwebs. Some books were damaged and missing pages to such an extent as to render them useless. Such books were put aside to be burned or repurposed. The shelves suffered the least damage, although the volumes on them lay haphazardly in uneven stacks and slouched against each other.

Hazel appraised the large room. "I wonder if we could have Lyvae-lan blow a wind through the library to get all the dust out."

Alistair considered it. "Can he do that?"

"I don't know. Probably?" Hazel responded hopefully.

"Well, I think even if he could, we'd have to be careful about the books. A light breeze will probably do little to remove dust, but too strong a gust could send some of these pages flying."

"True. By the way, I was sorting books on the other side of this shelf but had a hard time categorizing a few of them. Care to help?"

"What books are they? Maybe I can guess from the title," he said, placing a series of volumes on a shelf.

Hazel set down her stack and read the spines. "The first is called *Fall of the Gray Order.*"

"That sounds like history to me, though it could be historical fiction. Does it seem factual?"

"Hard to say," Hazel said, squinting at the pages. "It's a historical account but based on what I've read, it uses very poetic and flowery language."

"'Flowery language'?"

"*And on that day in the Year of the Empire 261, the execution of the Light Order was complete. The method was unclear, but their destruction was immediate, as every stronghold in their power was utterly destroyed within the span of a few days.*"

"Hmm." Alistair mused. "That doesn't sound 'flowery' to me."

"Hold on. *Their fall was only the start of the cataclysm yet to come. O Gray Order! You could not see what the dark had hidden from you! Mourn, though there are none yet left who can! What noble cause and ignoble demise! Did none of you feel the weight of your end at hand? Alas! If one had heard, then perhaps in secret, you might have lived.*

Now the legacy of gray fades into nothing more than a footnote in the interminable trek of history."

Alistair wrinkled his nose. "I... see what you mean. That's a history book, though lacking objective language. I'm going to guess it wasn't a modern composition. Still, it might serve as a good primer for those who find the subject boring. Maybe. Any others?"

"Yes. There's another called *Moth King: Theories, Attestations, and Legends.* I know nothing about this 'Moth King,' so it's a little hard to figure out where it should go."

Alistair frowned. "May I see it?" He took the book and flipped through several pages, rapidly scanning for information. "I can see why you would struggle with categorizing it. I think it should go with the myths and legends. The Moth King may once have existed, but this looks more speculative than factual."

"Who was the Moth King?" Hazel asked, taking the book back.

"He existed a few thousand years ago. Supposedly. He was some near-deity savior among a small collection of vampires, and a minor cult still exists that honors him. What few facts we have claim he was the child of a nosferatu and a camazotz, though that latter parent is *highly* debatable. He was a revolutionary king who became a symbol for the ambitious downtrodden."

"Huh, interesting. I'll put this with the other books on folklore and legends, then. The last one is called *Alder King, Alder King, Ride Not Hence!*"

His brow furrowed. "What is *that* about?"

"It's a series of fairytales and poetry centering on some creature who steals people away. It reminds me of stories for children, but some of this seems too frightening for kids."

"I understand the dilemma. Even though it has a mix, I'd keep it with poetry."

"Sounds good."

Hazel put the books away in their respective areas. Alistair had implemented a system of organization scholars from Scripthaven had been using for the last century that the empire only recently recommended. Hazel didn't understand all the specifics of how it worked, but Alistair labeled areas with distinct categories. He stated most libraries wouldn't contain the same quantity of information and this system—the imperial archival standard—provided guidelines for libraries with any combination of specialized or general texts.

Hazel smiled as they worked in silence. It was oddly refreshing, not feeling the need to fill the silence with conversation. Despite Alistair's politeness and the air of royalty surrounding him, he was easy to be around. He was comfortable with the quiet but didn't mind conversation either.

Hazel had continued to take Lyvaelan's training with her into all she did. She realized that months ago, when she sneaked out to be alone in the forest, she could feel something in the periphery of her awareness. Lyvaelan had helped her through his arcane meditations to expand her senses beyond what she initially knew. She could now sense living things around her; she didn't just notice people, but animals and plants as well. Sitting here in the library as she put books away, she expanded her consciousness to touch the minds of people walking in the street, plants growing between the cobblestones, and horses dragging carts. The people didn't notice her, but she felt an odd affinity to the plants in her vicinity. It reminded her of a friendly dog coming to greet its master. There were no distinct thoughts to these plants in the same way humans had thoughts, but they conveyed vague impressions, desires, and emotions. She asked Lyvaelan about this, but he was confused. Apparently, sensing the emotions of plants was an uncommon manifestation of telepathy.

Despite the oddness of the sensation, she enjoyed communicating with the plants. She sought vegetation anywhere she could. The plants seemed to glow from the attention, and even those which looked close to dying received a surge of new life in her presence. She remembered her mother telling her when she was very young that plants were sacred to Hemericanth, the god of life, and so she needed to treat them with respect. This claim later became problematic when Hazel refused to eat vegetables on account of doing what Hemericanth would want. Many plants, she could now sense, didn't mind being harvested. Trees especially laden with fruit expressed gratitude for being picked and many didn't mind pruning, although excessive or slow pruning annoyed them. Occasionally, she picked up on different emotions between plants that were simplistic but revealed a hidden world. Some of the ivy on one side of the library provoked several other plants to anger with its invasiveness. It felt to her like the other plants protested while the ivy sneered back. Not that ivy *could* sneer. It was a humorous display Hazel hadn't anticipated experiencing. The world around her was so much more alive than she remembered.

As she quietly placed books onto shelves, she listened to some plants grumbling about the ivy, several flowers excitedly waiting for a nearby bumblebee to visit them, and a tree contentedly enjoying the last rays of late afternoon sun on an otherwise cold day in early winter. Where she had once required absolute concentration to hear them, now she could listen without exerting any real effort. She also found she could feel life-forms in an ever-increasing circle. At first, she only noticed things within the same room as her, but then she felt birds on the roof and the occasional rat on the street. Now she could sense flora and fauna across the street from the library and into the shops nearby. She believed with a little more practice she might notice creatures as far away as Skilliven Tavern. She couldn't sense Thomas or Lyvaelan, however. When she questioned Lyvaelan about this, he informed her that those with magic preferred to shield themselves from unwanted attention, and doing so was relatively simple. He also warned her that creatures with greater awareness might notice she was observing them, which could create problems. Noting this, she limited her sense to plants, which rejoiced at her contact.

That night, they chose to return to Skilliven Tavern. Before their first visit—and upon deciding to go again—the group told Thomas of their whereabouts. The inquisitor appreciated the information and requested to be kept abreast of their whereabouts in the future in case of an emergency. This was reasonable, and so they warned him a few hours ahead of their departure whenever they left the library.

Hazel wore a white dress she particularly liked. It used to be her favorite dress, partly because she always got compliments on it, but also because she found she could run in it without tripping or constricting her movement. Along with the dress, she donned her sunhat and a thick cloak. She knew it was a little nonsensical since it was nighttime, but she enjoyed the look and it was chilly. It was also the same basic outfit she wore when she first came to the library. When she entered the living area, Lara gave a low whistle.

"Wow, Hazel, you're cute when you dress up!"

Hazel looked at her sideways. "And I'm not when I don't?"

Lara stuck out her tongue. "Don't play those games with me, Haze. They won't work."

"'Haze'?"

"No doubt her new nickname for you," Lyvaelan said, walking from his room. "You appear to be her latest victim."

"Aww, c'mon, Lyvie, you know you like it."

His scowl said more than words could.

"I'll echo what Lara said, Hazel," Alistair said, rising from his seat. "You look lovely. It makes me wonder if possibly some of us are underdressed." He glanced in Lara's direction.

Lara opened her mouth to protest when an idea popped into her head, and she disappeared into her room. A few seconds later, she reappeared wearing leather gloves with metal knobs affixed to the knuckles.

She threw several punches into the air, tossing her loose brown hair all over. "Well, what do you think? Haze gave me the idea after our fight with the shadow dog things."

"Aufhockers," Lyvaelan corrected absently, examining the gloves. "Are these silver knuckles?"

"Silver *and* steel. Like the prince's sword. I figured it was better to plan for anything."

"Wouldn't the silver hurt you?"

"Not with a nice layer of leather between me and the metal! I also put some additional padding in them to make them a little easier to slip on and off. They're enchanted, too. They won't break if I accidentally knock down a stone wall and they stretch to accommodate my claws when I go half-wolf."

Alistair lifted an eyebrow. "'Accidentally'? How do you accidentally demolish a stone wall?"

"You never know," she answered cryptically.

Alistair crossed his arms. "I would protest using weapons as fashion accessories, but I feel that would be lost on you."

She blew a few strands of hair from her face. "Keep up the snide comments, princeling, and your nickname will be Alice."

Chapter Twenty-Two
Strange Alchemy

Lara smiled with unbridled exuberance as they walked to the tavern. It was a special kind of joy to share something she enjoyed with friends. She hadn't expected anyone to agree with her idea of going out as a group. That they also let her decide the location bordered on surreal. She had half considered taking them to the strangest bar she could think of, but felt an odd sense of responsibility to live up to their expectations. A twinge of anxiety leaped unbidden into her heart that they might not enjoy Skilliven Tavern. Their desire to return each night proved that her fears were baseless.

The tavern was much the same as it had been, although there were more people tonight than before. The tavern was rowdy and Eustace Skilliven bustled about making drinks and ordering his waitstaff to different places. When he noticed Lara, he waved and gestured to their usual place, which had been reserved for them. They sat and talked while Eustace got their drinks and meals.

An hour passed, and patrons came and went. Lara chatted with patrons at the bar, and Alistair sat at another table listening to stories from some older men. Lara stopped listening when the hairs on the back of her neck stood on end. She glanced at Hazel and Lyvaelan, who rose with alarm on their faces.

"Lyvaelan, what's happening?" Hazel asked. There was an uncharacteristic urgency in her voice.

Lyvaelan's eyes dart around the wide room. "It's the glamour. It's wearing off on both of us."

Lara and Alistair immediately excused themselves from their respective conversations.

"I'm sorry, Lyvaelan," Alistair started. "I may have set things off by talking to that group."

"Don't be ridiculous," he muttered, heading toward the entrance. "You and Lara acted normal for both of you. There's someone in here who's searching for us." He nodded to Hazel. "We need to leave. Now. If the glamour wears off, it will be much worse than just one person who has discovered us."

Lyvaelan and Hazel exited quickly, with Lara bidding farewell and Alistair paying their bill. When they had just left the view from the windows of the establishment, Lara noticed Hazel shiver. The glamour had disappeared. Lyvaelan ushered the group into an alley across the street.

"Shouldn't we get going if you two are afraid of being seen?" Lara asked in a loud whisper.

Alistair looked at Lyvaelan, then at Lara. "Wouldn't it be better to find out who was looking for us?"

Lyvaelan nodded. This could be a special opportunity, and it would certainly not be one they would get again. They didn't wait long before four surly men trudged out of the tavern, searching the street. They wore heavy, stained cloaks but otherwise appeared no different from anyone else in the tavern. Lara had seen many men like these in the past. They were looking for trouble, and Lara was inclined to give it to them. She stepped out of the alley.

"Hey boys, did you lose something?" She cracked her neck and knuckles casually.

They all turned to look at her. The shortest member of their group spoke up. "Nothing so lost we can't find it, but maybe you can help."

"Oh, really?" there was a note of challenge in her voice. "Well, describe it to me and maybe I can." Judging from their heavy cloaks, she guessed they had weapons on them. They weren't as subtle as they thought.

The men stalked toward her. "We're seeking a fancy vampire, a green girl, a gray-skinned elf, and a shabbily dressed bitch who doesn't know when she's outmatched." The man whistled loudly and from down the street and hiding in a few alleyways came a dozen more men, each armed with clubs, daggers, hatchets, and spiked chains.

Lara glanced at each of them and resisted smiling. Maybe she'd have the chance to use her studded gloves. "Well, I've seen the first three, but that last one doesn't sound familiar. I should tell you, though, that I'm an officer of the Evenfall Vigil." She drew her badge, which flashed when she showed it. "I would really recommend you go home. Maybe I'll forget this happened."

"No, I don't think you will," the man said, drawing a shortbow from within his cloak. "I've got a message for you: 'You shouldn't mess with the Alchemist's business.'" He now stood across from the alley where the other Watchers were and took aim with two other thugs, who pulled similar bows out. They revealed small side quivers and drew arrows at Lara. They loosed, and she nimbly dodged away. The other men charged her, brandishing clubs, only to be disarmed by the blurred form of the vampire. Two more arrows were loosed, but she caught one and the other flew wide. She rushed toward the first three men, grabbing one by the shirt and throwing him into the other two. She picked up their bows and snapped them in half with her hands. Three more advanced but stopped abruptly, unable to move. Lyvaelan approached from the shadows, speaking under his breath at the immobilized assailants. He tossed a ball of force at another that threw him a distance away. In only a few brief seconds, the aggressors had been subdued.

Lara picked up the man she had been talking to and threw him back to the ground. "See? I didn't underestimate your abilities. You lost."

He grinned and spat out a tooth. "You sure about that?"

Lara cocked her head. She picked up a chain from one man Alistair disarmed and tied one of the man's legs to a lamppost before rushing toward the alley. He might have been full of shit, but she had the sinking feeling he wasn't. She paled at what she saw.

There, lying supine, struck in the abdomen and chest by arrows, was Hazel. "Lyvaelan! Alistair!" Lara screamed. Both rushed to her side and fell to the girl's side when they saw Hazel's wounds staining the white of her dress into a deep red. She remained unmoving.

"Lyvaelan, can't you do anything?" Lara begged. Mentally, she cursed herself for dodging aside and not thinking of who was behind her. *Idiot!* Based on the location of the wounds, both lungs were punctured, along with her intestines. Humans couldn't survive such injuries, especially without someone to heal them.

Lyvaelan shook his head in shock. "One of these wounds would have killed most humans. Three such wounds... I... I can't." He started hyperventilating and his pupils dilated, turning his eyes entirely black. Lara's dismay grew into horror as she watched Lyvaelan lose control.

Hazel coughed.

All three gasped in unison.

"Ow. What... are these things?" Hazel's voice was barely more than a whisper.

They all glanced at each other, speechless.

Hazel moved a hand to the arrows in her chest. Before any could stop her, she pulled both out with little resistance. She did the same with the one that struck her middle. She looked around at each of them. "What?" She turned to her side and coughed as dark gouts of blood stained the alley.

She frowned at her wounds and wiped her mouth. "They ruined my favorite dress." She propped herself against the tavern wall.

"Hazel!" Lara finally blurted out. "You're *alive!* I'd have a thousand of your ruined dresses over one dead Hazel!"

"Thank the gods." Alistair sighed. "Those wounds would have killed anyone and pulling out the arrows would've made it worse. Were you hiding armor under your clothes?"

"No," Lyvaelan said, checking the wounds, "look!"

They watched as each wound closed of its own accord before their eyes.

"Those wounds really pierced your vital organs," Lyvaelan said with wonder. "But you survived. You healed from what would have been certain death. You are incredible."

Hazel looked at the nearby plants curiously.

Lara heard the chains shift far behind her. "I don't think we're safe yet."

Outside the alley came suppressed, maniacal giggles. They dashed out to find the man Lara had chained doubled over, laughing. The chain holding him had snapped and a small, empty vial rolled at his feet.

"You're... too late," he wheezed through his laughter. His eyes blazed with a blue fire and his body vibrated. Instantly, he grew six feet taller. Massive muscles bulged across his body and his clothing ripped apart. His grin widened as he said through his persistent giggles, "Behold, the power of the Alchemist."

With blinding speed, the giant rushed at Lara and slammed his enormous fist into her gut, sending her thirty feet through the air before bouncing an additional ten. Lara rolled to her feet, though the punch hurt more than she expected. This creature was stronger than the one the soldiers of the Evenfall Vigil fought. *Much* stronger. Alistair drew his sword. He struck at random, inflicting gashes on the monster with lightning speed and precision. Each wound dripped no blood and closed moments after it was made.

Alistair's eyes flashed black. "If you give in now, no one will think less of you. Calm yourself, breathe. No one has died. You can still give up without trouble. Give up. Give in. You know it's the right thing to do. Surrender."

The alchemically enhanced man shook his head with a giggle and took an additional swing at Alistair, narrowly missing. The man's speed was almost the prince's equal. Lyvaelan pulled white wisps from the air and sent them toward the hulking mass. Previously, this magic froze the other criminals in place. Against this man, it did little to even slow him. After a few moments, Lyvaelan abandoned the effort and spun lightning between his fingers and shot a constant red electrical stream at the monster. The creature howled as the energy screamed across his body. He glowered at Lyvaelan with the same maniacal grin. The man moved sporadically, seemingly teleporting short distances unintentionally. He disappeared from the magic barrage for a moment and appeared before Lyvaelan. The dark elf stepped nimbly to the side and gestured, sending up a sparkling translucent barrier. Despite dodging the worst of the blow and using an arcane shield, Lyvaelan was not safe. The monster's arm swiped through the shield with the tinkling sound of breaking glass and batted the dark elf warlock away. Lyvaelan careened into a brick wall with a loud *thud* and slumped to the ground.

Lara wiped blood from her lip and gritted her teeth. That blow would've killed any human the moment it connected, but not her. She didn't break easily. She had a plan. Lara sprinted within ten feet and then advanced cautiously with hands held up in a defensive position. She feigned a left jab but sank a right uppercut into his stomach with such force he vomited a small quantity of blue liquid, alcohol, and bile. He threw a sloppy right hook in retaliation, which she evaded by bobbing and weaving to her right. She grabbed his arm as it passed and threw him over her shoulder. Rotating around—still holding his arm—she crossed her ankles around his shoulder and locked him in an armbar. She gripped his wrist with her right hand and crushed his upper arm between her left hand and thigh with all her strength. A *pop* followed by a *crack* indicated that she had both dislocated and broken his arm. He grabbed her with his left hand and ripped her from his arm—and would have ripped his arm too, if Lara hadn't let go intentionally. She chopped at the back of his wrist, and he released her. Both rose to their feet.

The monster roared, but she noted with satisfaction his right arm only twitched limply. If the potion dulled his sense of pain, it was actively working against him. Pain would drive him to self-preservation, but he had none of that. His perceived invincibility would be his defeat.

He grabbed at her, but clearly wasn't used to fighting with his non-dominant hand. She bobbed under his grasp and swept the legs from under him. With his stomach on the ground, she repeated a variation of her previous maneuver with a kneebar. Using her thigh as a fulcrum, she hyperextended his knee and twisted until it stuck out at an odd angle.

Lara yelled to Alistair, "Slash the muscles in his other arm!" The vampire flew to the other side and cut down hard on the monster's one good arm. Alistair struck deeper than before; the man's arm dropped to his side and the wound—which still didn't bleed—slowly knit back together. The creature flipped onto his back despite how it mangled the leg Lara held and kicked at her with his right leg. Lara grabbed and twisted it in its socket, dislocating it. The monster panicked but found he was helpless to do more than spasm on the ground. Lara panted and climbed on top of him, kicking the first knee she wounded to ensure he didn't heal.

"Why didn't you turn wolf?" Alistair asked, pushing the creature's gyrating body stationary.

"Because," Lara said, grimacing at the giggling creature whose eyes flickered between fear and manic joy. "This guy is no Lorkian zar Kalo." She slammed her fist into his nose, breaking it and his cheekbones. The back of his head shattered the cobblestone beneath it, and he finally lay still. She knew how strong she was but also knew her opponent. In the past, she had knocked trolls unconscious with a single strong blow to the head. She had no intention of holding back tonight against this intoxicated idiot.

"Who is Lorkian zar Kalo?" Alistair asked, bewildered.

"He's a vampire I went wolf for in the ring." Lara rolled off of the man. "Nice guy. We had drinks after." She surveyed the scene and noticed the other two.

Hazel had run to a still-motionless Lyvaelan. The dark elf was crumpled on the ground. To Lara's dismay, she noticed a blood smear where his head and body had impacted against the wall.

Lara glanced from Hazel to Lyvaelan, trying to think of what to do. The wound he sustained was severe. She watched as Hazel put a hand to his chest. "I didn't die tonight, and neither will you." Lara's eyes widened as smoky green light coalesced around Hazel. They backed away as Hazel stared at Lyvaelan with sheer determination. The green light wrapped itself around him, producing a low and comforting hum. Lara could only see a gash on his forehead close, but as the light enveloped him, Lara imagined it healed more than she saw. With a final push of power, Lyvaelan gasped and awakened. He blinked at them as the green light subsided.

"How..." he whispered to Hazel. "How did you do that?"

She smiled. "I learned that from you."

"Never once did I teach you how to do that," he scoffed, shaking his head. "I should have a terrible headache, but I don't. Actually, I feel better than I have in days. Weeks, maybe."

Hazel shrugged. "I got a sense from the plants that I could heal. If I could do it to myself without trying, then why shouldn't I be able to use it to help you?"

Lyvaelan fixed a flat look at her. "Because almost nothing else in the world works that way. You're saying *the plants* told you to do that?"

"Not *exactly*. They just wanted me to reach out to you like I do with them."

"Well, how about that?" Lara said, shaking her head. "Hazel's a healer."

"Oh, you're hurt too," Hazel said, noticing the multiple scrapes and bruises Lara sustained.

"No, Hazel, I'm alright, really, no need to—" Hazel, a few feet from her, put forth her green tendrils of light and Lara fell silent as her wounds mended. A warm, comforting sensation flooded over her. It was like thaumaturgy, but different. She felt like she almost wanted to laugh for joy. "Hey! That was pretty good! I feel *fantastic*, actually! My shoulder isn't doing that creaky thing it was doing!"

"'Creaky thing'?" Alistair questioned.

"Yeah, you know, a creaky thing. Wow, you could put other thaumaturgists out of work!"

Hazel smiled and rose to her feet with a slight wobble. Her friends jumped to catch her, but she waved them off. "I'm fine, really. Just a moment of dizziness. Besides, I think we might have to explain ourselves."

A dozen Evenfall Vigil soldiers approached on horseback with a prisoner wagon in tow. A centaur, dressed in the regalia of a lieutenant, led them. His short black beard and severe expression, coupled with his tanned and muscular physique, lent him an intimidating air. He galloped to them.

Lara held up her badge. The others did likewise.

He scanned them. "I'm Lieutenant Leo Hipparchus. What happened?"

The four gave an account to the lieutenant, who occasionally interrupted to issue commands to his men, who were gathering all the incapacitated criminals. Over the course of their report, his gaze softened.

"You've done excellent work. Few soldiers could accomplish what you have tonight. In fact, other soldiers have died against similar alchemically enhanced monsters. I knew of your division within the Evenfall Vigil but hadn't expected you to behave so competently. Not one death on either side—that's difficult to achieve. Although"—he examined the torn and bloody areas of Hazel's dress—"you seem to have managed it only barely. You did a good job of getting that brute to regurgitate the potion he took. That was a smart tactic, Watcher Lara."

"Thanks." She grinned. "It's an old fighting move."

He watched the man, who had been slowly shrinking as they spoke. "This person you've apprehended will be very helpful in some of our ongoing investigations."

"Has there been any other word on the Alchemist?"

He shook his head. "None. Tonight is the first we've heard from him since the aufhocker incident. I'll have spellcasters examine the stuff he coughed up. It might take a few days, but until then, you can rest easy. Or at least as easy as you can, knowing that you've drawn the ire of the Alchemist."

"Don't we need to fill out a report?" Alistair asked. Lara wanted to thump him for bringing it up.

"No, I don't think so," he said, smiling at Lara's sour expression. "You've been through enough tonight and you've given me sufficient details so I can write the report myself. You four have surmounted quite an ordeal. Rest up, and we'll send someone to check on you tomorrow if we need anything. You're dismissed." He saluted and trotted back to his other soldiers, who had just finished loading most of the assailants into the wagon.

The four journeyed to the library in silence. As Lara opened the door, Hazel spoke, "We need to find out who the Alchemist is because he definitely seems to know who we are."

Chapter Twenty-Three
Lyvaelan's Request

Two days had passed since the incident at the tavern, and the Evenfall Vigil had learned little of the Alchemist. They questioned the criminals they had arrested, but each confirmed they had not seen the Alchemist in person. Large, shadowy figures gave written instructions and payment. The individuals who had been chosen all had previous encounters with guards in the city or had been implicated in various crimes without evidence. Each of the men had received a substantial sum for killing the members of the Evenfall Vigil that night. All were paid one silver merchant for the initial job with the promise of double that upon proof of completion. These men were simple laborers and would not have made a single silver merchant in a week if they worked nonstop, though most found little fulfillment in honest work. The promised compensation—three silver merchants—was a small fortune to such men. This claim floored the Evenfall Vigil. The average soldier in the department made one silver merchant a month, which was slightly more than that of a soldier in the general city guard.

This was troubling for many reasons. While suspicion had long been on the alchemists in the city for being the alleged mastermind, none could throw such enormous quantities of money at problems.

Even if the claim of tripling their pay had been fabricated, the men involved were still paid fifteen silver merchants. Alchemists made more money than common soldiers, but not by such a wide margin. The number of practicing alchemists in the city with enough prestige to earn so much and have funds to spare was short to none and made the members of the Evenfall Vigil uneasy. It now seemed like the unseen threat they fought was much greater than any single individual. While selling illegal potions could garnish whatever amount an alchemist made, from what the investigation uncovered, the blue potion that turned the man into a monster was given freely. Who, then, were the potions being sold to that resulted in the Alchemist's wealth?

To further complicate matters, Thomas Eller and his inquisitors had clarified their role in the investigation. While alchemy was the least magical of all the arcane arts, it was still under the purview of the Inquisition. They had little interest in the more common thugs, but took the man, the bottle and much of the vomit he left at the scene as part of an ongoing inquiry. Thomas had been apologetic—yet firm—about the necessity of the Inquisition's intervention, but it did little to appease Commander Comrear, who led a one-man shouting match against the inquisitor who refused to waver. This made questioning the criminals they kept an effort in futility, since the man who drank the potion was the one who hired the others. Not that questioning him would have helped, since his memory and higher cognitive functions appeared to be severely impacted by the potion.

Hazel slept for what she later discovered was close to sixteen hours after that night. Lara was more chipper than usual due to her contribution in the fight, Hazel suspected. Alistair asked to see Hazel's torn dress and set about mending it with surprising skill and speed. Charlie, the diminutive redcap cook, helped Hazel remove the bloodstains, which she found ironic. Lyvaelan, however, stayed to himself. He meditated in his room and occasionally attended meals but was more aloof than usual.

Hazel had been working on expanding her mind and sensing the different plants outside when she heard a knock on the door. Rising from her bed, she opened the door to find Lyvaelan waiting for her.

"Oh, Lyvaelan!" she said with genuine surprise. "Uh, come in."

He glided in, briefly glancing around the room in silence. He strode noiselessly to the corner of her bed and released a sigh before slouching to the ground with his back against the bedpost.

Hazel hurried to him but stopped when he looked up at her. There was something complicated in his eyes. A storm of emotions she had never seen in him before.

"Hazel," he said, "I need to say something. I meant to say it sooner, but I didn't know how to adequately put it into words. I... want to thank you."

"Of course." Hazel sat on the floor across from him. "I was happy to help you. I couldn't leave you injured like you were the other night."

"No, that isn't why I'm thanking you, though I suppose I owe you some gratitude for that." She read the exhaustion on his face. "I came here to thank you for not dying."

She cocked her head.

"Or, conversely, I suppose I wanted to thank you for living. When I saw you dying..." she heard anxiety creep into his voice. He paused and took a deep, shuddering breath. "I didn't know what to do. I was experiencing powerful emotions and felt *it* rising in me. If you died, I might have done something truly terrible."

Hazel studied him. He was trembling. The emotion she saw in him—so strange considering his usual calm demeanor—was terror. Not of her, but of himself.

"You wouldn't have done anything wrong. You're a good person."

"No, you don't understand." An urgency took his voice. "It has nothing to do with being good. *I am dangerous.* I don't suffer from the weakness of lacking power; I suffer from the surplus of power I'm incapable of controlling. When I beheld you, pierced and bleeding, it welled inside me and I don't know why. It seized me, and I felt my power releasing along with my desire to control it."

He held his hand before his face and Hazel watched as black lines and cracks broke across his gray skin. His pupils appeared more dilated than usual. "I could have stopped them all with a gesture. A small wish, and my power would have crushed him like an insect." He lowered his hand and his voice. "But it would've been a short-lived victory. For everyone. When warlocks lose control of their powers, they draw on the surrounding magic until they cause an arcane cataclysm. Nothing survives. I can die; that matters little to me. But when you almost died, I nearly caused that arcane cataclysm. It wouldn't have just killed me; it would have obliterated the vampire, the werewolf, and everyone within half a dozen miles of my location if it were not contained. Thousands of people—dead, because of me. When you survived, I felt it dissipating. Everything was safe again. My life is inconsequential; it was the lives of everyone else that mattered.

"Life means little to me." His voice had grown increasingly steady and detached. "I think my existence may ultimately amount to a giant mistake. Dying fixes that. What I cannot stand— what I fear beyond all else—is the prospect of losing control and destroying so many inno-cent people at once. The arcane cataclysm is all I fear. To die like that would destroy me in a way a solitary end never could. It isn't my life I thank you for, so much as my soul."

Hazel gazed at him. He appeared so young to her. She had always felt like a child around her friends—and especially Lyvaelan—but now the role had reversed. In Lyvaelan she saw a boy terrified of what he might do, afraid of the shadows that held no threat beyond himself. She reached over to him and placed her hand on his. A green glow sprouted from her fingertips. "Lyvaelan, you'll be fine. I promise. I have asked so much from you and you have supported all of us with-out asking for anything in return. I'm here for you too, and I'm not going anywhere."

He glanced at her hand and then up at her. "Hazel, make me a promise."

"I will."

"If ever I should be on the brink of causing an arcane cataclysm…"

"Yes?"

"Kill me."

Hazel stared into his eyes without breaking contact. He meant it. Behind his expression, she saw desperation. She took a breath. "No."

"Please, Hazel, don't let me destroy so many lives."

"I will promise you, Lyvaelan, as Hazel Enda, daughter of Kyle and Lynn Enda, member of the Evenfall Vigil, and your friend, I will not kill you. If you are on the brink of an arcane cataclysm, I will pull you back. I won't kill you to save others. Instead, I'll save everyone by being there for you."

Various emotions played across his face. Anger, joy, fear, confusion. "That isn't what I asked for."

She crossed her arms, resolute. "When I was eight, I wanted a pony for my birthday, but I didn't get that either."

"What does that have to do with this?"

She smiled. "I eventually realized I was wrong and my parents were right, even though I didn't see it."

His face twisted into an expression caught between annoyance and amusement. "This is a little different."

"It is, but I'm still right, and you're still wrong. You're the smartest person I've ever known, Lyvaelan, but even you can be mistaken occasionally. This is one of those times. Trust me. I'll help you, just like you've helped me."

He sighed and shook his head. "I still don't think you're right, but I can see it's pointless trying to extract the promise I want from you."

"You shouldn't have come to a healer if you wanted someone who would hurt you."

He studied her, his expression turning to curiosity. "You've changed, Hazel Enda. You're more alive than when we first met. More… impudent."

"I think you mean impressive."

He eyed her sideways with a small smile. "No, impudent. You aren't as excessively polite as you were before."

"Is that a good thing?"

"If your impudence is a symptom of your liveliness returning, then I know of no way it could be bad."

Chapter Twenty-Four
Tactics and Planning

Alistair sat in an armchair in the common area, casually flipping through a book on early imperial literature. From this distance, he could hear the exchange between Hazel and Lyvaelan, but focused his attention elsewhere for the sake of maintaining their privacy. His ears picked up the sound of bare feet approaching. Based on the gait, weight, and direction, he guessed it was Lara when she was still fourteen paces away and out of sight. He glanced up when she approached and smiled. She surveyed the room briefly before sitting down.

"Where are the other two?" she asked.

"Upstairs. Talking," he said, continuing to read his book.

"A serious conversation?"

"Yes, from the little I inadvertently overheard."

"I imagine they'd have a lot to talk about. Lyvie's been withdrawn lately—more than usual. It's a shame. He seemed to finally be opening up."

Alistair turned a page. "I think he repeats mistakes he's made in his head until it's all he can think about. I've seen it in many vampires and a few humans. It can be paralyzing."

"It can be."

He felt her eyes on him, and he sighed, closing the book. "Yes?"

"You said it's a serious conversation about mistakes he's made. Mind if I take a guess at which mistake he has playing in his head?"

Alistair studied her. "I can't stop you from trying, but their conversation is not for me to divulge."

"How very diplomatic of you." She rose and fell to a knee just across the table from him and leaned over, meeting him eye to eye. Her voice quieted. "He's talking about how he nearly killed us when we thought Hazel died."

Alistair narrowed his eyes. He knew the content of their conversation, but he was unwilling to release any information. "We were all under stress that night, but I reiterate: it is not my place to reveal what they may or may not be discussing."

She nodded. "See, it doesn't actually matter, prince, because it's what *I* wanted to talk about." She leaned closer and lowered her voice still further. "We need to stop him."

Alistair folded his hands and briefly allowed his sense of hearing to bring him into the conversation some ways away, to ensure they were not being listened to. His voice matched hers for volume but allowed a sharpness to enter it. "What are you proposing?"

"Alistair," she said, shaking her head in disbelief, "we have a *warlock* in our midst. That makes him dangerous."

"So are we," he countered. "Neither of us is defenseless and could hurt many if we decided to, but we have not. Why? Because when goodness controls the dangerous, it is a buffer against all evils. Lyvaelan is good. We only need to trust him."

"I can't believe you're this naïve! Yeah, we're monsters—like Garo said. Yes, we're dangerous, but not like he is. He could level this city if he got annoyed enough and no one could stop him."

He stood and paced around the couch. "Nonsense. There's a magic university nearby. They could rein him in, if it ever got to that point."

Lara snorted. "If they knew in advance, then maybe, but what about now? What if there isn't a warning? If he suddenly caused an arcane cataclysm, there wouldn't be time for them to react. Oh, I'm sure their precious school would be fine, but the rest of the city? A pile of ash, rubble, and a memory of innocents screaming."

He bared his teeth and met her gaze. "I will *not* kill an ally needlessly!"

"But would you if there was a great need?" Her excitement cooled unexpectedly, throwing Alistair off-guard. "I never said we should kill him for no reason. As annoying as he can be, I like the guy. That said, his weakness will end us all if we aren't careful. We can't depend on the girl. Shit, she'd probably try to stop us if she ever learned about it. But we're different.

"I've fought alongside you twice now, and I know you don't let emotions get in the way. Last night, your only mistake was giving mercy to the wrong side. You could've severed that bastard's arms if you felt like it. You're faster and stronger than the other two realize. So why didn't you? Are you afraid to kill?"

"No," Alistair said, clenching a fist, "I'm not afraid to kill. I simply don't wish to when alternatives exist."

"A giant alchemical monster isn't enough reason, huh?"

He searched her face and saw that—despite her prodding—she simply desired the truth. Behind the bravado and harshness, she wanted to know.

"You're right. I made a mistake," he replied after several moments. "I should've gone for his head when I had the chance. I failed us, and I replay it in my head almost constantly."

"No, 'mistake' doesn't cover it. You might've miscalculated, but you didn't want to end his life. Why?"

"Because..." Alistair paused, his gaze hardening. "If I start killing humans, I'm not sure I'll want to stop."

Her eyebrows rose. "You think you'll return to hunting like your ancestors?"

"No, not like my ancestors." He ran his hand through his hair. "Like the rest of my kin. I'm the first in my family—and the first in Noxphetalis—to be born without the bloodcurse. I have never tasted human blood, save for what derivative exists within blood wine. My presence in Coruvaine represents a change in my kind, beyond simple diplomacy. I must set an example for others to follow and for humans to judge. Others would fear me, but if I show all the best virtues, then perhaps nosferatu can be brought back into the trusted circles of humanity. To degrade myself by killing a human—*any* human—would destroy the hopes of my people."

"You're putting too much pressure on yourself." Lara relaxed back into a sitting position. "Why do you have to be responsible for your whole race? That's crazy. Also, I've killed before. Humans, very rarely, but plenty of other things. Know why? It's *because* I'm a hunter. Life is one giant struggle for survival; you're either hunting or being hunted. That's why I intend to put down any danger before it gets to me. No matter who it comes from. I want you to join me."

"Why? Why do you need me if you've determined your own future actions?"

"Because I can't do it if you're against me." She forced out a breath. "Look, you're fast and strong. I've fought nosferatu before and they're challenging. Granted, I could possibly defeat you singly, but that would take time. If *he* needs to be killed in the moment, it must be fast, painless, and surprising. I probably can't surprise you like that. If I did it myself, you'd think I went crazy and would try to stop me while he explodes. You're faster than me. If we coordinate, we can make sure that if one of us falls that the entire city doesn't pay for it." When she saw him about to reply, she interrupted, "Don't give me an answer now. Wait and think about it. Just don't wait too long or it might be too late."

"Don't bring this up again," Alistair said. "Garo and King Aldric didn't put us together to kill each other. We can find another way. We *must*. I respect your skill, Lara, and I don't doubt that you care. That said, this talk is beneath you. Why speak of countermeasures when we can ensure what happened before never occurs again? Oil only burns when introduced to flame. If we protect the oil perfectly, then disposing of it will never need to happen. A cabal within our group undermines its integrity."

She relaxed back onto the ground, crossing her arms as she stared straight up to the ceiling. It seemed to Alistair that she wanted to continue arguing but decided against it. "I sure hope so. No two fights are alike, though. The next one could always be the last."

Alistair determined that a change of topic was in order. "I've been meaning to say you fought well the other night. You carried us. It was like you knew exactly where to hit and when to do it."

"Thanks, Al." She smiled. "I've fought guys like him before, though it's always iffy when dealing with alchemy. I don't know a lot about it, but I found when power-fighting alchemically enhanced opponents, the battle could drag out into an hour if I wasn't smart about it. If you see someone take a potion, then the chance of beating them is great. Punch the gut hard enough and the source of their power comes up. It's gross. The audience *loves* it. That also means they usually only have a few more minutes left of effects before they weaken. At least, that's how the enhancers work."

"That was a good move, but I was specifically impressed with the maneuvers you used *after* he vomited."

"It's all the same stuff, honestly. Know where to hit and when to do it. The most dangerous thing was his speed, and after that, his strength. If you can break a leg so he can't run, or immobilize an arm, then suddenly the fight gets a lot easier." She glanced at him as she flopped back onto the couch. "The blows you were landing on him weren't half bad. If you weren't holding back, you might have disarmed him, literally."

"I wasn't sure how much to do or what would hurt him without killing him. You may be right to say I shouldn't have held back as much as I did. As it was, I only inflicted a few scratches that healed immediately."

"Yeah, you shouldn't've held back, but at least it was for good reasons. The 'scratches' were more helpful than you think. If the potion was healing him, it's likely you caused the effects to burn more quickly."

"Yes, though if I had thought to do greater damage sooner, Lyvaelan might not have been nearly killed by that thing."

She sat up and looked at him seriously. "Yeah, but you didn't. You didn't know what would happen, and neither did Lyvaelan. So what? He clearly underestimated him, too. It isn't like you made the only mistake. If you get thumped in the ring, do you mope about how much it hurt or what you could've done differently? No, you get ready for the next punch and don't let it happen again. He caught us off guard. Next time, we'll be ready.

"Besides"—she leaned back into the couch but looked unsettled—"it was alchemy I'd never seen before. Usually, alchemical enhancements only do one or maybe two of those effects. Strength and rapid healing are pretty common, but it did that *and* increased his size and speed. I'm proud of how I improvised."

Alistair considered it. "Achieving that much with a single dose seems dangerous."

"Yeah. Imagine if he hadn't thrown up most of it. It could've been much worse for him and us."

"True. I guess we know how the Alchemist has been using the bluecaps. Perhaps they add to the potency of the concoction."

She sighed. "Poor little weirdos. We need to stop him."

"Agreed," said Garo as he emerged from the shadows. "Get Hazel and Lyvaelan. I need to hear what happened to all of you so we can put an end to this criminal enterprise."

When Hazel and Lyvaelan joined the rest in the common room one and a half minutes later, Alistair told the story. Garo listened to the account of what transpired that night with gravity and interest. Occasionally, Lara or Lyvaelan broke in with corrections or observations.

When the story concluded, he studied them. "What is your next move?"

"Honestly," Alistair said, "I was hoping you would have advice for us."

The grim shook his head. "I'm not sure. This isn't my area of expertise. With the training you've received and the experiences you've had, you're all more qualified than I am to find leads."

The group fell silent. Alistair thought of others who could help within the city, but no one was exactly right. He had fostered a few relationships, but most were in the castle.

In the middle of their silent musings, Lyvaelan spoke, "Isn't there another ambassador in the city?"

Garo cocked his head. "Another ambassador? There are several ambassadors from other kingdoms, but I don't see what good they would do."

"No, no—not *any* ambassador." Lyvaelan peered at the grim intently. "I mean another Seelie Court ambassador. Isn't Ambassador Relas in the city?"

The grim's eyes widened. "Lysander! Of course!"

"Who is Lysander?" Hazel asked.

Garo turned the idea over in his head as he spoke. "Lysander Relas is an ambassador of the Seelie Court, but is likely better known to all of you as the Archmage of Education. He is also the chancellor of Calixford University."

"Would he know anything about the Alchemist?" Hazel said.

Garo nodded. "He oversees all training of spellcasters and keeps a regular record of each student, even after graduation. Lysander is an expert in magic and was one of the key mages responsible for lifting the bloodcurse during the War of the Night. He is both extremely knowledgeable and very likeable. Lysander would happily cooperate with you. He spoke with Commander Comrear some months ago regarding the Alchemist, but since you only recently came to the realization that he is likely a conjurer as well, it would be a good idea to see if that narrows the number of suspects down."

Alistair's eyebrows shot up. They were talking about meeting with an archmage. An *actual* archmage! More than that, he helped end the bloodcurse. He shivered.

"Sounds like a solid lead," Lara said. "Should we start out tonight?" Alistair looked at Lara with alarm.

"No, I don't think so." Garo glanced between them. "I will check in on him first to ensure he can speak with you at length. Besides, it is a little late to start on that at the moment. I'll go see him immediately and inform him. You four should prepare questions to ask. If you do not see me before you leave tomorrow afternoon, assume he knows you're coming. I'll inform you if he is unavailable. I'll also tell your commander of this plan so he doesn't send anyone else out first." He dissolved into the shadows, leaving the group alone.

"Well," Lara said, folding her arms with satisfaction, "I get to meet an archmage. How about that?"

"It's kind of exciting," Hazel said. "I haven't met anyone that important before, aside from the king, of course. Archmages seem so majestic."

"I know what you mean," Alistair said. "King Aldric is very relatable, but archmages are harder to understand. Their connection to magic is said to be unparalleled."

"*Almost* unparalleled," Lyvaelan corrected. "There is only one other kind of human spellcaster I know of who can defeat an archmage."

"And who would that be?" Lara asked.

"A lich."

"Technically, yeah." Lara rolled her eyes. "But what's the likelihood of us meeting a lich?"

Lyvaelan pondered the question for a moment. "Probably about as likely as the prospect of us meeting the High Archmage."

"Yeah, not likely."

Alistair's demeanor fell. "It occurs to me the meeting will take place during the day. I may not be able to accompany you."

"It is winter, though," Hazel said hopefully. "It could be cloudy."

"Even if we have cloudy weather, it will still be difficult for me to move, and I'd slow the group down."

"What about an umbrella?" Lara suggested.

He sighed. "No, I'm afraid that won't work, either. It might help but not to the degree necessary."

"What about magic?"

The group turned to look at Lyvaelan, who had spoken.

"Magic. You know, the thing I do."

"Yes, we know you use magic," Lara snapped back. "Why didn't you mention this before?"

He crossed his arms and arched his eyebrows. "The magic involved is more complicated than you realize. It isn't especially powerful, but it is intricate. I have been thinking about it since I knew there was a vampire in our group, actually."

"Why didn't you use it sooner?" Alistair said.

"Partly because I didn't have it figured out, and partly because I preferred having you and the werewolf separate. You bickered too much. If you were stuck here while she could go out, then it was essentially optimal. Since you two argue less now, I can offer the possibility without perpetual headaches."

"Really?" Lara said. "You think we argue less?"

Alistair was taken aback. "I'm surprised as well. I don't think me and Lara fight much differently now than we did before."

"Is that so?" Lyvaelan shrugged. "Well, perhaps I just don't mind your arguments as much."

"I agree with Lyvaelan." Hazel smiled. "You two still fight, but it's like you don't do it because you hate each other."

The two glanced at each other and shrugged. "Whatever you say, Haze," Lara said, relaxing back.

"Yes, well, returning to the matter at hand, Lyvaelan, do you have some spell that can make me invulnerable to sunlight?"

"No. I have no spell that can negate your vampiric aversion to daylight. Such a spell would be far more difficult to achieve. You want to move around in daylight without the negative effects, correct? The solution is to make it so that you can walk around at night."

Alistair squinted at him, trying to sort what he said. "So... you are going to turn the day into night?"

Lyvaelan scoffed. "Ha! No. That's even harder than what you previously asked. No, I can cover you with the shadows of night, so you will keep your power but still be able to walk around outside. Observe."

Lyvaelan rose and gestured for Alistair to do likewise. He moved his hands like a weaver around Alistair as dark purple strands wrapped loosely around the vampire's form. Lyvaelan plucked at each thread and they stuck to his fingers, moving with the motion of his hands. He intoned softly, "By the power of Umbravelle the Ubiquitous and by Kistra, Lord of Stars, may you be enveloped in shadows of night that prevail before the dawn. Let night become you and let night surround you in open defiance of the rising sun." When he finished, the dark threads shivered and burst into wisps of black smoke that surrounded Alistair.

"This is... incredible," Alistair said, considering his smoky form.

"Yeah..." Lara wrinkled her nose. "Do you have any way of making him look less like the scariest of the Unseelie Court's bogeymen?"

"It's not *that* bad," Alistair said, more to comfort himself than convince her.

"No, Lara is right," Hazel said. "You look terrifying. Kind of like the aufhockers."

"Actually," Lyvaelan said, "that was where I got the idea. Your point is taken, however. The effect will be less pronounced in daylight. You should still carry an umbrella or hope for overcast skies, otherwise the effect will quickly dissipate. On a completely sunny day with no shade in the afternoon, it would probably last ten minutes. You won't appear as smoky when you're outside, but you won't be as strong as usual. The more you lean on your vampiric abilities, the faster the darkness will subside. It's temperamental, but it should work well enough for now. I haven't tested it, but I will need to see how it works in order to make any adjustments."

"Thank you, Lyvaelan. This means a lot to me. I deeply appreciate it." Alistair paused from within the inky blackness. "Also, I'm smiling at you, in case you couldn't tell."

Lyvaelan half smiled. "I couldn't see it, but I could hear it. You're welcome."

Chapter Twenty-Five
Calixford and Its Chancellor

They set out the next day, following Garo's instruction to seek the counsel of Archmage Relas if he hadn't returned to tell them otherwise. Inquisitor Eller was reticent about their meeting with the archmage, citing his many duties. When they informed him that Garo had already gone to announce their meeting, he relented but urged them not to take more of the archmage's time than necessary.

The sky was overcast—as Hazel hoped—and Lara confirmed after sniffing the air there wouldn't be rain until late afternoon. It took them less than a minute of walking to notice the telltale signs of Calixford University around them. The buildings looked new, and the air was electric with magic. Students wearing various colored robes and gowns carried books and talked while practicing minor fantastical feats, such as changing the color of flowers, or animating smoke. Dormitories on the outer edge of the campus served as a physical barrier to the rest of the city by design. Magic—while helpful—could endanger and frighten the uninitiated. Many merchants and craftsmen in the area had banners representing their loyalty to the college, and a few further flaunted the alumni status of their occupants.

At the intersection between the main boulevard heading westward out of Coruvaine to the ocean, and the road the group traveled on south from the library, a brick road split the buildings. Two magnificent statues, standing twenty feet tall, guarded the gateway leading into the college. One statue depicted Athelea, goddess of knowledge, and the other Selevara, goddess of magic. Both were stern and regal as they gazed down on those who approached. After passing the statues, the group found themselves with small, grassy hills on both sides, now enclosed by the wall of buildings that encircled the campus. From this side, Hazel noticed a paved road along the backside of the buildings flanked with intermittent magelamps. Students lay on the grass reading, some sat debating, and a few napped. Many of the students appeared to be Hazel's age, though some looked significantly older.

The road dipped into a small incline after a minute, and Hazel saw a large recreational field surrounded by towering buildings. She looked further down to a T split in the road where several small buildings dotted the pavement in each direction. Additional paths connected to the main road and the large buildings behind the field. Flower bushes lined the path with trees overlooking them. Hazel sensed the plants with little effort. In this place of magic and learning, everything was charged with arcane energy. The plants quaked with excitement, even over things plants rarely enjoyed. The grass rejoiced each time it was stepped on, and each time it was left to itself. Flowers nearly shivered with anticipation, waiting for the rain, the sun, or neither. The trees let out one long and continuous sigh of contentment. Each plant greeted her in their own way as they sensed her, which only added to their joy.

The group stopped at the T, deliberating. Alistair's dark appearance was—like Lyvaelan said—less noticeable, but he still remained more shadowed than the rest of the group. As they contemplated which direction to go, Lara grabbed the arm of a student walking by. "Hey, could you tell us where the archmage is?"

The student—a young woman about Hazel's age in white robes—retreated. "Why do you want to see the chancellor?"

Lara flashed her badge. "Official business. He's expecting us."

"Oh, um…" the girl stuttered, "sorry, I'm new here. I think he's in the administration building. The one in the middle on the other side of the quad. I've never tried to see him before, so I don't know for sure, but someone in there should be able to help you."

They thanked her and headed toward the administration building. Ornate carvings of battles and previous archmages adorned the exterior of the stone building, and the dozen deep steps leading up to the doors gave the opportunity to admire the reliefs. The huge wooden doors swung open to admit the group into a large foyer with hallways and rooms adjacent. A bald man wearing a black cassock with a matching sash around his waist sat at a large desk, writing. Hazel shivered.

"How may I help you four?" he asked without looking up. "The archmage is a busy man and cannot take unsolicited visitors."

"We have business with Archmage Relas," Alistair said, stepping up. "*Official* business," he added, flashing his badge.

The man glanced at it before returning to his work. He sighed. "Very well. I will inform the chancellor. Please, sit."

The group sat while the man continued what he was doing with no sign of rising. Lara tapped her foot, but after another minute, she stomped back to the desk. "Hi, yeah, when were you going to go tell him we're here?"

The man met her gaze, his sunken eyes filled with annoyance. "I already did, werewolf."

Her eyebrows shot up. "How do you know I'm a werewolf?"

He raised an eyebrow. "You're extraordinarily easy to read, Lara. I would think your magical ally would have told you something about sorcery. What? You come to a school dedicated to magic, and yet you're surprised by magic? Honestly." He went back to writing.

"Now you listen here—" she reached out to grab his collar but abruptly stopped. She returned to her seat with a sigh. She stayed seated for several minutes without talking.

Hazel regarded her surroundings with awe. The amount of skill that went into building this room alone was monumental. The floors and walls were a polished and unblemished white stone. She searched for signs of where each stone was laid but found no evidence to suggest the building was not carved out of a single giant rock. She knew such a place could not be possible, but then, magic was often touted as the art of making the impossible a reality.

"The chancellor will see you now," the sorcerer said after another few minutes. "Ascend the stairs and his room is at the end of the hallway."

Lara jumped from her seat, her eyes darting between the others in confusion. "Did you see that?"

Hazel frowned. "See what?"

Alistair shrugged. "You were sitting quietly for the last five minutes, so I suppose that was noteworthy."

"What? But I was just—" she growled and stamped over to the man at the desk. She reached out but stopped and climbed the staircase without comment or emotion. Hazel and Alistair shared a bemused look. The group continued through the hallway, eventually arriving before a pair of tall, white wooden doors, upon which were carved intricate designs of dragons, griffins, and manticores. Lara reached out to open it.

"Wait, Lara," Hazel said, "shouldn't we knock before going in?"

Lara blinked several times and jolted, searching around her. "What? What happened? We were just—" she trailed off, and swallowed.

Before Hazel or anyone could inquire what was wrong, the doors opened. Warm orange light from a fireplace and several magelamps lit the room. Two symmetrical staircases led up to a landing backed by a series of tall bookshelves. A desk occupied the middle of the room, with several chairs before it, and at the desk sat a man.

The blond archmage smiled. "Welcome, members of the Evenfall Vigil. Please, have a seat."

The light from the magelamps glinted off the gold trim adorning his white robes. Dark blue epaulettes sat on each shoulder, broadening his subtly muscular physique.

"Chancellor, it is our pleasure to meet you," Alistair said, bowing low. "If you would please, how would you like us to address you?"

"Well met, young prince." His voice was a friendly baritone. "Garo speaks highly of you. I am Lysander Relas, so you can call me Lysander if you desire—I don't stand on formalities. If you prefer, the formal address for archmages is *Your Eminence,* but you may also call me Chancellor, Archmage Relas, Ambassador Relas, or Colonel Relas."

"Are you in the military?" Hazel asked.

"Yes, but not the one you're thinking of. I don't belong to the standing army of Ethelian, but I am a colonel of the Imperial Armies." He sighed, settling back into his chair. "I fought during the War of the Night as a battlemage. I worked until my company was recruited by the late Archmage Lerethes to capture enemies for examination. He later requested my retirement so I could assist with the research that eventually led to the lifting of the bloodcurse. When I retired, I was a major, but for my research that led to the end of the war, I was given the rank of colonel by the emperor. Although I consider myself more a scholar than a soldier, I still wear my regalia to remind myself of the soldiers who never had the opportunity to do the same."

"I owe you a great deal, then," Alistair said earnestly, though Hazel sensed fear in the vampire. "In fact, all my people owe you... everything."

The archmage waved a hand dismissively. "I was just a research assistant. Hardly the genius behind it. You are the Firstborn, correct?"

"I thought you had older siblings?" Hazel asked.

"I do," Alistair replied. "What His Eminence refers to is my honorary title of Firstborn. I was the first nosferatu child born without the bloodcurse. There are several years separating me from my siblings, and each had the curse removed, though most were still young when it happened."

"I would love to continue speaking of this," Lysander said, "but I don't wish to take up too much of your time unnecessarily and I am fatally drawn to tangential topics. Please, what is it you came here to ask me about?"

The group explained the case they had been working on. They spoke of their encounter with the aufhockers stealing bluecaps and of their latest battle. They mentioned Hazel saving Lyvaelan's life and realized they had said more than they had initially intended. The archmage listened to them intently, showing little emotion beyond nodding occasionally.

His eyes moved from one person to the next, his gaze eventually ending on Hazel. Looking into his eyes, she saw both aged wisdom and sharp clarity. He studied her as if he could understand her by sight alone.

"I find this circumstance—and your group composition—highly unusual," he said at last. "I have been attempting to parse out the magic in you, Hazel, but I find it's a combination of unfathomable contradictions. The Inquisition knows of you?"

"Yes, Inquisitor Eller stays with us in the library, actually."

He frowned. "Really? Hmm. Well, I suppose it is not my place to interfere, but such behavior from an inquisitor is atypical."

"To the matter at hand," Lyvaelan interjected, "can you help us?"

He smiled. "You know, Lyvaelan, I think leaving Elliara has done you some good. You're different from when I saw you last, though that was some time ago. Yes, I can help you, or at least point you in a helpful direction." He stood and circled the desk. "Please, follow me."

He led them out toward the entrance of the building. "My work here is important, and I cannot focus on the microcosmic details, so I rarely engage with the students for lengthy periods of time. For this reason, I cannot say I would be the expert on gifted—albeit misguided—students. We keep records of student misconduct when it is dangerous enough to mention, but because of the longevity of spellcasters, it is challenging to know how far back we should look since each year there are hundreds of graduates."

They passed by the front desk. Lara gave the sorcerer who hadn't looked up a wide berth as she caught up to the archmage and whispered, "Hey, sorry to interrupt, but I think some magic was done on me and I'm not sure if it's still working."

"It's not," said the sorcerer, still attending to his work.

Lysander laughed. "I think I can guess what happened. You had a run-in with a master sorcerer. What did Kelsyn do to you?"

"I don't know." Lara shivered. "One moment I was reaching up at him and the next I was sitting down. Then when I went to get angry at him, I was suddenly at your door. It gives me chills just thinking about it."

He nodded with understanding. "Induced fugue. Many don't know how to protect against it. Some believe sorcery to be one of the lesser arcane arts because it requires much less magic compared to other fields, but the creativity and finesse necessary to make a person forget what they were doing and then switch memories is true magic. In the next few days, you will remember sitting back down and waiting, and you will recall retracting your hand so you could come upstairs to see me. At first, they will not seem like *your* memories, but they are. On the surface, it appears like little more than a trick, but to you, it was probably upsetting."

"Yeah! It was seriously freaky."

"Exactly. The chief tenet of sorcery explains this idea simply: knowledge of the self provides the means to alter reality. Your perception of reality changing altered your world every bit as much as if the world had actually changed. Your friends may not have noticed, but the spell could have affected them as well. Fugues are one of the many unsettling capabilities of a decent sorcerer, though I assure you, there are many stranger and more frightening spells a sorcerer can use."

The Archmage of Education led them across the quad to another building bearing the mark of alchemy. A large group of students, split into four teams, competed on the grass over a large leather ball. One student threw the ball and used the wind to direct it to a teammate.

Another student picked up a handful of grass which glowed before he ate it, instantly running at a heightened speed to intercept. A hawk swooped to catch the ball and deliver it to a smiling young woman, who immediately handed it to a smaller woman. The first woman blinked in disbelief upon noticing her hands were empty. The competition continued, though Hazel only caught glimpses.

"What are they doing?" she asked.

Lysander followed her gaze. "Ah. The students are engaging in a friendly game of squareball."

"Squareball?" Lara asked.

The chancellor nodded. "The point of the game is to have a team maintain possession of the ball for four minutes in ten-second intervals rounded down. Thus, holding the ball for thirteen seconds only counts as ten seconds, while possession for twenty-nine seconds only counts as twenty. This is played in four rounds with the winner being the team who won the most rounds. Students are encouraged to use magic to achieve this end. In classes, they focus on theory and mechanics. Competition such as this helps them think outside of their books and get exercise. The four teams I can see currently playing are wizards, alchemists, conjurers, and sorcerers. This looks like a group of second-years. They are clever, but you should see a game played by the graduating class. That's where you see some incredible uses of magic."

They entered the alchemy building. It resembled the administrative office, except for various glyphs and symbols inscribed on every surface.

"Isn't this a little excessive?" Lyvaelan asked, looking around.

"I can see why you would think that," Lysander said, "but we take every precaution to guarantee safety. Explosions are quite common."

"That seems careless," Lyvaelan said, studying the inscriptions.

"Well, it is, and it isn't. The instructors often lead first-year students into experiments intended to test patience. Every year there are at least a few who attempt a shortcut and end up with a headache and temporarily blue skin. It's almost a tradition. The lesson teaches the impatient student the dangers of shortcuts and rewards the patient students with their first successful potion, which could have failed miserably. Failure is often more instructive than success, whether it's a personal failure or the failure of another."

"I can understand the merits of that," Alistair said, looking around somewhat uneasily. "I must beg your pardon for changing the subject. We were in your office for an hour, weren't we?" The others in the group looked at him quizzically. "I ask because although it's overcast, the sun is in the same position from before and I recognized the students in the quad from earlier."

The archmage smiled slyly. "No, the campus isn't enchanted in that way. My office, however, is." He rested his hands behind his back. "You may have spent an hour in my office, but outside it was only a minute."

Lyvaelan's eyes widened. "How is such a thing possible?"

"Temporal magic. I confess, I am hardly an expert, but it is an essential key to my work here as chancellor. My office slows the passage of time. When I enter that room, I can do a few hours of work, take a nap, and do some reading. Out here, it will seem I spent half an hour in my office. It allows me to meet all my obligations in a timely fashion."

"I understand the *reasons* for it," Lyvaelan said, "but I want to know *how* you did it."

"The 'how' is unfortunately not extremely interesting. Time is a challenging force to control, and it requires certain external factors to balance it. Most commonly, there are specially enchanted crystal glasses and vases that absorb and contain the excess time. The siphoned time needs to be spent or else the containers will crack and many problems could arise."

"What do you do with the extra time?" Hazel asked.

He stared off into a memory. "I use it to keep a single flower alive." He smiled distantly. After a moment, he shook himself from his reverie. "Of course, I have to use bits of the slowed time in other matters as well. Magic must always balance itself, and temporal magic is no different. Slowed time is more challenging to handle, however. My room was filled with fast time and you likely barely noticed it. If my room were filled with slowed time, and you tried walking into it, you would find the experience akin to walking through a wall of mud. The moment your hand touched the surface of slow time, that part of your hand would move slower than the rest of your body, which would give the feeling of resistance. There are exceptions to this, however. Time seeks balance and will expand endlessly until it meets a containment field, similar to the kind we keep in this building. While slowed time is expanding, it is extremely liquid. It is only once it has been contained that it 'hardens up,' so to speak.

"Hopefully, that answers your questions. Now it is time for me to introduce you to the dean of the College of Alchemy."

Lysander opened the door to reveal a large laboratory. Many vials and alembics stood by unlit burners in a variety of configurations. Plants and minerals were organized into small boxes with clear labels. At the far end of the classroom sat a man marking papers with a quill.

"High Master Alchemist Drovir!" Lysander called out. "May we speak with you?"

The man looked up. Long and frazzled white hair stood on end, save for a large bald patch on the left side of his head that was burned away, leaving glowing green scars. His right eye was brown but his left eye, which had been afflicted by the same green scarring, had flecks of glowing orange. As he stood, Hazel realized he was a dwarf, though beardless.

"Chancellor! How good of you to visit, though this is unexpected."

"I hope we aren't interrupting anything."

"Not at all, just grading a few poorly written papers. You're saving me some frustration and possibly a student from getting a worse grade than merited."

Lysander smiled. "Then we have impeccable timing. These good people with me are Watchers of the Evenfall Vigil. They are investigating a series of crimes concerning someone who goes by the name of 'the Alchemist.'"

"I will help if I can. How can I be of service to you people?"

"We believe this alchemist is someone who may have studied here," Lyvaelan said. "According to the reports we've received, he appears to be extremely wealthy. Rich enough to hire dozens of ruffians at a month's wages with the promise of double upon success. He has been using strength-enhancing potions to make some thugs more dangerous. We fought an individual who was not only considerably stronger, but had also doubled in height, and his speed and rate of regeneration were astounding. We know the Alchemist used aufhockers to capture bluecaps, presumably as ingredients for his potions. If you know of any students who were problematic in the past, or who are currently rich because of their practice, we would appreciate your help."

The dwarf crossed his arms. "Hmph. It sounds like your 'alchemist' is actually a mage. Alchemists cannot control creatures like aufhockers. That is the domain of the conjurer or—less commonly—the sorcerer. Your criminal specializes in more than one arcane discipline, making him a mage. Fortunately, that narrows things down."

He opened a cabinet and moved a small ladder into place so he could reach a book. "Alchemists are the least magically gifted of all spellcasters. Some jokingly say if you walk into a crowd and blindly spin and point, the person your finger lands on could be an alchemist. Of course, that oversimplifies matters. Simply because a man can put two numbers together does not make him a mathematician. Alchemists require discipline, memory, and an entrepreneurial spirit. Now, I say it narrows matters down, because many of those who specialize in alchemy do so because they lack the capability to wield stronger magics. The list—while still lengthy—shortens, considering each aspect."

He paused, staring at the book. "Of course—just to be sure—are you certain the Alchemist works alone and not with a conjurer?"

The group looked at each other. "We are uncertain," Alistair said.

The dwarf shrugged. "Very well. I'll compile a list for you to follow up on that includes possible alchemist and conjurer partnerships, and mages with proficiency in alchemy. I'll also put a special contact on there. He is strictly an alchemist, but he's one of the best I've taught. He toyed with the idea of joining the Inquisition but abandoned that thought and opened his own shop. Many alchemists in the field stay in contact and compete for customers. He's avoided much of the competition by focusing primarily on topical agents instead of potions. I'm sure he'd be happy to help. Ha! It would probably fulfill a lifelong dream for him."

"The criminal also uses bluecaps for his experiments," Alistair said. "From what we've experienced, it seems to increase physical attributes. Do you know why he would use bluecaps?"

High Alchemist Drovir scratched his chin. "Hard to say. Ingredients in alchemy are altered by magic, but *when* they are altered, changes their effects. I haven't worked much with bluecaps, though a few years back I used a few bluecap hairs as a catalyst for a project I worked on. The issue is there are so many parts to any creature it would require dissecting it and experimenting to fully understand the alchemical nature of it. For example, chicken feathers reduce the weight of any creature, while raw chicken liver remedies hair loss. *Cooked* chicken liver, in contrast, strengthens teeth and nails, so the state of change the thing is in also matters. Three very different effects from the same animal. Beyond that, experimentation on fae has been outlawed for almost four hundred years, so there are no texts available cataloguing the details of bluecap components beyond what the bluecaps themselves have been willing to share. The Inquisition confiscates such research, which means each experiment is generally done from scratch. Fae ingredients tend to be more chaotic in their uses, which may be attributed to their natural tendency to amplify magical effects. The extreme potency of the fae extends to their alchemical uses. Put differently, those who use fae only do so to create something of world-changing power."

"Thank you for your insight," Alistair said. "When do you think you would have the list ready?"

"I imagine it won't take me longer than an hour. You've given me some decent information so I can start with the most likely students. I can give you a short list with a couple dozen possibilities and if I come up with any others, I will send them to you. Compiling an exhaustive list would likely take days—if not weeks—and as much as I hate grading papers, I still have to do it."

"Of course, and we appreciate all the work you do to assist us."

"If your group does not object," Chancellor Relas said, "I could take you on a brief tour of the facilities while we wait."

"That would be fine with most of us, Ambassador," Lyvaelan said, "but I will need to renew the magic I've placed on Alistair first. If he goes outside again, it will probably wear off."

"Ah, I was wondering about the spell you used. You wrapped him in a cloak of night, correct? Come out into the hallway." They took their leave of the dwarf alchemist, who flipped through a large tome and began writing on a sheet of paper.

Lysander Relas stood in front of Alistair with a smile and dusted the previous magic off of him, dispersing the shadows. "Lyvaelan, you are a gifted spellcaster. No doubt incredibly powerful with magic, despite your limited training. Let me work some enchantments of my own on your friend here." He stepped back a couple of paces and walked counterclockwise around Alistair. Blue light streaked from his fingers, leaving lasting lines in the air. The archmage drew circles and triangles in the air with the light and various glyphs and runes Hazel didn't recognize. After a minute, it was hard to see Alistair inside the circle of blue lines. When the symbols were completed, Lysander withdrew his hands but continued walking while humming a constant tune. The glyphs glowed brightly in response to the sound. The tune shifted to two notes held simultaneously, and the symbols split into double images, with red glyphs separating from the blue. For a moment, the wavering images solidified. The instant that happened, the archmage grinned and spun around in the opposite direction and, with his right hand, threw all the symbols he had drawn into a clockwise spin. The symbols became indistinct as he thrust his open palm into the circle, which erupted with a burst of wind that blew back the hair of all witnessing it.

The archmage stood straight and dusted his hands off. "There. That should do it."

Alistair appeared dumbfounded. "What did you do?"

"I reversed your aversion to sunlight until nightfall. The downside would be you're now weaker during the night, but I timed it so the spell will fade before then."

"How did you learn to do that?" Lyvaelan said, looking Alistair up and down.

Lysander shook his head. "I didn't learn it. I helped create it. During the War of the Night, we had some key vampires we needed to travel great distances with great speed. This was the solution I devised. Of course, I made many mistakes initially, but eventually I mastered the technique. With so few vampires around, I rarely cast it, so this was a treat. Come, Alistair, let's enjoy what little light we have on this overcast day!"

The group walked outside and Alistair—at first with trepidation—stepped out and into the afternoon. He glanced at the archmage, then at his friends, and floated a few feet off the ground. "This is incredible! I feel like it's the middle of the night, not the middle of the day!"

Lysander crossed his arms and looked kindly at the dark elf. "Your idea was good, Lyvaelan. We explored that same possibility you did but found the limitations were too great. It took us months to develop what you devised on your own with no research background. You did incredible work with what you had."

"I'm not upset you used a better spell than me, if that's what you're thinking." Lyvaelan arched an eyebrow and leaned against a pillar. "Archmages are beyond powerful. I know that. The spell you utilized was also more complex than any I've tried to create. I understood pieces, but the finer details were beyond my ability to comprehend."

"Only because you haven't been taught." The archmage smiled at him. "I have an offer. While you are in Coruvaine, why don't you come by occasionally? You could learn more from being here."

Lyvaelan observed the field and scoffed. "Be a student running around playing pointless games? I don't think so."

Lysander chuckled. "No, not as a student at the university. You aren't capable of being a typical spellcaster like these people, and such education would ill suit you. No, I want you to be *my* student."

Lyvaelan scrutinized him. "Your student? Aren't you busy enough without me? Isn't that why you have a temporal disaster waiting to happen in your office?"

"True." Lysander's eyes twinkled with amusement. "I'm not suggesting we talk every day, but I think I could help guide your studies when we both have an hour or two to spend. Honestly, I miss the teaching aspects of being an educator. Serving as chancellor is rewarding in its own way, but I've always found my passion was more in guiding others individually. I'm not asking you to decide immediately. I just want you to think it over. It could help your work."

Hazel smiled at Lyvaelan. "You should do it. Maybe you could teach me a few of the things you learn."

The archmage shifted his focus to Hazel. "Has he been teaching you about magic? You're gifted, then?"

"I suppose. Mostly, I can just feel living things around me and sometimes heal people."

He nodded. "You use thaumaturgy and sorcery, then?"

"No, she doesn't use thaumaturgy," Lyvaelan interrupted. "She doesn't require the use of her hands to heal others. She can also heal herself without conscious effort."

Lysander frowned. "Interesting. Of course, there are those who can use thaumaturgical magic without their hands or needing to be conscious, but they are much more powerful than average." He studied her and muttered to himself, "Alvaria would be very interested in you, I think."

"Who?" Hazel asked.

He shook himself with a smile. "A friend of mine would find you fascinating. That's all."

"I'll do it."

Both the archmage and Hazel turned to Lyvaelan.

The chancellor blinked. "You'll... do it?"

"Yes. It would be foolish to waste the opportunity of receiving instruction from an archmage. Besides, you were the Archmage of War before you were the Archmage of Education, correct? You could teach me about battle magic."

A shadow passed over Lysander's face, and to Hazel, he briefly appeared very old. "Ah, yes, I was once the Archmage of War. That was a long time ago, however." He shook himself and smiled. "I would happily show you some self-defense and immobilization strategies. Anything to keep you alive and chipper."

"Speaking of," Lara said, "do you have any way to make the sky sunny? I have a feeling Al would be giddy with excitement."

"Lara," Alistair said, "you shouldn't ask such things of one who has already done so much for us"—he looked hopefully at Lysander—"unless it's an extremely easy spell to cast..."

The archmage laughed. "No, I'm afraid changing the weather is more difficult than you think. But perhaps I can offer something better. Let us take our tour to the refectory. I'll treat you all to a late lunch."

Chapter Twenty-Six
The Cookbook

The archmage led them into the large refectory behind the administration building. Many round wooden tables stood on cream-colored marble floors. Ringed around them were dozens of businesses selling more foods than Hazel could imagine. Few students were present since their arrival fell between typical meal times.

Lysander smiled as he followed her gaze. "The refectory employs some of the best chefs in the country. All the cooks are former students as well, and so their food has students in mind. Meals are nutritious and delicious, and most have magical effects."

"Do you have any wizard's tea?" Lyvaelan asked.

Lysander frowned. "We do. While I'm typically against it, its use is nearly universal among practicing wizards, so I have allowed it so long as vendors mention it causes premature graying."

"The smells in here are amazing," Lara sniffed and rubbed her hands together. "I hardly know where to begin. What's the best to eat?"

"There are no bad choices. Some of these vendors sell food specifically to satiate for several hours quickly, so if you wanted food to savor and enjoy, I might suggest against going to the closest stalls. If you wanted a genuine work of art you will remember, one of my favorites is undoubtedly Talva's Cookbook."

"Cookbook?" Lara said doubtfully. "Do we have to make anything ourselves?"

"No, no, you just need to order and let Talva do the rest."

They approached a vendor on the far side of the hall. A woman hunched over her station with her chin resting on her palm as she watched them draw near. She looked a few years older than Lara, but a long streak of white hair in the midst of her otherwise black hair made her appear older.

She squinted at them and smirked. "Come to pay me a visit again?"

He smiled. "You know I can't resist your talents, Talva. The last meal captivated me from start to finish. I was a little unsure of how it would end and the middle had moments of blandness, but by the finish I was nearly in tears."

She shrugged. "I'm not the best with the middle stuff. It's the beginning and ending I really try to master. Who're your friends?"

"They're visitors. They want to try your cuisine."

She looked at them. "Alright, what do you all like?"

Excitement played across Lara's face. "I prefer meat, something really juicy I can tear into, but I could really go for—"

"That isn't what I mean," Talva interrupted. "What *genre* would you prefer, and how hungry are you? Would you like a short story or something spanning multiple volumes?"

Lara blinked. "Uh... what?"

Talva sighed and straightened with her smirk growing into a knowing grin. "What kinds of stories do you like? What books do you enjoy?"

"I don't like books; I just want some damn food!" Lara huffed.

"Hmm. Okay. I'll put you down for an action series. What else?"

Lysander stepped up. "I'll take a romance this time with a hint of comedy. Go light on the action. If you can incorporate some warm, genuine moments, that would be wonderful. Oh, and a sixteen-stanza poem—a ballad, if you have any."

"Having an early dinner, are we? Very well. Who's next?"

Alistair approached with an uncertain bow. "Greetings, madam. I'm a vampire, so I don't eat very often, so perhaps something meat-based. I enjoy carefully crafted literary prose the most, particularly in the style of Rathmarou, Cleridis, or Zaphnathius."

"Oh, yeah, I got *just* what you'd like." She wrote on a scrap of paper. "Historical drama with witty repartee. And you?"

Lyvaelan looked the woman up and down. "Do you have any-thing... calming? Perhaps refreshing as well. Nothing too stimulating."

"Sure. A long reflection about the beach on a summer night. How about you, green girl?"

Hazel didn't go to many restaurants, but this was not the way she was accustomed to ordering. "The books I like are usually about girls my age doing fantastic things. Something fun and light. Maybe some witty humor."

Talva glanced up at her and smiled. "A girl who knows what she wants."

"Could we also get a dozen epigrams as appetizers along with some water?" The chancellor asked.

"You got it. The meals will be out in half an hour. I'll bring the epigrams in a minute; I have a batch freshly baked as of an hour ago. Take your seats and I'll bring them out to you."

Lysander put two silver commons on the table. "Thanks, Talva."

"We're always happy for your patronage." She winked and scooped up the coins, disappearing behind her stall and into a kitchen just out of sight.

They sat at a nearby table when Lara burst out, "What was *that?* I thought we were getting food, not buying books! What good will a book do when I'm hungry?"

Shortly after, Talva returned and placed a basket in the center of the table, containing numerous small muffins with a glowing fruit jam in the middle of each. She smirked at Lara. "Enjoy the epigrams," she said, and repaired to her stall.

Each person took one. Hazel put the whole muffin in her mouth. It was sweet with a raspberry filling. She heard words speak not only into her mind but into her lips, tongue, throat, and stomach as they filled her being:

> I do not care for wisdom, not a bit.
> Far better's bits of folly with a savage wit.

Hazel looked around and saw her peers were similarly perplexed. Only Lysander appeared to genuinely enjoy the muffin.

"What *is* this?" Hazel asked.

He smiled. "It's an epigram. A pithy, often clever piece of poetry. I find they work as a nice appetizer before the larger meal."

"This is weird," Lara said, her mouth half full with a second one. "Why would you do this to food?"

"It takes a time to adjust, but I think you'll come to enjoy it."

Lara laughed and then coughed as she choked on the muffin. "Oh man, the lemon ones are my favorite. The one I had said:

> When it comes to lengthy journeys, I must pass,
> For riding donkeys too long is a pain in the ass.

"I think I'm warming up to these. Some are boring, but when they're good, they're great!"

The others in the group shared some of the epigrams they consumed, and before long, their meals arrived. Talva approached first, followed by four assistants whose arms were laden with plates and trays. The servers fanned out around her as she regarded the group with the same confident smile she had when taking their orders.

"For the esteemed Archmage of Education, I have a romantic comedy, prepared in the style of the Knights of Petrim with the gentle wit and humorous moments associated with southern Ethelic litera-ture. I sprinkled in moments of whimsy to give it flavor while focusing on realistic characterizations with a unique blend of personalities to make the dialogue unpredictable—"

"What is going on?" Lara cried in bewilderment.

"—and yet sophisticated," Talva continued, unperturbed. "You will find the entire piece familiar and yet fresh, for such are our ingre-dients. For your beverage, I have your sixteen-stanza poem. This is a heroic ballad, so you may want to cancel your meetings for the rest of the day. I chose the heroic ballad because you will find it pairs well with the romantic comedy you ordered without interrupting it or simply repeating it." Some attendants placed a dish of noodles with aromatic spices and diced pieces of pork in front of the archmage, along with a tall glass of dark amber beer.

Talva moved to Alistair. "For you, I have a meal that is small in quantity but rich in flavor. You may wish to chew slowly to savor each intricate moment rather than rushing through." The plate placed be-fore him was seven small pieces of beef with sauteed mushrooms mixed between.

"For the young woman"—she turned to Lara—"I have four courses." The assistants put down each plate as she spoke. "I recom-mend starting on this one and then going in order. You will find them highly enjoyable and easy to digest. The flavor is basic but appealing, and you will hunger for the next in the series almost immediately. It ends satisfactorily, but you may find yourself hungry for more in a few hours." Each plate held a very similar sizable chunk of meat with a large side of potatoes mashed together with garlic and cheese.

Talva strode to Lyvaelan. "To the dark elf gentleman, I give a po-em. It is also a lighter meal, but I think it will satisfy you for quite some time. It's relaxing and incorporates elements of mint and cilantro, as well as warm nights on the beach with a loved one. The poem is not a love poem, exactly, but contemplates the feeling of being at peace. It evokes feelings of calmness and tranquility, not to make one fall asleep but to help one escape to another world." A small seafood salad with shrimp and tomatoes was placed in front of him.

"For the green girl, I have a mid-sized meal. It contains elements of action and comedy but is primarily fun. It is created with teens in mind and features fantastical adventures that transcend ordinary life. The seasoning is a little heavier, but not overpowering. This helps bring out the colors in the dish and I think you will find the overall feel of the ingredients uplifting." Talva put down a plate of chicken pasta with a thick white sauce in front of Hazel. She stepped back and her assistants fell into line behind her. "With that said, I am Talva, and if you have any additional desires or if you would like to ask questions, call me over." She turned and strode toward her stall, but stopped at a table nearby and sat, taking a book from an adjacent seat and reading it.

Lysander had already begun eating and taking occasional sips from his drink. The others shared a look and ate.

Different from the epigrams, Hazel now gazed over a vast field, following a heroine her age who looked much like herself. She took a bite of the chicken covered in creamy white sauce and flew on the back of a friendly dragon to disrupt the plans of an evil queen who had kidnapped her family. Hazel twisted her fork to gather noodles, while the protagonist made friends, including a bumbling wizard, a farmhand she knew from childhood, and a giant talking wolf. Hazel slurped a noodle and—despite the threat of the queen—the protagonist had fun with her newfound companions. As Hazel enjoyed the creamy garlic of the sauce, the main character had developed romantic feelings for the handsome farmhand who was her age. He had helped and worked with her, and she found his simple kindness and genuineness appealing. With the last piece of chicken on her plate, they stopped the evil queen's plan to rule over the realm with a reign of darkness and an army of terrible monsters. Each bite refreshed the story, with details increased in color, complexity, and volume, depending how quickly Hazel consumed her meal. The protagonist defeated the evil queen in a fun and unexpected way, only to discover she was the rightful ruler of the land and that the queen had wiped the memory of all the people until she had been conquered. Hazel scooped the remaining noodles and chewed. With the girl's new kingdom and a reciprocated romance, the story came to a close as Hazel finished her last bite.

Hazel sighed, setting her fork on the empty plate. "That was *so good.*"

"I know what you mean," Lyvaelan said with his eyes closed as he swayed in his seat.

"This is the most delightful human meal I've had the pleasure of eating," Alistair said with uncontained joy.

"Mhmm urg, ummff," Lara said. She was halfway through her third plate and wasted no time in devouring it. She gave a triumphant fist in the air with one hand while shoving another handful of food into her mouth with the other.

Lysander laughed. "I thought you might enjoy it. Really, it is a unique experience. Talva is the only enchantress I know of who uses this method of cooking. The food is wholesome on its own, but the stories they tell are what really makes it a complete meal."

"Pardon me, Mistress Talva?" Alistair called, looking toward her. She put down her book and sauntered over.

"How can I help you?" she asked with a knowing smile.

"How did you do this? What is this?"

"This is my invention. I call it literary cuisine, but I may change the name if I think of something better. I used enchantment to give your food a little extra depth, you could say."

"But... how? My sword is enchanted to remain sharp and not break. How can enchantment be used that way? I thought enchantment required extensive time, energy, and magic."

"You're mostly right. About seventy percent right, I would say." She sat with the group. "You're just missing the answer to a more important question: what *makes* enchanting difficult? Your sword there likely has an enchantment that will last years if it doesn't last indefinitely. Same with magic rings, clothing, and so on. Enchantments can be temporary, however, or fade with time. Why would I enchant bread to permanently taste wonderful if it's practically inedible after a week? Your food was enchanted with stories that would only last for about an hour before degrading. If you saved some of the food on your plate for several hours from now, it might still taste good, but there would be no story, though whispers of it might still reach you."

"Is it hard to enchant food like that?"

She shrugged. "I wouldn't say it's 'hard,' exactly, more like it requires a certain finesse. I'm sure for anyone who has never tried it this would seem impossible, but I've been doing this for about nine years and I experimented with it for almost twenty years before that, so it's more or less second nature to me. I tried to do the same with alchemy, but it was all one big mess. Enchanting was much easier."

"Did you master enchantment and alchemy?"

"Yep. Mastered both. I knew I wanted to work in the culinary field, but I needed to make money, too. Alchemists do alright, but enchanters make a vast amount pretty quickly. I figured I could use alchemy for food and enchantment to finance my inevitable failures."

Alistair smiled. "Your 'inevitable failure' looks like success to me."

"That's just because you didn't see the failures, sweetheart." She pinched Alistair's cheek. "I had to fail a thousand times to succeed just once. When I finally succeeded, I knew I finally had it. The problem with alchemy is it just brings out the innate properties in ingredients. It's hard to create a story when all the ingredients already tell their own stories. Enchantment is the opposite of alchemy; rather than evoking the innate traits of each thing, enchantment alters what a thing is on a fundamental level without regard for its original purpose. I could enchant this table to fly, walk, or sing a song—if I felt so inclined—but regardless, it would tell the story I want it to tell rather than simply being what it is. This turned out to be a good career move because there are culinary alchemists out in the world who are absolutely cutthroat in the business, and they waste no time proving how much better they are than the competition. It would have been like being a small child with a wooden sword showing up to a joust with fully armed knights—a recipe for disaster, you could say. This way I can still use alchemy a little to help with the beneficial effects of the food while the enchantment makes the experience nothing if not"—she spread her arms dramatically—"enchanting."

"What do you have for dessert?" Lara asked, licking the last of the meal from her fingers.

"I rarely like creating desserts, so my options are limited, but I have some morals which I can send out. They are uniquely enchanted, and I think you'll find them delightful." She turned back to the stall. "Hey! Bruce! Bring out a couple rounds of morals!"

Within a minute, a server brought them a dozen small chocolate disks.

"These are chocolates infused with mint and tempered by sugar. They clear your senses and cleanse your palate. Enjoy."

Hazel took one and found the taste simultaneously comforting and refreshing. In her head she felt the words: *with friends, anything is possible.*

Lara ate three before looking back at Talva. "Hey, I got three different morals, but they all fit with the story."

"Perhaps it's because the morals are vague enough to fit?" Alistair suggested. "Although mine was almost impossibly appropriate."

"That would be the enchantment. Or at least one of them. Rather than have them stand on their own, to complete the full dining experience, the desserts you just consumed picked up on whatever story you previously ate and extracted an important lesson based on the information and the residual magic from the meal. As she discovered, there can be more than one moral to any story. In fact, I've tested this on my workers who were kind enough to eat a couple dozen each after eating the same story. Interestingly, none came away with the same lesson. There were a couple that were close, but because it draws from the consumer's experience in addition to the story, it means each person receives a tailored culinary experience that cannot be replicated."

Lara sat back in awe. "You're a genius."

Talva smirked. "I wouldn't deny it."

They sat and chatted with Talva for a few more minutes when the Archmage of Education reminded them of their work at the university. After offering profuse compliments and promises of future patronage, they left the dining hall to return to High Alchemist Drovir. A light drizzle of rain had begun to fall, but an invisible halo surrounded the group, keeping them dry as they walked back to the alchemy building. They ascended the stairs and returned to the classroom, where Drovir was busy writing on a piece of paper.

"Ah! You're back. Good, good, good, I'm almost done here." He scribbled a few more notes before rising. "Here are the names you've requested as well as their places of work, as far as I know. My records are mostly up-to-date, but a few I am uncertain of. Not all of my students keep regular contact with me, I'm afraid. I'm sure the city's registry will be more complete regarding all that information, however."

Hazel took the short stack of papers. Each page had a dozen names with addresses and areas of interest. "How many did you put in here?"

"There are a little over a hundred names."

"A hundred names?" Lara exclaimed. "Are there that many alchemists in this city?"

"More, actually, but your information narrowed it down. They aren't all distinct businesses. It's common for a group of students who get along to go into practice together. In fact, some of the most successful alchemy businesses in Coruvaine have upwards of five alchemists, and each often has some interns as well. Alchemy is such a popular subject that for a single moderately skilled alchemist, it's challenging to start a new business without prestige or a gimmick to catch the public's eye. Besides, most alchemists will cover any range of basic ailments, but there are some that require special knowledge. Not any one person can know everything. If you get three decent alchemists, one who specializes in animal products, another in roots, and another in minerals, then those three can collaborate to create the most effective potions for clients and pool their knowledge to treat ailments they might individually be unable to help. I tried arranging names of individuals to reflect groups they may be in wherever possible; however, these collectives change their makeup frequently once they're working in the field. Some decide after a few years to enter private practice, while others join another group that better aligns with their vision or is simply closer to their place of residence."

Alistair took the pages and flipped through but stopped at a specific name. "Who is Paxton Averly?"

"He's the one I mentioned before. The contact I would recommend you speak with. He is an excellent alchemist, and he visits from time to time. Occasionally, he acts as a consultant for the city guards, producing topical agents for healing various injuries. He can be a little odd, but he's just shy. I think his timidity and his inability to see anything bleed made his dreams of becoming an assistant to either the Sapphire Guard or the Inquisition unrealistic. He is friendly, though, and I cannot say that about all the people on that list. Alchemists work very hard and can be singularly focused, which can lead them to appear less than amicable.

"The alchemists on here all exhibited *some* abilities with conjuration. A few pursued mastery in conjuration and alchemy, but the vast majority simply expressed interest or showed some minor aptitude. The two skills together are not especially helpful in any way that would make money, unless one summoned creatures to experiment on alchemically, but such a thing would be highly irregular and not sustainable for the average alchemist."

"Why not?" Hazel asked.

"Because alchemists work so hard to stay afloat that expending the magic to summon creatures and maintain concentration on them would be exhausting. Especially if one were to do terrible things to them directly. Conjuration requires a certain level of charisma and rapport with the thing being summoned. Hurting something you summoned would cause it to struggle against its bonds, and it would be extremely difficult to maintain.

"Naturally, summoning a creature to kidnap *other* creatures would be much easier, but it still presents challenges. Most alchemists need to spend their time evoking properties and mixing materials for quick client turnarounds. The high number of alchemists raises expectations among the populace, you see. Also, I'm not entirely certain all these alchemists are still in Coruvaine. Our records are imperfect when it comes to tracking alumni."

"Thank you very much, High Master Alchemist," Alistair said with a small bow. "We appreciate your help in this matter, and the information you have given us is invaluable."

"Yeah, you've been a real help, but one more question." Lara leaned in close to him. "How do we know *you* aren't the Alchemist?"

His eyebrows shot up and he burst out laughing. "You are a funny one. What better assurance can I give you than my position? I'm the dean of the College of Alchemy. I'm in academia; I'm interested in research, not money. If I wanted to be rich, I certainly wouldn't be sitting around grading papers and teaching classes. I'm much too busy for any illicit activities, and I'm around people too much for that to even be possible. But thank you for your... consideration." He wiped away a mirthful tear. "Now I really must get back to those papers I was working on. I hope you find your criminal." He waved goodbye and returned to his desk, still shaking his head and chuckling.

Alistair slapped Lara's arm. "What were you thinking?"

She shrugged. "I figured I'd at least ask. Now we know, right?"

Lysander smiled. "I wouldn't worry about your friend's line of questioning. Drovir is not one to get offended, and the linear thinking of his students gets tiresome. I'm sure your random accusation was more amusing than anything. Though, I might recommend a more subtle approach with the alchemists outside the university. They may take your claims more seriously than you realize."

Chapter Twenty-Seven
Tea and Alchemy

Saving Salves Alchemy was located southeast of the palace, and on the opposite side of the city from the library. Rain had poured all day, but the group was determined to make the wet journey to the workplace of Paxton Averly. Each donned a thick wool cloak which both kept away the rain and obscured their identities.

They decided against visiting Paxton Averly the day after they met with the Archmage of Education on Alistair and Lara's recommendation. Alistair had observed increased foot traffic around the library, and Lara noticed familiar scents being left in the area. When they tracked different individuals, they discovered their paths intersected in the Temple District, which contained various churches, chapels, and temples for all the religious cults. Beyond this observation, they heard rumors the High Priestess of Semeleme had recently delivered impassioned sermons in the Veiled Chapel to an increasing number of congregants. The priests—known as the Undertakers—had recently procured many shovels. While this was hardly unusual given their line of work, it still did nothing to set Hazel or her friends at ease.

When they found no signs of dangerous people near the library, they went as a group to speak with their contact on the sixteenth of

Melantria, two days after speaking with Lysander Relas at the university. Although Hazel sensed the reluctance of the group at having her come to speak to the alchemist, she refused to let fear guide her actions. She remembered what Thomas Eller said about living her life while she had it, and it resonated with her. She believed her friends could take care of her.

After an hour of walking and navigating the streets, they found the small shop they were looking for. It was a single level brick building surrounded by a small garden with various flowers and herbs. Ivy climbed the side and crept along the frame of the sign, which was written in gold painted calligraphy. Three steps led up to the building, giving a slight sense of privacy despite several paned windows along the exterior. A wooden overhang provided a small respite from the downpour when they knocked on the door.

"Come in!" A man's voice called from inside.

Lyvaelan moved his fingers subtly and his gray skin shifted to pale peach while his red eyes turned green. With his disguise complete, they opened the door to a brightly lit room. An iron stove stood in the corner, providing warmth, while several lanterns cast warm light from each of the main beams. Several long tables surrounded by shelves stood to their left, covered and arranged neatly with various wooden and glass boxes and vials with prices and information written on paper around them. To their right, behind a long counter, sat a smiling man with short sand colored hair.

"May I help you?" His smile was genuine and warm, and the glasses he wore amplified the earnestness in his eyes. His expression changed to subdued shock when they doffed their hoods.

"Yes," Hazel said, "we are looking for Paxton Averly. Are you him?"

"I am indeed. What can I do to assist you?" His voice was gentle without being quiet. His eyes flicked between them rapidly.

"We're members of the Evenfall Vigil," she said. "We need to ask you some questions."

"Oh," he said, rising to his feet, his voice taking a note of alarm, "is... everything alright? What is this about?"

Alistair held up a placating hand. "We were advised to come here by High Master Alchemist Drovir. He said you might be able to help us."

Paxton put a hand to his heart and sighed with relief. "Thank Selevara. I thought maybe I misfiled my tax paperwork. You aren't the usual soldiers who visit me. In fact, you're quite *un*usual. But where are my manners? Let me put on some tea. You can hang your cloaks on the rack by the door."

Alistair smiled. "That really isn't necessary—"

"Oh no, I insist. I have a nice herbal blend I've alchemically altered to help calm the nerves and increase awareness and critical thinking. It helps me when I'm feeling lost with a client. Please, take some seats at the table and I'll clear a few things away."

He put the kettle on the stove as the others gathered stools to the place he indicated. He was smaller in stature, close to Hazel's height, with a mildness that put her at ease. His meekness did not appear to stem from a lack of confidence, so much as his natural temperament. When he put the kettle on, he sat at the head of the table with a smile.

"I'm afraid I'm at a slight disadvantage. You know my name, but I do not know yours."

Alistair opened his mouth, but Lara spoke first. "I'm Lara. The pale guy is Alistair, the half-elf is Lyvaelan, and the green girl is Hazel. We wanted to ask you a few questions about your business, but more specifically, about some of your associates. Do you work alone?"

He blinked several times, processing the information. "I—ah, it's a pleasure to meet you all. I'm glad to help however I can. I work alone; I don't have any assistants."

"Seems like a lot for one person to handle by himself," Lara said, studying the room.

He smiled and shrugged. "Oh, it gets busy from time to time, but I have a loyal base of customers and I don't need to compete for additional clients, since my specialty is rarely covered and not the most lu-crative on its own."

"What is your specialty?"

He pushed his glasses further onto his nose with barely contained excitement. "Topical alchemical agents. Salves, balms, unguents, poul-tices, that sort of thing. I've also been considering making cleaning products, but I'm busy enough at the moment that it's unnecessary and unwise to experiment."

"'Topical alchemical agents' doesn't sound like much of a special-ty to me," Lara replied.

"It didn't to me either when I first graduated from the university. I saw how amazing many of the alchemists were and realized I couldn't possibly compete directly. Instead, I looked for what nobody was of-fering except for special order. Lotions were not in high demand until I advertised them because no one was aware alchemists made such things. Whenever a person thinks of alchemy, one's mind leaps to po-tions and glass bottles of bubbling liquid. What many did not realize was the value of treating the skin rather than oral consumption."

"I'm curious myself," Alistair said. "Why would someone prefer to apply something to the skin rather than drink it?"

"It varies by individual." As the teakettle whistled, he removed it from the stove but continued talking as he poured the boiling water into a blue teapot with a white rose on it. "For some, they simply pre-fer the tactile sensation of applying my products. For others, they dislike the taste of potions. There are ways of masking taste, but mostly medicine is doomed to taste like medicine. This is especially true for children. If a child is injured and has a nasty gash, then it might be hard to get the child to stop crying long enough to drink a healing accelerant laced with a calming agent. Unfortunately, most children won't like the strange mix of garlic, chamomile, lemon, salt, and deer feces, even if non-alchemical berries are added to enhance the flavor. Taking those same ingredients and turning them into a topical analgesic the child can see working while relieving the pain can be much more effective.

Not everything can be turned into a salve, of course, but most can, and I've been actively looking at alternative ingredients to produce the same effects when applied topically. It requires more time than using a potion, but not so much that it's a bother." He placed five blue porcelain teacups with white roses that matched the teapot before the group. "Would anyone care for some tea?"

"Yes, thank you," Lyvaelan said. "If what you're saying is true, why don't more people prefer your products to others?"

He poured tea and passed cups as he spoke. "That is a complicated question, but I think it partly has to do with speed of effect. The biggest disadvantage to using a salve is its effects take the longest to work unless applied to specific areas of the body. I won't bore you with details, but topical application is slower than oral, and oral is slower than intravenous. The case of the injured boy works the most to my benefit because the wound is visible and the blood can readily absorb it. If it were an injury beneath the skin—such as a broken bone—then taking a potion would be faster."

"We heard you wanted to join the Inquisition when you were younger. Why?" Lara asked, blowing on her hot cup of tea.

He folded his fingers. "Well, Miss Lara, I suspect I wanted to join the Inquisition for the same reason many of you wanted to join the Evenfall Vigil. I wished to join because I desired to be part of something bigger than myself. I wished to make a difference beyond satisfying my own needs. I believe I have a good sense of justice, and it seemed to me like they were seeking justice."

"Why didn't you?" Hazel asked.

"Simple: I abhor violence. I am of a faint constitution and cannot handle seeing blood. The situations inquisitors get into can be perilous. Besides, inquisitors are gifted spellcasters with a variety of useful abilities. I have no great gift for wizardry, enchantment, or conjuration. My own magical capacity is embarrassingly small. Because of my inability to fight others and my lack of magical aptitude, I'm afraid I had to put that dream behind me. I still value the inquisitors and the

Sapphire Guard, but I'm a little too timid to be effective." He smiled at them. "Of course, I'm happy to collaborate with law enforcement whenever possible. What is it you need help with?"

"We are currently working on a case to find a criminal who has been selling illegal potions to people within the city," Alistair said. "The only information we have is this individual is known as the Alchemist. We believe the Alchemist also has some skill with conjuration and has greater monetary resources than most. We were referred to you because your business has little to gain or lose since you appear to have control of the market with salves. In essence, we want to know if you suspect anyone within your field of possible malfeasance. We recognize you likely do not possess enough evidence for us to arrest anyone, but we would appreciate guidance, as the number of alchemists on our list is rather extensive."

He looked at each of them. "Of course. I would be happy to help. Do you have a physical list or anything I can look through?"

Lyvaelan handed over the notes. Paxton scanned the document, shaking his head with a sigh. "It hurts to think any of them could be the one you seek. I had classes with many of them, while others I have gotten to know professionally. I suppose it's impossible to know anyone completely." He looked up at them. "Do you mind if I write a few notes on this?"

"Please do," Lyvaelan said, sipping his tea.

As he pored over the names, Hazel enjoyed the tea he poured. It was a light chamomile and mint tea and—true to what he said—she felt simultaneously more alert and more relaxed than before. It was strange to experience both sensations in conjunction. She listened peacefully to the sound of rain hitting the roof, the scribbling of the alchemist's pen on paper, and the wind whistling by the workshop. Lara, too, relaxed noticeably while the changes were less pronounced in Lyvaelan or Alistair.

Paxton examined the document and circled names while adding notes to others. Sometimes, he corrected information that was wrong or outdated. After a few minutes of muttering to himself and going through the pages, he leaned back and sighed.

"I think that's a good start. It's hard for me to truly narrow your list since I consider all of them my colleagues, and it pains me to imagine any of them committing crimes. With that noted, I have tried to give some character details that might be relevant. Your 'Alchemist' might be multiple individuals working together to a common goal, but I do not think it is necessary to give undue attention to groups. The five businesses I would start with are Peregrine Potions, Telemica's Alchemy Shop, Essentialists Alchemy, Jorgen's Potions, and the Elixir Emporium. Peregrine Potions, Essentialists Alchemy, and the Elixir Emporium are all groups focused on specific attributes that have made them especially successful. Peregrine Potions is actually a conjurer and an alchemist duo who collaborate and have an excellent delivery service. They emphasize speed and convenience and wouldn't be my first guess as a danger, but given the skills of the conjurer and the alchemist, I cannot ignore the possibility. Essentialists Alchemy is a group of five master alchemists who already had successful businesses but united to create the highest quality potions for practically any client request. They are the most expensive alchemists in the city, and at least a couple have magical gifts beyond alchemy. They would have considerable funds and ambition. I do not know if they would jeopardize everything they've built for that ambition, but people can be unpredictable. The Elixir Emporium is an enclosed outdoor market made up of eleven alchemists who sell their wares individually in part, but also pool resources. It is very popular for its pre-made cures and low prices, as well as the fun environment they create. I suggest them because—with how many alchemists practice in their business—it is entirely possible that more than one might have talents in a field other than alchemy.

"As for the two individuals, Susan Telemica of Telemica's Potions is a somewhat rough individual. I do not know about money, but she has always been a little paranoid about others stealing secrets from her. She also has an affinity for conjuration. Richard Jorgen of Jorgen's Potions has been competing with her directly for some time. Telemica and Jorgen have some history, but mostly as bitter rivals. He is extremely ambitious and could make potions illegally to boost his income to take her out of business. At one of the alchemist meetings we hold annually, the two got into a fight that resulted in him walking away with a bloody nose while she had a bruised cheek. It was awful, really. I doubt either would stop at anything to defeat the other, personally." He glanced at each of them nervously. "Oh, and please don't tell them I said that. I may not like the fighting between them, but I don't want to get in between them either."

Lara smiled. "Don't worry, your secret is safe with us. I think we're done with our questions. Could you give us a brief tour of your shop?"

"Certainly!" he stood. "I would be happy to."

He showed them around the shopping area where they had been talking, and then back to his workshop. The workshop was a small room with every inch of counter space covered with complex equipment Hazel was unfamiliar with. Burners stood beneath alembics of various sizes, and an array of pipettes lined the wall. Mortars and pestles of various materials and sizes stood to the side. Opposite this work area were cabinets reaching the ceiling, which he informed the group were filled with his most common ingredients. Against the far wall, only ten feet into the room, was a large shelf filled with neatly arranged books. The room was more cramped than Hazel would have thought, though she hadn't entered with any specific expectations. He then showed them a small door on the far side of the shop that led to his home, which was modest and simplistic. Paxton was orderly, and his home reflected his calm and open demeanor. Considering the reputation spellcasters had for extravagance and strange interests, Paxton was relatable.

They thanked him and excused themselves when they noticed a break in the rain. He waved them off at the door to his shop with a smile, inviting them to return any time. They weaved through the streets, avoiding puddles. They were cheery after their meeting, and the crisp, clean air with the light smell of petrichor invigorated them. Lyvaelan mentioned his first lesson with the archmage the following day more than once. While he appeared as calm as ever, Hazel knew he was excited. She was happy for him. Still, something bothered her despite the effects of the tea. The night before, she dreamed of fire and awoke in a cold sweat. It was not the same dream as before. This new dream felt imminent. It was hard to take it seriously when the weather was cold, but she still could not forget that horrible burning dream.

When they returned to the library, they found a large group of people gathered outside. Many were older bearded men holding shovels, while others were women carrying buckets or torches that crackled in the rain. There were almost a hundred of them arranged on the steps and all bore the same sour expression. Lyvaelan casually moved in front of Hazel, as did Lara. Alistair removed his hood and approached with a smile.

"Greetings, friends. May I help you?"

A tall man with a gray beard and muscular arms walked up, with the others in his group moving behind him. "We have no quarrel with any of you. We just want the girl."

Alistair frowned. "The girl? What do you mean?"

The man's steely expression didn't change. "The girl who returned from the dead. She doesn't belong to you."

"She doesn't belong to anyone," Lara spat back.

He looked at her sternly. "You're wrong. She belongs to our mother." He turned back to Alistair. "This is government overreach. It is well-known the Cult of Semeleme buries bodies once and for all. When she was exhumed, it was a terrible offense, but to allow her to exist and hide her existence from us and then to protect her is an act of flagrant sacrilege. I know who you are. You work as guards for the king. That's the only reason we're showing restraint. Give the creature to us and we leave peacefully."

"And if we don't?" Lara growled.

He looked at her placidly. There was no fear in his eyes. His was the gaze of a true worshipper of the goddess of death; peaceful and accepting, yet fueled by a fiery zeal that couldn't be extinguished.

Hazel shivered. It was cold, but it was their gaze that froze her blood. The night darkened.

Alistair smiled and put a hand on his shoulder. His eyes flashed dark for a moment. "Listen, my friend, you don't want to do this. I know you think the priestess wants you here, but she doesn't. If she did, she would join you. We should talk about this more, but not like this. Tell your friends to move aside and go home. It's cold and wet out here, and you want to get somewhere warm. This can wait until another day. Go home now or some of you will probably be arrested. I'm just trying to help you out, friend."

The man blinked several times and shook his head. "Yeah... you're right. It is cold out. I guess I let my love for the goddess cloud my better judgment. We can leave and talk about this later." He turned to his followers. "Hey! We need to return home. Let's do this another time."

The crowd whispered in confusion. "You heard me! Make room for them," he barked. The mob made a passage to the doors of the library begrudgingly. He smiled apologetically. "Sorry they're moving so slow."

"That's alright. Thanks, friend." He turned to those behind him. "I suggest we take advantage of this while we can."

Lara whistled. "Sometimes you come in handy, vampire."

He grinned at her. "Yes, but only sometimes."

As they slipped through the narrow hallway of people, Lara glared at each. Lyvaelan strode ahead as the group became single file to pass through the crowd. The cultists fumed, but made no move against them.

Hazel glanced at each of these faces as she passed. All were cloaked against the rain, but their animosity was undisguised. As she walked, she felt like a sheep paraded through a row of hungry lions. Each step took impossibly long as she crept between the rows of seething zealots. Despite her friends' confidence, a constricting dread clutched at her heart.

She trusted the strength of her friends to protect her.

But not now.

Once they reached the steps to the library, several things happened simultaneously. Two cultists on each side split as women on both sides emptied buckets they carried onto Hazel. Three more buckets were splashed onto the doors of the library. A voice from the group cried out, "Destroy the undead!"

Hazel could hardly understand what was happening as she spat out the liquid, but then she remembered her dream and recognized the smell and taste of what she was now drenched in.

Oil.

A roar erupted from the crowd as a cultist behind her threw his torch at her and she burst into flame. She saw nothing except the tongues of orange and yellow surrounding her, and she ran from them as they bit and tore into her. Searing pain devoured her, and she could do nothing but run as she tore off her cloak. Another cultist splashed her as she passed. Momentary relief surged through her when the flames sputtered, but horror replaced relief when the flames spread. More oil. As she fled from the heat, she could think of nothing but the screams she heard, the pain she felt, and the fire engulfing her vision. Those screams came from her. A force impacted against her face and she dropped to the ground, still surrounded by flames. As darkness took her vision, she was grateful to be sinking into that deep place, away from the burning pain that surrounded her. Perhaps it was better to die.

Chapter Twenty-Eight
Through Flames

The cultist loomed over the burning, unconscious girl. Lyvaelan watched—stunned—as the man raised his shovel, ready to dig into her neck and end Hazel's life. A rush of air swept by and the shovel stopped its descent. Alistair stood with both hands gripping the man's wrists. The shovel dropped as the vampire pried the cultist's hands away. The man screamed as both hands crumpled as Alistair crushed his wrists and ripped through the skin. He released his grip and lifted the man by his throat. Alistair brought him to his face, and the vampire bared his teeth and hissed as his canines grew into fangs. Alistair dropped him and, in the same instant, punched him in the middle of his chest with a *crack* that sent him hurtling backward. He turned to the cultists, his jaw dislocating as all his teeth grew and his face turned ever paler. His bloodcurdling shriek split the air and everything recoiled from the monster who lost all pretense of civility. The vampire stalked between them with almost imperceptible alacrity, shattering each shovel and emptying each bucket onto the ground. The torches sparked puddles of flame as the cultists scattered from the hellscape of the vampire's onslaught. Rain fell and fire raged. Alistair pursued them, knocking several to the ground and breaking limbs to prevent escape.

The sophisticated vampire who was willing to parley had gone; only the relentless monster remained. He released another shriek into the night, scattering water droplets as though they too feared the wrath of the bloody prince.

Half of Lara's body was covered in oil but she had removed and smothered most of the flames by flipping her cloak inside out while leaping toward the wet dirt adjacent to the library. Covering the garment with the mud, she ran to the library and hastily rubbed it over the fire to keep the building from burning further. She turned to Lyvaelan and yelled: "Help her!"

Lyvaelan had leaped clear from the cultists by pure reflex. He saw the library in flames and between the shouting and the running blur of fire; it was difficult to quickly piece together the situation. Lara's command shook him, and he instantly realized what happened and cursed his delayed reaction. He dashed toward Hazel and shouted at Alistair, "Move out of the way!" Lyvaelan raised both hands as white tendrils of fog rolled between them. He twisted his hands as he ran and released a swirling mass of white frost. The water of the street where it passed instantly froze, and the fire extinguished. When it reached Hazel, it gently burst into fog, leaving the burned girl covered in a thin sheet of ice.

Alistair ran and picked her up. "Did you need to freeze her?"

Lyvaelan panted. "I did what I could. It wasn't enough to hurt her, but it should help her wounds. Quickly! We have to get into the library!"

The vampire and the dark elf sprinted to the doors just as Lara had finished putting out the fire. She glanced at Hazel, then at Alistair. "Give her to me."

"Now isn't the time—"

"Give her to me," Lara urged. "You're the fastest. You need to get the rest of the Evenfall Vigil here to arrest those bastards. Go."

Alistair was about to protest but instead released a chilling hiss and handed Hazel to her. Lara had barely taken her when the vampire disappeared in a blur.

Lara burst into the library. "Inquisitor! We need your help! Inquisitor!" There was no reply.

Lyvaelan's heart pounded, and he struggled to keep himself in check. He needed to remain calm. For Hazel. For everyone. The temptation to use his power gnawed at him.

"I don't think he's here. We have to get upstairs."

"Just like a damn inquisitor not to be there when you want one."

They ascended the stairs and gingerly laid her on the kitchen table. She was unconscious still.

"Charlie!" Lyvaelan said.

The redcap appeared with a smile, which melted into horror upon seeing Hazel. Lyvaelan tried to meet his eyes. "Charlie, I need you to get me as many wet towels as you can. Hurry!"

Charlie hyperventilated as his expression shifted from horror to fury. His hair stood on end and he bared his needle-sharp teeth. The whites of his eyes became a murky, blood red. He crouched on all fours and drew his sharp talons across the floor, pulling up wood shavings. "Who—did—thissss?"

"There's no time!" Lyvaelan snapped. "If you don't get what I asked, she might die! I'm angry too, but right now she needs help, not vengeance!"

Charlie hissed and shook his head before disappearing. When he reappeared moments later, he carried a bucket of water with several folded towels. Lyvaelan wasted no time in applying a damp washcloth to Hazel as he removed pieces of her burned clothing. The thick wool cloak had all but turned to ash with his touch. He realized quickly the inadequacy of his abilities. Some of her clothes seemed to meld with her skin, making separation difficult without hurting her.

"Can't you do something?" Lara pleaded. "Can't you heal her?"

Yes, Lyvaelan, heal her. You only need to wish for it, came the dark voice of temptation in his head.

He tried to calm himself as he raised a hand to his brow. "I already told you I can't. I wish I could, but I can't."

He avoided the seductive thoughts by focusing on her. He dabbed at her wounds. "Something is wrong. She isn't healing like before."

"What do you mean?"

"Before she was struck three times by arrows, any of them should've killed her but didn't. Instead, she healed in less than a minute. Her wounds now are still open and burned. Why?"

"Maybe the cultists did something to the oil? Does fire hurt undead?"

"Yes." Lyvaelan clenched his fists. "Fire is one of the most reliable ways to destroy the undead. I assumed she was different. I was careless."

"Hey." Lara put her hand on his shoulder. "We're not to blame. The assholes throwing buckets of oil on girls are responsible. We're trying to help her. We're not the enemy."

"You're right. I'm—" he stopped and studied Hazel's face. "Lara, she's healing!"

"What?" She followed his gaze. "She looks the same."

"No, I know, but she *is* healing. She's just regenerating much more slowly. Actually"—he looked at his hands and then at Hazel—"I think it's the water."

"The water?"

"Yes, the"—he tried to lift Hazel but strained until Lara took her from him—"thanks. Bring her, I have an idea." He strode toward his room, with Lara following. "The places I dabbed water are healing the fastest. I don't know why, but I need to test this hypothesis."

"'Hypothesis'? We're talking about Hazel, not an experiment."

"I know," he whispered, "but this is all I can think of that might help."

A dark shadow emerged from behind Lara.

"Took long enough, you stupid dog!" Lara yelled, continuing forward.

Garo looked at Hazel, his mouth agape. "Hazel." He gasped, disappearing immediately.

"Great, some help he was."

"He's going to get help," Lyvaelan said, opening his door.

"How do you know?" Lara moved past him.

"It's the only thing he can do in this situation that's mildly useful. Charlie! Let anyone know who comes that we're in my bathroom!"

They hurried into Lyvaelan's room, and through to a large built-in bath of stone. Lara laid Hazel in gently. Lyvaelan closed his eyes and moved his hands in a swirl. Water drops flew from their clothes and air around them and spilled into the tub. Lara shouted for Charlie to bring more water. No sooner did the buckets arrive than the water flowed from them and onto Hazel. When most of her body was submerged, Lyvaelan stopped and breathed.

"Now what?" Lara asked, wringing her hands.

"We pray to Hemericanth I'm right."

They sat for a tense several minutes. Lara rose and paced the room while Lyvaelan sat cross-legged in front of the tub, reaching out with his consciousness to Hazel, trying to connect. He noticed occasional pulses of activity in her mind. He smiled slightly. Was this the joy she told him about? No, it was relief; relief she wasn't dead. Relief she still lived. He opened his eyes to examine her and caught his breath.

Lara ran over and released a shuddering sigh. Hazel's wounds, once so grievous, had mostly closed. They could see the water rise and fall with her breath. She was alive. She was going to be fine.

They heard many footsteps approaching as Alistair, followed by Garo and Thomas Eller, entered. Alistair—usually so put together—was a wreck. His hair was in disarray, and no part of him seemed aligned. To any other vampire, this would be impossible to tolerate, but Alistair appeared to have forgotten such petty concerns.

"Hazel, is she—"

Lara nearly tackled him with a hug. "He's going to be fine, Al. Lyvaelan saved her." Alistair stood stunned and then returned it.

"I *helped* her; she means," Lyvaelan said, not taking his eyes from Hazel.

Garo sighed and dropped to the floor.

"I'm sure you did well, Lyvaelan," Thomas said with a smile. "You need to give yourself more credit."

Lyvaelan felt Hazel's mind flickering rapidly. She was returning to awareness. "It's not modesty, it's a fact. I could only guess at what would help. Lara carried her, Charlie brought water and towels, and Alistair prevented her head from being removed with a shovel."

"What?" Garo roared. The black dog gathered shadows into him as he grew, his fur spiking out, his eyes a seething green that wafted smoke. "The cultists of Semeleme go too far! I shall rip out their hearts for this and send them to the goddess they so ardently serve!"

Lyvaelan frowned, sensing her consciousness. She was coming back, but something was different. Something strange was going on. Her mind was erratic, stressed, overwhelmed by...

"Garo, please," Thomas said, "we don't need to—"

Lyvaelan fell back and a loud splash came from the bath as Hazel rose without warning, levitated above the tub, surrounded by swirling green light. Her body floated upright and her arms spread. The green light covered her like a gown. Her eyes opened, but there was only the same green light. Her voice rang throughout the room and pierced each of them with its power.

"*The living lich of half a day shall rise with legions of undead that none can kill. Through betrayal of friends and oath, the living lich shall trample bodies and hearts. The world will quake as the impossible becomes the inevitable. The living lich of half a day may only be stopped by the slow progress of time.*" Her eyes burned into each person with a green, spectral glow. "*The day of the lich draws nigh.*" The light disappeared and her eyes closed as she collapsed into Lyvaelan's arms, who was waiting for her.

The room fell silent. Thomas Eller sat down, stunned, and Garo returned to his previous form. Moments felt like hours, as no one dared break the stillness. Finally, Thomas searched their faces with accusing eyes.

"Did you know?" Thomas asked.

"Yes," Lyvaelan whispered, gazing at the sleeping girl in his arms. "I've known for some time."

"Me too," Lara said.

"And me," Alistair said.

"And what about you, Ambassador? Did you harbor this lich-in-the-making under my nose with full knowledge?"

"Thomas, I know what this looks like and I know how it sounds, but—"

"Answer the question!" Thomas snapped. He stood and stared at the grim. "I, Thomas Eller, of the Inquisition of the Archmages by the authority of Archmage Alvaria Saccarra, the Grand Inquisitor, command you to answer! Did. You. Know."

Garo sighed. "No. I didn't."

"Even the leader is blind. Pathetic." He turned his attention to the others. "You idiots. You lunatics. Do you know what dangers you bring on yourselves? On the city? I should arrest you for this."

"Do what you want," Lyvaelan said quietly, "but you can't have Hazel."

"What was that?" The inquisitor's voice took on a dangerous edge.

"He said you can't have her!" Lara shouted. Fur had grown on her and her voice distorted.

"I agree. Take me in with them, but you will not touch one hair on her head without deeply regretting it," Alistair said, putting a hand on his sword. His eyes were icy.

Thomas shook his head in disbelief. "You're all insane. I can't believe you."

"Believe it," Garo growled, "because they mean every word."

"Even you? What spell has this girl cast over you? A friendly face can hide dark intentions."

"But not Hazel," Lyvaelan said. He continued to gaze at her face, now healed of burns and tranquil despite the water droplets and fragments of ash. "You heard the prophecy. The living lich may be someone else." He looked at the mage. "I refuse to believe she is responsible for anything she just predicted."

"What more proof do you need?" Thomas's voice broke. "She brings people back from the brink of death, she was brought back to life in a matter of weeks, and her powers grow far more swiftly than any I have ever seen. You know this, Lyvaelan. She regenerates like it was nothing and she can heal others. Why don't you see the danger?"

"Why don't you see Hazel?" Lara challenged. "Look at this girl! Have you ever, *ever* sensed even a grain of malice in her? Has she ever left you feeling anything other than happy? Has she?"

Thomas locked eyes with Lara for several long moments before looking away. "No, no, I haven't." He slumped to the bed, his voice hoarse. "But there are protocols I must follow. Even if Hazel is a wonderful person, this is no small thing. I need to report this."

"No, you don't." Alistair stepped forward. His eyes flashed. "We will stop the lich no matter what. It isn't Hazel, but if it is, we will be the first ones there to stop her. Until then, we will protect her. Don't report this."

Thomas shook his head. "Protect her? Like tonight?"

"We will do better." Alistair averted his eyes and clenched a bloody fist. Lyvaelan sensed shame in him.

"We shall have other members of the Evenfall Vigil monitor the outside," Garo said. "We *will* protect her. We will continue to investigate and find ways to ensure her safety."

"I... I must be crazy, too." Thomas rose to his feet. "I won't report this. Yet. You have done outstanding work in the city and Hazel... is a wonderful young woman. It's clear to me she has many loyal friends, too. But whatever you do, you must keep her from speaking that prophecy again to another person. The more people who know of it, the more dangerous it becomes. If the cult hears it... I shudder to think of what they'll do."

"Thank you, Thomas," Garo said.

"Please, no one thank me." He staggered to the door. "I feel sick. This contradicts all orders and half of my conscience. I just hope you're able to end this Alchemist business and justify my actions. I need sleep. Say nothing else."

He plodded out of the room, and each foot fell heavily upon the floor. The group sat in silence as the footsteps grew distant.

"I suppose that counts as a win," Lara said softly, "but it doesn't feel like it."

"It was, Lara," Garo said, "and possibly one of the most important victories of your career. If you hadn't stopped him together, then I think he would have taken her away and I doubt any of us would have ever seen her again."

"Where would they have taken her?" Alistair asked, leaning tiredly against the wall.

"Probably they would have taken her to Selevarian to be processed. If not there, then they would place her in Arcanathema Prison. In time, she would be dismantled safely and the magic in her would be unraveled."

"Dismantled?" Lara asked.

"Killed," Lyvaelan clarified bitterly.

Lara looked at Garo. "Is that true?"

"Well... in a way. I don't know everything the Inquisition does, but dismantling creations can take the form of destruction or storage. There are some powerful sorcerers within their order, so I suspect they may attempt to split her consciousness from her form or find other ways to reduce her power. They could also incarcerate her in Arcanathema Prison until she is 'healed.' If they were unable to kill her, heal her, or they discovered the underlying process to be less worthy of study than believed, then they could simply destroy her." He looked up. "Of course, I will work to guarantee that never happens, and Aldric shall likewise do his best to protect her."

Lyvaelan felt her weight in his arms and a much greater heaviness in his heart. "Can we really fight the Inquisition? Can Aldric resist them?"

"He will try. At present, we must hope the work you have all done will warrant a case against the Grand Inquisitor, should she come here. We must do what we can and pray, because that is all we can do. Pray to Hemericanth, the Lord of Life, perhaps. With one who has so much life within her, it seems right to ask that he not let her be taken from us."

"I think her wounds are mostly healed," Lyvaelan said, his voice showing signs of strain. "I do not think there will be much benefit to keeping her immersed in water. She needs to be changed out of these rags as well. Lara, can you take her? She's a little heavy for me."

Lara took her. "That's a rude thing to say."

"Physical strength was never my specialty. She's the lightest of us, but that doesn't account for my lack of developed arm muscles. Besides, she would likely prefer you to switch her into undamaged clothes rather than anyone else."

She nodded. "Well, at least *that's* true. Couldn't you use magic to get stronger?"

"Yes, but using magic like that is an unnecessary risk, especially with the stresses of the last hour. Would you feel comfortable drawing a straight line with a knife to your throat?"

"Is that what using magic is like?"

"It always has been for me."

"You should all rest," Garo said. "You are exhausted mentally and physically. I will speak with Commander Comrear when I leave to make sure everything is in order. After that, I will guard this library so you can all relax."

"Like a guard dog?"

He grinned at Lara. "That's what a grim is. We are guardians. Now rest. Sleep easier knowing that—at least for tonight—Hazel Enda is safe."

Garo melted into the shadows, which expanded into a dark pool before settling when he vanished. Alistair left to speak with Charlie and let him know everything was going to be fine. The vampire prince looked haggard, and his fangs were still out, which illustrated his fury had not yet subsided in full. Lara left to change Hazel into clothes that were not blackened by fire and did not smell of the oil they had been drenched in. Hazel, despite the ordeal and her prophetic outburst, seemed peaceful. It was almost comforting. Almost.

Lyvaelan stood and shut his door. He stumbled to the far corner of his room and rolled up his left sleeve. Along the light gray of his arm and down his fingers, fissures formed a spiderweb in his skin, pulsing with a dark energy as black as the void. His heart quickened at the sight of it. It appeared to spread with each breath. He slowed his breathing, focusing on the pleasant thought of talking to Hazel. She was going to be fine. Worry was unnecessary. He breathed through the anxiety, searching for a calming memory. He remembered her jumping into a puddle when she thought no one was watching. A smile touched his lips. Hazel's thoughts—so poorly guarded they could practically be seen—came to mind. How single-minded she had been that she could not destroy him should he lose control. How sure she was she could help him. He opened his eyes and the fissures had disappeared without a trace. He sighed and flopped onto his bed.

I guess we won't have to see today if she could save me without killing me, he thought. His gaze softened. *Then again, I suppose she already did, even if she didn't know it.*

Chapter Twenty-Nine
Monstrous Necessity

Alistair sank deeper into the darkness. They had saved Hazel, though she showed no signs of waking and almost a full day had passed. They prevented the inquisitor from taking her. Why he agreed was beyond Alistair. They had apprehended the majority of the cultists, though many still had escaped. To some, this might be a victory. He gazed at his hand and sighed, leaning back against the slanted top of the library. Despite the wetness of the gray-tiled roof, he slumped against it, painfully aware of the water increasingly soaking through his clothes with every moment.

"Painfully aware," he whispered to no one, "that's me."

Through the scattered drops of light rain, he heard voices in the distance to the north. He recoiled from them, only to be swept into a conversation on the eastern side of Coruvaine. Each escape ran him into a new distraction. The water had penetrated his cape and now worked its way into his shirt and pants. Thirty-seven miniscule droplets fell on him from the stormy sky, equaling a quarter of a teaspoon of water. It had taken him four and a half seconds from the time Hazel ignited to react. The man's screams stopped seventeen seconds after Alistair ripped his hands off. The color of his blood hinted that the man had not consumed enough meat in his diet and risked anemia if nothing changed. The number of buckets of oil dumped on Hazel equaled—

He jolted forward and buried his fingers in his hair. His vision swam, and he gritted his teeth. Tepid blood trickled down his brow as his elongated fingernails dug into his scalp. No peace. No silence. Only painful awareness. He considered flying away, drifting high into the sky to escape the endless noise, but it did no good. Above the city were the clouds, and above them were the stars. Countless stars he felt compelled to enumerate. There was no escape by flight, for he could never leave the single cause of fruitless pain: himself. These trifles could not hurt him alone. Conversations on the other side of Coruvaine meant nothing to him. The water—which now reached his skin and trickled slowly down his back—could not hurt him. He could be soaking wet in icy cold weather and would only be aware of its temperature, not discomforted or harmed by it. Not directly, at least.

Three drops of his blood fell to the roof. Four. Another two in rapid succession.

He withdrew his hands and stared at his long and sharpened nails. These were less hands and more claws. These were not the hands of a gentleman, but of a—

The door to the library opened far below. He heard sniffing and knew immediately who it was. A series of loud scrambling noises later and Lara landed on the roof eighty-seven feet away from him. She stood upright and strode awkwardly across to him, stumbling and slipping occasionally. She wore her typical tatters. Based on the lack of shivers or goosebumps on her skin, Alistair supposed the rain did little to change her body temperature. Unlike him, he sensed the warmth in her. Like a human. Like most creatures.

"Enjoying the beauty of the city?"

He could not even muster a fake smile and stared ahead. "If you say so. How did you find me?"

"I just followed the smell of soap and regret, and it led me right to you." She sniffed again and peered at him. "Are you bleeding?"

His eyes drifted back to his clawed, bloody hand, and a sudden energy surged through him with an irresistible violence. Shaking, he fought to contain it, gritting his teeth as his fangs extended and every hair stood on end.

"It's okay, Al," Lara whispered. "Scream."

A primal cry escaped from his soul as an inhuman screech pierced the darkness. Rain seemed to stop and tremble in the air, and the sounds of the city drowned beneath the scream of the vampire. After almost a minute, he stopped, his lungs bereft of air. The energy now smoldered in him like a bright ember. He took no breath and relaxed forward on the roof, maintaining balance through unconscious flight. Three minutes passed before he finally took a breath. He turned toward Lara without looking at her.

"Thanks."

"Sure."

He waited for her to say more, but she said nothing. His cry—which in humans and other creatures elicited a deep terror—did not affect her, it seemed. "I'm... sorry."

"Don't apologize, Princeling, this is the most I've liked you in a while. Don't spoil it by making it out as a bad thing."

"And I suppose the fact I killed someone yesterday helped me rise in your esteem?" His voice had more bitterness to it than he wished.

"No," she said softly, "but the fact you did it to save Hazel did."

Alistair gazed at his hands. The blood still on them reminded him of the blood he had spilled with them earlier.

"I've scrubbed at them," he whispered. "I spent the entire day washing, and cleaning, and using every kind of implement I have to get clean, but it's still there. The blood. I smell it and remember every detail. Even when I plug my nose or use perfumes, the blood is still there. It never leaves."

Lara put her hand on his shoulder. "You did what you had to. I know you didn't like it, but—"

"No," he interrupted, staring at her with wide eyes, "you're wrong. I enjoyed it too much. After I took off his hands..." He trembled and his voice dropped lower. "... I wanted to rip out his throat with my teeth."

Lara swallowed but held his gaze and did not move her hand from his shoulder. "It's okay."

"No, no, it's not. How can you say that? I'm supposed to set an example for my people and others. Last night I hurt so many humans and others will hear of it and come to hate my kind. I've failed."

"Would you have rather had Hazel die decapitated in that blaze?"

"I would have rather kept a level head and used my speed to stop him without hurting anyone. I could've run Hazel to thaumaturgists, or run her to the Luthain River, or—"

"Stop!" Lara exclaimed. "You'll go crazy thinking of all the ways you could've done things differently. It doesn't matter what we could've done; what matters is what we chose to do. Your emotions took over, but why? Why did your feelings lead you away from your important goal of being a pretty face for vampires? Because you cared even more about her. Maybe your execution wasn't perfect, but your reasons were. Nothing else matters."

"I don't regret saving her. I never would. Above all else, by Umbravelle, I wish I could've run with her the moment we saw the cultists so she would never get hurt. I just... I didn't want to be a monster."

"You mean you didn't want to be what you are," Lara said. She withdrew her hand and sat beside him, staring off across the city. "I understand, I really do. The War of the Night ended, and neither of us was part of it, and yet... we are. We can pass through them invisibly, but if they *really* knew what we were, they'd be terrified. There's a reason I haven't assumed either of my wolf forms in Coruvaine yet. I hate to admit it, but I don't want anyone to look at me differently. It's not that I'm afraid of their opinions, I'm just tired of it. We show our human sides because humans accept them." She snorted a humorless laugh. "You know why I don't shake hands? Hairy palms. The hairs are short and almost invisible, yet somehow humans know hairy palms mean someone's a werewolf. It's the dumbest thing, but I momentarily panic when someone offers a hand." She drew her knees up to her chin and hugged her legs. "We're monsters, Al. Why bother denying it?"

"I want to deny it. I want to be a hero, as trite as that sounds. Before, you mentioned that all people are hunters or hunted, correct? Well, what if all people are actually monsters or heroes? I think most see themselves as heroes but may be monsters to others. I want to be a hero in their eyes." He wiped the blood from his brow with a handkerchief and contemplated it. "That's hard to do when you're born a monster. Even a noble one. I showed the world something dangerous."

"True, but not so terrible. Unhinging your jaw was freaky, but still relatively harmless."

He gave her a wry look. "Thanks. Your support is unparalleled." He leaned back with both hands on the tile. "You sought me out for a reason, and although I appreciate your kindness, I don't think it was your intended goal."

"You're right, it wasn't." She stopped and pursed her lips. "When I said that we're monsters, I meant *all* of us. Including Lyvaelan." She met his eyes. "Did you see him? I mean, really get a good look?"

Alistair's expression softened. "Pupil dilation fifty percent more than usual indoors. Three black fissures on his left hand and five on his right."

Silence filled the space between them as they stared into the darkness. Neither wanted to speak, and a heaviness hung in the air.

"It's never been about the killing," Lara whispered, her small voice surprising Alistair with its meekness. "It's about saving Hazel. It's about saving everybody else."

He looked at her and saw genuine concern in her that bordered on fear. Her eyes searched him for something, maybe a sense of purpose or trust. No, it was more than that. She searched because she didn't wish to be alone.

He noticed his nails had receded but still held blood beneath them. "He doesn't deserve to die, but neither do they. Why should I deal harshly with him when I've lost control and been treated kindly?"

"You and me can afford to lose a little control. At most, four to six people might die before we get ourselves in check and they're mostly going to be people who have it coming. With him in this city, it'll be a thousand times that number. We would struggle to kill that many in a night if they lined up for it. We're dangerous, but not like him."

Alistair's gaze unfocused, and his posture relaxed. His fangs had receded, but his awareness of them lingered. "I'm a monster. I always will be. In the face of imminent destruction, I will act as necessity dictates. If I must do something monstrous to save others, then I will."

She nodded. No levity reached her face or voice as she said, "We're doing the right thing, Al. We're doing what no one else can."

"And Hazel?"

Lara bit her lip. "I would rather she hated me than for her to die."

"Agreed," Alistair replied in a hollow voice, "but I'd prefer neither."

"Same."

Thunder rumbled in the distance. A wind sprinkled cold droplets over them and then subsided. There was little comfort in their promise and no joy. On that cold and rainy night, they sat close on the roof of the library, wishing to be heroes but needing to be monsters.

Chapter Thirty
To Wait and Dream of Tomorrow

Alvaria Saccarra sat overlooking the lush gardens of Chateau Zariel-le, swirling a glass of white wine. A cool breeze blown from the west ushered in the salty humidity of the sea several miles away. The temperate sunlight belied the season. She leaned back in her chair, letting the sun fall over her face. She didn't always enjoy such warm winters.

This weather allowed her to wear a simple dress without a petti-coat. The sea-green gown she wore blended the lighter fabrics of Selevarian with the elegant style of Chastielle in the far northeast. The dress accented her modest curves without revealing too much. A high neckline flowed down into long, gossamer sleeves that terminated at her wrists. It was only at her hips that the gown gradually loosened into a shimmering ocean of satin, with waves curling and breaking at her feet. Minute threads of orichalcum were woven throughout, occasion-ally adding to the reflectivity of her attire. It was a dress for summer weather, and yet it was as far from summer as possible.

In childhood, winters struck with ice and gale. Far north and east, a few dozen miles from the imperial capital of Tellaris, was where she grew up. Her conscientious father stored enough firewood to survive the winter, but even so, it was difficult. She recalled being so cold she would imagine jumping into the fire and still not being warm enough. Her father sometimes sat behind her before the fire and held her shivering little body wrapped in a blanket and told her stories. Some nights, she fell asleep like that, wrapped in the warmth and safety of his arms.

It never snowed here, in Selevarian. The difficulties of living in frigid weather never touched the people here. For the rest of her days, she would never need to experience a cold winter or the draftiness of a small cottage. She would never need anyone to warm her against the chill of the snow.

She listened to the whisper of living leaves and the rustle of those that fell across the courtyard. There would be no leaves back home. Funny how she thought of that cottage as home after nearly a century away. It wasn't about the cottage, though. It was where her father was buried. He had transformed their house into a home. She sold their cottage after he died without needing—or wanting—to see it again. It was no more her home than the dead man she buried was her father. The Saccarra cottage was devoid of life. Its soul had left it. She wouldn't survive another winter in that cottage, not when its source of warmth had disappeared.

She gestured for a waiting servant to pour more wine. Alvaria watched the passing clouds and wondered how she lasted as long as she did in the Inquisition. There were many challenges, but necromancy brought personal feelings to the surface for her. She had witnessed necromancers bring children back as mindless zombies, just to maintain the fading embers of a family. Those overcome by grief and determined to change the past made such horrifying mistakes that the solution was either to search more desperately for answers or delude themselves into thinking the zombie was truly the beloved. Each alternative was heartbreaking in its own way. Some sought increasingly violent means of bringing people back, gradually dissolving their morals by incremental concessions. The Inquisition was not merciful by nature—and neither was she—but those cases hurt more than she admitted.

Perhaps bringing the dead back intact was simply beyond the abilities and resources of most spellcasters. If there was a way to accomplish it safely, it would have been done.

Or had it been done already?

Hazel Enda presented such a conundrum. An undead creature with intelligence to match a draugr but no sign of decay was unheard of. Miraculous, even. Revenants deteriorated mentally and physically within a matter of weeks, but this girl showed no signs of it months after her return.

Alvaria twirled the stem of the wineglass between her fingers. How did Hickory Allkirk do it? *Did* he do it? It seemed implausible, but if he stumbled across some secret method that had been lost to time, the Inquisition needed to know. Arresting him alone was out of the question, however. The fruits of his labor needed to be taken for testing as well.

She sighed and turned to the servant. "Fetch the chamberlain for me."

The servant bowed and retreated into the chateau. A minute later, Arlith arrived.

"My lady requested my presence?"

"Indeed, she did. Join me."

He bowed and took a chair across from her. He waited expectantly.

"The business in Coruvaine troubles me, as it often does these days. I would welcome your perspective."

"I would be happy to give it," he replied. "What troubles you?"

"All of it." She looked across the garden with a sour expression. "I think the greatest difficulty is the gamble of waiting. Waiting for the perfect opportunity. The first to the table gets her choice of the food."

"That may be so, but she's also the first to discover if it's poisoned."

"A fair point." She watched several pixies in the garden flitting through the trees and dancing on the grass. "Back when I attended university, I knew a student who had fallen in love with a young woman but didn't wish to make advances at the wrong time. Rather, he believed there would be a 'right' time and kept careful watch. Weeks passed. *Months* passed, and the right time had not yet presented itself. One day, in a particularly boring lecture on pre-imperial history, another young man leaned over to her and asked if she would join him for dinner. She said yes, and they began to court. The first young man was devastated and kicked himself for not acting sooner."

"I've heard similar stories. Would things have turned out differently if he openly asked?"

"Yes." She pondered her wineglass. "But not the way he would've imagined. I asked her later what she thought of the hesitant student and she laughed. She had no interest in him and the perfect situation would have done nothing to change that."

"Did you tell him?"

"No. What would be the point? No matter which path he took, there were none that would have resulted in her choosing him." She rose and walked to the railing. "Sometimes, careful planning will yield identical results to immediate action. Often what matters is the person executing the plan may not be the best suited for it."

"Lady Alvaria." Arlith joined her. "You *are* the right person for the task. You're the *only* person for the task."

"Even I can be wrong."

"True, but if you're wrong, then no one has a chance of being right. I know you do not enjoy waiting, but the advice of Archmage Varaldan was sound. Let the Coruvainians play with powers they don't understand. In the end, it will benefit us more than it will hurt them."

"And if compassion gets the better of me, what then? What if delaying is only my excuse to keep her with her family?"

"Then you will benefit from your compassion, regardless. Lady

Alvaria, you are attempting to save the world from ruin and the Inquisition will follow where you lead. I cannot make the decisions for you; I can only obey them. What are your commands, Grand Inquisitor?"

She took a deep breath and exhaled. "We will wait. Coruvaine will keep Hazel Enda as long as it can. For now, we shall watch and see what Inquisitor Eller discovers."

He bowed. "It shall be as my lady orders."

She gazed past the garden and toward the city of Selevarian in the distance. Much work needed to be done here. There was no reason to rush out to a faraway nation out of fear. She would not wait, she would prepare. Time would hurry past before she knew it, but she would be ready.

Chapter Thirty-One
From Ashes

Hazel awoke to the feeling of warmth against her cheek. She opened her eyes to see the midmorning sun peeking out from behind the third wall just beyond her bedroom window. Blinking in the bright light, she stretched a little to find herself aching all over. She rolled away from the sun and noticed Lyvaelan sitting in a chair beside her bed. She blinked, trying to remember what had happened the night before. It felt like she had slept for ages.

"Lyvaelan?" she whispered. Her voice was hoarse from disuse. "How long was I asleep for?"

He watched her with open, honest eyes. Concern and relief played across his face. He handed her a glass of water from her nightstand and leaned back into his chair with a sigh. "You have been asleep for the last four days."

"Four days?" She almost choked on her water. "What happened? I can't remember."

"The Cult of Semeleme happened." His countenance darkened. "They doused you in oil and set you on fire. You have been uncon-scious ever since." He hesitated. "At least, *mostly*."

"'Mostly'?" She sat up.

"Your dreams have gotten stronger, haven't they?"

Hazel nodded slowly.

"Well, your visions of the living lich of half a day were too strong for you to contain as you were. You spoke the words out loud and… the inquisitor heard it all."

A chill ran down her spine. "Is he going to take me away?"

"No, or at least I don't think he will. Not yet. He was irate that we kept such a secret from him, but he agreed not to report it. For now."

"What about my parents? Do they know?"

He folded his hands in his lap. "Commander Comrear spoke with them and mentioned you were injured but recovering. He spared any specific details but noted you were resilient." Lyvaelan half smiled. "Which is an understatement. Regardless, they were worried. He instructed them to stay home for now and posted Evenfall Vigil guards for their protection."

"Do you think anything will happen to them?"

"No, I don't. Even without the guards, I doubt they'd be in danger. They were after you and believe you're some soulless monster. It is unlikely they'd attack your parents, since they had nothing to do with creating you as you are now. They probably view your parents as delusional with sorrow over the loss of their only child and are willing to even accept an illusion if it alleviates the pain. If they want anything, they will simply attack the library."

Hazel fell back against her pillow and stared at the ceiling. "Maybe I should just let High Priestess Caeli use her power on me."

"What?" Lyvaelan snapped, bolting upright.

She sighed. "Maybe I should let her touch me. I've been causing people trouble. If her coming into contact with me would change that—"

"Hazel!" Lyvaelan interrupted sharply. "Do you *want* to die?"

"No, but—"

"Then *live*," Lyvaelan said, leaning closer. "There are no excuses, explanations, or justifications. If you want to live, no one should take that away from you, no matter how difficult, inconvenient, or annoying your existence may be to others."

"Thanks," she said sarcastically.

He kneeled before her bed and locked eyes with her. He lightly gripped her shoulders, though she sensed his urgency. "I'm serious. You hurt no one by living. These cultists are misguided extremists, nothing more. Even if the world lashed out against you, you would still deserve the right to live. The mage who brought you back may be responsible for what he did, but even he cannot give the right to live and die. Hemericanth alone can give life, just as Semeleme alone may take it. It is said you cannot live without the will of Hemericanth and you cannot die unless it is the will of Semeleme. The cultists may not see it yet, but you live because the goddess does not want you as much as the god does. Don't give up. We need you. Your parents, Lara, Alistair, Garo, Charlie"—He looked away—"me. We all need you. The afterlife can wait. Be with us now, for as long as you can. Please."

Hazel smiled and put a hand over one of his that still touched her shoulder. His hands and expression relaxed. He withdrew his hands, but Hazel held one for a moment. "Thank you, Lyvaelan. Really. I promise I won't give up on you if you don't give up on me."

A small but earnest smile crept onto his face. "Deal." He cocked his head, listening. "The other two are on their way. They must have heard your voice. I hope you're ready."

"After being set on fire, I think I can handle my friends being excited to see me."

His smile widened a little. "You say that now..." He moved to the foot of her bed, bringing his chair with him.

"Hazel!" The door of her room burst open, revealing Lara and Alistair.

"Is it alright if we come—" Alistair began but didn't finish. Lara grabbed and threw him through the doorway before diving onto Hazel's bed.

"Hazel! We were so worried! I'm so glad that you're safe." She threw her arms around the girl in a constricting embrace. "Promise me you won't die again. Promise."

"I—can't—breathe—"

"Lara! How do you expect her to make any promises to live when you're squeezing her to death?" Alistair said, rising to his feet and adjusting his shirt.

"Sorry, Haze," Lara said, separating from her. "I'm just really glad you're doing better. We were worried about you. Alistair spent all day yesterday counting the grains of wheat we have in our pantry. *Twice.*"

Hazel looked at him. "Really?"

He crossed his arms and averted his eyes. "That's an exaggeration. I did not count all the grains of wheat twice—"

Lara raised an eyebrow. "How many grains are there, Al?"

"Seventy-nine thousand, five hundred and twenty-one grains." He scratched his eyebrow absently. "I only counted them once."

Hazel giggled lightly. "That's incredible."

Alistair smiled at her. "Truthfully, I *was* anxious. I couldn't do anything to help you."

"The vampire prince is lying or else very forgetful," Lara said. "He stopped a cultist from decapitating you with a shovel."

"Really?" Her eyes widened.

"Well, I mean he would have tried, but it's probably hard to accomplish with a conventional shovel so someone could have stopped him before he got *all* the way through..." Hazel observed a slight reticence in the vampire.

"This is morbid. Even for me," Lyvaelan grumbled.

Lara laughed but turned serious again. "Besides that, Alistair was the first to protect you and react to the cultists. He ran and got help after we beat them. He may have felt helpless after, but his quick response might have really changed the outcome for the better."

Alistair shook his head. "Lara only speaks of what I did, but the other two did far more. Lyvaelan doused the flames that burned you and developed a way to heal you by putting you in a bath."

Hazel gave Lyvaelan a quizzical look. "You bathed me?"

Lyvaelan rolled his eyes. "Yes, we put you into a cold bath, along with all your burned clothes, when we thought you were dying. Don't make it sound weird. Lara was the one who carried you in from outside and helped me with the bath the entire time."

"Yeah, that's true," Lara said. "We actually worked like a team. All it took was one of us nearly burning to death."

The group fell into silence. A giant weight had been lifted from her companions. The bags under their eyes offset their genuine smiles. Seeing the care on their faces and hearing how each had contributed to saving her, something welled up inside her. It was akin to joy, but deeper. She took a deep, shuddering breath as a tear rolled down her cheek.

Gratitude.

"Hazel, are you alright?" Lara asked, concern wrinkling her face.

Hazel sniffed, wiped her eyes, and smiled. "I'm fine. I'm just happy to be with my friends. Thank you. All of you."

Alistair kneeled next to her bed and met her eyes. "You're welcome, Hazel. If our positions had been switched, you would have done the same for us. We're Watchers of the Evenfall Vigil; we work together and for each other."

"Even if you wouldn't have done the same for me," Lara said, "I would have done all I could to help you, regardless. I care about you, Haze. I don't care about many people, so you're staying safe for as long as I can help it—no matter what."

Lyvaelan gazed at Hazel. There was a softness in his eyes. Whether it was a recent memory or by some sorcery, she could not say, but she heard Lyvaelan's words echo in her mind: *the afterlife can wait. Be with us now, for as long as you can.*

"I'm lucky to have you. You're all wonderful. I know I can trust you with saving me again, should the time come." Her brow furrowed. "And that time might be soon."

"What do you mean?" Lyvaelan asked, his smile disappearing.

"I had another dream."

Silence.

Lara cleared her throat. "Was it the same one?"

"Yes—and no. I always have that dream when I sleep, though the details are clearer each time. The dream I had was much closer. I saw myself opening a door and saw rows of cages holding bluecaps. When I turned, I saw a person bite off the head of a bluecap and smear the blood over its arms. I couldn't make out the details of the person, but I saw the smile grow wider until it became the face of an aufhocker."

Lara whistled. "Hazel, you have the craziest dreams. In most of my dreams, I'm just chasing things. Why can't you have normal dreams, like showing up to classes naked, or giving a speech you haven't prepared for on a subject you know nothing about?"

She let out a breath. "Honestly, those dreams sound great compared to these. The more I hide my dreams, the more powerful they get and the harder it is for me to think of anything else."

"Understandable though that is, we need to take your dreams as they are: warnings," Lyvaelan mused. "They might seem inconvenient, but this latest dream tells me there are more aufhockers in the future as well as the Alchemist. It is challenging to fully understand the specifics of your vision, but hopefully, time will make it clear. Have you been transcribing your dreams?"

"Yes, I have." Hazel reached to her nightstand to pick up the empty book Aldric had given her. "I've written every dream I've had, as well as thoughts on exercises and other things. It's helped make them clearer."

Lyvaelan's eyes grew resolute. "Good. Keep writing them down and perhaps we can spring the trap on the Alchemist before the Alchemist can get to us."

"I find that unlikely," Alistair said.

"Why is that?" Lyvaelan turned to him.

"Well, apart from counting grain in the kitchen"—he glared at Lara—"I also did some reconnaissance. "

Hazel sat up fully, with a few minor groans as she struggled through the stiffness. "How did you know where to look?"

"Honestly? I didn't. That's why I didn't look. I *listened*." He pointed to his ears. "Vampires hear better than almost any other creature but sorting through the mess of sounds is challenging. I trained myself to selectively listen for certain words and then attend to them."

"How?"

"It's like when one is at a party with many conversations going on simultaneously. Amid one conversation, you hear your name spoken and turn to find the speaker. The speaker was not trying to get your attention, nor was the speaker saying your name any louder than any other word in the conversation. You recognized it and attended to it. That is the easiest example, but some individuals also train their ear to recognize interesting topics. The topics are so ingrained in that person's identity that mentioning it is enough to bring their full attention. My power is similar. I just needed to be interested in hearing 'the Alchemist' and then I can focus on that conversation."

"What did you hear?" Lyvaelan said.

"Unfortunately, very little pertaining to the Alchemist, or at least to *our* Alchemist. A few conversations about chores, or discussions of favorite alchemists, a couple of children wanting to be them in the future, and so on. No mention of the criminal, nor of the aufhockers."

"Too bad," Lara said, sitting up next to Hazel. "It was a good idea, though."

"But it isn't *entirely* a loss," Alistair rose and paced the room. "Actually, in the three nights I listened, there was no chatter about the Alchemist. Not even *idle* talk. Do you know what that means?"

"That people have stopped caring?" Lara guessed.

"It means the Alchemist is not doing business currently, nor is the Alchemist planning on doing business soon."

"So?"

"*So,* the Alchemist is lying low. Do you remember the original reason Aldric wanted us to join the Evenfall Vigil? It was because there was some alchemist in the city giving enhancers to citizens. The Alchemist has been active for at least a year, if not longer. Crime reports I've read show sporadic activity but most occur weekly, with multiple separate incidences occurring on some nights. The more recent the reports, the more frequent the incidents, until the last several days. The Alchemist hasn't lost the interest of others; the Alchemist is willfully *deciding* to stop normal business."

Lyvaelan's eyes widened in comprehension. "The Alchemist knows we're close."

"Exactly!" Alistair slammed his fist into his hand. "We are so close that continuing operations could jeopardize his safety. There are two different ways he could know we are close. What's one way?"

Lara rubbed her chin. "If we met him?"

"Yes, and the other?"

The group was silent as Lyvaelan frowned thoughtfully. His eyes opened wide. "If he was spying on us."

"Yes! All other options are some combination or type of those two. The first option on its own is the least likely. If the Alchemist knew us, then he would have met us before the attack at the bar. We have had limited contact with mages outside of those involved directly in our work. What we *do* know is several aufhockers escaped into the city and remained unfound. They would recognize us on sight and could hide easily in shadows and stalk us in the night. Given our role in law enforcement, it would not take much to have one wait until we made a report before tracking us. There was likely an aufhocker watching us as we fought against those ruffians some weeks ago. In fact, I believe there was an aufhocker watching as we went to Paxton Averly's house. At that point, the Alchemist likely understood we were close since we were consulting an associate who knew about the alchemists of the city, especially those with talents or friends in conjuration."

Lara's eyes widened, and her fists balled. "We're so close!"

"We are!" Alistair exclaimed with a grin. "We are getting closer every day."

"But..." Lyvaelan said, idly twisting his black hair, "how do we make sure the trail doesn't get swept away? How can we be certain the Alchemist won't cover everything up and disappear?"

"I've thought about that too," Alistair said. "I think the answer lies within the problem: the Alchemist is cautious. Very cautious. One could even say the Alchemist borders on paranoid. To leave the city now would be incriminating and unusual for any alchemist, since they don't need to travel for work. In addition, the Alchemist will want to return to his or her initial research and moneymaking, which means restarting business as quickly as possible. When will it be safe to restart?"

Lara frowned. "When no one is looking?"

"Precisely. When will the Alchemist know we've given up searching?"

Lara perked up. "When his spies tell him!"

"Yes! We are likely being spied on regularly. All we have to do is follow the aufhockers without them noticing. They should lead us directly back to the criminal in question."

"Alistair, that was amazing," Hazel said in awe. "How did you come to realize all that?"

He shrugged. "Counting grain is repetitive, but it helped clear my head for some good ideas. You might think about trying it sometime."

"I'm gonna pass on that one, thanks," Lara said dryly. "But nice detective work. I'm going to go see if your theory holds any weight." She jumped off the bed and sauntered to the door.

"Where are you going?" Hazel asked.

"I'm going to sniff around the library and the surrounding alleys and rooftops. If an aufhocker has been watching us, I should catch the scent. Since today is a clear winter day, they should be hidden far away to avoid the sunlight. While they're gone, I can find their hiding places. It hasn't rained the last two nights, so I should catch any traces. If they notice my scent, it probably won't matter, since we're expected to be around this area."

Lyvaelan looked at her and stood, walking between her and Hazel. "Let us know if you find anything useful. There are some logical leaps in Alistair's thinking, but if you can confirm the aufhocker presence, then at least we'll have a start."

"Will do, Lyvie. Make sure Hazel's doing alright."

"I feel fine—" Hazel struggled to rise from her bed, only for Lyvaelan to push her back down.

"No. You just woke up. I can tell you still hurt. Sleep another few hours and you will be much improved. I will inform Charlie of your progress. If you rush to get up now, then you will risk feeling worse for longer. Trust me. If you need any help falling asleep, I can assist with that as well."

She sighed. "No, I'm fine. I could sleep a little longer, though I feel kind of useless."

"The only one doing anything this instant is Lara. We will be much more helpful tonight and hopefully better rested. After all"— Lyvaelan looked at Alistair—"vampires need sleep too, don't they?"

"Yes, I suppose so."

Hazel just noticed Alistair had been wavering slightly in place and avoided the sunlight on her bed.

"Sleep, vampire," Lyvaelan said. "We may need you to track the aufhocker from the sky to avoid detection. If you fall asleep when flying, then you're less than useless."

"Rude though that was, you have a point. I will take my rest and see all of you in the evening." Alistair left the room with Lara, who was several steps ahead of him.

"I should sleep too," Lyvaelan said, though he showed no signs of leaving.

Hazel stared at him. "Are you planning on just sleeping in that chair?"

"No, but I wanted to make sure you fell back to sleep first. You might do something reckless otherwise."

"You mean like standing up?"

His eyes narrowed. "I mean anything that isn't sleeping."

She shook her head and settled back in. After all the excitement, she was more tired than expected. "What if I promise to go to sleep? Couldn't you leave then?"

"I could, but I'd rest better knowing you're slumbering peacefully first."

She smiled and yawned. Her eyelids felt heavy. "I won't make you wait long."

"I know you won't. Sleep well, Hazel Enda."

She closed her eyes with a smile. Hazel Enda. That was her name. It sounded so much better when he said it. With those final warm thoughts, Hazel drifted into a peaceful slumber.

Hazel awoke a few hours before sunset. She was less achy and could already tell Lyvaelan's assessment had been correct. She stood and stretched. Energy flowed through her limbs, waking her. She checked herself in the mirror to see if there were any signs of the burns she sustained. To her surprise, there were no marks on her green skin. Similar to the three puncture wounds she received from arrows, there was no evidence the injuries had happened. Her clothing from that day told a very different story, however. Little remained but scorched tatters. Attempts to clean her clothes only aided in their disintegration.

The fire hurt, too, more than the arrows. Truthfully, getting pierced had only stung slightly and was dull in a way that her emotions had been blunted when she first returned. The fire, however, was the most powerful sensation she had ever experienced. Whatever feelings of invincibility she possessed after being shot had since been replaced with justifiable caution.

She had time to prepare for their adventures that night, but still needed to leave time to eat, speak to Thomas, and figure out how she could help. It might be useful having someone who could heal, but neither Lara nor Alistair ever seemed to need mending. She wondered if her powers would even be capable of healing Alistair should the need arise, since thaumaturgy tended to hurt vampires.

Just as Lyvaelan instructed, she continued to write dreams in her journal. Even though she had a good nap after speaking with the others, she still had the recurring vision. She supposed it wouldn't be helpful to mention to the others that they were getting harder to control since they witnessed it. She reconsidered the thought of *any* dream being easy to control and amended the thought. *Her* dreams were hard to stop from entering the waking world. Now, even though she was awake, she felt the need to express it aloud. Speaking it helped, so she would write the dream in her journal while saying the words under her breath. She knew this was only a temporary fix, but it was the best she could do.

She was heading toward a major juncture that would connect her dream to reality. The closer she got, the more it became an eventuality and the harder it would be to contain. Hazel got the impression she was less foretelling the future than she was speaking the future into existence. In some strange, core part of her being, she knew the last time she would speak her dream would be as the prophecy came to fruition. She did not want to tell her friends, or burden them with the knowledge she had, but the coming days were tenebrous. She wanted to believe Lyvaelan. She wanted to believe it might not be so bad, but it *was* going to be bad.

What she beheld would be monumentally horrifying.

Her pulse quickened as she remembered the vision. Breathing slowly, she calmed herself. She promised she wouldn't worry her friends more than necessary, and she'd already weighed them down enough with her outspoken concerns. As morbid as the thought was, she almost wished they'd let her burn if it meant stopping the coming horrors. She didn't want to worry her friends, but some part of her desired to seek the High Priestess of Semeleme and submit to her. If the god-given power the priestess possessed was as powerful as she'd been told, then even Hazel should be capable of being destroyed. It would certainly cause fewer problems for her friends and family. But she made a promise. A promise she struggled with now that she had a clearer head.

She sighed in frustration. Even if she wasn't confined by her vow, Lara and Alistair could track her down with speed and ease. They would discover she was missing before she had gotten halfway to the Veiled Chapel. Not only was she bound by an oath, but she lacked any ability to do otherwise.

She chuckled. Friends could be such a pain for trying to keep each other alive. The smile faded from her lips. In the end, they couldn't do anything to prevent the horrors she saw from happening. They weren't strong enough. They were only strong enough to keep Hazel from taking action alone, which was a profoundly irritating level of power.

A tugging sensation in her mind pulled her from her reverie. She strode to her balcony, where she felt something calling to her. She smiled and looked down at the daffodil bulb she'd planted a couple of weeks before. She'd planted it out of season, hoping to be one of the few people in Coruvaine with a healthy daffodil in the winter. Looking over the ledge and down the side of the library, she noticed jasmine near the base, climbing up the building toward her window. It was a small plant that had grown between the cracks in the flagstone around the library. Its small tendrils reaching up reminded her of a small child asking to be picked up. The highest vine bore a single white star-shaped flower, as if offering it to Hazel. She looked back at the flowers she was tending. She extended her consciousness and noted a feeling plants rarely showed. Concern. It was not a fear of being trampled or destroyed, as some more delicate plants possessed, but a worry for something else. For someone else. For Hazel.

Hazel gazed at the small, flowerless leaves of her daffodil. They appeared sad and beaten by the heavy rain. Perhaps it was her imagination, but the daffodil seemed afraid for her. Hazel ran her hand over the leaves gently.

"Don't worry about me. I'm fine. I'm not going anywhere."

The leaves strengthened a little, and Hazel extended some of the peace she felt when healing Lyvaelan to the plant. The leaves wiggled with excitement as a stem emerged from the foliage, and a bud reached out and opened before her eyes into the healthiest daffodil she'd ever seen. She beamed as she felt the rush of plant emotions from the daffodil, but also noticed the emotion of the jasmine below. The jasmine strained to reach her window. It was such a small thing, but it put forth such great effort. Hazel grinned as she looked down at it.

"Come on up! You can do it. You're so close!"

The jasmine was not, in fact, close to her window at all. It was over thirty feet from the bottom of the ledge. Hazel reached out to the jasmine and closed her eyes. She pictured coaxing it, like a mother encouraging her child to walk for the first time.

"Come on!" she whispered. "You can get up here if you want to."

She mentally cajoled the jasmine until she felt a tickle on her finger. She opened her eyes and smiled when she saw the small, star-shaped flower had crawled its way to her balcony.

She giggled. "It's a really beautiful flower. Thank you for sharing it with me."

The vines shivered with glee at the praise. Along the rest of the jasmine, white flowers instantly bloomed and a sweet fragrance washed over her. Hazel glanced up and noticed the sun had finally set. She turned to leave when another mental tug came from her flowerbed. She cocked her head back at the single blooming daffodil, then to the jasmine.

Hazel sighed and placed her hands on her hips. "Look, there's plenty of space for both of you. Daffodil, be welcoming to the jasmine. I know you don't trust it, but I think you two can get along without stealing from each other. Jasmine, you can grow anywhere there is metal or on the side of the building, but you may not take over the daffodil's flowerbed! If you do, I will be very annoyed because the daffodil was there first. I don't want to prune either of you, but I will if you don't do as I say. Do you understand?"

She could feel the uneasiness of the plants, both because of proximity to each other and the possibility of being pruned. Their uneasiness shifted into wary acceptance.

"Good." Hazel left the room, grinning.

The remarkable and rapid growth of the flowers didn't immediately strike her as unusual, though to any on the street who witnessed the exchange, it would have appeared like a long and leafy arm had reached from the street to give the green girl a flower.

Chapter Thirty-Two
Falling Into Victory

*T**his is stupid.*

Hazel sat outside the library, whistling on the steps. The night was clear and cold. Her breath was visible with exhalation. It was only half an hour after midnight, but her annoyance grew by the minute. She had been there for almost three hours.

The group agreed that someone needed to keep the attention of the hidden aufhocker long enough for them to determine its location. Lara discovered three places where the aufhockers watched them. Since the other three had different observational skills that could be useful in finding the spy, Hazel sat in front of the library, trying to look inconspicuous while also drawing attention to herself by talking out loud.

"I really wish we knew what the Alchemist was up to," she said. "As it is, it's like the trail has gone cold." *This is a stupid way to catch them,* she thought, then loudly droned: "I wonder how the Alchemist always outsmarts us? Must be a super genius."

She frowned into her now-cold cup of hot chocolate. Charlie, when he learned she recovered, made an unbelievable number of sweets for her, along with a lavish feast. It was strange to think such a demented-looking creature could be such a culinary savant. She had only had enough time to scarf down a light meal with the promise she would return to eat more. On her way out, he gave her a warm mug of hot chocolate to keep her going through the night. She was grateful to him, but still cross with her friends.

She glanced at the rooftop across the street and east of the library, then at the southern sky. Nothing. Lara and Alistair sought the aufhocker using their advanced senses. When the creature was found, one of them would flash their badge using the innate magic in it to produce a flicker of light. If the creature focused on Hazel, it likely wouldn't notice, or else it might mistake it for a shooting star or a late-night traveler flashing a distant lantern. Lyvaelan, too, was hidden, though he could mentally communicate with Hazel within this range, so flashing the badge was unnecessary.

She sighed and sprawled out on the steps. She recognized she'd be open to attacks this way, but she didn't feel whatever sinister presence might stalk the darkened alleys of the street would want to attack her at this moment. If only her parents could see her now. Last year, they practically demanded she go to bed no later than two hours after sunset, and now she often stayed up until sunrise. They told her if she couldn't go to bed early and wake up early, she would never be capable of getting and keeping a job. Evidently, her parents hadn't expected her to get *this* job.

She noticed a dim flicker out of the corner of her eye. Alistair. The aufhocker was in the area he watched. She hesitated a moment before stretching, trying her best to stay collected and casual. She rose to her feet and glanced toward the pink crescent of Kythis.

"What a beautiful moon tonight. Well, I guess I should get some rest and go to bed, just like the others. Maybe we'll find the Alchemist tomorrow."

By mentioning the moon, she signaled to her friends that Alistair had eyes on the creature. That would give the other two the opportunity to get into position so they could track the aufhocker as well. If Lara had seen it, Hazel was supposed to make up something about seeing a baker. If it was Lyvaelan... she couldn't remember. Lara had been eager to develop codewords, but Lyvaelan decided to simply communicate the message to each of them telepathically using sorcery. She was glad he offered because staying outside, rambling about nothing for hours, was not conducive to remembering specific codewords that had only just been developed.

She reentered the library and slumped into an armchair and defiantly picked up a book and started reading. She realized she'd asked to be helpful, but this felt silly and like the most useless way of being useful.

Hazel, she jumped at hearing her name in her thoughts. *The aufhocker is on the move. We'll track it and then I'll return to get you before we make the raid. It shouldn't be long.* They had said the same thing about being the bait outside, but that hadn't been true. She noticed a slight movement out of the corner of her eye as the short and unnerving form of Charlie appeared.

She sighed. "Hi Charlie."

"Not happy?" He cocked his head.

"No, not happy. Just annoyed."

His long, pointed ears drooped, and his wide mouth fell out of its toothy grin. "Issorry."

"No, no. It's not your fault. It's not a big deal. Honest."

His face perked up a little, and he touched the mug with one claw. "Want more?"

She smiled. "Yes, that would be nice."

He grinned and disappeared with the mug.

"Sometimes letting others help us is the best way we can help them," a deep voice said with a chuckle.

"Hello Garo," she said without turning. She felt him coming to see her moments before he spoke, so his sudden arrival didn't surprise her.

"I'm glad to see you're well, Miss Enda." He observed her posture and sat. "What troubles you?"

"Mostly it was having to wait outside for three hours, pretending to be clueless while the others did all the work."

"Hmm? Really? Do you think they were doing more work than you?"

"They were trying to find the aufhocker. I just had to distract it."

"Interesting. It sounds like you were doing more work than they were. You watched out for each of them while keeping the attention of the enemy. They only needed to listen to you and notice the aufhocker. In that way, you all had a very similar task."

It was aggravating, but he was right. "Yeah, but I felt useless. All the pretending just seemed stupid and unnecessary."

The grim cocked his head. "'Stupid'? Out of curiosity, Hazel, did you truly feel useless, or was it closer helplessness?"

She looked at Garo. His glowing green eyes reminded her of her own glowing green emanations, even if his eyes were a darker shade. He looked at her with as much concern as she had ever seen in the face of a dog. "I... guess it could have been helplessness."

He nodded. "Since I first met you, you've struggled with feeling emotions at all. While they've gradually returned, I sense turmoil in you unrelated to your present tasks. What's wrong, Hazel?"

She put her book down and looked straight ahead. "My dreams... they're coming true. Some are not terrible, but others—the worst ones—they're going to happen and there's nothing I can do to change that. I know the others mean well when they tell me we'll fight whatever the problem is, but they can't prevent this. No one can. It's like I'm being pushed in front of a speeding cart but everyone around me says 'it's going to be fine,' 'we can handle it,' 'it won't be so bad,' and so on."

He looked off distantly. "I know some of what you mean. The Shadow World allows me glimpses into the future. Different from the experiences you've had, but I've had a taste of what you've seen. Utter helplessness. Sometimes I wonder if it'd be better to just let matters run their course than interfere the way I do. I gathered all of you here for a good reason, but even I can't tell if it will end well or poorly. Do I doom the world by bringing you together, or do I save it? Do my actions even have any bearing on the situation, or am I just another insignificant piece in the grand puzzle of existence that could easily be replaced or substituted with another? It's hard to say, and there are no easy answers. These are questions I've never stopped asking myself."

She clenched her hands in her lap. "How do you deal with it? Knowing you're powerless to stop a bad thing from happening, I mean."

He sighed and shrugged. "I focus on what I *can* do instead. Since I couldn't save the world myself, I resolved to gather a group who could. I have kept searching and seeking to understand the future. In the end I need to remind myself I am just one grim and I can't protect everyone, much as I wish I could. You can't do everything yourself, nor can you put all the blame or all the success on your own shoulders. You are an incredible young woman, but you are still just that: a young woman. You can do great things, but you have limitations. Accept those limitations. *Embrace* those limitations. We are not the infinite gods, and we shouldn't strive to be. If you do what you can whenever you can, that will be enough. I was there when you spoke your prophecy, so I can only imagine how dark and terrible your dreams must be. I'm sorry you have to live with so many horrors, but I'm glad it's you and not another. No one else could handle such pains. Lara wouldn't know what to do and would lash out and seek seclusion or drown herself in alcohol. Alistair would overanalyze and drive himself past the point of insanity, losing all confidence and sense of independence. When vampires are stressed, their obsessions and compulsions grow exponentially worse, and he is no exception. As for Lyvaelan, the poor child is already so dark and tormented that to add prophetic dreams would likely lead to suicide."

"'Child'?"

"Yes. Although he has lived almost forty years, he is close to the same maturational stage as you, Hazel. Elves are not true adults until they've passed their second century, but his warlock blood ages him faster. He is physiologically and psychologically a young adult, though he may seem more mature to you because of circumstances beyond his control. Such is the way of those who suffer as children: they grow up faster, but not necessarily better.

"That aside, despite his maturity, he would crumble under the weight you carry. You may not realize it, but you're the leader of this group."

She wrinkled her nose. "What? No. The others decided what I would do tonight and I doubt any would follow orders if I gave any."

He chuckled. "Is that what it means to be a leader?"

She shrugged. She hadn't given it much thought.

His open green eyes regarded her kindly. "Allow me to posit a different perspective. Many believe leadership is standing at the top of a pyramid and dictating the actions of those beneath them. I'd argue the leader is actually the cornerstone the rest relies on to maintain order. They depend on you. If you decided you were through with the Evenfall Vigil, how long do you think it would be before the rest of them separated as well? If Alistair left the Evenfall Vigil, would the others leave, too? What about Lara? Lyvaelan? Your visions may give them a direction to go in, but it's your attitude, personality, and strength of character that gives them a reason to go where you choose. You aren't above them; you *support* them. I doubt even they realize that yet. You may not fit the archetype of a leader, but then this group doesn't fit the archetype of crime-fighting heroes. In time that will change, and as you change so will each member. You will all learn to grow together into something new."

She smiled and raised an eyebrow. "Should I brag when they get back about how you made me the leader?"

He barked a laugh. "You could try, but I would flatly deny it."

"Oh, well. I guess there go my plans of bossing people around."

"You still have time. I suspect in your long life you will have ample opportunities to tell others what to do."

She shrugged uncertainly. "We'll see how long my life is. All it takes is a little fire to put me out of the fight."

"True, but the severity of the burns you received would have had any normal human out of the field for much longer than three days."

"I guess." She looked up thoughtfully. "This is a random question, but can something be considered a weakness if everything else is also weak against it? I mean, I heard one of the few ways to kill a vampire is to put a spear in its heart and decapitate it. Is that really a weakness when every other creature would also die from that?"

"That..." He smiled. "... is a good point. I hadn't really thought of it, but now I'm not sure I'm going to *stop* thinking about it."

A tray popped out of the air, bearing a steaming mug of hot chocolate and a plate of cookies. The redcap gradually appeared along with it, starting with the talonlike hand that held the tray down to its feet. Charlie grinned and removed his cap in an elegant bow and somehow kept the tray steady.

"Thank you, Charlie," Hazel said, taking the mug and a cookie. The cookie was warm and freshly baked.

"Welcome, miss."

"It's good the two of you have continued to be better friends. You should be careful with yourself, Hazel. When Charlie saw you were hurt, he was very close to dying his cap a different shade of red with the help of those cultists."

Charlie looked sheepishly at the ground.

Hazel smiled at him. "Thank you, Charlie. It means a lot to me to know how much I mean to you. I also know how you helped me, even though you were furious. That was a good thing. I don't want you to attack anyone who doesn't like me. If someone hurts me, help me get better, but don't hurt them instead. Okay?"

He nodded with a bashful smile and disappeared.

"Garo, do you know how long it will take them to track down the Alchemist?"

"No idea. There's a chance it will be quick, but the aufhocker may try to stick to the darkest path which might not be the most expedient. The aufhocker will not want to be out close to daybreak, so it likely won't wander for more than a couple of hours. Does Inquisitor Eller know of your plans?"

Hazel nodded. "We told him earlier. He said he'd inform Commander Comrear and have Evenfall Vigil soldiers stationed with wagons near the general areas with the highest density of alchemy shops."

"Excellent. I suppose all we have to do now is wait."

An hour had passed when Lyvaelan finally returned. Hazel jumped to her feet, but he slowed her down. He closed his eyes and snapped his fingers as several pieces of paper glided through the air from upstairs to create a neat stack in his hands. He rustled through the notes, checking each name and address before settling on one.

"Ah, I think we may have the identity of the Alchemist. It turns out Paxton Averly pointed us in the right direction. We saw the aufhocker disappear into Telemica's Alchemy Shop, which makes Susan Telemica our prime suspect. We should leave before anything else happens. The others are still there, but the longer we wait, the more opportunities she'll have to escape if she discovers our plans."

Garo stood. "Do you need any help?"

Lyvaelan examined the grim. "We need to get there swiftly. I don't suppose you can walk us through the Shadow World, can you?"

"No, but I can do almost that much. Let's go."

The grim led them to the middle of the street where he examined the alleyways and crevices cloaked by shadow. He smiled at them. "Try not to be too amazed." He closed his eyes and his fur stood on end. Black darting things sped to the grim and absorbed into him. As Hazel glanced between him and the shadows, she noticed the darkness stretching toward him as if pulled by a magnet. When they could extend no further, they ripped from their place and surged into him. With each shadow, the already large dog grew bigger. In less than a minute, the black dog had become as tall as a horse and nearly twice as long. Garo had been intimidating before, but now he was truly terrifying.

"Can you always do that?" Hazel asked.

"Only when there are enough shadows for me to borrow. The brighter it is outside, the harder it is for me to call shadows to me. Get on. Both of you. I know the shop you mentioned and I can take you there much faster than you could get there on foot."

Garo laid down to make it easier for both to get on. When they were both firmly in place with Lyvaelan behind her and holding Garo's fur in front of her, the grim sprinted from the library. Despite the initial lurch, Hazel found riding on Garo much easier than riding a horse. Despite his spiked appearance, Hazel noticed his fur was soft and similar to other dogs she had petted in the past.

He dashed through the empty city streets with only the soft sound of his padded footfalls to warn of his approach. Despite the speed of their travel and the lack of any harness or reins, he maintained the equilibrium of his riders without trouble. He seemed to know when one of them was losing grip and adjusted himself to make it easier for them. They passed houses and the Evenfall Vigil building at breakneck speed, although Garo showed no signs of fatigue.

They neared the alchemy shop, on the eastern side of the city, roughly fifteen minutes north of Paxton Averly's business on foot. The pair dismounted, and Hazel came around to face Garo.

"Thank you for bringing us so quickly. Are you going to leave now?"

"No, Miss Enda, I don't think I will. I'll stay out here and make sure the aufhocker doesn't escape."

"Can you really fight and win against one of them?"

A wide, toothy grin spread across his face. "Tonight, we may see which creature of darkness claims mastery over the shadows. I am not legal law enforcement, but the fae are not citizens. Stopping that monster would be viewed similarly to killing a rat on the street."

"And just as easy...?" Hazel suggested with a smile.

"Ha! Unlikely, Miss Enda, but I appreciate your optimism. Although iron and light are the easiest ways to destroy them, those are not the *only* ways. A word of warning when dealing with aufhockers: when they are weak, they'll resort to trickery. They'll attack from behind and tear out your neck, especially if they're outnumbered. Good luck with your capture of the Alchemist. I await your inevitable success." Garo dissolved into the multitude of shadows he had summoned.

Lyvaelan led her to Telemica's Alchemy Shop. It was a small, two-story building, built to house workers above while work could be done below. Small planters lined the front of the shop while a wooden sign bore the name of the business scrawled in a swirling, mysterious script. The sign itself was weatherworn, but the age only added to the mystique of the store. Alistair and Lara waited in an adjacent alley that had been partially converted into a small park with a young tree and clover groundcover. Hazel waved to her friends. She then smiled at the young tree and waved at it, too. The branches of the tree swayed, although there was no discernable wind. Lara glanced between the two rapidly.

"Did you—did the tree—what?" she whispered. "Did that tree just wave *back at you?*"

Hazel shrugged coyly.

Lara shook her head. "Green girl, you keep getting weirder every day."

"Not to interrupt the conversation, but we're on a schedule," Alistair hissed. "We've already checked the perimeter. There's only one small back entrance, and we have other members of the Evenfall Vigil stationed directly outside, guarding it. The aufhocker sneaked in through the back, but we've seen no lights go on, nor heard any noises from inside. We don't know the layout, but I think the three of you can enter while I detain anyone who attempts to flee."

"You're not going in with us?" Hazel asked.

He shifted feet uncomfortably. "No, I... prefer not to enter places I haven't been invited into if I can help it. Besides, we need someone outside who can prevent any escapes. If matters get too challenging, let me know and I will dash in to assist."

"Thanks, Al, but we got this. I brought my special gloves for the occasion. Those aufhockers won't know what hit 'em." Lara grinned, but to Hazel it looked like she was baring her teeth.

"Good. The other members will rush in the moment they hear any commotion, so expect additional backup within thirty seconds of any altercations."

"Then we're all set," Lyvaelan said. "Let's enter through the front door."

They crept to the front. The interior of the shop was dark, and whatever light nearby magelamps provided did little to illuminate the area within. Lyvaelan approached the door and tried the handle. Locked.

"Can you get it open?" Hazel whispered.

"There are some spells that could undue it. One moment." He moved his hands and muttered a few quick words as small blue sparks alit on the handle. He tried the door again. Locked.

"Hmm. Well, that's one spell. Let's try another." He rubbed the surface of the lock and reddish smoke lifted and formed into the vague shape of a key. He drew his hands back and then pushed them forward as he controlled the key. The key fit into the lock and turned without a problem. For the third time, he tried the door. Locked.

He frowned. "Troubling."

"Do you know any other spells that could help?"

"Not really. I think the last spell worked, but it's missing a component. Given she's an alchemist, it's probably something alchemically altered she uses to unlock the door. Without that, I have no simple way to get us in. There might be a spell—"

"I have a spell." Lara pushed ahead and with one swift punch broke through the door, knocking the handle and locking mechanism onto the floor with a loud clatter. She turned back to them and waggled her open palms at them. "See? Magic."

Lyvaelan's frown deepened. "That wasn't exactly subtle."

"Well, it worked, didn't it? Now, are you going to get inside, or do you want to find a different way in that won't work?" She held the door open. Lyvaelan sighed and entered. Hazel followed, with Lara behind.

Hazel squinted as her eyes adjusted to the dark. The vague shape of tables and alchemical tools lined her sight. The hair on the back of her neck stood. She searched but saw nothing unordinary. It was quiet. Deathly quiet. She put her hand against her neck, thinking of the warning Garo had given her.

She felt a long, wet tongue lick her hand. *"Am I lost?"* a grating voice whispered.

"Hazel! Drop!" Lara yelled. Hazel fell to the floor and flipped over in time to see a huge scythe-like claw rake through the air where her head had been. Crawling along the ceiling was a creature with six legs. A long, sluglike neck extended and ended in a head with a single white eye and an oozing black tongue. The stench of sulfur suddenly filled the air. The creature licked its lips and reformed its claw into a long, nine-digit hand with more knuckles than any human hand. The creature reached back to Hazel.

"I wish I'd asked for directions—" Lara leaped over Hazel's supine form and slammed her fist into the creature's hand. The hand splattered against the wall as the aufhocker roared, screamed, and howled in unison. Its head split in two, each with a large fanged mouth and three small white eyes.

"I told you it was right at the fork!" the other head responded to the first. *"We just need to go a little further."* The creature crouched as if about to strike, then it scuttled backward and disappeared behind a table.

"Shit! Lyvaelan, do your magic!"

"Get out of my house!" A crash and a flash of red light illuminated the interior.

Hazel recoiled from the blinding flash of light, losing her sense of direction. She blinked rapidly, but all she saw was dazzling crimson.

Lyvaelan shouted out, "We are members of the Evenfall Vigil, we demand—"

"You demand nothing!" yelled a woman's voice. "You break into my home in the middle of the night and you expect me to—"

"Listen up, bitch!" Lara interrupted. "You've made a big mistake! We know you're the Alchemist. Surrender!"

"You're in no position to make demands!" said the woman Hazel assumed was Susan Telemica. "Not when I have all the power."

Hazel's vision began to clear when she heard another crash of broken glass, and a feeling of heat and itchiness flooded over her. This was going poorly. She reached out to the plants mentally, unsure if it would help.

"A dark elf breaks into my home, and I'm to believe he works for the city? I'm no fool! I—oof!" An impact on the floor followed by a third sound of shattering glass resounded as the woman fell. "Ow! No! Damn—!"

A voice came from the front door. "Susan Telemica, in case these incompetents didn't mention, you're under arrest by order of the Evenfall Vigil." Hazel saw the half goat form of Sergeant Mellius Concornus looking in with undisguised amusement. "You're under arrest on suspicion of creating and distributing illegal alchemical compounds, resulting in widespread panic and destruction." Four human soldiers entered the room from behind him and restrained her.

"What—I—no!" she protested as two members of the Evenfall Vigil hoisted her to her feet. Her face was covered with a light brown liquid and a few cuts where the shattered phial had broken her skin. She rose but appeared incapable of maintaining her balance.

Hazel rose to her feet and looked around the other side of the table. Multiple Evenfall Vigil soldiers had entered carrying torches and several candles had been lit for more stable lighting. The aufhocker was nowhere to be seen. Hazel walked to the place where Susan Telemica had fallen and noticed roots sticking out from the floorboards, close to where the tree stood outside. She smiled painfully and turned to her friends. Neither one looked happy about the capture, though it could have been the blinding light followed by terrible itching that made them irritable. Lyvaelan rifled through nearby potions quickly as he itched uncontrollably until he found one and drank a sip before handing it to Lara, who snatched it from him. Hazel drank next and immediately felt a wave of relief as the heat and itching dissipated.

They stepped outside as Sergeant Concornus took over the investigation. Alistair waited with a drawn sword. He followed Susan Telemica to the wagon and made sure she entered without trouble. When the wagon departed, he returned to the others. He looked at each of them and opened his mouth to speak, but Lara held up a hand. "Not now, Al. Not. Now."

Hazel searched the street. "Garo? Are you alright? Garo!" The black dog stepped out of the shadows, back to his usual size. He panted raggedly. His fur was mottled in areas and a dark red gash broke through the black on his right flank. He limped to them.

"Miss Enda! How good to see you alive and well!"

"Garo! What happened?"

He grinned wolfishly and his tail wagged. "I won."

Her eyes widened. "You fought the aufhocker?"

"I *killed* the aufhocker. I have to admit, I'm terribly out of practice and made a few mistakes I'm now paying for."

"Oh, let me heal you!"

"No, thank you, Miss Enda. I would actually prefer to let my wounds heal on their own. I regenerate quickly, so you need not worry. I'd like to feel the reminder of my mistakes just a little longer before I let them disappear. It feels good to know I accomplished something immediate. I spend so much time in courts speaking with dignitaries that this pain reconnects me with my born purpose as a fae watchdog."

"I know what you mean," Lara growled, "but I don't feel that way tonight. That was... embarrassing."

"Embarrassing, maybe, but you succeeded in your mission, nonetheless. You should return to the library. There are professionals searching the business for signs of the missing bluecaps and for any additional evidence proving Telemica is the Alchemist."

"I second that assessment." Commander Comrear approached. Dark circles ringed his eyes, but he lacked his typical sour disposition. "You've all performed adequately. We've been tracking the Alchemist for months and now we might have her. Veratheragan's peace! We didn't even know if the Alchemist was a single person, let alone the manner in which the Alchemist operated. You might have tactically made a dozen terrible decisions, but everything turned out alright so I'll let it slide. Besides, you've helped more than you've hindered and shown you're at least decent investigators, even if your methods leave much to be desired. I want all four of you in my office tomorrow evening at eight. I'll brief you on what we've learned and what evidence we find. You're dismissed."

They saluted as he walked away. Now that the excitement of the situation had subsided, Hazel noticed her exhaustion. She looked to the sky and saw the light blue in the east preceding dawn. It would likely be another overcast day, but it was wise to get inside before Alistair felt the effects of the sun. With Garo partially injured, it was improbable they could ride on his back this time. They departed for the library.

"Well," Alistair said after they spent a minute in silence, "it's hard to believe we finally caught the Alchemist. It was a little... anticlimactic."

"Yeah, talk about a boring finish," Lara grumbled. "If I finished a fight like that in the ring, I would've been booed off the stage."

"I suppose that's the reality of it, though," Lyvaelan said, gazing absently at the stars. "Real life is rarely as interesting as we'd like to imagine it is."

"Yeah, except that aufhocker." Hazel shivered. "It licked me! Does that do something? Do I need to amputate my hand?"

Lyvaelan smiled thinly. "No, their saliva doesn't have any dangerous effects. It's just disgusting."

Lara grimaced. "If I were you, Hazel, I might amputate the hand, anyway. That was pretty gross."

"I think washing your hands might suffice, though doing it more than once could be helpful," Alistair said. "Also, why did it lick your hand?"

"I used my hand to cover my neck. Garo said they sometimes like to leap on people from behind and tear out the neck, so I protected it. Maybe it was trying to lick my neck?"

Lara gagged. "Ugh, that's even worse. Yuck."

Lyvaelan thought about it. "I think it's more likely it licked your hand so you'd reflexively pull it away from your neck to check it. Though, admittedly, it was disturbing."

"I think that describes the aufhockers," Hazel said, shaking her head. "The way they talk, the way they act, what they are... they are basically the definition of creepy."

Her companions nodded. Nobody disagreed with that.

Chapter Thirty-Three
Celebration and Success

They slept soundly that day. Thomas Eller hadn't returned to the library when they arrived, which suited them given their exhaustion. Although in Hazel's mind she had done little worthy of note, she felt more tired than expected. Whether it was more draining emotionally than she anticipated or she needed another day to recover from her burns, she could not say. Regardless, by the time she awoke, it was early evening and the rest of the group waited eagerly to return to the Evenfall Vigil headquarters. She skipped a meal and grabbed some bread and cheese to take with her before leaving.

The same recurring dream plagued her sleep. The images of aufhockers and the person eating bluecaps were more present than it was the night before. It made her uneasy, but she pushed the feeling aside to enjoy the victory they'd won over the Alchemist.

The wind carried the scent of approaching rain beneath clouded skies. This made traveling easier for Alistair, who desired to leave before sunset. They walked in high spirits and veiled excitement, their embarrassment regarding the night before evaporating at the prospect of closing a major case. They'd captured a dangerous criminal and earned the respect of their superior officer.

Sergeant Concornus was not at his usual place to greet them and heckle Lara. Instead, a young woman informed them the commander wished to see them immediately. They entered the office and saw Comrear flanked on each side by Ellen Honrick and Mellius Concornus. The satyr pointed to notes on a page the commander examined while Ellen shook her head. When the commander noticed the group arrive, he ushered them in and asked Sergeant Concornus to fetch a couple of extra chairs.

"Well done," he said. "Based on our investigation, I think she really is the Alchemist."

Lara looked excitedly at the others, who shared her enthusiasm.

"Did you find anything about the bluecaps?" Hazel asked.

He glanced at Hazel and then back down at the page. "Yes, we did. I have the report right here but haven't had the time to go through it completely. Fortunately, Concornus and Honrick interrogated the suspect and investigated the material. I'll have each of them discuss what they've found."

Mellius winked at Lara before starting. "I handled the bulk of the interview. Miss Susan Telemica is an unpleasant woman. Gruff, lacks a sense of humor, is business-oriented, prefers early mornings to late nights—"

Comrear growled. "Get to the point, Mel."

"She refuses to acknowledge any involvement with the materials we've confiscated from her home and claims she is not the Alchemist, despite much evidence to the contrary. Several times she claimed she'd be open to sorcerers examining her mind, but that makes me think she has some trick to employ that will make her appear innocent. Certain clever mages are capable of such deceptions and sorcery is usually only able to extract information that lies on a gradient between true and false rather than being wholly one or the other. If she's been a criminal mastermind for as long as we believe, then it's likely doing as she says would play into her hands. We may hire a professional sorcerous interrogator, but that must come later.

"Regarding the evidence we collected, there were several unmarked potions similar to the kind found in the stomach contents of the gentleman you apprehended previously. We collected three bluecap bodies in various stages of decomposition and dissection, which we suspect are related to the potions. Beyond that, we found a cache in her home where she kept a decent quantity of money, potentially to pay off thugs like those you encountered. We also gathered ashes from the alley beside her house, where Ambassador Garo fought the aufhocker. Preliminary tests show remnants of fae magic surrounding them, belonging to some previously living creature. Given the odor of sulfur surrounding them, it is safe to confirm Ambassador Garo did, in fact, kill an aufhocker as it left the business of Susan Telemica."

"For my part in the investigation," Ellen took over, "I analyzed the blue liquid and discovered its effects are functionally similar to the one utilized by the man you fought against on the eleventh of Melantria at night on Faelsday outside Skilliven Tavern. The exact components are unclear to me since I am strictly a magician and not an alchemist proper, but the next phase of our investigation is to see if the pieces of missing bluecap correlate to the uses in the potions. Based on the number of bluecaps we discovered, we suspect she is hiding more and simply refusing to tell us, or she disposed of the other bodies immediately after using them. Given the size of her shop, she lacked sufficient space to contain a great number of bodies, even those as miniscule as the bluecaps. Her specific research on the subject has not been located, although she has several books on fae and specific alchemical properties of fae byproducts, which *could* be circumstantial evidence."

"Pardon my interruption, but do you recall how many bluecaps were estimated to have gone missing?" Alistair asked.

She looked at him. "The foreman was unclear, but he believed the number to be somewhere in the hundreds. It's difficult to say. We don't know how many bluecaps were used to create a single potion. Maybe a single bluecap is enough, or it might require dozens. We need to have this analyzed by a dedicated alchemist."

"Which brings me to your next assignment," Comrear said. "We have an alchemist on staff, but I always get a second opinion. I heard Paxton Averly helped narrow down the list, and he's assisted our department in the past. I'd like you to take a sample of the potion along with a list of the parts missing from the bluecap. With any luck, Paxton will either discover more than what our alchemist will or at least come to the same conclusions. If you could deliver it immediately, it would be an immense help. He should then deliver the results back to us once he's finished."

"Does he get paid to do this?" Lara asked.

He folded his hands on the desk. "As a consultant? Of course. Actually, consultants get paid more than our resident alchemist, simply because they have to use their own resources and juggle that with their work schedule. Besides the pay, he gets to feel accomplished knowing he did the right thing. Don't all of you feel accomplished?"

Lara hesitated. "I guess a little..."

Comrear chuckled. "Well, a little is better than not at all. Deliver the package to him tonight. I sent a courier earlier to ask if he would help and set a specific time when you would come by. He should expect you in an hour."

"Really?" Lara said. "We're here almost an hour early. What were you going to do if we'd gotten here late?"

"I knew you wouldn't." He shrugged, leaning back. "I saw the way you walked off last night and figured you'd be eager to hear the full story. Besides, I could've sent someone else if you arrived late."

"Don't you mean 'on time'?"

"Nope. In this business, early is on time and on time is late."

"Shit," Lara mumbled, "I'm in the wrong business."

He frowned at her. "You're fortunate Watchers can set their own schedules. You should also learn to speak with more respect to your commanding officer. Get the job done. You're dismissed."

The walk to Saving Salves Alchemy from the Evenfall Vigil headquarters took slightly less time than it did from the library. A sparse drizzle and a strong breeze sent glowing watery sparks through the light of street lamps. Many people they passed had eschewed umbrellas, not deeming the intermittent rain to be worthy of the trouble. The magelamps had just ignited, staving off the gloom of the overcast winter night. They passed close to Susan Telemica's shop on their way south. Upon reflection, Hazel realized Paxton Averly's shop was removed from many other alchemy shops and closer to residential areas, which likely made his clientele larger families and laborers rather than wealthier customers. The merchants could usually afford specialized treatments, which would make for a more lucrative business. While living further away would grant Paxton an opportunity to fulfill a greater number of client needs, it was unlikely they could pay as well as those within the second wall or in the main mercantile districts of Coruvaine.

Hazel volunteered to take the list of questions and ingredients while Lyvaelan kept the phial. After the previous night, she wanted to feel useful, even if it was simply delivering a list. Lyvaelan surrendered the list but kept the potion on the grounds that he had the most experience with magic and could neutralize it if necessary. Neither Lara nor Alistair made any argument for either and led the way to Paxton's home and business.

As they approached the door, Hazel smiled at the plants in his garden as she passed. The vegetation bowed as she neared. Each leaf of ivy growing on the building waved at her, though it could have been mistaken for the rustle of a breeze blowing. Lyvaelan studied Hazel but made no comment.

Lara knocked on the door, which opened to reveal the smiling, spectacled face of Paxton Averly.

"Ah! Right on time. Please, come in. I've prepared tea for us as well as a place to sit. I'm still a little embarrassed by my lackluster hosting the last time you visited." He moved aside and gestured to a table in the center of the room, where he removed potions and displays. A blue teapot with a white rose rested in the middle of the table, lightly wafting steam from its spout. Five matching teacups were arranged around the table with teaspoons and folded napkins. Biscuits sat beside the teapot, along with a bottle of cream and a sugar bowl. He extended his hand to Lara. She hesitated, but Alistair stepped up to shake it. "Congratulations," Paxton said warmly.

The vampire brightened. "You honor us with such a reception! Everything is so neatly arranged and symmetrical!"

Paxton polished his eyeglasses and shrugged. "Oh, it's nothing special. Besides, I wanted to acknowledge your tremendous success! You caught the Alchemist. Capturing one terrible criminal who makes the rest of us alchemists look bad is a worthy reason to celebrate. Please, let me serve you."

They took seats across from each other, with Paxton at the head. He held the teapot and poured the steaming brew into each person's cup as he moved around the table. "The tea is a special blend I made myself. Peppermint, chamomile, fennel, and a bit of ginger. The chamomile and fennel are alchemically altered, which should simultaneously relax you and give you a sense of accomplishment. Alchemical fennel can energize too much, and alchemical chamomile can act as a soporific, but using them in conjunction brings out the best in both without creating an overpowering effect. The peppermint and ginger are naturally refreshing and good for digestion, though I decided against extracting their alchemical essence. I will say some find the taste of fennel a little bitter, so a small quantity of sugar and cream can help if you find it overpowering, others enjoy the crispness of the tea on its own without the additional sweetness. Whatever way you wish to enjoy it is up to you." He set the teapot down and raised his cup. "To your victory."

The tea was invigorating and soothing. Hazel felt an energy and relaxation at once contradictory and complementary. The others enjoyed it just as much. Even Lyvaelan, who was usually taciturn, gave a small smile as he closed his eyes and smelled the sweet aroma. Hazel usually detested the taste of licorice so common in fennel, but the balance with the other ingredients kept it from being too much.

"This is excellent." Lyvaelan opened his eyes, looking at Paxton with appreciation. "How did you come by such a blend?"

Paxton beamed. "The way every alchemist does: trial and error. Sometimes I used too much fennel, or too little chamomile. It took time, but I suppose it's in my nature. I try new things and tweak the recipe slightly until I get it where I want it. I'm happy with the proportions I used here."

"I think we can all agree with that," Alistair said. "It is truly exquisite. Even the best attendants in the king's palace have struggled to create anything that approaches this."

"Oh-ho, please, you flatter me. You make it sound like making tea is such a terrible challenge when it is simply a pleasant pastime." He gazed into his cup, his smile dwindling. "What all of you have done is so incredible I can hardly compare to it. Arresting criminals, I mean. Changing the world for the better. It's... truly commendable. I would be out there with you, but I abhor violence. I must content myself with riding behind the parade of your accomplishments." He blinked, rousing himself from his reverie. "By the by, I should probably have the phial before I forget."

Lyvaelan handed it to him. "For what it's worth, your work helps people, just in a microcosmic sort of way."

"True. Still, some days, it's hard not to feel like I'm stuck in a loop. I help one person, then another, then another. By the time I've finished with the last person, the first person returns and wants something else and the process repeats. It's like the spoke of a wagon wheel: constantly moving and yet never going anywhere."

"Do you dislike what you do?" Hazel asked.

"I wouldn't say that. I think the problem is one of expectations. When I was in university, I had dreams. So did everyone else. We all had essentially the same vision: we wanted to amaze the world and save lives. We wanted to create the perfected panacea, discover the philosopher's stone, invent some other usable apotheotic alchemy, or uncover a great wonder that would lead to a revolutionary discovery. Unfortunately, if you have time to learn about a subject in a classroom, it usually means most of it has been figured out. Some might say it is akin to climbing a great mountain. All the earliest alchemists gave us the foundation so we could research at higher levels without starting at the bottom. The trouble is the higher up a mountain you are, the harder it is to walk the same distance as those below because of altitude, air, and weather. My problem is in moving as far as the pioneers of alchemy."

Lara cocked her head. "What makes it so difficult to go further?"

He shrugged, holding his teacup with both hands. "Most convenient cures have been discovered already and those that haven't are termed unethical."

Lara frowned. "What do you mean by unethical?"

He sighed and held up the phial. "To my knowledge, this Alchemist is the first to attempt anything like this. And why? Because he— or she, rather—had to use some portion of tissue from a living creature. Certain animals such as rats, pigeons, mice, rabbits, and the rest wouldn't pose a problem, but taking parts from a fae—particularly one ostensibly sentient like a bluecap—would be considered fundamentally wrong. There are other examples, of course, such as test subjects. Obviously, humans are the best to test alchemical agents on, but if one doesn't know its effects, is it ethical to experiment on a human? Even if the individual consents, is it ethical given the limited understanding a willing adult might have? These are the difficult considerations and standards alchemists are held to. The rules protect, they don't promote." He gazed at the phial. "In a certain way, I empathize with the Alchemist." He looked at their shocked faces. "I really do! The Alchemist wanted to find some knowledge or create some potion that could change the world. Isn't that what being human is really about? Attempting to matter and leaving this world better than we found it?"

Lara leaned back in her seat, rolling her eyes. "I wouldn't say hiring the scum of the earth to attack us and giving them powers is exactly changing the world in a positive way."

"Perhaps not, Miss Lara, and I wouldn't argue with the terrible methods she employed. I merely meant that—despite the terrible things the Alchemist did—at its core, there was an understandable reason. That's all. That doesn't justify it, it just makes it less black and white. All spellcasters operate in a space between moral extremes, which is why so many move to either end of the spectrum. The Dark Order—which is supposedly nonexistent—pushes magic to create and do terrible things, though new knowledge is discovered as a result. On the other hand, the Council of Archmages prevents anyone from doing anything terrible with magic at the cost of our growth of knowledge. Preventing knowledge is bad, but so is torturing others. Both groups have faults and flaws, it just depends on which is *most* at fault." He stared absently into his tea for a moment and then jolted upright. "Forgive me! I've been more talkative than usual. It's likely a combination of the tea and my work. I'm not used to staying up so late, you see."

"Oh." Alistair stood. "Forgive us for taking so much of your time. May we assist you with cleaning before we go?"

"No, I should be fine. It isn't much, and I'm rather particular about where I place my tea supplies."

"Of course. I completely understand."

"You would," Lara said under her breath.

Alistair scowled at her.

"In any case," Alistair said, "we look forward to working with you again in the future, Mr. Averly."

"No need for such formalities. 'Paxton' or even 'Pax' is fine with me. I look forward to seeing all of you soon. Safe travels back home!

Even with the Alchemist in custody, the roads can be dangerous at night."

The group smiled and waved at Paxton, who was busy picking up his teacups when they egressed.

"He's a nice guy," Lara said, when they were out of earshot, stretching. "He makes awesome tea, too. I would've preferred alcohol, but that alchemically enhanced stuff is pretty enjoyable."

"Indeed," Alistair said. "I will have to ask him if he could make us some to take to the library."

"If he gave me the ingredients, I could probably make some myself," Lyvaelan said.

"Really? You could do that?" Alistair asked.

"Sure. Alchemy is easy. It's just the memorization and quantities that make it challenging. If I had a list with instructions, it would be exceedingly simple."

"Sweet Caleptis!" Hazel exclaimed. The others looked surprised at her outburst. She gaped at them. "The list! I forgot to give it to him! I was so busy with how good the tea was, I forgot." She felt embarrassed she had insisted on performing a task and then failed to perform it.

Lara chuckled. "He's probably still awake. I can handle it."

"No, it's my fault. I'll give it to him. Just wait for me, alright?" She ran off without waiting for a response.

Hazel ascended the three steps and opened the door, which happened to still be unlocked. She looked around but didn't see him. The dishes had been cleared, but Paxton was nowhere to be seen.

"Paxton?" She continued deeper in and moved to where she believed his kitchen was when her eye caught something strange in his workshop. She walked into the small workshop, uncertain of what she found odd. It was as tidy as ever, but the bookshelf stuck out at a slightly different angle than before. Forgetting her mission, Hazel touched the bookcase and found it gave way with negligible force. She moved it toward her to reveal a large black room. She heard a noise from somewhere inside. A small candle at the end of the room cast a bit of light on the surrounding area. The room appeared to be a series of... shelves? It was difficult to make out since sheets covered them. Whatever they were, they were arranged in rows as far as she could see to her left. To her right, a wall with a long table attached to it continued around the perimeter of the room. There were no windows. She approached the candle.

"Paxton?"

As her eyes adjusted to the light, the sheet covering the shelves to her left wavered as she passed. The table had various papers and diagrams, as well as a plethora of implements that could be useful to an alchemist. Shears, scalpels, burners, mirrors, files, forceps, mortars, pestles, and other equipment were arranged with the same characteristic precision as the teacups they used earlier. Hazel reached for the candle and then heard a rattling from the shelf behind her. She whirled around and saw the sheet sway slightly. Without taking her eyes off the sheet, she picked up the candle and brought it closer. She lifted it and gasped.

A dozen tiny blue flames scurried in the cage. She pulled the sheet off and as far down as she could see were bluecaps in cages. She turned back to look at the table that continued to the other side of the room. At first, she couldn't understand what it was, so she got closer. Stretched out and transfixed by pins was another bluecap, the skin of its belly split down the middle with surgical precision and stretched back to reveal its internal organs. She recognized this one. It was Zigglepet. Dozens of blue phials dotted the sides, interspersed with the dried blood of many bluecaps.

Hazel staggered back. The hair on the nape of her neck stood on end.

"Oh dear, you weren't supposed to see that," said a voice from behind.

Hazel whirled around, nearly extinguishing the candle. Standing at the hidden entrance to the laboratory was the slim and smiling figure of Paxton Averly. Creeping, sulfurous fumes wafted from the entrance.

"Such a pity," he said as he rubbed some kind of blue ointment on his arms. "I hoped we could part ways as friends. I suppose it was not to be." Throughout the room, black shapes with glowing white eyes appeared. Growls and sniffing came from the shapes as they fixed their attention on her. Hazel found she couldn't move; stunned by what she saw and what unfolded before her.

An aufhocker with six glowing white eyes spoke, "*What... do you want... us to do... Alchemist?*"

Paxton pursed his lips and stared at the ceiling, pondering the question. He had the same mild but assured demeanor he always possessed, but in the dark, surrounded by countless horrors, the sense of safety and kindness had melted into something monstrous. He smiled and nodded, as if coming to a conclusion.

"*Alchemist?*" the aufhocker asked again.

He pushed his glasses up. "Take her outside and kill them all. Don't let any escape and leave no witnesses. And be sure you don't get any blood on the floor. I abhor violence."

Chapter Thirty-Four
Illuminating Shadows

"She's changed a lot from the beginning, hasn't she?" Lara chuckled as Hazel disappeared into Paxton Averly's shop.

Alistair smiled and leaned against a magelamp. "She has. In some ways, she's a more normal girl than before, but—given the circumstances—that only makes her more unusual."

Lyvaelan studied both of them and wondered if they were right. Had Hazel truly changed, or had *they* been the ones to change? In the beginning, both vampire and werewolf were practically at each other's throats, which constantly vexed him. Recognizing the changes in Hazel may have more reflected the change in each of them than any difference in her.

He conceded she was unique. Perhaps more than unique. She was powerful in a way he'd never encountered. The magic within her teetered on the edge of the unfathomable. Could a half-crazed mage really have been responsible for her transformation? It was a riddle. But perhaps it was not just the objective power she possessed that amazed him so much as the effect she had on each Watcher of the Evenfall Vigil. They had shown—beyond any reason—they would protect her at all costs. Even he noticed she had effected some change within himself that was difficult to describe.

Why did he care for her? Why did he care for any of them? Life was easier without attachments and he'd already nearly lost control on two separate occasions and neither instance was due to some overwhelming danger to himself. Why did he care whether she lived or died? Was this a mistake? There was a pain he felt around her he didn't understand. It was a pain he couldn't ease, nor did he want to. He turned from contemplating such thoughts and pushed the emotion and everything else down. Nothing good would come of it. His selfishness would level this city if he wasn't careful.

Kiran had told him there was nothing wrong with caring for someone, but he needed to maintain control over his feelings. Was such a thing even possible? He felt he'd lost any sense of middle ground and risked falling exclusively into one extreme or the other. Was it careless for him to grow attached to these people? Loneliness was painful, but he understood it. Losing a loved one was unbearable and devastating. Some part of him wanted to release the fear and care for them without reservation. Then he remembered: he was part warlock. His magic was unstable and powerful, far beyond the abilities of his kin. His two bloodlines mixed and—rather than diluting each other—multiplied the powers of both.

When he lived in Elliara, Kiran had once brought him to a place in the northeastern section of the forest. The canopy of the trees had abruptly ended and all around, almost a mile in diameter, was a crater leaking magic. Images of individuals within the crater reenacted the same ghostly scenes without end. He witnessed lifeless, floating husks of those who died, their souls long fled into the afterlife but their memory living on in a perpetual state of agony and sighs. Black and purple tendrils of magic seeped from the cracks, poisoning the world around them with the last feelings of the warlock who died there. Lyvaelan remembered touching one spark of magic and feeling—for a moment—the overwhelming power, desire, elation, and agony of the warlock. The tendrils didn't speak; they screamed. Their shrieks filled his soul and though but a moment had passed, it felt an eternity. He knew the futility of the warlock's desire, and he understood it. The more magic the warlock used and drew upon, the closer he came to ultimate arcane power. It was a desire not born from hubris but from uncontrollable longing. The more the warlock consumed, the hungrier he became. When he died, it was a death of horrific euphoria.

The stream of magic had been utterly and irreparably disrupted. The resultant crater, with every painful feeling and drifting phantom, was the attempt to fix and *cure* the destruction. Elves and mages worked to undo it and succeeded tremendously, and *that* was terrifying. That what he witnessed was the solution to the problem shook him to his core. The memory haunted Lyvaelan's nightmares.

The warlock who had died was middling in power but lacking in control. It was not a massive surge of energy brought about by the mightiest of their kind; it was the mistake of someone of mediocre power. Kiran hadn't shown him to scare him, but to inform him. It served that purpose well but demonstrated so much more than that. He understood the terrible risk of staying in the lofty branches of Chaldra. Despite his dislike of the light elves, he dreaded hurting them. They took him in and allowed him to live, despite his dually damned lineage. If he created an arcane cataclysm, it would kill many and destroy that area forever. If he lost control in Coruvaine, it would kill everyone in the capital city and turn the land into a desolate wasteland of unending screams. Warlocks were rightly reviled. Joining the Evenfall Vigil was a mistake. Kiran should've let him die when he found him.

Looking at Alistair and Lara, he knew he could rely on them in ways he could not rely on Hazel. They would kill him if he ever lost control; he'd known since the day before Hazel awoke. Both experienced guilt over the decision, but it was unnecessary. Their pact had given him a sense of peace. One of them could stop him.

The world belongs to you. Take it. He shook his head, clearing his thoughts. He wouldn't let those ravenous temptations overwhelm him. Turning his attention back to the conversation, he said, "Hazel has changed, though her personality may be the least of her relevant alterations. Each day brings fresh surprises."

"No kidding!" Lara said. "How many new powers does she get each week? Eight?"

"That's an exaggeration," Alistair said, "although her abilities have grown and changed. The new powers I've noticed besides prophecy are regeneration, healing, talking to plants, making plants respond—"

"—that last one is incorrect," Lyvaelan interjected. "The plants respond on their own."

Alistair opened his mouth as if to argue, but then thought better of it. "That point notwithstanding, are there any other abilities she possesses?"

Lara jolted upright and walked toward the alchemy shop. She stopped and slipped on her silver and steel gloves, listening intently. Alistair's eyes widened, and he drew his sword, which glinted in the light.

"Yeah, she has one other ability, Al," Lara said, moving into a fighting stance. "She's fantastic at finding trouble."

The door blew off its hinges as the alchemy shop vomited out a shapeless black stream, and with it, Hazel Enda. Hazel careened into Lara. The werewolf leaped to catch her, but the force of the throw sent both of them tumbling into the street. The black mass grew a giant mouth with countless pin-like teeth. A dozen legs sprouted from each side as the creature gurgled and clicked, its head rotating around its neck.

"No! Please! I don't want to die!"

Behind the black centipedal creature, five more dark shapes darted to the sides and around. They surrounded the group, each one moving to a different magelamp and bending the metal poles until they snapped. The orb within each magelamp shattered and darkened. The creatures stalked closer and took a conglomeration of unique traits.

Their voices varied as much as their shapes, with some growling, others screeching, and all laughing in a maddening din.

One aufhocker remained silent. It adopted the form of a slender human over ten feet tall with horns, looked at the others. Six white eyes on its face burned with no other visible facial features. On the ends of its long and willowy arms were tentacled fingers, writhing like a mass of worms. The aufhocker held its claws to its brethren. "*Beware...*" it whispered, "*elf... has... sunlight... magic.*" The other aufhockers regarded Lyvaelan and circled him cautiously, with at least one white eye of each tracking him. Lyvaelan's eyes narrowed. This was the special aufhocker they encountered the first time. It saw what happened to its allies and now strategized. This differed from how most fae would think. Perhaps its thoughts melded with those of its conjurer, lending it a cunning human element. Lyvaelan would have been frustrated, but the situation differed from before. These creatures had better cover now, and unleashing sunlight would severely cripple Alistair, and might harm the other two as well. Paxton had deceived them and had the upper hand. The desperate sunlight spell Lyvaelan used previously would weaken the entire group too much for them to face him.

Lyvaelan's ears picked up the sounds of the neighborhood stirring. It was only a few hours after sunset, but many windows were dark. As he watched, shutters opened and citizens began searching outside their homes to find the source of the commotion. Some brought daggers, clubs, and hatchets to meet the threat. *Useless,* Lyvaelan thought with gritted teeth. *They'll only get themselves killed.*

This conflict needed to end swiftly. He spooled magic around his hands, beginning a spell that would take time to cast. "The Alchemist," Lyvaelan muttered, "if we defeat him, his summoned lackeys will disappear and be incapable of interfering."

Lara grunted an acknowledgement and drew her fingers into fists as she popped the vertebrae in her neck. She grinned. Frenetic excitement gleamed in her eyes. "I might have to fight as a wolf by the end of the night. That's exciting." She lunged toward the giant black nightmare centipede that barred entry into the alchemy shop. The creature screeched at her, turning two of its front legs into crablike claws. She ducked beneath one as it snapped at her and rolled out of reach as the other slammed the flagstone, shattering it with a thunderous *crack*. She leaped for its head. The aufhocker, surprised, reared back to protect its face, but exposed its neck. Lara punched through it, bursting its neck with a sickening squelch. The shadowy body expanded and dissipated like confined smoke, given freedom. The head with three glowing eyes released a porcine squeal as it landed a dozen feet away. The head flopped on the ground like a fish struggling to return to water as tiny black legs emerged spiderlike from the remnants of its neck. Lara landed on her feet and raced toward it as it righted itself. It looked up at the werewolf, its white eyes open wide.

"*Mommy?*"

Her fist slammed down on its head. Its eyes burst with light and then were no more. The other aufhockers stood transfixed before screeching, roaring, hissing, and crying in a cacophony that conveyed one emotion: *rage.*

Lara turned to run into the shop. The intelligent six-eyed aufhocker collected itself and appraised the situation. It gurgled into a harsh cackle and extended its arms and fingers, which writhed and grew. It sent its fingers through the window of a nearby room where a candle had been lit. Lyvaelan's pulse quickened. He heard two screams. The aufhocker withdrew its fingers, holding a man struggling desperately to escape the tentacles to no avail. Lara hesitated.

The man drew close to the tall, horned aufhocker. It gave a deep, guttural laugh as it observed Lara's uncertainty and how the rest of the group froze. "*You care... too much.*" A third arm extended from the chest of the creature toward the man. Three spikes emerged from the hand and skewered the captive.

Lara leaped back from the door toward the aufhocker. The creature appeared unconcerned as it looked at its peers. "*Leave no witnesses alive. Make them all witnesses.*"

The other creatures laughed and howled, turning away from the four and toward the citizens who retreated into their homes or sought help.

"How do I get home? I'm so lost..."

"Gods preserve us! Oh, it was just a shadow."

"Daddy is going to be so mad when I get back..."

During this time, Lyvaelan had finished gathering magic. He could use the magic within himself, but it would be more dangerous and less effective in this case. He caught wisps of it in the air and rolled it in his hands, feeding the scraps with his own power until it crackled with energy. Finally, he threw the invisible orb of power into the air. It rose twenty feet above the tallest building in the area and burst into a tiny sun that bathed the street and almost every alleyway with bright light. It wasn't daylight, but it would limit the powers of the aufhocker even if it didn't kill them. With any hope, it would also alert the Evenfall Vigil.

The shadowy beings recoiled. Lengthy appendages disintegrated in the light, and their forms shrank to more compact forms. "Go!" Alistair yelled. "Flee, citizens! Run! Vacate the street!" The people needed no further prompting as they fled in all directions, with several aufhockers in pursuit. One aufhocker picked up a screaming woman, only for its hand to drop with the woman as Alistair severed it. In the next instant, the woman and Alistair disappeared as he dashed away. The vampire reappeared just as the aufhocker regrew its claw. With the woman out of harm's way, Alistair advanced with longsword in hand. The creature erupted into dozens of spiny claws that reached for him. With lightning speed and the impeccable precision one would expect from a thinner and lighter blade, the silver-steel sword slashed through every attack while Alistair approached, cool and unrelenting. The creature squirmed back in panic after losing so many limbs but could not move fast enough. Following Lara's example, he decapitated the creature and made a swift X through its eyes in a fluid motion. It burst into light and dissipated.

Hazel ran to the side of the man who had been speared. *He's dead,* Lyvaelan thought. *Let him go.* Hazel's green glow exploded and swirled around her as the man's wounds knit back together. Potted plants and nearby trees grew tangled and large, as if feeding off the green aura surrounding her. Lyvaelan's eyebrows lifted. *I suppose Hazel has more surprises than I realized.*

None of the aufhockers appeared to pay him any attention. He ducked into an alleyway and breathed, focusing on imagining the screaming people he saw. The appearance of the frightened young woman Alistair saved wrapped around him. His fingers twitched as he wove a glamour into his voice and appearance, creating the irresistible sense of one who was helpless and in trouble. He drew upon the dark magic of the aufhockers to make the spell doubly enticing. With any hope, this would draw all the unoccupied aufhockers to him and away from those who were actually helpless. He took a deep breath and screamed a loud, feminine scream. He drew another breath and sharpened his natural and supernatural senses by using sorcery. In the dark of the alleyway, the odious presence of an aufhocker crept toward him. Its hunger and lust for blood filled his mind. He turned, feigning fear. The creature rose with giant fangs, and four small white eyes on its head as it reached for Lyvaelan.

"Don't worry, honey, you're going to be okay."

Lyvaelan rolled his eyes. "I will, but you won't, idiot." He pointed his hand at the monster's head and a concentrated yellow blast of sunlight shot from his palm. The aufhocker was totally obliterated. The ruse attracted fewer than he'd hoped, but at least it worked. Lyvaelan emerged from the alley and surveyed the area. Alistair killed a second aufhocker, decisively slicing its head in two and wheeled on another, who moved to ambush him and avenge its comrade. Lara stood between the intelligent six-eyed aufhocker and several more people it had dragged out and attempted to attack around Lara. The closer she moved to it, the closer its tentacles got to the prey behind her. She could defend them when she was close, but her reach was limited and her speed was easily outmatched by the vampire.

As Lyvaelan watched, a realization dawned on him. He knew Lara struggled to protect these people, but he also saw she wasn't truly standing between the monster and its goal. It wanted her to protect them. She wasn't shielding the people from the aufhocker; the aufhocker was shielding the Alchemist from her. Lyvaelan stepped behind the aufhocker, though one of its white eyes traveled around its body, watching him. Alistair dispatched the penultimate monster and rushed to another side, cutting off the final aufhocker's escape route back to the alchemy shop. Another white eye tracked him. Hazel stood opposite from him, green glow still emanating from her body; the previously injured man now taken back inside by his wife. Yet another white eye watched Hazel. The intelligent aufhocker showed no signs of emotion, just that sleek, black humanoid form with horns. It silently regarded them. It retracted its tentacles and stood still, showing no signs of aggression.

Lyvaelan mentally reached out to the creature. Invisible strings controlled it on some level, though its intelligence was its own. The monster shifted its focus to Lyvaelan. It studied him impassively.

"You are all... fools." Its voice had the same dark, whispering quality it had before, but now it was loud enough to shake the air, and ended with a series of insectoid clicks.

"Your allies are dead, and you are surrounded," Alistair said, brandishing his sword. "Surrender. Tell us about your master, the Alchemist."

The creature gurgled a laugh. *"Fools. You have... no idea. So small. You save twigs while the forest burns."*

Alistair pointed his longsword at the monster. "Answer our questions or die."

The aufhocker's single eye that was trained on Alistair shifted up slightly, then returned to the vampire. Without warning, it rushed at him and thrust the sword into its middle, holding on to Alistair's arm with both hands. It slowly drew the sword up its body as the vampire regarded its suicidal actions with shock. It leaned close to Alistair. "*Though I seem to die, the night returns tomorrow.*" Its head jolted upright. "*Kill him!*" The aufhocker pulled the vampire's arm along with the sword through its head as all the white lights in its head blinked out but didn't burst like the others. In the same instant, Alistair screamed in pain as a bloody human hand exploded from his abdomen.

The Alchemist had arrived.

Chapter Thirty-Five
The Burden of Limitless Power

"Alistair!" the three shouted in unison.

"I can't risk you damaging my plans. You're too fast."

The Alchemist withdrew his hand from the vampire with a loud *crack*. Several vertebrae were clasped in his fist. Alistair collapsed to the ground. He struggled to pull himself up, but his legs remained unmoving as blood and entrails spilled from his wound.

Paxton looked at his hand and retched. He threw the pieces far from him and flicked his hand with a movement that made the wings of hummingbirds look slow. Reddish purple blood and colorless spinal fluid disappeared from his hand in a puff. He adjusted his glasses and smiled, drawing a notebook and a pencil from his pocket. Lyvaelan staggered back, stunned. That speed! It wasn't a spell that cleaned his hand, but a swift vibration so strong it rid his hand of Alistair's blood instantly. Paxton's outward changes were minimal. His body was only slightly more muscular than before, but every vein and artery in his body glowed with a pale and bright blue light, as did his eyes.

Paxton inspected his hands and nodded as he wrote in his book. "The present iteration condenses power without abnormal growth in size. Speed is greater than baseline, as are strength and regenerative properties." He glanced at the vampire. "I wanted to put my hand through your heart, but you must've heard me coming and jumped. I was right to fear your speed."

Hazel rushed to Alistair who, despite his injuries, protested through forced groans he was otherwise fine.

"You bastard!" Lara leaped over her companion and lunged at Averly but missed. She swung again, punching, kicking, and leaping with ever-increasing speed, but each blow was as fruitless as the last. He moved with such alacrity that it bordered on teleportation.

Paxton evaded another punch. "Heightened reaction time"—he slapped away one attack with a hand and wrote in his book—"and temporal perception, or existence"—Lara kicked, but he caught it and flipped her over—"appears simultaneously slowed and increased"—she tried to sweep his legs out from under him but he jumped over remaining in place—"with recovery for any exertion near instant." She leaped to her feet and circled him. "Feelings of elation and energy are coupled with a growing sense of invulnerability. Whether this is because of some innate property of the compound or is a byproduct of success is unclear. Further tests are necessary." Lara feigned a roundhouse punch with her right but jabbed with her left. Paxton caught the punch with one hand and looked into her eyes. "No cognitive impairment or enhancements noted." He twisted Lara's hand and threw her a couple dozen feet away.

"Oh, but where are my manners?" Paxton bowed. "I should thank you for helping me test my new product. I think it will be quite popular."

Lyvaelan reached out mentally to Paxton. Most magical attacks Lyvaelan knew of the Alchemist would be able to dodge, but a psychic assault required only one mind to invade another. He ignored the surface thoughts and emotions of his companions—Alistair's pain, Lara's frustration, and Hazel's shock. Random whispers came from Paxton, showing that his mind was unguarded. Lyvaelan could paralyze him on the spot. When he finally touched his mind, he slipped. He tried again and got closer when his attention shifted away again. Thoughts and memories popped from Paxton without context or connection to the present. What strange alchemy was this?

Hazel stood and gritted her teeth. She was the angriest Lyvaelan had seen. *No,* he mentally pleaded to himself, trying desperately to concoct a plan. *Please don't fight him.* Green light erupted from her in all directions, filling the street. She raised her arms and a giant root emerged from the middle of the street beneath Paxton. He moved swiftly enough to avoid it but didn't notice the ivy covering his home had grown and reached for him. The ivy wrapped around him, drawing him into the air in a multitude of slithering vines. Hazel raised her hand and threw it down multiple times as the ivy slammed him repeatedly into the ground, following her every motion. As she brought him down once more, he grabbed the street and slipped free from their grasp. He tossed a handful of broken stone at her with that same absurd speed. Several pieces hit and stunned her momentarily. He hefted a heavy piece of flagstone and hurled it at Hazel, which caught her in the head, knocking her to the ground, unconscious, but still glowing.

He turned and narrowly prevented a giant, furred claw from slicing into him as he caught it above his head. Lara stood over eight feet tall in her half-wolf form, dark brown fur covering her entire body. She snarled at him, her paw pushing him slowly down. For a moment, Paxton's eyes revealed panic before he disappeared from under her as her paw shattered part of the street.

"Note to self," he said. He stood several paces away, and his voice shook ever so slightly. "Strength is limited and appears inferior to that of a transformed werewolf."

"Damn right," she growled as she sprang at him again.

Paxton flipped onto his back the moment before she made contact, and using his legs and her momentum, sent her sprawling a few feet from Alistair. He rose to his feet and advanced on Lara. As he passed near Alistair, he tripped and narrowly dodged Alistair's sword. Despite grievous injuries, Alistair continued to fight.

Lyvaelan watched in horror, transfixed by the scene. They had fought powerful individuals before and the aufhockers were dangerous, but this? This was beyond them.

They couldn't win.

They were going to die.

As he continued to assail the Alchemist's mind, he struggled to ignore the dark side of him, hungering to be let loose. *Your power is unbeatable. They are weak. Destroy.*

Paxton glared at Alistair and dodged backward to avoid Lara's fist to his midsection. He underestimated her reach and had the air knocked out of him, along with some bile. Lara grinned triumphantly. If they could get the potion out of his stomach, then his power would fade. Lara's amber lupine eyes widened. Her grin faded.

His vomit wasn't blue.

"Ugh, disgusting." Paxton spat and smiled when he noticed her dismay. "Didn't I tell you my specialty? Topical alchemy agents. They take longer to work, but they don't need to be ingested and so they can't be regurgitated. That alleyway thug you fought just had an early prototype. I added some white lotus and a dash of henbane to the brew I gave the hired muscle. I couldn't have them remembering anything important, now, could I?"

Lyvaelan watched as Alistair struggled to prop himself up on his elbow, holding his sword in his other hand. While Paxton's back was to him, the vampire threw his sword with accuracy and speed at the Alchemist's head. Lara lunged for a second strike. The Alchemist noticed the flash of steel and silver out of the corner of his eye as he readied himself and caught the blade. Lara slashed at his abdomen but only clipped him, tossing him a few feet away with the sword still in his hand.

She leaped at the Alchemist, who lay prone before her. Lyvaelan saw the glint in Paxton's eye.

Lyvaelan reached out desperately. "No! Lara!"

Paxton flipped the sword in his grip and ducked beneath her, running the sword through her middle as he twisted aside. Lara gasped. She tumbled forward from the momentum and then fell to her side.

One trembling paw pulled the blade from her middle. Her skin smoked where she clasped the metal. The sword fell to the ground.

Lyvaelan redoubled his efforts, sweat beading on his brow despite the cold. He worked feverishly to develop a plan or remedy to the situation while he continued to fruitlessly besiege the Paxton's mind.

The Alchemist was uninterested in waiting. He sauntered to Lara's side and kicked the werewolf in the ribs.

"Stupid wolf! Did you think your cheap martial arts and amateur wrestling moves that worked against an addled half-wit criminal would defeat me?" He stomped on her back and she cried out in pain. "I've beaten you, Lara. Me, a weak, fragile, talentless human! No more!" He kicked her again with greater force. "Not so strong with silver piercing you, huh?" He grabbed the back of her head and slammed it into the ground. He glanced back at Alistair. "Don't think I've forgotten about you. I think it's about time I returned this pretty sword back to its owner. Wouldn't you agree?"

Lyvaelan leaped forward. He had wracked his brain trying to devise a strategy or some magic that would work. Paxton's mind moved in strange ways that made sorcery almost impossible for Lyvaelan, especially under stress like this. Finally, upon observing the horrifying power before him, he settled on something desperate that wouldn't hurt the others. Null magic. He'd heard of null magic before, but never used it. Some archmage of dark elf lineage had discovered it. He hoped that, despite his inexperience, he could use it. Summoning up the dark, terrible feelings he had inside, he pictured everything being swallowed in an unfathomable abyss. He imagined opening this darkness within himself, wider and wider, and then threw his hands forward as black gouts of flame burst from him, screaming like steam escaping a teakettle as they enveloped Paxton Averly. The flames wouldn't hurt Lara, but they would disrupt the Alchemist's magic. Paxton raised his arms against the blast and struggled toward Lyvaelan like a man pushing against the flow of a mighty river.

"This won't work, Lyvaelan," Paxton yelled over the scream of the flames. "I can feel my power decreasing, but the difference is negligible. You'd have to do this for hours to drain me of enough magic to defeat me, and you'd be long destroyed by that point. Admit it. You've lost."

Lyvaelan felt the resistance to the flames disappear abruptly. He grabbed both his legs, sending a jolt of thaumaturgical energy into them and jumped ten feet up, narrowly escaping a punch from the Alchemist. Lyvaelan reached the side of the building and climbed into the shadows of the alleyway. He imagined blending with the shadows and used his dark elf heritage to aid him as the night swallowed him.

Paxton searched for him, the same pleasant smile on his face. "You really have lost. I've been generous, even if you fail to see it." He glanced through the different alleyways and at the rooftops. "I'm through playing games, though. Look at your friends, Lyvaelan." He gestured to them. Lara still breathed and remained in werewolf form, struggling on the ground, bruised and bloody. Alistair could barely crawl, an ever-widening pool of blood surrounding him. Hazel just began to stir after being knocked unconscious. "You cannot win. All you can do is die." He giggled. "With this silver sword, I can kill the werewolf *and* the vampire at once. Then I can kill the green girl. After that, it should be simple to kill every witness in the neighborhood. Shouldn't be more than a couple hundred, on the safe side."

You can destroy him. Slay him, the dark whispers said to Lyvaelan.

He pushed the intrusive thoughts away, but his resistance waned. "What I want to know is how a simple alchemist managed to conjure aufhockers." Lyvaelan's voice came from the shadows. He struggled to control his breathing and hoped the implied question would buy him time to think of something.

"Every professional has his secrets." Paxton's eyes shot to the location but found the echo of the dark elf's voice reverberated through every shaded alcove. He sighed in frustration. "You're stalling. Time to start the executions. I'll kill the werewolf first. Then Alistair and Hazel.

I'll kill every single person in this Mirnak-damned city until only two of us remain, and then you can see how your cowardice annihilated the sovereign city of Coruvaine!"

Lyvaelan's head pounded. The voice in his mind got louder and multiplied into a roaring chorus, urging him on. He looked at his hands as small black cracks wove through his skin. Electrifying energy drew into him from every alley, street, and house as he became a living funnel for the magic.

No. His hands dug into his scalp. *They won't die. They can't. I have the power. I* am *the power.* His eyes turned utterly black.

The light that floated above the street flickered and disappeared. Paxton squinted and blinked, adjusting to the dark. He smiled when he saw Lyvaelan emerge from an alley. "Oh, so you decided to—" his smile vanished when he noticed the dark elf warlock's expression. His pupils had completely dilated. The area surrounding his eyes had blackened, with shadowy fissures reaching from the epicenter of his eyes. Lyvaelan's gritted teeth maintained a horrifying expression between hatred and glee.

Averly gasped and staggered back. "You're a warlock." He turned to run, but Lyvaelan was there. Everywhere he looked, he was there, staring. Unable to escape, Paxton sprinted at Lyvaelan, but a shield separated them and every blow the Alchemist landed damaged it less than leaves in autumn damaged the earth when they fell. He stepped back to retreat but found his speed no longer availed him. Lyvaelan heard the thoughts of the Alchemist, and his grin widened as he transfixed him mentally. He no longer relied on years of training in sorcery to achieve his goal. Wizardry, sorcery, enchantment, conjuration, alchemy, and thaumaturgy were disciplines reserved for weak humans.

He was a warlock. His perfect will manifested through magic. Reality was his to bend and break. And he would.

Lyvaelan raised one hand in the air and Paxton's feet lifted from the ground. Lyvaelan squeezed and Paxton shrieked as his body compressed, gripped by the unseen hand of the warlock. Lyvaelan moved his fingers violently, and the Alchemist convulsed with frantic screams as each bone in his body broke with a series of individual snaps. Lyvaelan levitated him higher in the air as darkness gathered in smoking tendrils from the ground. Thunder rolled and red lightning streaked across the sky.

"Paxton Averly," Lyvaelan spoke with many voices at once as a storm rumbled overhead. "I lay upon you all the curses of the goblin witches and the dread and thrice-accursed Oathbreakers. I draw you into the shadows of the Unseelie Court and the forever bloodied claws of the Morrigan that will ravage your soul. You shall find no peace, no respite from the sidhe who will haunt your dreams with nightmares of the blackest reaches of the Otherworld." The Alchemist's eyes bulged. The shadows around Lyvaelan stretched and filled with the fanatical giggles of vile and twisted beings, incomprehensible in their madness and unfathomable in their cruelty. Lyvaelan stood amid this darkness, like some monstrous king of legends past who these phantoms obeyed without question. They swarmed Paxton with gnashing teeth and fangs, frightful eyes, and searching tongues. Lyvaelan lifted his other hand to Paxton. "Writhe." Black lightning shot from his hand and coiled around the Alchemist, who screamed from the pain and terror of the countless horrors ripping into his flesh.

The world descended into chaos. Lightning arced across the sky and struck innumerable times nearby as thunder boomed and rattled the earth. The wind whipped in every direction as a howling, omnidirectional gale. Hail the shape and size of daggers poured from the sky but were whipped by the wind, breaking into walls and smashing windows. Random flames burst in every color through the air.

Amid this pandemonium, Lyvaelan held Paxton. The lightning surrounding the Alchemist bit into him as blood vessels burst in his eyes. Lyvaelan savored the overwhelming power flowing through him. He never lacked power, he merely had to set it free. Now that it was released, it was taking over. He looked at his hands. His fingertips had gone completely black, and the darkness spread along his arms as each fissure pulsed and connected with others. The exhilaration transcended anything he had ever experienced. Intoxicating euphoria flooded him with the immense magic he channeled. If he died, it didn't matter, so long as he could experience this until the end. Even if he wanted to stop now, he couldn't. The magic would immolate his entire being, and he would enjoy it.

He glowered at the struggling Alchemist. *So weak.* He grinned and continued to exert his power. The blue had faded from Paxton's body, and he stared forward in vacant terror as not even the pain of multiple broken bones could shake him. There was no more magic left to drain. *I'm going to kill him. Just like I killed*—Lyvaelan winced. *No. I... can't.* He struggled inside, with one part begging him to continue, urging and demanding to fulfill his bloodlust and pour all his hatred into his hapless prey. The other side was softer, gentler. He didn't know why, but he found that kindness push him with greater strength. Lyvaelan whipped his hands away, releasing the broken Alchemist. The black lightning from his hand streaked across the street, ripping up parts of the road and collapsing part of a building. He cut off the power.

He stood, panting, the swirling storm around him intensifying. Lightning cracked, and the sky turned purple. Shapes of vast monsters flying behind the clouds appeared and disappeared with the intermittent lightning flashes. He dropped to his knees and watched as fire rained from the sky. In the distance, a massive funnel cloud reached for the ground. Then he saw another. And another. All around Coruvaine, funnel clouds formed, destined to become devastating cyclones.

"Lyvaelan!" Hazel yelled over the gale. She had risen to her feet and pushed against the storm to reach him. His blackened eyes turned mournfully toward her.

This was the end.

A black tear fell from his eye.

This was the last time he would ever see her.

He opened a tunnel in the maelstrom for her to walk to him. It was selfish for him to bring her to his side, but it was okay to be a little selfish, wasn't it? He wanted his last moments to be with her, thinking of her. Hazel dashed to his side. "Lyvaelan, you have to stop this." Her eyes held urgency and concern. She didn't know.

He extended his hand to Alistair's sword which flew to his palm. He pressed it into her grasp. He gazed at her with his pure black eyes reflected in her beautiful hazel eyes. "They can't help me," he whispered. "You have to end this."

"What?" Phantoms screamed behind her. Another blast of iridescent lightning shattered the street.

"Kill me."

"No." Behind her, a tree uprooted and soared skyward.

"Please," he pleaded, "It's too much. I'm going to kill *everyone*."

She threw the sword away. Her eyes welled, but she looked at him resolutely. "I won't do it."

"Then I must try." The sword lifted in the air and flew point first to Lyvaelan's chest but stopped short when Hazel threw her arms around him and it pierced her instead. "Hazel," he whispered, black tears now flowing freely, "why?"

"I told you before," she said. Sparkling tears fell from her eyes, but her expression wasn't sorrowful or pained. "I won't give up on you if you haven't given up on me." Green light surrounded her and the sword slid from her body.

"Everyone will die," he rasped.

"Then so will I."

His eyes widened. He felt a cold shiver down his spine as more tenebrous tears fell. "No."

"Yes." She held his shoulders and stared into his eyes. "I'm with you until the end. If this is the end for you, then it's the end for me, too. I won't let you go."

"No." Lyvaelan whispered. The green light around her ignited a distant spark in his heart, and he remembered. He remembered the first time they met. She was an intriguing mystery. His memories flashed through all the lessons he gave her, all the dreams she told him.

He thought of her challenges in feeling her emotions and personally connected with her struggle. He remembered how she wished for him to one day feel true joy and found it strange that someone he barely knew would be the first to wish that for him.

The storm churned around them.

"No!" He remembered his terror at seeing her pierced by arrows. He saw her concern and unwillingness to give up as she healed him from a previous battle. He saw her smile of relief. He recalled walking back and feeling the smallest fragment of a positive feeling. Hope?

Hazel held him close as the falling fire became floating embers. The lightning flashed distantly, and the thunder grumbled instead of roared. Chunks of the street gradually descended back to the ground.

"*No!*" He remembered her insistence she would never kill him and she would find some other way to help him or die in the process. A lump formed in his throat. How had she come to speak so authoritatively to him? How could she look at him so warmly and genuinely when he was such a dark and twisted creature of hate and confusion?

The funnel clouds receded into the sky and the cutting wind slowed. Hazel glowed a faint green as the black lines receded and disappeared from his light gray skin.

"*NO!*" he cried as he remembered. A blast of magic exploded from him, releasing his hold on the world. She had sought him out to learn, but he had a debt to her that he could never repay. He would try, though. He refused to let this be the end. He refused to let Hazel, Lara, and Alistair die because he had given up. His life meant nothing to him, but their lives were worth fighting for. He flattened the rapturous intoxication with the even stronger desire to see his friends live. As he cried out, the black retreated into his eyes. The warlock hugged her close, unwilling to let go. Unwilling to lose her. The remaining disturbance calmed, and the night fell quiet. He blinked several times before collapsing onto her, feeling weak. His eyes had returned to red.

Lyvaelan could do nothing but lean against Hazel and weep. They wept together.

Chapter Thirty-Six
To Heal and To Be Human

Other members of the Evenfall Vigil—no doubt brought by the bright lights and the cataclysmic storm—had just arrived. They stared in stunned silence at the destruction and its conclusion. Lieutenant Leo Hipparchus and Sergeant Concornus surveyed the scene with shocked wonder. Three dozen other Evenfall Vigil soldiers approached, hesitant to wander into the stilled madness. After the blast of the storm, the world was unnaturally quiet as a soft drizzle fell from the sky.

Lara rolled to her side. Blood gushed from her belly before she held her claw over it to stanch the flow. She reverted gradually into her human form, which shrank the wound slightly. This wouldn't kill her, but she felt a long way from healthy. Reverting would help prevent her from losing too much blood until she received medical attention. Thankfully, the Alchemist missed piercing anything too essential. She kneeled in place for some time before she felt she could move. The battering he gave her hurt more than normal, a side effect of getting stabbed with silver. She noticed Alistair rise to his feet. He retrieved the vertebrae that had been ripped out and had healed just enough to stand, though he still held a hand to his bleeding stomach, which already showed signs of closing. The vampire prince averted his eyes and struggled to remove his cape as he approached. He offered it to her. "Here, cover yourself up."

She wobbled to her feet, taking the garment. She had nearly died. She hardly cared that she was now nude. "As injured as you are, you still worry about modesty?" she croaked. The sting of blood in the back of her throat made her wince.

He smiled weakly. "Always."

"I think if you had any blood left in your body, you might be blushing."

He coughed up blood. "Just put on the damn cape."

She almost laughed but grimaced at the pain. He handed her the bloody cape. A hole had been ripped through the fabric where the Alchemist struck. Alistair teetered precariously, and she supported him despite his protests. She observed the street. The once calm area was ripped to shreds. Miraculously, most of the homes in the area hadn't sustained tremendous amounts of structural damage. She watched Hazel and Lyvaelan, who still held each other. "You know, Al, I think she has another power."

Alistair tracked her eyes to Hazel and glanced back. "What's that?"

She shook her head and shivered. "She's the only one who can keep us from destroying ourselves."

Chapter Thirty-Seven
Drinks After Work

The Watchers of the Evenfall Vigil returned to the library via carriage. Even if their physical injuries hadn't warranted such conveyance, the emotional toll of the confrontation with Paxton Averly was enough. The group spoke little on the way back, save to answer questions asked by an Evenfall Vigil soldier who needed to get their preliminary account. When they arrived, Lyvaelan retreated immediately to his room and Hazel shortly after retired to hers. It was only an hour after midnight, which was early for them, but the night had seemed endless and exhausting. Inquisitor Eller was neither in his office nor in the library, but the group didn't care. They could brief him the next day if necessary.

After donning a robe from her room, Lara joined Alistair in the common area where he reclined supine on the couch. She smirked. "A little while ago you scolded me for lying in the same position in the same place."

He opened an eye at her. "Yes, but you weren't suffering from severe blood loss."

"Point taken." She settled into a wingback chair with a groan. "Literally *and* figuratively." She let out air as she felt pain where she was stabbed. Werewolves could regenerate from most wounds quickly, but getting stabbed with a weapon of alchemical silver made healing difficult. Hazel helped, but even with her extraordinary healing abilities, the wound only scabbed over, although her other injuries were gone. Too much movement risked reopening the scab. She supposed she shouldn't complain too much, since Hazel's healing appeared to have no effect on Alistair.

She sniffled. "I failed."

"None of tonight went as planned."

"No, I mean—" she bit her lip, not trusting herself to speak.

Alistair met her eyes and nodded. "Neither of us could make good on our pact. Thank the gods."

"I just—I wanted to help," a tremor reached her voice that she tried to suppress. "I wanted to keep her safe."

"I know," he whispered.

"I haven't tried to be a good person in a long time, not consciously. But I didn't think I was a horrible person. Not like I do now."

"You're not, Lara. Not even a little." Alistair sighed and closed his eyes. "You made hard choices and attempted to solve it the only way you knew how. You were right to form a contingency plan against him."

"Hazel helped him without hurting him. She found another way. If we were closer to him, could we have helped?"

"Maybe. Regardless, our agreement still stands since he's alive. What do you want to do?" Alistair opened his eyes and studied her impassively.

"I want to be better," Lara whispered. "To be better, I need to see the good in him and trust that it's greater than the evil. I need to be like Hazel."

"So do I. I agree."

They sat in silence for a couple of minutes, both focused on their respective wounds and the emotions they held. He made no pretense of gloating over the decision, nor did he add to her guilt. Perhaps the vampire was as perfect as he liked to appear.

Shrugging off the uncomfortable feelings, she instead admired how much he had recovered. It amazed her he could walk, let alone speak. Vampiric healing put even werewolves to shame.

"Ugh." Alistair groaned. "I need a drink. Maybe some food too. Would you care to join me?"

"I never turn down an invitation to drink. Who knows? Maybe with all the blood loss I'll finally be a cheap date."

He chuckled and fell to coughing. "I can't imagine with your tastes you'd be an expensive date, regardless." He raised his head a little. "Charlie!"

The redcap housekeeper appeared almost instantly, watching Alistair expectantly.

"Charlie, could we get a platter of the leftover meat from earlier? I would also love if you could bring me a bottle of blood wine and a glass."

"W-warm food, or cold food? W-warm w-wine, or cold w-wine?"

"Whatever is fastest, if you please. It has been an arduous night." Charlie nodded solemnly and turned to Lara.

"Whiskey for me. Some of the meat too. I'm not picky if it's hot or cold, just bring a lot." Charlie nodded and disappeared. A few moments later and a bottle of wine with a glass appeared before Alistair and a bottle of whisky with a shot glass on top appeared before Lara. She moved the shot glass aside and opened the bottle.

Alistair turned with a grimace onto his side. He stared at the wine bottle on the table. From his present position, he was not quite close enough to reach it. He strained with his arm and closed his eyes as if willing the bottle into his hand. The bottle didn't move one iota. He gave up trying with a sigh. "What I wouldn't do to have the gift of psychokinesis right now."

Lara slid to the floor so she could sit near the table. She uncorked the bottle of blood wine and poured Alistair a glass. "There's always tomorrow."

"Right." He smiled and raised his glass. "To learning psychokinesis tomorrow?"

"To learning psychokinesis tomorrow." They both drank deeply from their respective glasses. "Hey, is that actually something vampires can learn? That's moving things with your mind, right?"

"Yes, but it's challenging. Most of the masters learned to fly first and then trained to use psychokinesis, but I've also heard it's difficult regardless of what one learns first."

"Well, you can already fly, so it shouldn't be too long."

He laughed and winced at the pain. "Do you know how long it took me to get to this point in terms of flying?"

"How long?"

"Nineteen years."

Lara whistled.

"Precisely. It takes time to learn and master any vampiric skill."

She leaned back, her bottle of whiskey in one hand as she gazed at the ceiling. "Still, it'd be great to move things with my mind. Sometimes I'll forget to extinguish a candle before bed and then I have to get up to douse it. It'd be worth it for that alone."

He turned his head and squinted at her. "You'd spend twenty years of diligent practice just to save yourself the trouble of getting out of bed? That would be worth it?"

"Yep." She grinned. "Not that I wouldn't want it for other things, too. I could spend all night at a party and psychokinetically tap a person on the shoulder every few minutes and act like nothing happened. It'd drive that person crazy."

His smile spread uncharacteristically wide. "I never would have thought to use it that way. Now I'm tempted to learn it. I assume you'd do it with people you hated?"

She shrugged. "Probably. I mean, there would be pranks I'd play on you, Hazel, or maybe Lyvaelan, but you'd know I had that power, so you'd probably suspect it was me the entire time."

"Fair point." He took a deep drink from his wine and sighed.

"Is the wine really that good?"

"It is to me."

"Charlie! Bring another wineglass!"

The redcap appeared with two large plates of cold, cooked meat from the last couple of nights. He set one tray before each of them and produced another wineglass, which he handed to Lara.

"Are you sure?" Alistair asked. "It probably won't be to your liking."

"What, are you afraid I'm gonna drink all your wine? I'll *try* to be moderate." She poured a glass and took a sip. She contemplated the taste. It reminded her of both wine and blood in equal measure. The aroma and consistency belonged to a red wine, but it also had the iron-taste of blood with the slight sting of alcohol. "You know... it's not terrible. I like it."

"Really?" Alistair's eyes widened with interest. "You're the first non-vampire I've met who didn't find it revolting."

"Well, my kind fought alongside yours during the War of the Night, in case you'd forgotten. Neither of us were alive back then, but I'll bet on some level we both desire human blood."

He nodded. "Much though I hate to admit it, you're right. I assumed because my race depends on blood to exist while yours can eat any meat, the desire for human blood wouldn't be in you."

"Don't get me wrong," she said, downing the rest of her wine. "I still prefer the hard alcohol, but drinking this stuff feels nutritious."

"It is. Honestly, I feel significantly better since I started drinking."

"I always feel that way."

He gave her a wry smile. "I'm sure you do."

She studied him. Although he wasn't showing it, she could tell he was still in considerable pain. She wondered if vampiric healing could really repair a broken spine so quickly.

"You can't really walk, can you?"

He stared into her eyes, icy blue meeting fiery amber.

"No," he whispered.

"Why didn't you say something?"

He stared at the ceiling. "It wasn't the right time for me to draw attention away from others who needed it more."

"You've just been flying all this time and barely moving your legs. I assumed you were wobbly because you were healing slowly."

He gave a small smile. "That's technically true, just not for the reasons you guessed."

"How long will it take you to heal?"

He shifted his head back and forth uncertainly. "I will likely be able to walk again in the next few days. I won't be able to use my full speed for another two weeks or more after that, I would guess."

"Well, if you need a crutch, just let me know. I'm strong enough to support both of us."

He closed his eyes. "Thanks, Lara."

She leaned back. This was nice. Pleasant, even. Despite the rocky start to their acquaintanceship, the two were closer than she would've expected. He was still prissy and obsessive, but she admired his fighting spirit. He seamlessly combined speed, skill, and strategy. She was better in the nitty-gritty aspects of combat, but he changed his tactics when they worked for her, and that level of quick adaptability meant he had to keep a cool head. Most vampires were good at maintaining composure—or at least the appearance of it—but Alistair kept calm in stressful situations without sacrificing intuitive action. If he saw someone in trouble, he took the swiftest path to them and acted in a way to best benefit the situation. Rather than pushing a person out of harm's way, he stood between the danger and the victim and fought. It was a rare thing, in her experience, and she respected him for it.

"Hey Al," she said after a minute of unbroken silence, "why do you wield a sword? Most vampires I know don't use weapons."

He opened his eyes. "Most don't. Personally, I've always found swords to be fascinating. The concept of fighting with one seemed right. It also symbolized something important to me. Not long ago, my clan was little more than a collection of ravenous beasts. By wielding a sword, I separate myself from most other vampires by being a positive symbol of civility. A beast does not wield a weapon, but a man does. I'm the first vampire born without the bloodcurse and so even though I'm the youngest of my siblings, I'm in some ways a leader. I think that's why my father sent me to Ethelian. He wanted me to live as an example of what vampires could be if given the chance."

She thought about her own relationship with her father. "That sounds like a lot of responsibility."

"It is, but I bear it gladly. Any way I can help my parents and do my best as the youngest child."

"I've always wondered what it'd be like to have older siblings."

"You don't have any?" He turned to look at her. "Forgive the intrusive question, but don't you have littermates?"

She laughed. "Werewolves have as many children as normal, depending on what form the parents are in when they—"

"—procreate?"

She winked coyly at him for his interruption. "Exactly. If it's in wolf form, then it's a litter. If it's in human form, it's usually single children, but twins are common too. My dad left us when I was about twelve."

If he noticed how she sidestepped the question, he politely left the matter alone. "I'm sorry to hear that. Do you know where he is?"

"No idea. Probably causing trouble for people who don't deserve it. That bastard and I cross paths now and then, and it's never pleasant. Werewolves who aren't part of a pack are vicious."

"I've noticed."

"Hey," she laughed, "that isn't what I meant, though you're probably right."

"You've gotten a lot better from before, though," Alistair said, as he flipped onto his back again. "I don't wish to be presumptuous, but you may have found your pack."

"Maybe I have," she murmured. "And what a pack it is. We're all so... out of place."

"Perhaps that's why we work so well together."

"Yeah." She looked over at him. "By the way, what's the name of your sword?"

His brow furrowed. "That's a random question."

"I'm good at asking those. I figured I should at least know its name after getting so intimately acquainted with it."

He opened an eye and glanced at her. "It doesn't have one."

She frowned. "But isn't it magical?"

"Yes, but only a little. It mostly has enchantments against breaking and dulling, along with alchemical alterations to the steel and silver."

She scoffed. "All magic swords need names."

"Oh, really?" He smiled quizzically at her. "Says who?"

She grinned. "Um, *everyone*. What kind of legendary hero has a nameless blade?"

He rolled his eyes. "Oh, am I a legendary hero now?"

"No, but it'll be really embarrassing when you become a legendary hero and people ask what your sword is called. All the other legendary heroes will end up laughing you out of the legendary heroes' club."

"Well, I wouldn't want *that*." He chuckled. "But given how much good it did us in this last battle, I don't trust myself to give it any appropriate name at present. What kinds of names do you give to weapons anyhow?"

"Something really awesome and meaningful. Something like Godcutter, or Dawnrazor. Oh! I know. You can call it Vampirefang. What do you think?"

He scrunched up his nose.

She sighed. "Yeah, okay, it's not my best work. I'll come up with something better."

"Don't feel the need to hurry. It seems like an unnecessary human convention to me."

"Maybe, but I've heard enchanted weapons can take on personalities of their own once they're given names."

He nodded. "I've heard that too, but I assumed it was superstition."

"It could be. You never know, though. We live in a crazy world."

Alistair's eyes widened. "Certainly crazy enough for me."

Chapter Thirty-Eight
Aftermath

They slept in the day after their confrontation with the Alchemist. Although they had an early night—despite their occupation—not one of them woke before early evening. Hazel rose to a small headache, the first she had since before she died.

She exited her room and walked to the common area. None of the others had come out yet, but she thought she heard sounds from Lara's room when she passed. She gazed toward Lyvaelan's room but didn't approach. The previous night was... exhausting—as much emotionally as physically. To some extent, she knew Lyvaelan hadn't been lying about his power, but what he unleashed was unimaginable. Beholding such impossibly terrifying and yet beautiful magic staggered her. The world rippled and changed at his command, unliving things responded to his words and actions. She'd heard stories of djinn who could grant wishes and warp reality to accommodate the desires of those who asked, and this was the closest she had come to witnessing such raw power.

She sat in the common room, barely noticing Charlie had laid various sweets and breakfast food before her. How should she approach Lyvaelan? Their emotional moment felt awkward in retrospect. Was it better to pretend like it never happened? Would he be embarrassed or grateful? Should he mention it, or should she? She recalled having problems with these thoughts in previous years, but she hadn't come to any definite answer then, and she certainly didn't have one now.

"I heard you had a hard night."

She looked at Garo, who had just appeared and sat across from her. His voice was gentle, and his canine face was filled with concern.

"Yeah, it was... challenging. The hardest we've had."

"You seem deep in thought. How can I help you?"

She considered the problem before speaking. "Somehow, Garo, you know exactly what to say when someone is struggling. How?"

"Years of practice, Hazel. I may not be you, but the ordeal you suffered bothers you and so I want to help if I can."

"I always thought the fae were strange and hard to understand. Most stories I've heard involve difficulties with miscommunication."

He chuckled. "How much do you know about grims?"

"I know you walk through shadows. I know they usually protect some place, although you're different from most. You can also get bigger if you want to. Besides that, not much."

He nodded. "Grims are also known as church grims, by some. When a dog dies, it's sometimes buried by a human at a church, temple, or other holy place symbolically to ask the gods to watch over them. Many other conditions must be met, and some are innate to the dog, but it's possible for the spirit of the dog to return to life to protect whatever area it was interred in. This risen spirit dog is a grim."

"You were a real dog? Do you remember what happened to you or what your life was like?"

"I do, though it seems like a distant dream." He looked away with nostalgia in his eyes. "Dogs are smart creatures, but simpler than humans and other sentient beings. They have thoughts and feelings, instincts and predilections. The difference between a dog and a grim shifts by an order of magnitude regarding personality and intelligence. A dog that's suspicious of strangers would be paranoid and distrustful of others as a grim. A dog that could understand multiple commands may comprehend complex politics and discern potential intentions in others as a grim. When you were a young child, your parents saw parts of who you would be in the future, though it wasn't until you got older that they understood how it would manifest. So it is with grims."

"If grims guard the places where they were buried... where were you buried?"

Garo smiled. "Smart girl. My master was a traveler who called no place home. I died from wounds after we struggled against a pack of wolves. He survived, but my injuries were too grievous for him to treat. He understood me better than any. Better than most humans understand their animals. He buried me at a crossroads. It is unusual for a grim to rise at a crossroads, but I did. He wrote an epitaph for me that became my motivation: *He wandered the roads of the world in life, now let him protect all who wander those roads from beyond the grave. Thank you for choosing me as I had chosen you.* I became the guardian of the world, or so I interpreted my mission. Fae magic is temperamental, and it's unclear how it works or who decides how it works. Is it the doing of the Fae Nobles, or some other force? I don't know. What I *do* know is the sense of purpose I received."

"Do you miss him?"

"Miss who? My master?"

Hazel nodded affirmatively.

"Sometimes, yes, but time makes it easier. He died not long after I did. Old age walked with him but did not kill him. A couple of years after he buried me, he hiked a mountain path and slipped. He died but had a beautiful view from where he fell. To some it might seem like a sad or sudden end, but he died doing what he loved, and it was the most I could hope for him. Komora looked out for him that day."

"You handle his death well."

"It took time, but I moved past it. Grief is natural when one has lost someone dear, but death, too, is natural. To grieve forever is not what the dead would wish for us. When we refuse to accept that a loved one has died, we have died with them and are only phantoms. The living must continue and the dead must rest." He shook himself. "But that's enough about me, Hazel. What about you? You seemed pensive when I first saw you."

She looked toward Lyvaelan's door. How could she explain that moment? The night was harrowing, and there was so much she didn't understand that it was difficult to explain. "Lyvaelan had a really hard night. He told me before how serious it was, but I couldn't believe it would be as bad as it turned out. I calmed him down, but it was really emotional. He was crying, I was crying—it was a mess. I'm not really sure how I'm supposed to face him or what I'm supposed to say."

"Lyvaelan isn't like most young men you've met. He's lived much longer, but in terms of maturity, he still has some growing to do. With that said, he is straightforward with communication. Skirting the issue is unlikely to ameliorate the situation."

"I know what you're saying, but I don't know how to express myself in a way he'll understand."

"That's true of anyone, Hazel. The nature of your ordeal may have been emotional, but remember: he's still the same Lyvaelan you know. Does he matter to you? Do you trust him? If so, trust he will know you have his best interests in mind when you speak. You're not a vindictive, petty young woman, Miss Enda. You brighten the world around you simply by being in it. Your kindness—even if clumsily conveyed—will never be confused for cruelty."

"Thank you, that's sweet of you to say."

Garo chuckled. "It wasn't a compliment, merely an observation. I also get the sense you'll have your chance to speak with him soon enough."

The sound of a door opening came from the hallway. With silent footfalls, Lyvaelan stepped into the room, heading toward the kitchen. His eyes never drifted from the floor, even as he noticed the two. Hazel watched as he walked away. *He's embarrassed,* Hazel thought. *He must feel alone. He must wish he was*—Hazel jumped to her feet.

"Lyvaelan!"

He jolted and looked at her with surprise.

"I—" Hazel stammered, "—I'm glad you're alive."

He stared at her, and his gaze softened as a genuine, warm smile spread across his face. "So am I," he whispered. He then disappeared into the kitchen.

Hazel felt her ears and cheeks warm and she sat down as swiftly as she stood, covering her face. "Why did I say that?" she whispered.

Garo smiled and his tail wagged. "You said it because you felt it. You spoke well, Hazel."

A door opened from the opposite hallway, and a loud yawn preceded Lara's arrival. Her brown hair was tussled chaotically and her half-open eyes betrayed the fact she was still half-asleep. She wore her usual shabby clothes but was also wrapped in a large blanket. When she saw Hazel and Garo, she smiled and walked over to the couch. She sat beside Hazel, curled her legs up onto the couch, and leaned against her. Lara laid her head on Hazel's shoulder and closed her eyes. "Hi Hazel," she mumbled. "Don't mind me, I'm just waking up."

Hazel smiled. "This looks more like falling asleep to me."

"That's how I wake up. Just a few more minutes."

"Perhaps you should ask before imposing on her, Lara," Alistair said, walking gingerly from the hallway. His feet hardly moved.

Lara put her blanket over her head. "Give me a break. I was stabbed last night."

"And I had my spine partially removed, but you don't see me falling all over someone."

A single gleaming eye peeked out from under the blanket. "Maybe you should." She giggled. "I already claimed Hazel. You can cuddle with Lyvaelan."

Alistair's jaw dropped. Lyvaelan strode past him with a steaming cup of tea. "Please don't," he said.

"What—I—no! No! Lara, don't say such ridiculous things so casually. Umbravelle, keep me!" He drifted into the kitchen with a huff.

Hazel noticed his gait was slower than usual, and he walked stiffly. His injury hadn't healed completely. She looked at Lara's blanket-covered head.

"How is your wound, Lara? Can I help you heal it?"

Lara's head poked out again with a smile. "Nah, I'm alright. You did enough last night. It's just a little achy. If it were a normal steel sword, it wouldn't bother me this much, but the silver in the sword slows my healing. I'm mostly fine, though."

"If you say so."

"It could have been much worse. Luckily, Lyvaelan stepped in after Al gave Paxton his sword to stab me with."

Alistair's voice broke in from the kitchen. "I didn't *give* him the sword. I thought I could end the conflict swiftly by hitting him when he was off-guard. Unfortunately, you couldn't distract him enough for my blade to make contact."

"Yeah, sure, blame the girl who was *stabbed*. Where did you even get a sword like that?"

Alistair exited from the kitchen with a glass of blood wine. "The king gave it to me as a gift to celebrate the tenth anniversary of my arrival here. He saw my interest in swordplay and had the sword specially made for me and enchanted."

"What kinds of enchantments?" Hazel asked.

"Mostly sharpness and durability. The protection on the sword makes it harder to break than dragon scales, or so I'm told. It also helped with melding the steel and silver to make them both equally effective."

"That's a boring enchantment," Lara mumbled from under her blanket.

"Is something extremely useful boring to you?"

"Yes, it's *very* boring. I mean, why not have the sword burst into flames or something?"

"Fire on a sword?" Hazel said. "That sounds like a bad idea."

Lara looked up at her in surprise. "What?"

She remembered lessons her father had given her in his forge. "Heated metal is usually pretty weak. If I hit something with a fiery sword, the sword would dent or bend really easily."

"And besides that," Alistair said, gingerly taking a seat, "the wound would cauterize immediately. I don't doubt it would look intimidating, but it would be less effective than a conventional sword."

"I've heard the Paladins of Kalendril use flaming swords," Lara countered.

Alistair scoffed. "They do not."

"They do too! Everyone talks about them."

"If I may weigh in," Garo said, "You're both half-right. I've worked with the Paladin Order of Kalendril, and they *do* use swords that appear to be on fire—"

"—Ha! See!"

"Ahem," he looked at Lara, "their swords are not *actually* on fire. Paladins are accomplished thaumaturgists, and in battle their power spreads to their weapons, which usually manifests as white flame. It does not weaken their weapons, nor does it cauterize wounds, but the magic can cut through extremely hard materials with ease and prevent enemies from regenerating should the foe possess such capabilities."

"That's disappointing." Lara sighed. "Having a flaming sword sounds awesome."

"Not to shift the subject," Garo said, "but I spoke with Thomas Eller earlier today. He spent the night with his fellow inquisitors but will return this evening. He wished me to express his earnest congratulations on your recent success."

Lara grunted. "You mean our borderline disaster?"

"True, but had it been any other members of the Evenfall Vigil, then it would have *actually* been a disaster. No casualties—as far as I know—which is more than most could've accomplished in your circumstances. You feel out of your depth because none of you have experienced challenges like this. The enemies you've faced were ferocious. The Evenfall Vigil has some of the most skilled soldiers of any division within the entire kingdom. I didn't want you all working together to fight easy battles. Every conflict you navigate together reveals strengths and weaknesses you may not have realized were present. If you learn and grow, then you can continue to accomplish great things."

"Yeah, I guess." Lara yawned and then sat up. "Speaking of revealing strengths and weaknesses, did you know Hazel hit the Alchemist repeatedly with a tree last night?"

Garo looked stunned.

"It wasn't really a *tree*," Hazel said quickly. "Just some ivy. It wanted to help, so I told it what to do."

"Stop being modest, Hazel. You'll never get fans that way," Lara said. "She used the vines to pick him up and bash him into the street. It was pretty awesome."

Garo was uncharacteristically flabbergasted. "I... how... when? When did you realize you could do this?"

Hazel shrugged. "I just did it. I've been able to talk with plants for a little while, but when I woke up after being burned, I helped the jasmine outside my window grow and that's when I suspected I could get them to do things for me."

Garo considered this. "So... wait, were you responsible for making that tree root appear in the alchemy shop the night before last?"

"That was the first time I asked a plant for help during a fight."

He shook his head. "Incredible. I'll have to share this with Aldric. I'm sure he'll find this intriguing. Any other powers we should be aware of?"

"Not that I know of, but if I suddenly gain the ability to breathe fire, I'll let you know."

Garo chuckled. "Cheeky girl." He turned to Lyvaelan. "You've been oddly silent. How are you?"

Lyvaelan raised an eyebrow. "I'm not sure I know what you mean by 'oddly silent.' I've never been one for idle chatter. I thought I'd spend the time enjoying my tea instead."

Lara rolled her eyes. "Yeah, he's fine."

"I am, yes. At least, I'm doing as well as expected. Do we have a time when we need to debrief our experiences with Commander Comrear?"

"I would assume," Alistair said, "similar to last night, he would like us to report as swiftly as possible." He shifted uncomfortably and frowned. "Though if he asks us to deliver another sample of the potion tonight, I think I'll politely decline."

"You can politely decline," Lara said, "and I'll beat the shit out of him. That should get the message to him loud and clear."

"I would recommend against assaulting a superior officer," Garo said, "though I understand your dismay at repeating the events of last night. The captain has given you leave to report tomorrow night. Based on what he's told me, you all sustained grievous injuries. He has agreed you can have a full day to rest and recover if that is amenable to you."

The group looked at each other and nodded. Nobody seemed against the idea, at least.

"Good. I'll let him know. Besides, the details of the Alchemist are beyond your range of expertise."

Lyvaelan mused on this. "Might I ask for a favor, Garo? I have a lesson tomorrow with Archmage Relas. He wishes to go through the library for potential study materials. I think it would be best for us to postpone our meeting until after we've talked with Commander Comrear. I hate to make him wait yet again, but—"

"That sounds like a wise decision," Garo said. "Lysander is a good man and will understand. I'm glad he saw the potential in you and wishes to foster it."

Lyvaelan looked aside. "Potential can be good or bad."

"Yes, but he wouldn't want to foster your abilities if they were something terrible."

"Unless he sought to contain it."

Garo sighed. "As pessimistic as ever, hmm?"

"Not pessimistic at all. Realistic. An explosive sitting next to open flame should be guided away from it. I assume that's what he wants to do with me and I don't fault him for it."

"Regardless, I should like to see him again and discuss your training with him. Perhaps I'll drop by if it doesn't interfere with your lesson."

Lyvaelan shrugged. "Sure."

Garo gave a curt nod. "Of course, that is all business for later. Let us discuss much more important, immediate affairs."

Lara raised an eyebrow. "Like what?"

"Dinner. Charlie! I'm feeling a little hungry. How about an early meal?"

Epilogue
The Approaching Storm

Garo emerged from the shadows and onto a balcony rising high above Coruvaine. The view from the palace extended over the western and southern sections of the city. Leaning against the railing, staring into the darkness, stood Aldric.

"Hello Garo," he said without looking.

The black dog cocked his head. "You seem troubled, Your Majesty. After a victory such as what we've won, I would expect a more enthusiastic response. Matters could have fared much worse than they did."

Aldric cast a withering look at Garo. "I shudder to think of how it could've been worse. You assured me the city would be safe from Lyvaelan's power. Against my better judgment, I consented to have him here."

"Coruvaine *is* safe," the black dog replied in his most placating tones. "No one died defeating the Alchemist."

The king snorted. "The fae have a strange sense of safety if a multitude of imminent tornadoes surrounding an inhabited land is considered 'safe.'"

"My apologies, Your Majesty. While they have proven adept, I underestimated the danger of their work. I was blind to this. The Shadow World provided only a meager glimpse of the future, which told me little of this particular event. Only the broadest strokes are revealed to me, much to my displeasure. In the last month, I have been continually confronted with the painful reality that my knowledge is woefully lacking. Despite planning this for decades, surprise after surprise has rendered me little more than a passive actor when I believed myself to be the director of the future."

Aldric calmed gradually as Garo spoke. He rested against the balcony, concern still lining his face. "I wonder if we haven't made a mistake. If *I* haven't made a mistake. I can't resist the creeping dread that everything is falling into place a little too neatly."

"We're following the shadows. Maybe you're sensing the fulfillment of the prophecy?"

Aldric met his eyes. "Or the fulfillment of another." He stood straight and gestured to the west. "Hazel predicts the coming of a living lich. A metaphor, perhaps, but if not, a disaster. It could take dozens of scholars and sorcerers well-versed in foresight to determine the actual meaning of what she said within a fraction of clear comprehension. And yet an inquisitor hears this and decides to sit on the information and keep it from his superiors."

"For our benefit."

"Is it?"

Garo narrowed his eyes. "Are you insinuating that Eller has some ulterior motive?"

Aldric scoffed. "Oh, I know he does, but I don't know what it could be. Hiding this from the Grand Inquisitor could cost him more than his job."

"Do you think he was unaffected by our supplications?"

"I think he was as affected by yours as he was by mine," Aldric replied after several seconds. "Something bothered me after our meeting. He was too willing to delay reports to the Grand Inquisitor. I wonder if I didn't somehow give him exactly what he wanted while I begged him to receive it."

"If you suspect him of treason to the Inquisition, then you could report it to the Grand Inquisitor herself."

"No." Aldric looked sharply at Garo. "No, I wouldn't want that. I feel like I've walked into a cage and only now see the bars. Speaking to the Grand Inquisitor is a mistake, but I don't know what else to do."

"Is Eller the only problem? You could ask for a replacement. If he has kept the secret so far, it's unlikely he'd jeopardize his career to take revenge on you by mentioning Hazel's transformation or prophecy."

"It isn't just him, though. I've read the preliminary reports, both on the capture of Paxton Averly and of the debacle at Susan Telemica's alchemy shop. Someone wanted her to take the blame. They found evidence she was tied to the attacks that was evidently planted there by someone who knew the raid would occur beforehand." He looked at Garo. "Who would have known the attack was happening that night?"

Garo gasped. "You're right. We've been betrayed."

"The question, then, is who and why? Averly's capture was undoubtedly a victory, but it was won more by chance than effort, if we are to believe Hazel's account."

"What do you mean?"

"Was it truly by accident she forgot to deliver crucial documents to him, and he forgot to lock his door when entering his workshop?" Aldric walked to the door. "Follow me. We need to talk with someone who has more answers than we do."

They entered the palace and descended the stairs.

"Aldric, accidents happen and in the space of absentmindedness prophecy can find its foothold. Both Hazel and Averly may have been fulfilling the prophecy accidentally."

"Maybe," Aldric replied, huffing as they reached the ground floor of the palace. "Maybe not. It still doesn't explain who provided Averly with the funds he required to obtain the setup he enjoyed. Based on a rough approximation, his patron would have needed to be wealthy."

"Could he have not made the money himself?"

Aldric glanced at the grim before striding to another staircase. "It's doubtful. Even the most successful alchemists in the city would have struggled to make what he had in a lifetime. He'd only been practicing alchemy for a decade or two in Coruvaine."

Garo looked around the corridor they were in. "Aldric, why are we going to the dungeon?"

Aldric knocked on the heavy wooden door. A small slot opened up at eye level. When the person within saw who it was, the slot closed and the door opened. The king entered as the Sapphire Guard spellcaster stepped aside with a bow.

"We're going to the one who started it all."

"My lord," the Sapphire Guard said, "how may I help you?"

"Take me to see Hickory Allkirk."

The soldier retrieved a hooded lantern from his desk. They descended deeper underground. Candles dimly lit the area and Garo noticed a dampening effect to his magic immediately. He glanced at a few glyphs and symbols he suspected were responsible for the lack of magic in the area.

As they walked, Garo heard a man humming in the dark some distance forward. Several passages turned to the sides, but they continued straight in the direction of the sound. Garo ignored the dank air and smell of mold within and instead wondered what Aldric could learn from speaking with Hickory that the spellcasters could not.

They emerged into a flat area with benches on either side of the room. A single large cell took up the space. Its bars were eight feet back from the benches. A figure, lying on his belly with his head propped up by his hand, faced away from them. He continued humming, slapping one foot against the other to the tune.

The Sapphire Guard hung the lantern in the middle, admitting a little more light.

"Thank you," Aldric said, "that will be all. Please wait back at your post for us."

The man bowed and left. Garo watched the prisoner, who hadn't shifted except to scratch his leg.

Aldric approached the bars and crossed his arms. "Hickory Allkirk? You're up rather late."

Hickory jumped in surprise. He rolled over, dropping the book he had been reading. His gray hair grew unruly, and a beard sprouted from his face without any sense of direction.

"Oh, well, I like to read before sleeping and I got to a good part in the book—" he frowned. "Why would you come to see me if you thought I'd be asleep?"

Aldric sighed. "We came despite the possibility that you'd be asleep, not because of it. I have questions I want answered."

"And it couldn't wait till morning?" Hickory frowned at the light, blinking his eyes.

"No, it couldn't."

"Hmph. Well, it can wait until the next chapter is finished." He picked up the book and dragged himself over to his cot.

"Allkirk," Aldric said, his voice taking an edge. "Put down that book and talk to us. Now."

"You're awfully demanding," Hickory said, unperturbed. "Who do you think you are? The King?" Hickory turned the page.

Aldric sighed.

"Mr. Allkirk," Garo said, "we've come to talk to you about Hazel. We would like to hear your thoughts."

Hickory snorted. "You and the rest of the Inquisition."

"We aren't the Inquisition."

"No?" He looked up, blinking. "Sapphire Guard?"

"Not quite."

He peered closer. "What is a dog...?" he turned to Aldric and threw his book down. "Ah! Your Majesty! I wasn't expecting—I mean, you were not—why are you...? Oh." He bowed mid-genuflection, throwing himself off balance and onto the ground. He scrambled up and began making his bed and fluffing his pillows.

"Look, Hickory," Aldric said, "I don't care if your bed is made. You're in a prison. You're not expected to be orderly."

"Oh, ah, of course." Hickory stood and smoothed out his ragged clothes. He seemed incapable of controlling his hands as they continually patted, adjusted, and fiddled with his garb. "Why are you here?"

"My friend already explained that."

"Who?"

Garo cocked his head. "Me."

"Oh!" Hickory's eyes widened. "You're the other voice! A talking dog! I never thought I'd see the day. I thought the king was just doing two different voices."

"Why in the world would he do that?"

"I don't know, maybe as an advanced interrogation technique?"

"We're getting off-topic," Aldric said testily. "You've been unreasonable with everyone else who's talked with you, so now I must ask you myself. What did you do to Hazel Enda?"

Hickory's face hardened. "I can't tell you everything."

Aldric matched Hickory's determination. "We will settle for anything useful."

Hickory nodded and then glanced at the book on his bed. "I'll tell you, but you have to get me the sequel to this novel. There's only a little left and not everything will be concluded by then. Too many incomplete plot threads. I need to know what happens next."

"Fine, we'll bring you the sequel tomorrow, if there is one. You have my word as King of Ethelian."

"Good. What do you want to know?"

"What is she?" Garo asked.

"I don't know. Next question."

"What do you mean, you don't know?" Aldric demanded. "How could you not know what you did, or did you experiment with others?"

"No, no." Hickory jolted. "I swear by Selevara's eyes I never tried to revive anyone else before her. I just knew it would work."

Garo's eyes narrowed. "What do you mean?"

"It was a feeling—a compulsion. I always wondered if it was possible to use natural magic to raise undead, although my studies were purely theoretical. Using life magic instead of death magic to bring the dead back seems rational, doesn't it? I hypothesized the viability of multiple different creatures to serve as a building block for the enchantments I would need to bring her back. Each had a potential drawback I couldn't eliminate. I lived close to the Enda family, although we never crossed paths except for when Hazel would run by with her friends. When I learned she died, I realized I needed someone vivacious to serve as the subject. Of course, the cemetery is guarded by more than just the Cultists of Semeleme, so I took almost two months to gather my notes and determine which method I would use. Then I used a censer burning alchemical thyme to dig Hazel out of the ground without being noticed by the grim or the cultists and brought her back."

Garo nodded. He had spoken with the grim of that cemetery who was irate she had failed in her duty. "You mention several methods. Which did you try?"

Hickory grinned triumphantly. "All of them."

Garo and Aldric shared a look. "All of them?" the King questioned. "And that worked?"

"Well, she's walking around, isn't she?" Hickory's expression changed when he saw their pensive faces. "Isn't she?"

"Yes," Aldric said, "she is." He blinked and smiled. "Thank you for your time, Hickory. We must be going. I'll have the book sent down tomorrow."

Aldric strode away without further explanation. Garo glanced between the perplexed mage and the king before following. They continued through the hallways and out of the prison. Frustration emanated from the monarch.

"Do you believe his method worked?" Garo asked.

Aldric snorted. "Of course not! I've never heard anything so absurd in my life. It's like saying you've found the perfect dish by combining every ingredient you found in the kitchen."

"Then you think he's lying?"

Aldric slowed his pace. "No, I don't think that either."

"Then what are we left with? What other possibilities exist?"

"Chance is a distant prospect, but I think we both know better than to hope it was an accident that created her."

"Indeed, and much as prophecies fulfill themselves, they do not alter probability to the extent that would cause such a haphazard experiment to succeed."

"Which means someone—or something—is behind this. Something powerful." Aldric stopped to look out of a window. "But what?"

"I don't know," Garo said. "Fae Nobles possess such power, as would the gods or some especially gifted spellcaster, perhaps. We should also question the motives. Was this done for good or ill?"

"In the end, it doesn't matter," Aldric said. He looked at Garo, and his tiredness shone through. "Whatever is evilly made may serve a good purpose, and that which is good may be used for evil. We knew we would have to coax the group in the right direction. Now, we simply know the limits of our information."

"I will stand by them," Garo said. "I have grown closer to them than I wish to admit. I feel like I am one of them."

"You are." Aldric cracked a smile. "You were the first to behold them in the shadows. Whether or not you are employed by me is irrelevant to the group. They are so much more than just protectors of this city, even if they don't realize it yet."

"They will," Garo replied. "You sensed something coming. I do too. A storm rumbling in the distance, approaching Coruvaine. The Alchemist was the first drop of rain in the looming tempest."

Aldric nodded. "Will they be ready?"

"No," Garo said, gazing toward the library, "but regardless, they will fight."

Appendix A: Glossary and Pronunciation Guide

Alchemy: One of the seven arcane arts practiced by human spellcasters. It requires a high level of memorization but little magic. It is known for creating potions that cause a variety of potent effects.

Aldric Valmore (ALL-drik VAL-mohr): King of Ethelian, he rules from the capital city of Coruvaine.

Algendis (al-JEN-diss): The name of the world.

Alistair zar Erythis (AL-iss-tur ZAR air-ITH-iss): Youngest son and child of the vampire royal family of Noxphetalis and member of the Evenfall Vigil.

Alvaria Saccarra (AL-VAR-ee-uh suh-CAR-uh): Archmage of the Inquisition and Grand Inquisitor of the Council of Archmages.

Alza'varathede (AL-zuh VAIR-uh-THEED): A famous dragon.

Amphisbaena (am-fiss-BAY-nuh): A small serpentine creature with an identical head at the end of its tail. They are venomous but generally skittish. They use their four small legs to aid in locomotion as they roll along the ground similar to a wheel.

Arcanathema Prison (ar-can-ATH-em-uh): A penitentiary containing those who used or abused magic to commit crime. The prison is run by the Council of Archmages and directly overseen by a warden.

Arcane Arts: The seven methods used by humans to manipulate magic. These seven arts are Alchemy, Conjuration, Enchantment, Lesser Magic, Sorcery, Thaumaturgy, and Wizardry.

Arcane Cataclysm: An immense release of magic causing unpredictable and dangerous changes in the vicinity. This can occur when a warlock loses control of magic and emotions.

Archmage (ARCH-MAYJ): An individual with high mastery in two of the seven arcane arts and mastery in the others may become an archmage. Once this minimum requirement is met, the candidate must be recommended by a current archmage. The entire Council of Archmages then votes, and the individual becomes an archmage with either a two-thirds positive vote, or a one-half positive vote with the express blessing of the High Archmage.

Arlith Kovak (ARR-lith KOE-vak): Chamberlain of Chateau Zarielle, he is a mage and confidant of Alvaria Saccarra.

Athelea: See Appendix C.

Aufhocker (OWF-hawk-er): A generally malevolent shapeshifting fae of shadow, known for leaping on the back of its victims.

Avrael (AV-ray-el): Archmage of Nullification, he is also the Warden of Arcanathema Prison. He is half dark elf and maintains a neutral affect.

Black Dog: A variety of fae which may be malevolent or benevolent, depending on the specific kind. They generally appear to be black dogs of greater size, intelligence, and power than normal.

Blood Wine: A human invention designed for vampire consumption. It uses a few drops of human blood and a gallon of wine to create a drink that provides substantial nutrition for vampires.

Bloodcurse: A spell found in vampires, therianthropes, and other nocturnal monsters which increased aggression and predation against humans. Those afflicted exhibited a loss of conscience, decreased intelligence, increased strength, and feral tendencies.

Bluecap: A generally benevolent fae that usually appears in the form of a flickering blue flame and is known for mining.

Caeli Relinon (KAY-lee RELL-ih-non): High priestess of Semeleme and also the beloved of the same goddess.

Caleptis: See Appendix C.

Calixford University (CAL-icks-furd): An institution for higher learning regarding magic. It is one of the chief magic universities on the western coast and is located in Coruvaine. Lysander Relas acts as chancellor.

Centaur (SEN-tar): A species of daimon, they appear as a human from the waist up with a horse's body and four legs. They are known for their strength and speed. Centaurs are also notoriously dangerous when they consume alcohol.

Chaldra (CHAL-druh): The name of a massive tree and the city that surrounds it in the heart of Elliara. The surrounding area is inhabited by fae and elves. It is also the regular meeting place of the Council of Light.

Charlie: The redcap cook who lives in the Calixford University Library and prepares meals for the Watchers of the Evenfall.

Chateau Zarielle (ZAR-ee-EL): The home of the Grand Inquisitor.

Conjuration: One of the seven arcane arts practiced by human spellcasters. It uses a variable amount of magic depending on the rapport the conjurer has with the creature being summoned. It is known for controlling monsters, casting spirits from those possessed, and for creating summoning circles.

Coruvaine (cor-uh-VAEN): The capital city of the country of Ethelian. It is the location of the primary garrison of the Watchers of the Evenfall.

Cult of Semeleme: A religious group dedicated to the proper treatment of the dead. They perform the majority of funerary rites within any given city. Their priests are also known as Undertakers.

Daimon (DIE-mon): Any of a class of beings with a range of special abilities and ties to nature that are not classed with fae. Nymphs, satyrs, centaurs, and minotaurs are examples.

Dark Order: A group of spellcasters known for practicing magic illegally. They orchestrated the destruction of the Light Order and the Gray Order.

Draugr (DRAW-gur): A form of undead stronger than a zombie but weaker than a lich. They possess intelligence and a myriad of special abilities unique to each.

Drovir (DROE-veer): A dwarf high master alchemist and dean of the College of Alchemy within Calixford University.

Elchoran: Historical Archmage of Sound who devised a special spell bubble that prevented sound from entering or exiting it.

Elimia: See Appendix B.

Ellen Honrick (HON-rik): A mage working for the Evenfall Vigil, she reports directly to Commander Marcus Comrear.

Elliara (EL-ee-AR-uh): The vast forest region bordering the Vernal Sea and the Noxphetalis Mountain Range north of Ethelian. It is a place of great magic and home to many fae and elves.

Elves: A race subdivided into phylogenetically different subspecies and cultures, they share some core traits which separate them from fae, humans, and daimon. While they possess the pointed ears common to many fae, their culture exists independently of other fae and has little interest in humans. They are related to the fae but their exact relationship is unclear. Wars have been fought between light elves and dark elves for millennia and only came to a tipping point when humans aided light elves and pushed the dark elves further north and into the mountains. Elves are generally known for their capriciousness.

Elves, Dark: Generally feared by humans, they are the darkest in complexion and disposition of all elves. Their magic tends to involve illusion and stealth.

Elves, Light: Since they allied with humans during the War of the Night, they are generally viewed positively, even if their behaviors are poorly understood. Their magic tends to involve healing and light.

Elves, Wood: Humans regard them with healthy suspicion and fear. They maintain forests and the balance between flora and fauna. Their magic tends to involve speaking with beasts and plants.

Enchantment: One of the seven arcane arts practiced by human spellcasters. It uses generally large quantities of magic, depending on the enchantment. It is known for imbuing objects and creatures with magic effects which may be beneficial or detrimental.

Ethelian (eh-THEL-ee-uhn): A kingdom on the western coast of the continent, governed from the capital city of Coruvaine by King Aldric Valmore.

Eustace Skilliven: A friendly barkeep and owner of Skilliven Tavern.

Evenfall Vigil: A subset of the Ethelian city guards which handles nocturnal and supernatural threats.

Fae: A class of beings gifted with considerable magic and in possession of rational thought. They are broadly divided into the Seelie Court—for generally benevolent fae—and the Unseelie Court, for malevolent or hostile fae. They generally dislike use of the term "fae" and prefer to be called "sidhe," "the good neighbors," or "the fair folk."

Faelsday: See Appendix B.

Garo (GARE-oh): A grim, he works as an ambassador for the Seelie Court and advisor to the Watchers of the Evenfall Vigil.

Garson Varaldan (GAR-son vuh-RAL-dun): Archmage of Dragons. He used to study them and now he resembles them.

Garvey: A bluecap.

Gazrilan (GAZ-rih-lihn): A dragon little known by others. He is considered lazy by some and is given the epithet of "the Indolent," as a result.

Gharazan'nar'rakesh (gah-rah-ZAHN NAHR ruh-KESH): A famous dragon, known for his cruelty.

Glamour: Magic used primarily by fae to disguise their appearance and influence the attitude humans hold toward them.

Gnostrevaine: See Appendix C.

Gray Empire: The largest human governing body on the continent. It is a confederacy of countries overseen by the emperor. Each country maintains considerable autonomy but must obey rules, laws, and standards put forth by the empire.

Griffin: A large creature with the head, wings, and forelimbs of an eagle with the hindquarters of a lion.

Grim: Also called "church grim," they are mostly benevolent fae who guard particular areas or individuals. Garo is an example.

Hazel Enda (HAY-zuhl EHN-duh): Only child of Kyle and Lynn Enda. She died when she fell from a tree. She returned from death and became a member of the Evenfall Vigil.

Hemericanth: See Appendix C.

Hickory Allkirk (HIK-or-ee AHL-kerk): A mage illegally experimenting in Coruvaine. He brings Hazel back from the dead.

Hippogriff: A large creature with the head, wings, and forelimbs of an eagle with the hindquarters of a horse.

Irid (EER-id): A diminutive daimon closely related to nymphs, known for their speed and proclivity to gossip.

Kelsyn (KELL-sin): A human master sorcerer working as secretary to Archmage Lysander Relas at Calixford University.

Kiran (KEER-ihn): Lyvaelan's deceased teacher and father figure. He was a human mage.

Kistra: See Appendix C.

Komora: See Appendix C.

Kyle Enda: A blacksmith by trade. He is the father of Hazel Enda.

Kythis (KI-thiss): The small pink moon orbiting retrograde around the planet. In poetry and colloquially, it is referred to as either the sister or the lover of the larger moon, Progon, and is occasionally regarded as feminine. Children born under the full moon of Kythis are believed to be of cheerful disposition.

Lara (LAH-ruh): A werewolf, previously famous for power fighting. She now works for the Evenfall Vigil.

Lesser Magic: One of the seven arcane arts practiced by human spellcasters. It uses generally variable quantities of magic depending on the type of ability being used. It is known for its practical application of the other arcane arts, including pest control, medical potions, healing, and agriculture but eschews complex theories and spells with a narrow range of uses.

Lich: The most powerful variety of undead, capable of summoning great undead armies and wielding massive amounts of magic with ease.

Living Conduit: A former mage who experimented on himself. He is an inmate of Arcanathema Prison.

Luthain River (LOO-THANE): A river that passes through Coruvaine.

Lynn Enda: A midwife by trade. She is the mother of Hazel Enda.

Lysander Relas (lih-SAN-dur RELL-us): Archmage of Education and former Archmage of War. He is the chancellor of Calixford University.

Lyvaelan (lih-VAY-luhn): A half dark elf, half warlock young man who lived in Elliara until he joined the Evenfall Vigil.

Mage: A human spellcaster who has attained proficiency in two or more arcane arts.

Magelamp: A magical construct that emits light.

Malvex Sorrelle (MAHL-vex sur-EL): Archmage of Sorcery, and half dark elf. He was the previous Grand Inquisitor before Alvaria Saccarra.

Manticore (MAN-tih-cohr): A large creature similar in shape to a lion but possessing a humanoid face and innumerable venomous quills at the end of its tail.

Marcus Comrear (COM-reer): Human commander of the Evenfall Vigil. He appears gruff to most people.

Melantria: See Appendix B.

Melantros: See Appendix C.

Mellius Concornus (MELL-ee-us cun-COR-nuss): A satyr working for the Evenfall Vigil. He possesses the rank of sergeant.

Minotaur (MIN-uh-tar): A monstrous daimon that appears to be a combination of human and bull. They are known for their strength and ferocity.

Naiad (NI-ad): A nymph with the ability to control water. Usually found in areas of fresh water, such as rivers and lakes. They appear as generally beautiful humans with blue skin.

Necromancy: The illegal use of magic to resuscitate, control, or speak with the dead.

Nosferatu (NOS-fehr-AH-too): A particular kind of vampire known for aversion to sunlight, close resemblance to humanity, and social allure. Alistair is an example.

Noxphetalis (NOCKS-feh-TAL-iss): A mountain range known for harboring vampires and Unseelie fae.

Nymph: A particular subspecies of daimon, known for their beauty and generally positive disposition toward humanity. Nymphs are either all female or only the females of species are known.

Oleisia (uh-LEE-see-uh): A naiad who works for the Evenfall Vigil.

Orichalcum (or-ee-KAL-cum): A rare coppery-gold metal derived from ore found in areas of high magic. Its physical properties as a metal are most similar to copper but with a slightly lower melting point. It is valued by spellcasters for its magic conductivity that even exceeds gold.

Palace Valsidan (VAL-SIH-DAN): The headquarters of the Council of Archmages and the home of the High Archmage. It is located in Selevarian.

Paladin Order of Kalendril (cuh-LEHN-dril): A group of warriors possessing magic skill in thaumaturgy dedicated to the mission of their founder, Kalendril, and guided by the triune worship of Veratheragan, Melantros, and Caleptis.

Paxton Averly (PACKS-tun AE-ver-lee): An alchemist living in Coruvaine, he occasionally works as a consultant for the Evenfall Vigil.

Pegasus (plural: pegasi): A winged horse known for its speed.

Petrim (PEH-trim): A country to the south of Ethelian and bordering Selevarian. It is governed by an aristocracy of knights. The country is known for the chivalry of its ruling class and the high magic that permeates the land.

Pixie: A diminutive fae of the Seelie Court.

Power Fighting: A recreational sport where nonhuman creatures and magically enhanced humans fight one-on-one in a minimally regulated brawl. It is a popular event among gamblers.

Progon (PRO-GON): The large white moon that orbits prograde around the planet. In poetry and colloquially, Progon is referred to as the brother or lover of Kythis, the smaller moon, and is occasionally regarded as masculine. Children born under the full moon of Progon are said to be more serious or ambitious than others.

Redcap: A generally malevolent fae, it is known for its talonlike claws, short stature, and eponymous red cap. Charlie is an example.

Revenant: A human returned to life through necromancy. The creature shows signs of mental and physical deterioration within a few weeks before dying again.

Riglin Carstaff (RIHG-lihn CAHR-staff): A dwarf living in Coruvaine, he works as the chief foreman of the fourth wall and oversees his bluecap workers.

Sapphire Guard: Coruvaine's city guard that confines and interrogates criminals with magical abilities, consisting of normal humans and spellcasters. They operate from within the palace.

Satyr (SAY-tur): A specific species of daimon known for their halfway appearance between human and goat. They are known for their agility, exuberance, and magic.

Selevara: See Appendix C.

Selevarian (SEL-uh-VAR-ee-uhn): The city-country of spellcasters. It is ruled by the High Archmage and Council of Archmages. The city is noteworthy for its size, high population, and prevalence of magic.

Semeleme: See Appendix C.

Shadow World: A partially formed realm that runs parallel to Algendis, showing reflections of the world in the form of shadows. Some creatures pass through it to travel great distances in a short time.

Shadowseer: An individual who uses the images of the Shadow World to predict the future or interpret the past.

Skilliven Tavern: A bar and inn operated and owned by Eustace Skilliven.

Sorcery: One of the seven arcane arts practiced by human spellcasters. It uses little magic but requires significant creativity and mental fortitude. It is known for reading the thoughts of others, moving objects without touching them, and creating illusions.

Spellcaster: A human who uses magic.

Spellweaver: One who uses magic to create garments or cloth, which gives the item an innate magic that differs from a normal enchantment. Such artisans are rare and expensive to hire.

Spheres of Elchoran: A spell devised by an archmage to aid with studies. It creates a spherical area of silence. The spellcaster can choose whether it blocks sound from entering, exiting, or both.

Squareball: An athletic game played by spellcasters. It consists of four teams vying for control over a ball. Each group uses magic to maintain possession over several timed rounds.

Succubus: A generally malevolent spirit who seduces others in the guise of a woman but drains their life force.

Susan Telemica (tel-EM-ik-uh): An alchemist practicing in Coruvaine.

Sylph: One of the great prime elemental races representing air.

Talva (TAL-vuh): A human enchantress and alchemist who pioneered literary cuisine. She runs her own shop called Talva's Cookbook.

Tavek: See Appendix C.

Terekmalamae: See Appendix C.

Thaumaturgy (THAW-mat-erj-ee): One of the seven arcane arts practiced by human spellcasters. It uses little magic but requires a specific spiritual alignment to function properly. It is known for healing and enhancing physical traits.

Therianthrope (THER-ee-an-thrope): A being formerly human but now capable of assuming the appearance or abilities of specific animals at night. A werewolf is an example.

Thomas Eller: Chief Inquisitor of Coruvaine.

Thyrsus: A staff topped with a pinecone, used by certain daimon to induce a state of extreme intoxication.

Treland (TREH-lehnd): A city along the northern border of Ethelian known for its amphitheater and power fighting.

Umbravelle: See Appendix C.

Vampire: A class of being with nocturnal habits, pained by thaumaturgical healing, and generally human appearance. Camazotz and nosferatu are examples of different species of vampire.

Veiled Chapel: The home of High Priestess Caeli Relinon and the primary place of worship for the Cult of Semeleme.

Venarius zar Erythis (veh-NAR-ee-us ZAR air-ITH-iss): The King of Nosferatu, located in Noxphetalis. He is the father of Alistair.

Veratheragan: See Appendix C.

War of the Night: A conflict between humanity and vampires, therianthropes, and Unseelie fae, spanning several centuries and ended with the removal of a curse from vampires which stripped them of reason and morals.

Warlock: A human who broke the oath of Selevara in order to cast in the manner of the fae. They possess magical prowess far exceeding the majority of humans but limited ability to control it.

Wizardry: One of the seven arcane arts practiced by human spellcasters. It uses generally large quantities of magic and requires significant education and knowledge to function. It is known for altering the physical world in dramatic ways.

Wyvern (WI-vurn): A draconic creature bearing wings and two legs.

Zigglepet (ZIG-uhl-peht): A bluecap working on the fourth wall.

Zombie: An undead creature possessed of no will of its own except for what its creator desires. It is an animated dead body manipulated by a control spirit to continue moving and acting in whatever way it is told.

Appendix B: The Imperial Calendar

The imperial calendar was devised early in the formation of the empire to assist with commerce between nations. Before the unification, each country had widely varying measurements for the year, with a new year starting at different times, weeks of differing lengths, and months devised regardless of season. Scholars collaborated to create a calendar that was reasonable, accurate, and incorporated the cultures of the countries within the empire.

There are twelve months, which are composed of four weeks each. The first day of the year is also the first day of spring on the first of Verathia. Each season lasts for three months. The months in order are: Verathia (vare-ATH-ee-uh), Hemeria (hem-AIR-ee-uh), Rylith (RI-lith), Faerake (FAE-rayk), Kryvsta (KRIV-stuh), Kistria (KISS-tree-uh), Caleptia (cuh-LEPT-ee-uh), Reapwell (REEP-well), Elimia (el-IHM-ee-uh), Melantria (mell-AHN-tree-uh), Athelia (ath-EL-ee-uh), and Venamor (VEN-uh-mohr).

A week has eight days, each named after a different god. The first five days are named after gods of order whose months were renamed (with the exception of Versday which honors Veratheragan and recognizes his primacy among the gods), while the last three days—or "weekend"—are named after the first three gods of chaos to unite with the gods of order (see Appendix C for additional details). In order, the days are: Versday, Kalsday, Faelsday, Kaesday, Selsday, Komsday, Talsday, and Semsday.

Appendix C: The Pantheon

While there are regional deities and beings worshipped by those in the countryside, the Gray Empire recognizes twenty-two "true" gods whose existence is known through history and direct revelation.

The general understanding of the first age is that a conflict arose between the gods. Eleven gods held that it was best to create new things (these are now referred to as *Gods of Order*) and the eleven remaining gods disagreed, claiming that the nothingness of the beginning was beautiful and ought to remain unspoiled (these are now referred to as *Gods of Chaos*).

The powers on each side were equal until an accord was reached by Veratheragan and Semeleme, who represented the greatest of the gods of order and chaos, respectively. After Semeleme agreed to join with the Gods of Order, Komora abandoned the mission of her fellow Gods of Chaos, as did Skizivik Tal. With three Gods of Chaos adopting their cause, the Gods of Order quickly forced surrender or defeated the remaining deities.

In the ensuing peace, it is believed the gods collaborated on the fundamental structure of the universe, with each God of Order creating the rule and a matching God of Chaos providing a limitation to the rule.

Below are listed the Gods of Order followed by the Gods of Chaos. Some believe the order they are traditionally presented in correlates to their order of importance in the pantheon, since Veratheragan and Semeleme appear first on both lists. This is questionable to some scholars since various cultures and texts refer to gods as varying in strength, while others think discussing relative "power" to be a purely human invention and one as inappropriate to the gods as discussing the relative intelligence of stones. While each god is attributed a specific domain of influence, the listed qualities are those most acknowledged throughout the Gray Empire.

Gods of Order

Veratheragan (VAIR-uh-THAIR-uh-gin): Ruler of the gods, Lord of Peace (but considered a god of war). Usually depicted and referred to as male.

Selevara (SEL-uh-VAHR-uh): Lady of Magic, patron of spellcasters. Usually depicted and referred to as female.

Caleptis (cuhl-EHP-tiss): Lord of Healing, the Lifebringer, usual patron of doctors and thaumaturgists. Usually depicted as male, though some cultures see the deity as female.

Athelea (ATH-uh-LAY-uh): Lady of Earned Knowledge, said to favor those who toil for knowledge, including scientists and students. Usually depicted as female.

Melantros (mel-AN-trose): Lord of Hospitality, said to protect the household and guests. Usually depicted as male.

Faelvirma (FALE-VEER-muh): Goddess of Freedom, it is said the god favors those who are ambitious. Usually depicted as female.

Kalignus (kuhl-IG-nuss): Shepherd of Many Herds, considered the god of animals, specifically those domesticated. Usually depicted as male.

Hemericanth (hem-AIR-ih-canth): Lord of Life, traditionally considered the guardian of plants but also of life itself. Usually depicted as male.

Kistra (KISS-truh): Lord of Stars, considered the one who designed constellations and placed the moons into orbit. Generally depicted as male or genderless.

Elimerita (el-ih-MARE-ih-tuh): Lady of Elements, considered the creator of weather and the elementals. Usually depicted as female.

Kaerestra (KAY-RESS-truh): Lady of Reality, considered the patroness of philosophers and those seeking the truth. Usually depicted as female.

Gods of Chaos

Semeleme (seh-MELL-ehm-ee): Lady of Death, the Veiled Maiden, ruler of the Gods of Chaos. Usually depicted as female.

Terekmalamae (TAIR-ek-MAL-uh-may): Lord of Magic, considered the patron of fae and those who use magic innately. Some attribute Arcane Madness to him. Usually depicted as male.

Mirnak (MEER-nak): God of Destruction and Violence. No cult exists that worships this god officially, though some invoke his name as an extreme malediction. Usually depicted as male.

Gnostrevaine (NOES-treh-VAIN): Lord of Secrets and Forbidden Knowledge. This god favors those who wish to know what should not be known. Usually depicted as male or genderless.

Komora (KOE-MORE-uh): Lady of Lonely Paths, she is the goddess of wanderers, travelers, and those who are metaphorically alone. Usually depicted as female.

Fal Inderva (FAL ihn-DERV-uh): Lord of Fate and Prophecy. Usually depicted as male.

Stezelra (STEZ-EL-ruh): The Wild Lady, she is the goddess of the wilderness and untamable animals and monsters. Usually depicted as female.

Zerkendra (zuhr-KEHN-druh): The Inexorable One, this goddess is considered to cause all physical laws to function without regard for human desires. Usually depicted as female.

Umbravelle (um-bruh-vell): The Dark Lady, she is the goddess of night and all nocturnal creatures. Usually depicted as female.

Tavek (TAH-vihk): Lord of Inevitable Motion, he is thought to power the hands of smiths and craftsmen beyond their control. Usually depicted as male.

Skizivik Tal (SKIZ-ih-vihk TAHL): Lord of Madness and Poetry, he is considered the patron of those obsessed with their work. Often thought to be the most colloquially chaotic of the gods. Usually depicted as male.

Acknowledgements

Many deserve gratitude for helping this book become a reality.

First of all, I must thank those friends who completely read my book and offered feedback. I would especially like to thank Mary, who read the book in its earliest days. Her input helped me better reshape my novel into what it presently is and gave me the motivation to continue on when I doubted myself. I must also thank Peter, who read the book and informed me that it disrupted his sleep schedule (which I take as a compliment of the highest order). William offered valuable insights into the early chapters of my book and gave honest, blunt feedback. His and Peter's knowledge of the fantasy genre, coupled with their critical thinking, aided me in reshaping my thoughts on various characters and plot points. These three friends finished my book and gave me hope that others might finish it too.

Tomas and Jack helped me test my world through tabletop gaming, which is how the Paladins of Kalendril came to be. Tomas read some of my book and stated that it seemed professional and not like something I had written (a wonderful compliment).

My parents have supported me my whole life—and continue to do so—and were willing to listen to my stories and ideas. They allowed me to pursue writing and my creative interests without dismissing them, which they certainly could have done. My sister also took it upon herself to read my novel, even while taking care of her baby.

My beta readers and critique partners provided helpful insights both individually and when taken collectively. In particular, Melanie read my early draft and made me realize I needed to split the book into two smaller novels. Maddy gave me perspective into what to include in various parts of the book to make it seem a bit more finished. All other beta readers were also helpful in different ways.

Finally, to everyone who expressed interest in reading my book. Even if you never read it, I appreciate the sentiment for what it is. Thank you.

About the Author

Joe Field is the author of all books set in the world of Algendis, and *Watchers of the Evenfall* is his debut novel. After submitting his manuscript to numerous literary agents, Joe decided to self-publish so he could be rejected by a much wider audience. He is a student of psychology and an amateur YouTuber. A true nyctophile, he has actually hissed at the sun before. He loves world folklore and mythology and wished to see a greater range of monsters in fantasy than dragons and unicorns which is one of the inspirations for his work. He lives with his two cats in Texas.